James Leasor's two preceding books in
his chronicle of the Far East a century
and more ago – FOLLOW THE
DRUM and MANDARIN-GOLD –
have been acclaimed by critics on both
sides of the Atlantic. THE CHINESE
WIDOW is their equal. It combines
the ferocious force of the Dutch
mercenaries who seek to destroy Gunn's
plan; the pathos of a young woman left
alone to rule a fierce and rebellious
people; the pawky humour of Gunn's
partner, the rough, raw Scot
MacPherson; the mysterious yet
efficacious practice of Chinese medicine,
handed on through thousands of years . . .

Also by James Leasor

GREEN BEACH

and published by Corgi Books

James Leasor

The Chinese Widow

CORGI BOOKS
A DIVISION OF TRANSWORLD PUBLISHERS LTD

THE CHINESE WIDOW

A CORGI BOOK 0 552 10512 0

Originally published in Great Britain by
William Heinemann Ltd.

PRINTING HISTORY
William Heinemann edition published 1975
Corgi edition published 1977

This book is set in Intertype Plantin

Corgi Books are published by
Transworld Publishers Ltd.,
Century House, 61–63 Uxbridge Road,
Ealing, London W5 5SA
Made and printed in Great Britain by
Cox & Wyman Ltd., London, Reading and Fakenham

For Dr. Louis Moss,
who pioneered acupuncture in Britain.

CHAPTER ONE

As Robert Gunn stepped down from his cab into the fog that blurred the buildings in Harley Street, the full irony of his extraordinary situation all but overwhelmed him. Here he was, still under thirty, a doctor of medicine who had become an Eastern merchant so successfully that he was already a millionaire – and yet, unless he found swift help in this unimpressive street of medical specialists and quacks, he stood doomed to die within months from an illness that defied all cure.

The evening felt chill as a damp blanket; he shivered. He had been in the East for too long. His blood must be running thin – or maybe this was just another sign of his disease? England, he recalled, had a cold raw climate, but this knowledge he carried within him made it seem even bleaker.

'One shilling and six pennies, sir,' said the driver hoarsely from somewhere inside the layers of coats and rugs he had wrapped round himself against the January night. Gunn handed him up half a crown and irritably waved away both the change and the old man's amazed gratitude. What use were a few odd coppers to him, except to weigh down his pocket – even if the cabby had overcharged him?

The nag clopped away wearily into the deepening gloom, and Gunn stood for a moment, taking his bearings, leaning on his silver-topped stick. He was a big man, and in his black cloak lined with shot red silk, his opera hat brushed to a mirror-shine, he appeared even taller.

The fog muffled the clop of other horses' hooves and the raw grinding of iron wheels on gravel; dampness lay like dew on black railings. The air held that peculiar London smell of dust and sulphur he had remembered over the years. Street lamps flared dimly above his head, stretching like a necklace of captured stars into the infinity of darkness ahead of him. A few people hurried past, heads down, anxious to be home.

Gunn glanced at his gold hunter; five minutes to five on Wednesday, the fifth of January, 1842. He was on time for his appointment. He strode along the pavement of this street which, when he had first qualified eight years earlier, he had held in higher awe than any other thoroughfare in the world. But for his recent experiences in the East, he would still have felt inferior and unaccepted here. Yet so swiftly and so completely had the golden wheel of fortune turned, that as he began to walk, looking out for Number 58c, the residence of Sir Richard Bankhausen, acknowledged to be Britain's supreme authority on illnesses of the blood, Gunn allowed himself a brief and wintry smile. Now all was changed. Now, if he wished, he could afford to buy every freehold on both sides of Harley Street right down to Oxford Street, and barely miss the money. Indeed, there was nothing in London, or anywhere else, he could not buy, provided it was for sale, and he wanted it. But, recognizing the symptoms of the cruel malady from which he suffered, his wealth was useless; it could not buy recovery. Therefore, rich as he was, he felt poorer than even the wretched girls who stood about, cheeks hollowed and luminous with hunger and fatigue, hopefully hawking tawdry trays of matches; or the crossing-sweepers, the iron rings of whose shovels, removing horse manure, struck his ears like a knell.

Number 58c was a tall, red-brick house; the gilded points of its iron railings looked like spear-blades, to keep away all who could not afford Sir Richard Bankhausen's fees. Gunn strode up the scrubbed steps and rapped imperiously on the polished black door with his cane. A butler opened it instantly. Fog drifted between them like a shapeless ghost, hungry for admittance.

'Dr. Gunn, sir? Sir Richard is expecting you.'

The butler closed the door behind him; instantly, street sounds diminished, and so did the cold. A fire burned in a well-blacked grate, but fog still hung faintly under the high ceiling by the gas mantles. These were new since Gunn's last visit to London; everything had been lit by oil or candles then. Gunn had forgotten there would be changes, as he had forgotten so many other things. He had been away too long.

The butler took his cloak and hat and stick and gloves and ushered him into a waiting room. Leather chairs surrounded a circular table piled with copies of *The Illustrated London News*, *The Times*, *The Morning Post*. Another fire burned low in the grate and coals fell with a sudden sigh as he entered. He wondered how many others had also waited in this impersonal chamber, like the strangers' room of a London club, hoping that somehow Sir Richard would give them a different diagnosis from the one they dreaded; maybe a longer lease of life, or, at least, hope.

He turned the pages of *The Times* and moved instinctively to Foreign News. China was quiet. The four new treaty ports of Shanghai, Ningpo, Amoy and Foochow were operating smoothly. Trade was increasing between East and West, as Gunn had predicted it would. It had been a pity that Britain had been forced to mount a punitive expedition to bring this about, but pain accompanied all births, and results were what mattered. And results, so far as he and his trading company, Mandarin-Gold, were concerned, meant profits. He glanced at the Shipping Intelligence. The *Hesperides*, one of his company's clippers, in which he had sailed from Macao, the Portuguese island off the China coast, was recorded as having docked the previous day with a full cargo of silk and tea.

There was always a race to bring in the first cargo of tea for the New Year, because this commanded the highest price. He would give a bonus of £200 to the captain and officers, for their seamanship had enabled him to buy cheaply and still sell at the peak price. The early crops in China naturally fetched the highest price there, too, but such was the speed of *Hesperides* that Gunn had bought the second crop much more cheaply – and then overhauled the slower rival vessels that had set sail weeks before him. Nothing about that in the newspaper, of course; trade secrets should stay secrets of the trade.

He read on. The *Swallow* was due at Tilbury within days from Hong Kong with a cargo of spices, and the *Jupiter* from

9

Calcutta with jute; *Red Rover* was three days overdue, owing to storms in the Bay of Biscay.

How strange to sit in this warm room, at the heart of the world's greatest city, while across the seven deep seas *his* crews were toiling in *his* vessels to increase *his* profits! What miracles of effort and organization these few lines in *The Times* concealed. Clerks in offices in Canton and Hong Kong, in Macao and Manila, perched up on their stools like writer-birds, scratched away with thin pens, making out invoices, bills of lading, details of bonds and credits. Coolies on a dozen waterfronts sweated in his service. Overseers and native labourers were at that moment supervising the new opium crop in India; and mahouts on elephants were hauling teak logs in Burma. And all in his company's name, for his eventual profit.

But how ironic that while these hired men doubtless envied him his money and influence as one of the youngest and most successful merchant princes in the East, he envied them their health and vigour and expectation of life.

Gunn stood up and glanced at himself in the gold-framed mirror above the Adam fireplace. His face was sallow, with a little dusting of brown spots around the chin. The long voyage home had not burned his skin; the symptoms were of anaemia, and the kind for which, as a doctor, he believed there was no antidote.

The butler appeared at the door.

'If you would come this way, sir?'

Gunn followed him across the hall, into Sir Richard's consulting room. Sir Richard, a small fussy man, with pince-nez clipped precariously on the bridge of his peaked nose, stood behind a desk. As Gunn entered, he adjusted a few papers with his fingertips, and then strode around the side, hand outstretched.

'Please be seated, doctor ... um' – he consulted a note on his desk – 'Dr. *Gunn.* I received your letter. Delighted, sir, to be at your disposal. And, pray, how can I advise you?'

He sat back in his chair and pressed his fingertips together as though to try their strength. Gunn had written to him when the *Hesperides* called at Cape Town to revictual. The letter had been dispatched by fast mail boat through the Red Sea and then overland by camel caravan to Alexandria; in a paddle-steamer to Marseilles, and finally by rail and ferry to England. Such was progress now that a letter could cover the distance in under two weeks and beat the swiftest clipper from the Cape.

'I have been in the East, Sir Richard,' began Gunn. 'Largely employing myself in commerce in Macao and Canton and Hong Kong island. I gave up the practice of medicine shortly after I arrived there about eight years ago. I am now back in this country to see my mother in Herne Bay in Kent. She has been in poor health.'

'You are married, sir?'

'No. The opportunities for marriage in the East are limited, Sir Richard, and my mind has been taken up over diverse and complicated business matters. And as you will have read in *The Times*, we have recently been to war with China.'

'Ah, yes. I read about that. But China is a long way off, Dr. Gunn. Here, I fear, one tends to become involved with events of, shall I say, a more parochial nature. Now, sir, your problem?'

'During my last months in the East, and on the voyage home, I have suffered from a totally alien lassitude, to such an extent that I could not concentrate on my business affairs. I have had almost constant headaches. Heat became unbearable. I tell you frankly that sailing up the coast of Africa, I felt so ill and debilitated, I kept closely to my cabin, with all blinds drawn.'

'In what vessel did you sail?'

'The *Hesperides*.'

'What line is that? I ask, because my wife's brother is a director of a shipping line.'

'It is one of my own company's vessels. A Mandarin-Gold clipper.'

'Indeed?'

Respect hushed Sir Richard's voice. He had consulted the medical register, of course, before seeing Gunn, and knew that he had qualified adequately, if unspectacularly, at St. Andrews University. But to control a company that owned its own clippers – that was one up on his brother-in-law.

'And what did you diagnose?' he asked.

'I believe I am suffering from a serious form of anaemia.'

'In practice in this country, or in the East, did you ever treat any patients for this type of anaemia, Dr. Gunn?'

'No, Sir Richard. After I qualified, I found employment as a surgeon aboard a merchantman. My patients were crew, who mostly suffered from pox, from scurvy, and the after-effects of native drink.'

'A representative collection of lower deck maritime ailments,' agreed Sir Richard with a small smile. 'Since you are a brother physician, I can admit what I would be reluctant to confess to most other patients. We know relatively little about anaemia, its cause and its cure.'

'You are too modest,' replied Gunn shortly. 'You are the country's greatest specialist in this field. I have come not for generalities, but for your specific opinion on my condition.'

'Let me examine you. Please remove your outer clothes, and be so kind as to lie on this couch.'

Gunn crossed behind a lacquered screen that depicted Chinese dragons and mandarins with long drooping moustaches, their feet invisible beneath their robes, folded hands lost in wide sleeves. Behind them loomed the cone-shaped hills he had so often seen behind Canton in the blue mist of evening, and for a moment he was far away from the fog of London, Sir Richard's pomposity, and this stuffy room. Wearily, he began to unbutton his jacket.

Half an hour later, Gunn was dressed again. Sir Richard opened a silver snuff-case and offered it to him. He refused. Sir Richard took a sniff at each nostril, and snapped shut the lid.

'I regret that I must corroborate your diagnosis of anaemia,' he said slowly.

'But what *kind* of anaemia?' asked Gunn. Some were relatively harmless.

'It is impossible to say,' said Sir Richard. 'I just do not know – yet. It may take weeks, perhaps a month, for the type to declare itself.'

'But what is your *opinion*?'

'I do not like to indulge in personal opinions. Both of us are men of science. We should deal in facts.'

'I accept that, Sir Richard, but living in the East gives one a new view of human life. We are all living on borrowed time, and I wish to know when my debt may be demanded. I am used to bad news – to ships being late or lost in storms, to have warehouses and godowns destroyed by fire or typhoons. Please do not spare me out of reasons of reticence.'

'You speak as a man of courage and resource, Dr. Gunn. Since you demand to know, I must admit that it is my opinion you *are* suffering from a malignant form of anaemia.

'On the other hand, anaemia can wear many masks. You might find after all that this is not the gravest kind. I will, of course, prescribe for you what no doubt you have already prescribed for yourself – a diet of lean meat, liver, oysters, with daily glasses of port and champagne. I suggest also that you have blood let, to relieve the pressure on the main body arteries and other vital vessels.'

'I am in your debt, Sir Richard, for your candour, which I fear is too rare in men of our profession, and so all the more valued. Should I recover under your treatment, I have no problem. But should my condition not respond, then please be so kind as to tell me how long – at the worst – you think I have left before my strength leaves me and my ability to conduct my business diminishes.'

'I would estimate you have twelve months ahead of you, Dr. Gunn. In the tenth, eleventh and twelfth months, of course, you may notice a steady increase in lassitude, and a greater general feebleness in your person. Efforts to walk any distance or to take exercise will quickly tire you. But your brain should be undiminished in its vigour until the last few weeks, although towards the – ah, end – you may lose the power of coherent speech.

'It grieves me to have to tell this to any of God's creatures, let alone a fellow disciple of Galen and Aesculapius, and I pray to God that He and you may prove me wrong.'

They sat silently for a moment. I am like a judge pronouncing sentence of death, thought Bankhausen. This man, my patient, is condemned to die, a prisoner of time and of his own thoughts. He opened his snuff-box and inhaled in each nostril.

'Now, sir,' he continued. 'How long will you be staying in Herne Bay?'

'I have no fixed plans,' replied Gunn, 'but I expect to spend a week or so there. Then I may take chambers in London.'

'I happen to know, sir, of a very fine set at present vacant, belonging to a friend of mine, Colonel Parker, who is on service in Ireland with his regiment. No. 13 Jermyn Street.'

'Pray be so kind as to give the colonel the address of my company in London. It is on my card. I will take those chambers as from today. It is good to have a personal recommendation. I have been out of England too long to know who to consult on such a matter. Also, I have no time to waste.'

'I will see to it at once,' promised Bankhausen briskly. 'Now, sir, if we could fix a time for a mutually convenient second appointment?'

Lady Patricia Bankhausen sat in her bedroom, facing her cheval glass lit by three candles on either side. Her maid hovered in the background, holding two silver-handled brushes engraved with her initials, P.B., beneath her husband's crest.

Lady Patricia slowly turned her head to one side and then to the other, and still found no wrinkles in her neck. She was thirty-five and told herself she looked ten years younger. That was good, very good. She derived an immense pleasure from her own body and the prettiness of her face. She wore a bustle and long linen petticoat, but her breasts were bare, and, pouting slightly, as though in deep thought, she placed her hands under each one and forced them up slowly so that the delicate net of veins gorged with blood and her nipples darkened. The maid looked the other way; her ladyship embarrassed her with such manipulations of her body.

A knock at the door.

'Come in,' Lady Patricia called over her shoulder. The maid handed her a silk shawl to drape across her breasts, and as she did so she glanced again at her reflection; her nipples pointed through the stuff of the shawl.

Sir Richard came into the room.

'We are late,' he said gruffly, loath to show his irritation openly in case he displeased his wife; she was twenty years younger than him.

'The carriage has already been waiting for half an hour, and it will take at least forty-five minutes in this fog to reach Holland Park.'

'I am ready,' replied Lady Patricia, tossing away the shawl and holding out her arms for the silk blouse. 'You are delaying me, Richard, talking like this. Go downstairs and have a sherry to put yourself in a better frame of mind.'

'I am in a perfectly good frame of mind, my dear. It is just that I hate being late for *every* appointment.'

'It's bad manners to arrive on time for dinner. You know that quite well, Richard.'

'It's even worse manners to arrive an hour late. To come in at the fish course or even the remove, as we will be lucky if we can do now.'

'Then the longer you stand arguing, Richard, the later we will be.'

Sir Richard went out of the door, and pulled it shut behind him, not noisily but hurriedly, in case he forgot himself and slammed it. His wife made a face behind his back. Poor weak fool, who always sought to appease her when what she so desperately wanted was a man to do exactly the reverse, to dominate her.

The maid helped Lady Patricia on with her dress. She glanced again at herself in the morror. No lines, no wrinkles, but already the face had the soft puckered contours of discontent. Soon this frustration would etch itself permanently with little crow's feet around her eyes and at the edges of lips now so full and red and warm. Then her wide passionate mouth would look withered, tight and unpromising as the snap-mouth of a purse.

Her husband was a bore, of course, but then were not all husbands? He was rich and successful, and in her mother's trite phrase – 'he gave her everything she wanted'. But how could Lady Patricia's mother, a widow living in a small house with only two servants in one of Hove's more unfashionable squares, know what her daughter so desperately wanted – the hard vigorous thrusting advances of a young and virile lover? How could she guess that she longed to be dominated and flung on a bed; to have her clothes ripped off, to be shouted at, beaten, insulted, so that, naked and fulfilled, she could crawl abjectly to the man and acknowledge him as her master.

But instead, she had the soft marshmallow politeness of an ageing almost impotent husband, with his furtive, tentative caresses, prefaced by such meek requests as, 'Do you mind?' To be asked whether you minded was to imply that you would, and so, of course, you did. You hated it all, and turned away your face as you endured in silence his panting, pathetic exertions without any feeling beyond contempt. But then, was not this an inescapable wifely duty? How else could she live in this style, unless married to a wealthy man – or kept by one? Some day, maybe, she would have the chance to grow rich on her own account – or so a fortune-teller had seriously assured her only last summer. She doubted it; these gypsies told you what you longed to hear. But it was still a pleasant thought; if nothing more. As secret wish – and surely every woman deserved at least one?

She turned, the maid curtsied her approval, and Lady Patricia walked slowly down the wide marble staircase. The butler, waiting in the hall, bowed and opened the front door with a white-gloved hand. A footman held the carriage door as she stepped up and inside. Sir Richard was already hunched in the far corner, smoking a cigar and looking ostentatiously at his hunter. He snapped it shut with the same finite gesture he had used when he snapped shut the lid of the snuff-box. He forced himself to smile and produced a grimace. The footman climbed up on the box and, above their heads, beyond the brocaded roof, the coachman cracked his oiled whip. Instantly, the two matched greys leaned into their supple harnesses, and the carriage rolled forward.

Lady Patricia patted her husband's hand, not because she

wanted to touch his flesh, which felt dry and repulsive to her, but because there was no point in making him angry and miserable. If he was unhappy, he would drink too much at the Harcourts, and make a fool of himself, and perhaps others would smile, not with him, but at him; and, worst of all, in pitying him, would also pity her.

Was every marriage like this? Or was theirs unusual, even unique? Two lives out of step, two people out of touch; a misalliance. All her women friends seemed to be blissfully happy, bound up in their children, their husbands' careers, their London homes, their country house, busy organizing servants for winters spent in Nice and summers on the Isle of Wight. Or were they fooling themselves and her?

'You seem distraught, Richard,' she said at last. 'A busy day?'

'I have had several disagreeable tasks, I admit,' her husband replied thawing instantly at the false warmth in her voice. 'Several cases have simply not responded to treatment. One was a little girl of twelve. She could have been my daughter – our daughter.'

'You must consider it fortunate at such times that we have no children,' said Lady Patricia icily.

'Yes, my dear. But sometimes, when I see a dying child, it is infinitely more sad than when I attend a mature person who has lived out the full measure of his days.'

'I do not like thinking about such things, let alone talking about them. We are supposed to be going out to enjoy ourselves. Who else did you see today?'

'A fellow physician, similarly affected, poor man. And barely in his thirties. Robert Gunn.'

'Does he practise?'

'Not now. I believe he owns some Eastern trading company, Mandarin-Gold, and so he must be one of these new potentates we hear so much about these days.'

Sir Richard looked out of the window, already misted with their breath, at the phantasmagorical shapes in the fog. He saw a shop-window filled with huge cheeses, like wheels; the flare of naphtha above a stall selling skinned rabbits. The hoarse cries of the street vendors sounded like lost souls calling from the outer darkness of desolation. That poor devil Gunn must feel like one of them, he thought: a man hearing the march of the dead.

'What is he like, this doctor? Handsome?'

'Yes. About six foot three tall.'

'Is he married?'

'No. Says he has had no time for marriage. His business in the East has been too pressing.'

'Seems a waste of an attractive man.'

'He might not agree.'

'I would not know, of course, unless I met him.'

'Which is extremely unlikely,' said Sir Richard shortly.

'Why? We know several of your patients socially.'

'Only a few lonely souls who visit me for reassurance, or simply to talk about matters they feel they cannot discuss with anyone else lest their confidence is abused. Everyone needs someone in whom they can confide.'

How true, she thought. But there is no-one I can talk to. My mother could not even begin to understand why I am unhappy. She envies me my servants, my houses, my social life, for she wanted these herself and never achieved them. But I want other things – which I did not realize existed when she talked me into this marriage. I am like an actress, always pretending, playing a part. But when does the curtain come down? When can we go home and be ourselves – and who exactly are we?

'Why wouldn't I meet this doctor?' she went on, speaking to drive away these disturbing thoughts.

'Because, my dear, he lives in China. Or somewhere in that area.'

'But he is not in China *now*. He is in London.'

'Briefly.'

'But he is not returning to China tonight, is he?'

'So far as I know, my dear, he is travelling to Herne Bay, a fishing village in Kent, to see his mother.'

'That's near Canterbury, isn't it, Herne Bay?'

'About twelve miles away, I believe. Why?'

'You haven't forgotten we are going down to the de Veres for

18

their ball next Friday at Sturry House, have you? We might see him there.'

'I think it extremely unlikely that you will see a merchant from the East at the de Veres.'

'He is a *rich* merchant, though?'

'Indubitably. And most likely from peddling opium. It is to protect the bank balances of men like him that we have recently gone to war with China. I think it extremely unlikely we will meet Dr. Gunn at the de Veres.'

'Life itself is unlikely,' replied Lady Patricia shortly, making up her mind to write to her hostess the very next morning.

She looked out of the other window so that she would not be forced to see her husband's face. It was easier to bear his hand on her knee if she did not have to meet his eyes.

CHAPTER TWO

THE train slid jerkily to a halt as the brakes began to bite the wheels. The driver blew his steam whistle, and the porter at Sturry station started to run alongside the only first-class carriage. Not many people travelled first-class to Sturry; but then not many people travelled there in any case, for the branch line from Canterbury had only been in operation for a few months. He opened the door and saluted hopefully. Gunn stepped down on to the windswept platform.

'My luggage is in the guard's van,' he informed him.

The porter pulled out the matching calfskin suitcases, bound with cross straps, and the black wooden travelling trunk with its polished brass corners.

'A cab, sir?'

'Of course.'

The hackney driver and the porter heaved up Gunn's luggage on the roof of the one-horse carriage; Gunn felt in his back pocket for a florin.

'It is some years since I have been in these parts,' he told the driver. 'Fair View Cottage, Herne Bay.'

'Near the beach, sir?'

'Yes.'

'I had a commission there only two days ago, sir. A funeral.'

'Whose?'

'An old lady's, sir. Mrs. Gunn.'

He paused.

'No relation, I hope?'

He did not wish to say anything that might prejudice the size of this obviously wealthy man's tip; trade was very quiet at this time of year.

For a moment, Gunn stopped breathing. So his mother was

20

dead. He had raced home from the other side of the earth, taking only 93 days from Canton to the West India Docks, one day under the record of the voyage. As they set off, he had ordered his skipper, Captain Fernandes, to set his sky-sails and royal studding sails and not take them in during the passage unless the vessel's safety was at serious risk. Because of the vast spread of canvas, Fernandes's seamanship had been taxed to the limit of his endurance, for the danger was that, in an unexpected squall, the clipper could heel over on her beam ends, and even break the masts. Sometimes, Fernandes had only managed three hours sleep out of 24, but he had realized Gunn's reasons for speed, and had brought the *Hesperides* through safely – and all in vain; death had beaten them by days.

'Is her husband still living in the cottage?' Gunn asked the driver.

'Oh, yes indeed, sir.'

'Then pray proceed.'

He sat back on the cracked leather seat which smelt of damp camphor, and looked over thorn hedges, naked of all leaves, towards the fields, grey under the winter sky. Beyond them, the sea lay like a wide strip of pewter; a few fishing boats tacked heavily against the wind, which rattled the glass window pane in the carriage door.

How odd that this cold, wave-whipped water stretched from here, down the vast west coast of Africa, on south of India to Singapore, and then to Hong Kong and Macao, changing colour all the time, grey to green, then to blue and finally to gold in the setting tropical sun. And even stranger to consider that his company's clippers were sailing all those differently coloured seas. Yesterday, today, tomorrow.

The driver turned away from the lanes, past a few slate-roofed cottages. A quick glimpse of a shingle beach with tarred fishing boats drawn up in rows, and he saw his father's house. He remembered the discreetly drawn curtains, the yellowish privet hedge, the minute front garden, but thought it had been somehow larger and grander; this was little better than a labourer's cottage. Then he remembered that, as a schoolmaster, his father had commanded no more than a labourer's wage, and felt shame for his thoughts and his own prosperity.

The carriage stopped. Gunn handed the man a five shilling piece – almost a week's wage for a farm labourer – and walked up the straight path, still edged with shells and bordered by wallflowers, beaten down by the wind.

He tapped on the door with his stick while the cabby toiled in with his luggage. The door opened a few inches. A small old man looked out cautiously.

'I buy nothing at the door,' he said, and then regarded him quizzically, eyes narrowed as though peering into mist.

'Why, *Robert*!'

As he recognized his son, he stretched out both his hands in welcome, and led Gunn into the little hall. His father also seemed to have shrunk, like the house. He wore a dark suit, the same watch-chain across the waistcoat that Robert remembered from boyhood, but his face now was puffy and grey and soft.

'You received my letter saying I was coming home?' Gunn asked him.

'We did, my boy, but your dear mother was too ill to read it herself. I read it out to her, of course. I think she understood.'

The hall had the same decorations: brown paint, heavy, old-fashioned wallpaper with raised scrolls that he used to prick with a fingernail when he was a boy. A barometer on the right wall was tinted purple and green and blue by the edging round the frosted glass front door window. Everything smelled of old age and dust.

He followed his father into the front room with the bow window. Antimacassars protected the backs of the three easy chairs; the glass-fronted book case with the collected works of Shakespeare which he had never read still appeared too large for the tiny room.

They stood awkwardly, looking at each other, dredging for words.

'I didn't know when to expect you,' his father said at last. 'I am sorry that you have arrived too late.'

'I know. The cabby told me.'

'What a pity you could not arrive even a week earlier.'

'I did my best,' said Gunn simply. 'I came as soon as I received your letter.'

How could he explain to this shrunken stranger in the little over-furnished room all the complications he had overcome in order to leave Macao at only hours' notice? Or how he had continually urged Captain Fernandes aboard his clipper to clap on all sail, to pillage every wind and current and shorten every revictualling stop drastically so that he should be home as speedily as possible? He had failed. But he had done his best to succeed.

'Was she in pain?' he asked his father.

'Not towards the end.'

'What was the nature of her illness?'

'Internal. And then complications set in.'

'Ah, yes.'

Whenever doctors could not diagnose a serious illness quickly, complications invariably set in. He had used the oddly comforting words himself. Perhaps if he had been here he could have brought in other doctors, specialists like Sir Richard Bankhausen, people of that calibre? But even among the rich, patients' complications were mortal in the end; death was the certain cure for all diseases.

'We still have Gladys.'

'Oh, yes, Gladys,' said Gunn. This was their only maid; a woman from the village who had looked after his parents for as long as he could remember.

'She is out shopping at the moment. As I say, we did not know exactly when you were arriving. But I have got something special in for you.'

'You shouldn't have bothered,' said Gunn. 'Just being home is enough.'

'It's a bottle of sherry,' said his father proudly. He crossed the room and opened a cupboard door and took out a new bottle with two glasses. He drew the cork, and they raised their glasses.

'To absent friends,' said his father, his voice suddenly strained. 'To your mother, and all those good times we had. Remember?'

'For as long as I live.'

The sherry was not the quality Gunn was used to drinking, and tasted bitter and metallic on his tongue. But even nectar would have tasted bitter on that day. Here he was, home with a fortune, but home too late, and with less than a year to live. Why, his father, enfeebled and old as he seemed, would almost certainly outlast him.

'You will be wanting your old room, I expect? Gladys has had the bed aired this past week.'

'How kind of you.'

Gunn had forgotten the necessity of airing beds, the winter dampness of living by the sea, the cold smallness of everything. Windows rattled like loose teeth in their bow frames as he stood watching the cabby turn his horse back to the station. Why did realization always fall so short of what you anticipated? In imagining his home-coming, his thoughts had soared unfettered on wings. Reality was sharing cheap sherry in a shabby room with an old man with whom he had now almost nothing in common.

Gunn lay between sleep and wakefulness, looking up at the ceiling of a strange room, hearing gulls call and gusts of wind blow down the chimney, scattering soot into the empty grate. It took him a moment to realize where he was, in that once-familiar room, with the toys of childhood still piled on top of the cupboard.

Then he remembered Sir Richard's opinion: if he had been right in giving him exactly a year of comparative health two days ago, he now had three hundred and sixty-three days left. The thought was an almost insupportable weight on his mind, but despite it, the cold English climate had sharpened his appetite. He did not *feel* ill; his lethargy and lassitude had diminished. But an apple can have a shining red skin and yet be rotten inside, and appearances in many diseases were invariably deceptive.

He glanced at his watch on the bedside table; eight-fifteen. Gladys always prepared breakfast for eight-thirty. He swung himself out of bed, and then sat on the quilt looking out at the sea and the little fishing boats on the beach. An old man was slowly walking a dog along the shining shingle. He might have been the last person left alive. The scene seemed cheerless as his thoughts.

What was he going to do now that he was home? It was one thing hurrying back across the world to see his mother before she died. It was altogether another to arrive, too late, after her death. He could have taken them on a foreign tour; perhaps to Italy or to some German spa. But now what would his father wish to do?

Gunn shaved, washed, went downstairs. The house felt chilly; there was no heating apart from the fire in the little breakfast-room, and that was only a handful of glowing coals in a black-leaded grate. Yet several million people lived in this climate and did not complain. He had been spoiled by the East and its warmer, richer multi-coloured life; in the East even the food had fire.

His father, already seated at the head of the breakfast table, bowed his head gravely.

'For what we are about to receive, may the Lord make us truly thankful,' he said. The simple words took Gunn back to boyhood, yet his secret knowledge endowed them with a terrible irony that made him want to cry out at its unfairness.

Gladys, now to his surprise, a grey-haired old woman, in her familiar black bombasine skirt, and white apron and cap, curtsied, hands folded demurely, and echoed, 'Amen.' She held out a plate, warm from the stove, and his father served her with two strips of bacon, an egg, half a slice of fried bread. She curtsied again and carried her breakfast out into the kitchen.

'I still don't eat with her, even though your mother has gone,' said the old man defensively. 'She's happier eating out there.'

'I suppose so,' said Gunn indifferently. He had never considered important the delicate nuances of social caste in a small English town. Now, they seemed meaningless. He and his father ate in silence. Apart from clichés – 'the weather should improve; the glass is set fair' – they had little to say to each other. He had had more in common with his mother, for he had lived out her Scottish dream of the 'lad of parts' who worked unceasingly while others played, and by so doing achieved a great reward. But his mother, who of all people could most have appreciated his success, was not alive to see it.

His father was content that he owed no man, that the local parson and shopkeepers and three generations of pupils he had taught in the local school regarded him as a man of honour. Gunn also admired his uprightness, but honour was not love, and his father had never been a demonstrative person. Perhaps he had given too much affection to other people's children, and so had none left for his own?

Gunn said, as though the idea had just occurred to him, 'I was going to suggest that mother and you might accompany me to the Continent. Maybe Florence or to Baden-Baden. Now that you are on your own, the change would do you good, and we could leave within days. Will you come – as my guest?'

Anything to escape from this chill, measured, ordered life he had outgrown and gone beyond for ever. His father swallowed, wiped his mouth carefully with his table napkin, and nodded.

'That is a most generous invitation,' he said. 'But I could not possibly accept.'

'Why ever not?'

'It would be ruinously expensive for a young man making his way in the world.'

'Expense is only relative, father. I can afford it. I am not poor.'

'I am aware of that, but I would not feel at ease if I allowed you to spend so much money on such a frivolous expedition.'

'I would not consider the trip frivolous, father. After all, rich young men have made the Grand Tour for generations.'

'I am neither rich nor young, Robert. As you know, I was born in Kent, not five miles from this house. There are many places I have not yet visited in my own country, let alone travelling abroad among foreigners, with their disgusting ways and filthy habits.'

'Then let us travel in Kent or elsewhere in this country. I can hire a carriage and engage servants.'

'No, Robert. You are very kind and I appreciate your offer as only a father can. But I would prefer to stay at home among

26

familiar things. The older one grows, the less one is able to accommodate to change and novelty. Now, tell me, what are *your* plans? Would you like to visit the grave?'

'Mother's grave? Yes, I shall do that, of course. In the meantime, is there anything I can do to help? Clearing up any papers she had, or a will?'

'Your mother owned no shares, as you are probably aware. We both drew up wills leaving all we owned to each other. The local solicitor in Whitstable can deal adequately with that. I take it that you will now be wishing to buy a house in the locality – since you seem to have given up trade – to return to the infinitely more worthwhile calling of medicine, for which you trained at my considerable expense?'

'I have not really given up trade, Father. I have only returned here for a holiday.'

'Will your superiors not wonder if you stay too long? I heard only last week of a young fellow who worked for John Company and apparently overstayed his leave – owing to adverse winds – and his superiors regarded this very coolly. Indeed, he had to resign. Young fellow named James Brooke. An uncle of his told me about it. Came from Bath, I believe. Of course, I understand he had private means or at least expectations, so no doubt this was not such a blow as it would be to someone like yourself.'

Gunn smiled inwardly. How could he ever make his father understand that he was his own man, his own master, not an East India Company clerk or a hireling; and he could stay for as long as he liked, wherever he liked, for his wealth ran into millions? But it was impossible to explain this to a man who had lived out all his working life in one schoolroom, dreading the visits of education inspectors, lest his efforts should be found wanting.

'I am largely a free agent in these matters,' Gunn told his father gently.

'Then your employers must be very generous. There is altogether far too much slackness among young people today.'

'I'm sure that is so,' Gunn agreed. 'But then youth leaves us all quickly.'

'You are speaking like me, and you are not yet thirty.'

'I think I need a holiday. That is partly why I wish you would accompany me abroad. In seeing new people and places we could temper the sadness we both have in our hearts.'

'I know you mean well, Robert, but I cannot accept.'

Gunn bowed his head. He had thought at first of telling his father about the shadow that darkened his future, but now he decided against it. The old man had already endured enough suffering through the illness and death of his wife; nothing could be gained by adding to his burden of grief.

'I wonder,' said Gunn to change the subject, 'whether you have any news of Marion?'

'Marion?'

His father's brow wrinkled slightly in distaste; she was a local girl who had been engaged to Gunn years ago, before he sailed east. Robert remembered, as though it had happened yesterday, his arrival at Canton as surgeon aboard an East Indiaman, and the letter that awaited him from his father, with the news that Marion had eloped with a local married man, Joss Cartwright, who owned two sweet shops. How long ago, how remote it seemed now, and yet, with that strange ability time possessed of telescoping events in between, how real and sharply he recalled that day. Sun on the yellow Pearl River, the sweetness of spice blowing off the mainland, the wood deck rail warm beneath his hands. That letter had spurred him on to commercial success; it had hardened his determination to become so rich, so important, that no-one would ever again slight him. If he had never received it, he would no doubt still have been a ship's surgeon; or maybe the local doctor here, married to Marion. And if so, would he now be mortally ill?

'Marion has moved,' his father replied shortly. 'Mr. Cartwright was made to feel unwelcome here. A number of parents – wisely, I feel – forbade their children to buy his sweets. After all, his own wife, poor woman, had been put in an unforgivable situation. The last intelligence was that he and Marion were living in South London as man and wife. A disgusting episode. I am glad you got over it. But you have still not married anyone. Are you engaged to wed?'

'No,' said Gunn. 'I have no plans for matrimony.'

'You may not have heard that old Dr. Golightly, who brought you into this world and who was our doctor until he retired quite recently, is selling up and is going to live with his daughter in Birmingham? His house would make a fine home for you.'

'I remember it,' Gunn replied unenthusiastically, recalling a yellow-brick villa, which by local standards was imposing. Any country practitioner might find it ideal, but would a *taipan* be at home there? But then, would he now be at home anywhere?

'I think I will visit the grave, as you suggest,' Gunn said, standing up.

'I'll come with you,' said his father.

They put on their overcoats against the chill January wind, and Gladys brought in a red woollen scarf, warmed from the top of the kitchen stove, to wrap around his father's neck. The old man selected an ash walking stick from the umbrella stand in the hall, and they set off. His steps were short and his breathing hard; walking was an effort. Gunn had not expected his father to be so feeble, any more than he had anticipated how the town – it was really no more than a large village – had apparently shrunk to minute proportions: two or three shops, a church, a new post office, a public house. Grass grew in the middle of the road, and he only counted two carriages, both shabby, with scratched varnish and raw-boned, scabby horses, and one coal cart pulled by two Shires.

In contrast, the Praya Grande at Macao, the main thoroughfare of the port, would at this same hour be crowded with a throng of people. Servants would be pushing Chinese masters in huge, richly ornamented wheelbarrows, coolies would be trotting between rickshaw shafts, open carriages would bowl along, bearing pretty ladies to drink coffee in each other's houses, past bold-eyed Portuguese officers riding prancing chargers under a burnished sky. And as a background to all this cheerful activity, the white houses with their identical green blinds, and the balustrades on the roofs. But here was nothing but grey sea and small cold dwellings. The wind made his gums ache and his eyes smart, and even pushed its freezing fingers through the cloth of his overcoat.

The church was also pathetically small; only a handful of people had been buried there in the previous hundred years, and his mother's grave was still covered with rain-beaten wreaths. They stood looking at the trodden earth and the sodden petals in embarrassed silence, and then turned and walked away. It was difficult to assimilate that the person he had travelled from the other side of the world to see lay only feet beneath them, and yet separated forever.

'It is very cold,' said his father hoarsely. 'You feel it more at my time of life. When I was your age, even the winters seemed warm.'

'Then why not come back to the East with me?' said Gunn suddenly. 'I have a house there, with servants. It is always warm in Macao, even when it rains – which you may find difficult to believe.

'I cannot begin to explain the uplift you feel when you wake up every morning to sunshine, father, to blue skies and a bluer sea, to warmth and gaiety and music. Here everything seems so cold and flat and bloodless by contrast. A washed-out country-side.'

'It is my home,' said his father quietly. 'I am too old to move now. When I was young, that would have been different, but I did not have the opportunity then, my boy. I have lived here all my life. I know the people. They know me. I taught most of them and their fathers, even some of their grandfathers. Who would I know out in, where's this place – Macao?'

'I would introduce you to friends,' Gunn promised. But even as he spoke he knew this was impossible; he possessed no real friends, only acquaintances. When you were ambitious and eager for early wealth, you had no time to form friendships. A man travelled fastest when he travelled alone. And, of course, with or without introductions, the old man would never fit into the bright, exaggerated world of the East, where men regularly drank themselves to sleep, or discharged guns in the main streets, or indulged in outrageous affairs, regardless of what people would say, or think, because what did it matter *what* people thought? Your life might be short, with one of many unknown and deadly fevers. You might be bitten by a snake or scorpion, or shot by a jealous husband, or even marooned – as he had been – so you lived each day, each hour, to the full, for it could be your last. Here, in this cold country, near this grey, wind-ruffled sea, life was only marking time to keep your feet warm until they buried you in the wet, chill earth.

They walked back to the cottage in silence and, at the gate, both waiting for the other to lead, bumped into each other in the little path. Gladys had prepared two cups of hot beef tea and they sat, again in silence, drinking slowly and warming chilled fingers around the thick china mugs.

The second day at home was almost a parallel of the first, and so was the third; the only difference was that they did not visit the grave, but walked briskly along the beach, smelling the salty seaweed, his father nodding to fishermen he knew, and then back to the beef tea in the room that was warm close to the fire but cold and damp everywhere else.

On the fourth morning, a post-chaise arrived at the front door. It was beautifully turned out in royal blue varnish with fine red and gold lining around the doors and on the mudguards and spokes. The coachman and footman on the box wore cockades in their hats, and livery of dark blue-double-breasted coats with breeches to match the paint.

The footman walked up the narrow path and beat on the door as though he were a beadle.

'A personal message for Dr. Robert Gunn,' he told Gladys. Gunn put down his cup and went to the door.

'What is your business?' he asked.

The man saluted smartly and held out a white envelope. Gunn turned it over; the paper was thick and smooth and sealed with red wax under the imprint of a crest, he slit open the envelope and pulled out a heavily embossed card edged with gold, and at the top the arms he had seen in the sealing-wax.

Sir Vernon and Lady de Vere request the pleasure of the company of Dr. Robert Gunn at a ball to be held at Sturry House on January 15th.

Gunn's father stood by the bow-shaped bedroom window, looking out to sea. Spears of afternoon rain pocked the grey water and windows rattled wearily: it would be a rough night at sea. The room was cold, and his breath misted the glass; he wiped it away with his hand and remembered playing games when Robert had been a little boy, breathing on the window with him, outlining a face with a finger, wiping it off, starting again.

It seemed so long ago, but such events often seemed clearer than those of the last few days. It was pleasant to look back at the past, where time had rounded roughness from any discord, so that all recollections appeared happy. He looked through the rain and did not see an empty winter beach, but the sands of summer. Every year, on Robert's birthday, from the time he had been five or six, they had raced each other across that shingle, father and son. At first, he would have to hold back to let Robert catch up with him. Then, as the boy grew older and his legs longer, the contests became more of a race; and on Robert's thirteenth birthday he had to struggle to keep up with his son, and he realized that now Robert could beat him, but somehow, out of loyalty, he did not want to do so. Nothing was said, but after that there were no more races.

Now, his son had overtaken him completely.

In those days, he and Robert would walk along the beach, and watch the fishing boats come in, and he would tell his son stories of far away countries with strange foreign customs about which he had read. Schoolmasters, he sometimes thought, were like priests in one particular way; they passed on other people's experiences and beliefs as their own. Now his son had sailed to Cathay after the manner of Marco Polo, and established himself as a merchant, while he had stayed behind, watching the wind fill other men's sails. His son had done things that he had only heard about through the words of other men, and he was proud of him and the way he had transformed dreams to deeds.

It was kind of Robert to suggest he should return with him to Macao, but he was too old to leave home; it was too late to become a traveller, for the journey would take months, and he could never adapt to a hot climate and an alien land. He must be content to have sailed the farthest seas by proxy, in the pages of books read in his armchair by the fire, when the wind blew in the chimney and sea-birds cried through the dark. He had been content to live his life at second or third hand, but only now, when confronted by his son, did he realize this.

He sensed that Robert, despite the wealth about which he never spoke directly, but to which he only alluded in the most casual way, was not completely concerned with the gathering of gold. He was unhappy; something was worrying him, and the old man did not like to ask what this might be. After all, it was none of his business, and his son was no longer a boy. But although commerical success was commendable, that was not the whole duty of a man, which, according to the Good Book, was to worship the Lord God. And how could anyone worship God satisfactorily in the money-changer's temple?

Lady Elizabeth Mavourneen de Vere stood on the first landing of the white marble stairs, down which a red Wilton carpet cascaded like a crimson river. The clash of colours, the glitter of jewels reflecting the lights, excited and charmed her.

Her husband, Sebastian, a thin, tall man with an aristocratically small head and narrow eyes, stood symbolically a pace behind Elizabeth, surveying the scene with equal approval.

The ballroom stretched away under a forest of white candles, hundreds of tiny flames glittering like fireflies. At the far end, the orchestra, in black evening suits, with wide red silk lapels, played a polka. Sebastian had ordered the butler to instruct a waiter to give them two measures of whisky each. The night was cold; all musicians played better with spirit inside them.

A log fire, in a fireplace so wide it could hold trunks of trees, blazed to welcome the couples who were drifting in, the women in crinolines and new ball gowns, hair piled upon their heads in intricate coils, some displaying combs shot with jewels, others wearing tiaras. The men wore tails or regimental mess dress.

Waiters in the de Vere indoor livery of dark blue with gold

buttons, with freshly ironed white gloves, carried silver trays of glasses brimming with champagne. As the bubbles rose in each glass, Sebastian's spirits soared with them. He liked to tell himself he was a simple man, who appreciated nothing better than an evening with a few friends, but for him simplicity was not what everyone else understood by the word. He would spend 1,000 guineas on an evening's entertainment – as he was doing now – inviting people he did not really know particularly well, and if he knew, did not altogether care for, simply because the fact that they all invariably accepted his invitations brought a warmth to his otherwise chilly heart. They accepted with alacrity because he was who he was; one of the wealthiest landowners in Kent. The fact that he owed this distinction entirely to an accident of birth gave it an added dignity; there was nothing *nouveau riche* about Sebastian de Vere. He could trace his pedigree back through the male line for several hundred years, and frequently did so for his own reassurance as to his superiority, and the edification of any upstarts who dared to doubt it.

An ancestor had prudently allied himself with Henry VIII, and for his loyalty, his king had awarded him with these and other estates, which had previously belonged to a local order of friars in dispute with the monarch. Equally honourable men had chosen to stand with the Church on that historic confrontation long ago; their cause had not prevailed, and they had lost their lands as well as their heads. But then all life was a lottery, as Sebastian liked to claim grandly, and fortunately his family had been among the winners.

'Are you happy, my dear?' he asked his wife.

She smiled brightly and nodded. Elizabeth was always happy when she appeared as the star in any assembly. Other women, she conceded, might be more beautiful; a few might have richer husbands; quite a number could be wittier. But no woman of her acquaintance could beat her on all these three points all together.

Every one of these guests was in some way beholden to her or her husband. He was by far the richest man present, whose acres marched in thousands from Sturry almost to the sea. He could ride all day (and frequently did) and by dusk he had still not reached the extreme boundary of his land.

Her dark sharp little eyes flitted from one couple to another. She recognized Lord and Lady Rigby – such bores – but then Lady Rigby could really be rather sweet in a quaint kind of way, and she was one of the Leicestershire Rigbys, which was by far the oldest branch of the family.

There was Admiral Critchley, dancing with his plain, unmarried daughter, and Elizabeth need look no farther than the daughter's face to understand why she was, and ever would remain, unmarried, poor girl.

She saw Sir Richard and Patricia Bankhausen at the far end of the hall, and raised her fan and gave a small bow in their direction. But who was this stranger who stood by their side, clearly not with them but at least known to them, because Patricia was talking to him while her husband engaged someone else in conversation?

He wore a suit cut with a slightly unfamiliar and almost continental flare. He stood, champagne glass in hand, surveying the wealth and privilege the dancers represented, almost ironically, as though he had no part in it but was an observer above and beyond such frivolity. This must be the person Patricia had asked her to invite: Dr. Gunn. Well, he certainly looked handsome enough. Elizabeth had asked Sebastian to check that he really was a merchant and, more important, a successful merchant (one could not entertain people in one's own house who were involved with petty trade and sordid commercial transactions). Sebastian had dutifully asked a friend, who had inquired of someone else who owned a private bank, and the response had been gratifyingly favourable. Gunn was rich, unattached, and in the East his name was already spoken in the same breath as Dr. Jardine and Mr. James Matheson, whose Eastern trading company was probably the largest and most distinguished east of Suez. But what was he like? She would speak to him herself and form her own judgment. Elizabeth swept on down the stairs, and the dancers parted to let her pass, and the band switched from a polka to the Gay Gordons. Like a queen, bowing towards guests to right and left, she walked the

35

length of the oak floor that glowed like glass beneath her golden shoes. Her husband followed her.

'My *dear*,' Patricia greeted her hostess with sincere insincerity, 'I would like to introduce a friend of my husband, who has lately returned from the East. Dr. Gunn.'

Gunn bowed to Elizabeth and shook hands with Sebastian.

'You must be finding it very cold in January after the heat of the tropics, doctor?' said Sebastian stiffly. He classed doctors with barber-surgeons and tradesmen; not the sort of person he would usually invite to his house by the front door. But then Elizabeth had been so anxious to oblige her friend Patricia.

'As a cold hand is held to be evidence of a warm heart,' replied Gunn, 'the generous welcome I have received on my return home has more than compensated for any inclemency in the weather.'

'You are home for good, sir?' Sebastian went on, not that he really cared. And there was another reason he strove to conceal; something about Gunn irritated him intensely. For a start, he was a good three inches taller and more heavily built than Sebastian, and had a look in his eyes that seemed almost sardonic; as though he realized he was invited because of his own achievements, and was not a gentleman through generations of breeding, and the fortunate gambles taken by forebears hundreds of years before his birth. He was his own ancestor and owed no man servility.

'The words "for good", sir,' Gun replied, 'sound too permanent for my intentions. I hope to return to China in the spring. There is an attraction about the East which, as a doctor, I would say resembles that of the electric magnets that our scientist Michael Faraday has recently been experimenting with so successfully. It draws everyone back irresistibly.'

'You do not sound as though you rate the attractions of Society or this country very highly?' said Patricia, pouting and turning slightly away. She always thought her left profile was the best, and so displayed it whenever she could.

'Then, madam, the fault is mine in that I have been away from Society too long to express in proper degree the pleasure I derive from an evening such as this.'

'Surely life is very crude in this trading post I read about in the papers – Macao? How do you pronounce it, exactly?'

'Hard. As in Canterbury, ma'am. I would not agree that life there is in any way crude, although naturally we lack some of the amenities of culture that so enrich life in this country.'

'But all those interminable wars and insults we have been reading about in the papers by Chinese and Indians and so on – and the dangers to the lives of quite ordinary people—'

'Quite ordinary people, ma'am, among whom I would not presume to include yourself, or indeed any of your guests here, are always subject to insults and dangers. And a man can die of fever as easily in a castle as on the coast of China. The ancient indigenous races to whom you refer possessed a civilization which was in full flower when our ancestors were painting themselves blue with woad.'

'You speak of your ancestors, sir,' retorted Sebastian stiffly. 'Mine were always of the nobility.'

'In that case, sir, you have the advantage over me,' said Gunn. 'In this matter I would tend to agree with Seneca.'

'And what did he say, pray?'

'He who boasts of his descent praises the deeds of another.'

Gunn expertly exchanged his empty glass for a full one from a passing waiter's tray, and the band swung into the Lancers. Elizabeth hastily introduced Gunn to Admiral Critchley's daughter, and he asked her for the pleasure of the dance. They swirled away under frozen waterfalls of crystal candelabra, beneath the disapproving painted gaze of Sebastian's ancestors in their gilded frames. One partner led to another. Gunn danced with his hostess; with her sister, who wore thick glasses in an attempt to conceal a cast in her left eye; and then with Patricia Bankhausen.

'I have no idea why Lady de Vere should invite me to this ball,' Gunn told her, as they sat out a waltz in two gilt chairs, sipping champagne. 'I have never been introduced to her before this evening.'

'Are you glad she did invite you?'

'Delighted,' said Gunn. 'But, as I say, puzzled.'

'There are some puzzles that even the cleverest can never solve,' Patricia replied enigmatically.

'Seemingly so.'

Gunn had sized up the woman easily enough; she was passionate, frustrated, and she wanted an affair, or at least a man. He had met many other women like this, in Macao, in Hong Kong and Singapore; but in a hot climate, where death from a dozen causes seemed much closer than in this cold island, the passions always burned near the surface. Here they could be more readily concealed or disguised beneath layers of breeding and social customs. But, like a latent volcano, they smouldered on just the same. Sometimes, too, they could no longer be denied and burst out with all the heat of a pent-up furnace. Could this be one of these things, so far as Lady Bankhausen was concerned?

He found himself drawn to her, interested, and in turn flattered by her interest. Already, the chemistry of attraction was producing a heady, potentially dangerous amalgam of desire after months of worry and depression about his health. She had a gaiety that amused him, perhaps because, before he sailed East, he had never met women like her or his hostess. Indeed, as an impecunious medical student, he had met scarcely any women at all; and out East, he was never sure whether a woman wanted him for himself or because she wished him to give her an expensive present; or simply because he represented power and wealth, and to some feminine minds the equation could be irresistible.

'Have you seen Sebastian's library?' Patricia asked him, breaking into his thoughts.

'No,' said Gunn. 'This is my first visit to his house.'

'He had relatives who, I believe, were in Eastern trade. He has gathered a considerable collection of accounts of their early voyages . . . if you wished to see them?'

'It would be a pleasure,' Gunn assured her.

They walked past the dancers, out through the double-doors, instantly opened for them by a bowing periwigged flunkey. Another log fire burned in an inner hall; the library was to the right, with a bust of Solon over the door, and underneath his words: 'Call no man happy till he dies; he is at best but fortunate.'

The books on their polished oak shelves had their own peculiar smell of old damp leather and crumbling paper. Patricia handed one to Gunn. He glanced at it and then replaced it carefully on the shelf and turned to her, a wild mad thought exploding in his mind. He could have her here on the chaise-longue, and they could return to the ballroom and no-one would ever know they had been away. The idea was insane, of course, brought on by the unusual proximity of a passionate woman; by drinking iced champagne in an over-heated room with the chill of winter outside, and the prospects of death before a year was out. As Gunn analysed his feelings, the need receded.

'Are you and your husband the house guests of Lady de Vere?' he asked her.

'Yes. We are staying here for several more days.'

'But you usually live in London?'

'Yes.'

'I have taken temporary chambers at 13 Jermyn Street. I would be greatly honoured if you would accept an invitation to take tea with me there after your return. Next Thursday, at four o'clock to be precise. Your husband will no doubt be engaged with patients at that time?'

'Yes. He has engagements all next week. But I feel I could be free on that day. It is my pleasure to accept your invitation.'

'And mine to anticipate your arrival,' said Gunn. 'Now, if I am not mistaken, here is a very rare edition of Hakluyt's *Voyages* . . .'

The shadows of a late February afternoon painted the bedroom with darkness. The familiar outlines of dressing-table, leather chairs, the carved bedside tables, merged gently, almost imperceptibly, with the brown encrusted wallpaper, until even the air seemed the colour of dust.

Outside, in Jermyn Street, the muffin man's bell clanged as he hoarsely called his wares.

'Hot, steaming muffins! All hot, steaming muffins!' He went on his way, balancing the square wooden tray on his head.

Gunn sat up in bed, struck a lucifer and lit the pink-shaded oil lamp on the table. Patricia Bankhausen stirred lazily and luxuriously beside him, blinking like a cat against the gentle glow of the flame.

'It is four o'clock,' Gunn told her. 'You said you would have to leave at half past.'

He ran a finger gently down the alabaster skin of her back. She wriggled.

'Do that again,' she said huskily, 'and I will never leave.'

She rolled out of his reach and turned to face him. They were both naked, with only a sheet around their trunks. The fire had sunk to a red comforting glow. He saw its warmth reflected in her eyes.

'To think it is only weeks since we first met at Sturry,' she said dreamily. 'It seems as though I have known you for years.'

'That is because we meet so seldom. And when we do, our meetings are hedged around with subterfuge. We do not hope for years or months together, but barely hours. This heightens our feelings of mutual passion. As Dr. Johnson wrote once, "When a man knows he is to be hanged in a fortnight, it concentrates his mind wonderfully." '

'Why do you think about death when you are young and rich, when you have the greater part of your life ahead to look forward to?'

'I do not think about death a great deal,' replied Gunn. 'But as a physician I am ever conscious of the long fight we wage against it, and that, in the end, we all must lose the last battle. My chief counting house clerk in Macao told me a story about the human condition. There was once a Chinese merchant in Canton, he said, whose servant came to him one morning in a state of terror, and begged for the loan of his fastest Arab steed. He explained he had been shopping in the bazaar, and was astonished to see Death appear before him, in a frightening vision. He wished to ride to Peking so that Death, if he came to seek him out, would never find him. So the master gave him his fastest horse and then went to seek out Death in the bazaar himself. He also saw Death and asked why he had terrified his hireling. And Death replied: "I did not mean to frighten him. I was simply surprised to see him here – when tonight we keep an appointment together in faraway Peking," The moral is that when we imagine we are running away from events we fear or dislike, we often in fact are only running towards them.'

Patricia sat on the edge of the bed, looking at the fire. Then she turned to him.

'How many more visits will you have to make to my husband before he cures you of whatever your ailment is?'

'I scarcely can meet his eyes when I visit him,' admitted Gunn, not answering her question. 'Do you imagine he could suspect how you spend so many of your afternoons?'

'No. No-one could possibly guess.'

She stood up and began to put on her clothes. Gunn also dressed, and embraced her as she stood by the bedroom door. But now there was a faint chill between them; something had left their relationship – if it had really ever been there.

'I may not be hanged within a fortnight,' Gunn said, trying to make a joke, 'but I have received intelligence that forces me to return to Macao quite unexpectedly in about that time.'

'But you will come back? You will only stay briefly in Macao?'

'Yes,' he assured her, weighing the irony of her question and his answer. 'I will only stay there briefly. You have my word on that.'

He rang for the manservant and ordered him to call a hansom to the front door. He watched Patricia walk down the lamplit staircase. She paused on the last landing and waved up to him. He smiled after her and waved in reply and then he crossed to the window, and saw her climb into the waiting hansom. When she was gone, Gunn remained standing at the window, holding the deep red curtain, not seeing the street outside, filled with shoppers, and the blazing shop windows, but thinking of his lonely cabin in the *Hesperides*, panelled like this room, and dim like this at evening, when he would watch the sun dip into the inky sea and darkness sink from the sky.

He had not told Patricia that Captain Fernandes had called on him that morning with information that he had unexpectedly been offered a full cargo of cotton at a good price, on condition he sailed as early as possible.

Gunn had made up his mind at once; they would leave on the midnight tide. Sir Richard's treatment was having no effect whatever; Gunn was only delaying his departure because he felt convinced he would never return to England, and he was reluctant to bid farewell to the land of his birth. This would, no doubt, be his last visit to London, his last voyage East. Soon, within months at the most, there would be other finalities. He would take his last walk unaided, visit his offices and godowns for the last time. The prospect depressed him immeasurably, heavy on his heart as a vast physical weight, almost beyond human ability to bear.

Patricia would soon forget him, as more sombre thoughts would drive her from his mind. There had been nothing more between them than the unexplainable alchemy of attraction; they had both needed someone. It was purely fortuitous that they had found each other.

He would leave her a present, say a thousand guineas in a bank deposit in her name, to buy herself some jewellery to help to soften her sadness at his precipitate departure. Not that she would grieve greatly or for long; she would soon find another lover. Gunn was the one who should grieve. He had no need now for money or love, and little inclination left for either. What he lacked was time; and only God disposed that priceless gift.

A knock at the door interrupted his thoughts.

'Come in,' he called, without turning. The colonel's manservant entered and bowed.

'Is there anything you wish, sir? Shall I bring in a little more coal, perhaps, and light the lamps?'

'No thank you,' Gunn told him. 'I will stay in the dark. The fire is good enough, too. But there is one thing you can bring me.'

42

'Of course, sir.'

'Go to the wine merchants up the road, and buy me three bottles of champagne. Charge them to my account.'

'You will dine in your chambers, then, sir, with guests?'

'No,' said Gunn grimly. 'I will drink in my chambers. Alone.'

CHAPTER THREE

Captain Fernandes knocked gently on Gunn's cabin door.

'Singapore Island sighted starboard ahead, sir. One hour's sailing away.'

'Good.'

Gunn slid the curtain from his porthole and adjusted his glass over the glittering, dancing sea. The island lay green as a giant emerald in the morning sun, with tropical forests stretching down to a white rim of breaking waves. Above the trees he could see church spires and high buildings – several new since his last visit. On Flagstaff Hill the Union Jack stood square in the wind. Dozens of ships and sampans lay at anchor in the harbour.

He opened the porthole, and a thousand half-forgotten, now-remembered scents poured in, faint with distance; the sweetness of hibiscus blossom, the smell of curry, of spices and fish that had dried in the sun. He heard Fernandes shouting orders above the crack of the huge main-yard, which was 78 feet between boom irons and the urgent patter of bare, hard-soled feet on the deck. As the *Hesperides* turned slowly and gracefully towards the harbour-mouth, Gunn recalled the first time he had savoured these siren-scents of the East.

He had been a ship's surgeon, on his first trip to Canton, and going ashore, he had been drugged in a Chinese eating house and carried off to Macao. There, a rich Parsee merchant made him an astonishing proposition.

He was to pleasure the Parsee's young married daughter and get her with child by a white man. Her own husband's seed was barren, and her father desperately wished to keep the line of succession fair-skinned. Finally, they had agreed a price: three thousand guineas on the Parsee's note of hand.

44

But Gunn had been innocent then in the ways of commerce in the East, as well as the ways of love, for when he had successfully completed his part of the agreement, the Parsee offered him passage back to Canton in the *Hesperides*, a clipper in which he owned the major share. But instead of returning to his own merchantman, Gunn was marooned down the coast, for the Parsee believed that hostile Chinese would soon murder this Red Bristled Barbarian who had dared to land uninvited on the forbidden shores of the Celestial Kingdom. And then the Parsee's secret and his money would both be safe.

But although the Chinese had indeed pursued Gunn through the jungle, he had escaped and met another castaway, a Scot, MacPherson, the former mate of a British merchantman that had been seized by pirates some time previously. The Chinese tolerated MacPherson's presence because he spoke their dialects, and so could translate accurately the prices that itinerant British and American opium dealers demanded when they landed to seek new markets for opium, or, as the Chinese contemptuously called it, Foreign Mud.

Gunn had persuaded MacPherson to help him seize the *Hesperides* when next she put in for this purpose. Together, they had sailed her back to Macao and, under cover of the vessel's guns, Gunn had forced the Parsee to make over to him his shares in the ship and the company that owned it. On these unlikely foundations, Gunn had built the vast business enterprise he now controlled, which he and MacPherson had renamed Mandarin-Gold. Everyone in the East knew and respected the power of a mandarin – and did not the whole world of commerce revolve on a golden axle?

He dressed quickly, washed and – almost mechanically – now – examined his face once more to see whether those tell-tale brown spots had increased or diminished. But so far as he could judge, they remained as they had been for months. He felt a sudden excitement at the prospect of landfall, for this was where he belonged; Singapore was like a lodge at the gates of the East, leading to his mansion of adventure and achievement in Canton and Macao. It would be fascinating to see how his business had grown, what his new house in Macao was like –

45

work was only half done when he had sailed to England – and to examine the new warehouses he had ordered to be built on Hong Kong island. Despite the doubts of some of his friends at the small size of the island, he was convinced that its magnificent harbour compensated for all other faults. Any investment in it could be repaid 100 times.

Gunn had been away for months – a lifetime – and indeed longer than he could reasonably expect to live. Fernandes had taken the *Hesperides* to Singapore and back to the West India Docks in that time, and brought him word that, with all restrictions lifted regarding China trade after the successful outcome of the short, savage clash that the newspapers had dignified by the name of an Opium War, his business was still growing at an astonishing pace, and with it, his wealth.

The face of a man who realized how hollow all this was when measured in the scales of eternity, looked back at him from the cabin mirror.

He glanced at the calendar pinned up beside the mirror. Assuming that Sir Richard Bankhausen's diagnosis had been correct, he had about a hundred and fifty days left before life would become a burden, and the heat that now excited as much as it wearied him, would become unbearable, and he would long for evening, and then for merciful oblivion.

Gunn had not kept any more appointments with Sir Richard. He had sent a letter by messenger, giving the excuse of unexpected and important business that claimed his attention, and had asked for the specialist's account to be sent to his London agents for them to settle. He had not added that he would be at sea by the time Sir Richard received his letter. He had also given instructions to his bank in St. James's to open an account to the value of 1,000 guineas in the name of Patricia Bankhausen; then he had sailed on the midnight tide.

He unstoppered a bottle of whisky and took a deep draught to flush out these sterile thoughts of the past. He had begun to drink earlier in the day on this voyage, and also more frequently, for the surge of alcohol into his tired blood brought its own brief feeling of well-being and comfort. He disliked being alone. He hated the long nights when the sound of the sea

46

shanties sung endlessly by the crew in the fo'c'sle mocked his own weakness with their male legends of sexual and drinking feats. He would dose himself liberally with laudanum, and then wake late with a heavy head and thudding heart, and an increasing distaste at the prospect of another day.

He wiped his mouth and went up on deck. The heat of the sun hit him like a fist. The ship's rail was already hot to his touch, and the wind, although cooled by a stretch of sea, held all the burning warmth of a distant furnace.

The helmsman steered *Hesperides* in between sampans, lorchas and a cluster of little prahus, and past a flotilla of gigantic rafts made from newly-hewn tree trunks, 600 feet long and 70 feet broad. Each raft contained up to 2,000 trunks lashed together by rattan rope, and they provided homes to their crews of 25 men, with their families, in small attap-houses. Children played with hoops and smoke spiralled up from cooking fires. To move against the current, the crew would sit on a bench facing a horizontal barrel mounted on an axle, with holes cut in it for their feet. To this barrel was lashed a rattan rope 200 yards long with an iron anchor at the far end. One of the crew carried this anchor in a small rowing boat to the full extremity of its rope and dropped it in the sea. Immediately, the others began to turn the barrel with their feet, and so winched the great rafts along. When the rope was wound in, the whole operation would begin again. Eventually, the rafts would reach their destination, the lumber would be sold, and then all would journey back to the forests to cut down more trees, a cycle of events that occupied the whole of each year.

Fernandes approached Gunn.

'Will you be going ashore, sir?' he asked him.

'Of course,' said Gunn. He maintained an agency in Singapore and a staff of clerks under a European manager, who had been appointed while he was in England. He wished to meet him and assess his potential and his character. It would also be pleasant to stretch his legs on firm ground after so long at sea, with only the briefest stops at Madeira, St. Helena and Cape Town for water and provisions. The next brief stop after Singapore would be at Anjer Point in North West Java, 80 miles from Batavia, where a record was kept of all British and American ships entering and leaving China seas, so that a report could be sent on their movements to Lloyds in London.

'We will stay here for about a week,' Gunn told Fernandes. 'See that the vessel is completely revictualled. And show me all bills before you approve them.'

His wealth was no reason why he should allow anyone to cheat or overcharge him.

Even as Gunn spoke, he mentally subtracted seven days from a total he believed still remained to him. He still tried to measure out his life in months, but soon this would shrink to weeks and then to days. The thought made him start up from his sleep, crying out against the injustice of it all. How infinitely preferable, as with the vast majority of God's humblest creatures, not to know the time and manner of your death!

The *Hesperides* sailed on, the seas calm now as a blue glass floor, dotted with clusters of tiny islets, covered by trees of astonishing greenness. On some of the islands stood houses built by rich merchants, and boasting white stone porticos. Others seemed entirely deserted, save for rich-plumaged birds that fluttered from the trees at their approach.

Singapore Island – Lion Island in the vernacular because lions had roamed its forests in bygone days – was dignified by several hills. The largest was Bukit Timah or Mirror Hill, overlooking the harbour and so named because the sea reflected its cone-like shape in a mirror image.

The water was clear now as well as calm, and Gunn, leaning on the rail, could see a stretch of pink coral beneath its surface; shoals of fish flickered between clumps of seaweed, with trunks thick as a man's thigh, like a forest of sunken trees. The beauty of land and sea, with the fresh warm scents of the wind, accentuated the aching loneliness he felt within him.

They were coming in now under Flagstaff Hill, where flags could signal to vessels as far as sixteen miles away. Gunn saw the wide round mouths of the mortars built into the hillside, the blunt barrels of fifty-six pounder guns, and then the barracks for British and Indian troops. Buglers were already sounding morning calls, and their metallic echoes beat back from the hills and across a shining sea towards him, like a welcome.

The *Hesperides* sailed past the P. & O. wharves and the ugly sheds recently built to house the mountains of coal needed for the new steamers; past other wooden ships lying at anchor for repair. Relays of Malay divers were working on them; diving with sheets of copper to rivet in place under water, then bobbing up for air every few moments, then diving again.

Gunn spotted a Jardine, Matheson clipper in harbour and next to her one flying the Mandarin-Gold flag at her mast head; the *Waverley*, newly tarred and painted, out from Macao with silk and sugar for London, so Fernandes informed him. As the *Hesperides'* anchor chains went out with a roar, the longboat was already being lowered to take him ashore. It was no idle claim that his company's ships were the smartest or his crews the best disciplined.

How strange, he thought, as he watched them, that as a ship's surgeon only a few years ago he had to beg his passage ashore with any officer who might be generous enough to allot him a place in a gig or longboat! Now his intimation to Fernandes that he was going ashore had been instantly relayed to his personal cabin steward. His clothes were packed, and at that moment were being carefully lowered in two wooden cabin trunks bound with polished strips of brass. That was another difference between wealth and mediocrity; you commanded experts and servants of all kinds to carry out your wishes, even to anticipate them. But at what price had these distinctions been bought?

An officer saluted.

'Longboat ready alongside, sir,' he reported.

Gunn nodded his approval, climbed down the white gangway, and sat in the stern of the boat. Behind him, flags run up to the masthead informed his manager, Mr. Murgatroyd, waiting on the quay, that the founder and principal shareholder was coming ashore.

The manager was a red-haired man in his early thirties, wearing light trousers and a dark jacket and a black stovepipe hat. He sweated nervously in the heat. He had only heard about his employer; they had never met.

'Welcome to Singapore, sir,' he said as Gunn stepped ashore.

'Thank you.' Gunn took the man's hand. It felt clammy to his touch. He did not like men who sweated profusely; cold damp hands reminded him of corpses, and he would be a corpse soon enough without further reminders. They climbed into a waiting gharry.

'Will you be staying ashore long, sir?'

'As long as I please,' replied Gunn shortly. What the devil was it to do with this creature how long he stayed?

'Do you wish to see the office, sir?'

'Is there anything that requires my presence there?'

Gunn had a sudden sharp distaste at the prospect of watching Eurasian clerks on high stools, of hearing their scratchy pens splutter nervously on rough paper, and smelling the sweat of their labours, heavy on used-up office air, dull with the mustiness of old contracts inscribed on parchment and stored in greasy drawers. He longed for fresh air with a salt wind from the sea; for wine, witty conversation and the company of friends to divert his mind from thoughts of his own mortality.

The manager looked sideways at him uneasily. What could he say? Dr. Gunn was a legendary figure; one of the richest men in Eastern commercial life – and he had nothing to show him except figures. His Singapore office had no problems, only rising profits. So he said cautiously, 'I don't know, sir.'

'What do you mean, you don't *know*? You manage my interests here. You are in charge of the whole enterprise in this crucial pivot of Eastern and Western trade, and the first thing you tell me on meeting is that you do not know if there is anything I should see! Who engaged you?'

'I joined just after you passed through on passage to England, sir. It was confirmed from Macao, by Mr. MacPherson.'

'H'm. Then doubtless you are well qualified for the position. But, remember, do not indulge my good humour by asking me what I should see in *your* office. If you have nothing to show, pray say so. Now be so good as to lead me to quarters.'

Gunn put out a hand to steady himself against the roll of the two-horse vehicle. Above his head, the scrubbed white canvas canopy flapped its scalloped edges in the breeze. He felt suddenly dizzy and weak; sweat was running down his back, and his flesh crawled with fever. He had spoken more sharply than he had intended. He had not meant to be irritable, but nausea had provoked him and he did not wish to admit he felt ill. Once this happened, once he lowered his guard, he would be done for. And how could he explain to an unknown employee who had twenty, thirty or even forty years of working life ahead of him, that he was measuring out his own future by days, and so had neither stomach nor time for fools or procrastination?

'I have put you up in my bungalow, sir,' Murgatroyd told him. 'I thought it would be more convenient for you than an hotel.'

'Thank you,' said Gunn more calmly. 'That is most hospitable of you. You are married?'

'Yes, sir. We have a son of five.'

I also have a son, thought Gunn. A son who does not even know me: a half-caste I have never seen, who has probably never heard of me. He could be any of these children who ran along behind their wheels, hands outstretched, hoping for gifts to be thrown them – a coin, a piece of fruit, a sweetmeat. In fact, my whole fortune is based on this act of connection with a Parsee woman whose father paid me to get her with child.

The gharry moved along Orchard Road, following a winding stream with flat rocks where dhobi men crouched beating clothes and chanting with each blow. The road was bordered by tall bamboo hedges with thick shrubs planted behind them as an additional screen to houses. White-painted stone gates opened on to private drives. Here and there, small open stalls had been set up, with natives squatting on their haunches and passively offering for sale such unexpected items as slices of crocodile flesh, dead pythons and dried octopus. Elsewhere along the road were Chinese death-houses, where old people waited with resignation for the end of their lives, and almost next to them, funeral shops full of incense and joss-sticks and paper money to burn on behalf of the newly-dead.

Singapore was growing quickly, adapting to its rising

importance as a commercial port. In the centre of Commercial Square the principal European business houses were built around a green lawn, white-washed, with red tiles and arches and pillars leading to inner rooms. There was even a telegraph office now, and as their carriage passed the four banks, built close together as though for reassurance, the rattle and chink of metal dollars sounded like an avalanche of falling coin. These Chinese cashiers tested all dollars in case they were counterfeit by pouring them from one hand to the other as they counted them. So expert were they that by the ring the coins gave they could instantly detect a forgery. And how much of that money is mine? Gunn wondered, as though it mattered; as though anything mattered now.

'Mrs. Murgatroyd is looking forward to meeting you, sir.'

'Mrs. who?' Gunn asked him; his manager's voice returned his thoughts reluctantly to the immediate future.

'My lady wife, sir.'

'Oh, yes, of course. And I am looking forward to meeting her.'

But, of course, he was not. Indeed, he found infinitely depressing the prospect of spending an evening with an employee anxious to impress him. Yet how else could he spend the time save in an impersonal hotel suite, dining alone; and every time he glanced at his watch, literally seeing the hands measure that ever-shrinking distance between him and the gates of eternity? And no doubt the man meant well, or at least he had a wife who did.

'It is a great honour to have you in our home, sir. We have taken the opportunity of inviting some friends to meet you.'

'How very kind of you.'

And again it was, of course, but also unnecessary and unwelcome. Gunn sat well back in the carriage, feeling the sweat chill on his shoulders, and his brow cold like the flesh of a corpse. These confounded attacks! He hoped he would not suffer from one during the dinner in front of strangers, who would only repeat and amplify how ill he looked. For, no matter how ill he might feel, he must at all costs preserve an outwardly calm appearance, although his mind might fume like a volcano, erupting and exploding with alarm. What would death be like? How would he make the passage from life to endless oblivion? Could the Bible stories he had learned as a child in Sunday School about heavenly choirs and the fires of hell possibly be true? No-one could say until they made that ultimate journey; and then no-one returned to report what they had experienced.

'My home, sir,' announced Murgatroyd proudly, as the carriage stopped. Gunn had been so concerned with his thoughts that he had barely noticed they were gradually leaving behind the new mercantile buildings, and then the imposing houses of the merchants, until finally only an occasional bungalow stood, white and isolated, like a milestone to progress in the thick green expanse of jungle. They were outside such a bungalow now, with a porch high and wide enough to shelter a gharry during the monsoon. Some attempt had been made to hack down the jungle creeper and plantains and to cultivate a rudimentary garden; a post and rail fence formed a square about a hundred yards wide around the house, embracing the servants' quarters.

'Very pleasant indeed,' Gunn said, wondering what Mrs. Murgatroyd would be like, and how early he could escape on the morrow. Perhaps he should pat the head of their small son. He began to search in his waistcoat pocket for a suitable coin. But how much did you give a child? Sixpence, a shilling, a guinea? Money was the only currency he acknowledged for friendship and compassion; what he had no knowledge of was the going rate for such petty transactions.

Malay servants were already running out barefoot to take down his cabin trunk from the roof of the gharry. He followed Murgatroyd into the house, and was pleasantly surprised by the coolness, due to the high ceiling and slatted bamboo screens, against which Indian *bhistis* were throwing hog-skins of water to cool the air.

'My wife, sir,' said Murgatroyd. A pale woman in a white dress, whose hem trailed on the varnished maroon tiles of the floor, came out of an anteroom. Gunn shook her hand.

'It is a pleasure to meet you, sir,' she said, curtsying slightly. 'I have heard a great deal about you from my husband.'

Gunn bowed, and said nothing. What could a man he had never met possibly have told her about him, except what he had learned by hearsay, which was usually worthless?

'Perhaps you would like to rest and take a bath before dinner?' she went on.

'You are very kind, ma'am,' said Gunn. 'As a matter of fact, I was feeling unusually and uncharacteristically fatigued. It must be the change from sea travel to land travel.'

Mrs. Murgatroyd clapped her thin pale hands, and a Malay houseboy led Gunn into his bedroom.

'Dinner will be at seven-thirty,' Murgatroyd told him through the door. 'We dine a little early here because most of our guests have quite a distance to travel home afterwards, and the roads are not up to English standards.'

Gunn removed his shoes, his jacket and his waistcoat, and loosening his braces, he lay back thankfully on the bed, looking up at the plain pine ceiling. Shades covered the windows, like great bamboo eyelids to filter the merciless heat of the afternoon sun. Through the triangular crack in one of them he saw a patch of blue cloudless sky, and heard the splash of water, Indians hawking in their dusty throats, the grind of iron-tyred wheels as the gharry went round to the coach-house.

The disease must be taking a firmer grip on him; this enormous lassitude felt like fighting an unseen adversary in a fog. Perhaps he had been foolish to return East, but what lay ahead of him if he had stayed in Herne Bay, in a cold narrow house with an old man grumbling throughout the long chill of an English winter? But then what lay ahead for him anywhere?

Gunn sat up, crossed the room and washed his face and hands in a china ewer, and then looked at himself again in the mirror: the brown rash of spots was still there.

He lay down on the bed again and unexpectedly fell asleep. When he awoke, the bright blue sky had deepened to indigo, and frogs were croaking in the bushes. In the kitchens, Indian servants were chanting over a rattle of metal cooking pots. Someone had lit a candle in Gunn's room, and, feeling refreshed from his sleep, he crossed to the bathroom. A tin bath stood near a rush mat on the stone floor; lizards scuttled away at his approach. The water was only tepid; it must have been heated an hour or more ago, but he bathed and changed into his dinner suit. By his watch, the time was seven thirty-one. Two gharries arrived and left with a brisk clop of hooves, and he heard voices raised in greeting. He walked into the hall, where Murgatroyd sat in a cane easy-chair, pretending to read, while he waited for his employer.

'You feel refreshed now, sir?' he asked Gunn respectfully.

'Much refreshed, thank you.'

'Then I would be pleased to introduce my guests.'

Murgatroyd led him into a smaller room, hung incongruously with hunting prints and pictures of English fields, golden with harvest. Several guests were already there; Malay servants in white moved among them carrying trays of glasses and decanters of sherry and whisky.

'First, sir,' said Murgatroyd, 'I would like you to meet Captain and Mrs. Macrae. He is serving with the Yeomanry on detachment here.'

Gunn gave his hand to a red-faced man in his thirties, with bright blue eyes and skin as raw as if it had been sandpapered. His wife wore a dark moustache. She looked at Gunn with interest. She had heard of his wealth and his achievement. It was not often that the wife of an army captain, without private means and in an unfashionable regiment, met someone of his importance.

'Now, sir, we have our padre, the Reverend Cuthbert Royce and his lady wife. And here,' Murgatroyd went on rather nervously, 'a young man only lately in the East, Mr. Mark Greene, who is desirous of entering the mercantile field.'

'In other words, Mr. Greene,' said Gunn, smiling, 'you wish to work for Mandarin-Gold?'

'No, sir,' replied Greene promptly. 'Although if the proposal were uttered, I would esteem it a considerable honour, and a distinction I would be reluctant to refuse.'

He stood almost as tall as Gunn, but was younger and slimmer, with high cheek-bones and a sensitive mouth. He looked as

Gunn imagined a poet might look; but then he had never met a poet. As they shook hands, he noted with approval that Greene's hand-clasp was warm and firm. Gunn liked him on sight; he was direct, and this in itself was a rare quality. No doubt, Murgatroyd had only asked him here hoping that Gunn might somehow absorb him into the Mandarin-Gold empire, and maybe, indeed, he would make Greene an offer of employment. But what commanded itself to Gunn was that Greene had not asked him. When so many virtual strangers did ask Gunn for jobs or favours, either for themselves or for friends and relatives, this spoke well for him.

They took their places at the long table, lit by candles in silver holders. Moths flew blindly into the flames, throwing brief trembling shadows on the walls. Behind each chair stood one Malay servant to hand them their plates, with a second to pour the claret. Conversation flickered briefly between the guests. The Murgatroyds' young son was suffering from a fever, but their doctor held out good hopes of an early recovery. The Reverend Cuthbert Royce and his wife were shortly moving up country, but a bridge had been demolished on the road to Kuala Lumpur, and so they were delayed until it was repaired. This could take days or weeks – probably the latter, knowing the speed at which local coolies worked nowadays. Was not the derivation of the word *coolie* interesting? It stemmed, Murgatroyd assured them, from the Chinese *kuli*, which often meant a female labourer. And of course, in the East, women did physical work on the roads, just as in England, of course, they worked in mills and coal mines.

Gunn sat on the right of Mrs. Murgatroyd who made nervous, inconsequential conversation, crumbling a roll with her left hand, eyes flitting from one guest to another. She was uneasy at the prospect of entertaining her husband's employer; the knowledge that he held her husband's whole career in his hands made her sweat slightly. She also felt resentful that this ill-looking man could wield so much power. The knowledge that he had started from nothing so recently only increased this irritation. What gifts did he possess that her husband lacked?

Her face, thought Gunn with distaste, resembled a pale,

slimy slug. Yet she could be ambitious, and probably was, if not for herself, then for her husband; she had a hard mouth and a strong jaw and wintry, dissatisfied eyes.

To Gunn's right side sat Greene, sliding steadily under the influence of the wine. He was engaged in animated conversation with Mrs. Royce about the condition of the natives her husband strove to bring to a belief in the Christian faith.

'You can't trust any of these natives,' she told him earnestly. 'Why, only last Tuesday my husband christened a little Malay boy, Akbar Mohammed, and gave him the Christian name of John, after the Apostle. On Friday he paid the lad a surprise visit and was amazed to see him eating a slice of pork. Naturally, he asked the reason why.

' "It is *not* meat," the lad told him spiritedly. But my husband could see it was, and this absurd lie annoyed him, naturally.

' "Not only are you breaking the stern Christian custom, but you are also a liar," he told the lad.

' "No, Tuan," said the little boy. "Me no liar. *You* sprinkle water on me and say I no longer Akbar Mohammed, I now John. So *I* sprinkle water on pork and say, you no longer pork, you now fish!" What *can* you do with such people?'

Conversation lagged while servants removed plates that had contained a mild curry of Malacca prawns, and replaced them with bowls of peeled mangoes. Greene turned to Gunn.

'Tell me, sir,' he said suddenly. 'As one of our premier merchants, are you at all acquainted with James Brooke?'

'Brooke?' Gunn repeated the name slowly. He was conscious that people and places his companions were discussing were quite unknown to him – just as Canton and Macao and the Treaty Ports in China would all be alien territory to them. He was a stranger here. Perhaps when he reached Canton, he would find that everything had also changed there, or maybe it was just that illness and travel had changed him. Brooke. The name rang a distant bell in his memory, but in what connection had he first heard it, and where and when?

'What does he do?' he asked, carefully not admitting his

ignorance. And then he remembered his father telling him about this same man.

'He is now virtually a rajah in Sarawak, sir,' Greene was explaining. 'A province on the north coast of Borneo.'

'And he is English?' asked Gunn. Success in any field of endeavour interested him. To be a white rajah must be a rare distinction.

'Yes, indeed. He was formerly in the employ of John Company, and held a commission in the Company's service in Burma. During the Burma War in 1825 he was left for dead, but his colonel later found he was still breathing, and so he was brought in. They sent him back to England, and gave him a pension of £70 a year on account of his wounds. But owing to a hold-up on the voyage back to India, his ship arrived late. He had technically outstayed his leave – and so he left John Company.

'Fortunately, his father was a man of means, a former Judge in Benares, I believe. He died and left his son £30,000.'

'Which,' said Royce, butting in on the conversation, 'James no doubt speedily dissipated, in the foolish way of most rich young men it has been my unhappy lot to meet.'

'Not so, sir,' said Greene vehemently. 'He took passage in a vessel he bought himself, the *Royalist*, and sailed back to the East.'

'With what in mind?' asked Gunn. 'To treble his inheritance in business?'

'No, sir. James Brooke simply wished to help the natives in Borneo.'

'But why?' asked Gunn, astonished at the answer. 'And how?'

'Two sound questions, sir,' agreed Greene approvingly. 'First, he is not interested in commercial ventures, but in genuinely improving the lives of his fellowmen. He believes that natives, heathen though they may be, are as much his fellows as his own kith and kin and colour.'

Gunn said nothing. He had met missionaries before; he had even employed one, an American pederast, as interpreter on his opium trips. One day Gunn had discovered this man selling

58

religious tracts over one side of the vessel while Gunn was negotiating the highest price for his 'mud' over the other! The more money Gunn made from opium, the more tracts the missionary could afford to buy in order to convert the minds of the buyers and addicts. Gunn considered this a curious equation of conscience. No doubt, missionaries meant very well, but Gunn personally believed it was impossible to make another, younger religion replace the more ancient, indigenous beliefs of the East. In the end, converts became confused, and the missionaries were cast down with despair at the poor results they obtained at such enormous sacrifice.

'Next, Brooke feels that natives are generally exploited for monetary gain. He is trying to help them understand the benefits they could bring to themselves by hard work and industry and order. He wants to establish – as he told me himself only last week when he passed through this city – what he calls an Eden of the East, where they may live without fear that we of the West will despoil their enterprises or convert them to new religious faiths – with apologies to you, Mr. Royce.

'Already he has won the affection and loyalty of the Dyaks who inhabit Borneo. Next, he has the trust of the rajah of that country, which incidentally, sir, has the distinction of being either the smallest continent in the world – or its largest island. It is roughly five times the size of England and Wales.'

'But how did he do this? And how permanent is the trust of these people likely to be?' asked Gunn. Maybe Brooke had some secret he could use with advantage in his own company? In any event, he might be an interesting man to meet; their aims and interests need not be opposed.

'He sailed there in the *Royalist*, and arrived at a time of revolution. The rajah, who had earlier shown he was kindly disposed to persons of our race by succouring some shipwrecked British sailors, asked for Brooke's aid in subduing this insurrection.

'Apparently a stalemate of siege obtained between mutineers and loyalists. Both had prudently surrounded themselves by stockades of sharpened bamboo sticks and neither side had the advantage. Brooke instantly summed up the situation.

'A sharp attack by his crew with bayonets fixed, in the British fashion, and the mutineers scattered in disarray through the jungle, leaving the rajah secure upon his throne as the ruler. Such was his gratitude that he declared he would give over the state of Sarawak to the man who had saved his kingdom. I make bold to say, sir, that this is the only instance of a man of European blood being asked by the indigenous ruler of a native state to assume such a position of power. And, of course, no corruption or bribery whatever was involved.'

'Now that indeed *is* a rarity,' agreed Gunn, sipping his claret, so that Greene would not see him smile, for his whole fortune had been built on the venality of Chinese officials. Although employed by their Emperor to stop the opium trade that enfeebled his subjects, they had willingly lent their authority, and influence to what they called 'the Coast Trade' so long as they received a share of the profits. Without their help, indeed, there would have been no trading in opium, and no quick fortunes for the traders.

'I have enjoyed a modicum of success through such unhappy practices,' admitted Gunn dryly. 'But clearly Brooke's achievement is infinitely greater than mine.'

'I knew that you founded Mandarin-Gold, sir, but being only lately arrived, I did not realize that it was founded on the shifting sands of bribery.'

'You do now, sir,' Gunn replied, 'and I would say that the sands shifted significantly in my direction.'

'I came prepared to admire you as someone who had opened up whole areas of darkness to British mercantile and commerical ingenuity. Instead, I find that, like Jardine and Matheson, and so many others, although no doubt you have a legitimate side to your great enterprise, there is another side of which I am sure you will agree, sir, no Englishman can be justly proud.'

Greene turned towards Gunn, and Murgatroyd saw with alarm that the younger man's face was darkened by wine and the strength of his feelings.

'Please,' he said nervously. 'Remember that Dr. Gunn is our senior guest.'

'I apologize, Thomas,' said Greene readily. 'It was not my intention to insult any guest, but, like James Brooke, I feel strongly about these matters. Britain is a Christian nation, and a country of immeasurable ingenuity and endeavour, with much to teach these simple peoples that would raise them to something approaching our own standard. Not equal, of course, but at least towards a more equal footing.

'True, we have stopped the transport of slaves from China to India. We have stamped out many iniquities, such as *suttee*, in India, whereby wretched Hindu widows were forced to fling themselves alive on their husbands' funeral pyres and perish in the flames. But in assiduously advancing our commercial interests, I submit we stand in danger of corrupting whole continents, and ruining entire nations through opium, and in so doing, amassing a fearful debt that our sons, or our sons' sons, will one day be called upon to pay at a terrible rate of interest.'

'I beg you to desist,' Murgatroyd told him sharply. It was intolerable that this young fellow, who his wife had suggested he should invite, presumably as a makeweight to help balance the numbers, should insult the founder of the company, on whose regard his whole future depended. Had Greene gone mad? Or was the combination of claret and a hot climate too much for him to bear?

The room was suddenly silent. The hostess looked nervously at Gunn beneath lowered eyelids. The Reverend Royce wiped his mouth daintily with his napkin, and wished he were elsewhere. His wife looked in an embarrassed way over the guests across the table, a forced smile on her lips, as though viewing some distant sight of which they were oblivious.

Only Greene remained unrepentant, glowering belligerently at Gunn, almost challenging him to refute his opinion. Gunn sipped his wine thoughtfully. He was neither annoyed nor insulted, but in a strange way, interested. The young man had character and opinions, when so few men of twice his age had either.

'I must say, sir,' he said slowly, 'that for one so lately arrived here, you possess views of considerable strength which might in some quarters give cause for offence. I never deny that I have built a company on the foundation of selling opium. But, as a medical man, I have used opium, or laudanum, as you may know its English name, in nine out of ten of the drugs I have dispensed. It can bring peace to those in pain, and hope to those who have lost all else. It also gives comfort to the tormented and the bereaved. Opium is thus not so totally evil as you would suggest.'

'But in the end, sir,' retorted Greene, thumping the table with his clenched fist so that the silver rattled and wine trembled in the glasses, 'it brings death. For whereas one pipe a day may suffice a beginner for a year, then he becomes addicted, and demands two. Then three or four, until soon he is nothing but a living rotting chimney, where once he was a human being.

'Do you not find James Brooke's notion of a proud and fearless native state, untrammelled and undespoiled by such sordid transactions, of greater worth as a lasting monument to our country? And, indeed, sir, to yourself? How much better than to force cowed and subject people to puff their lives away through bamboo pipes, drifting hopelessly and helplessly into a foggy eternity of numbed sensations and dulled animation!'

'If you insist on insulting my guest,' said Murgatroyd sharply, 'please be so good as to leave my table.'

'I do not wish to insult anyone,' said Greene, standing up a little unsteadily, 'but if you feel that my views have gone beyond the limit of courtesy and social intercourse, then, sir, I will accept your invitation and withdraw.'

'Please,' said Gunn, putting his hand on the young man's sleeve and pulling him down again. 'You are both young. You take these things much too seriously.'

He turned to Murgatroyd reassuringly.

'I accept what our guest says, and I admit that it would be better to be remembered as James Brooke will no doubt be remembered, if his experiment succeeds, even to a limited extent, than to be recorded in the annals of time as a privateer who forced opium down the throats of peasants.

'Certainly Mr. Greene speaks with conviction, and he convinces me. So please do not think I'm insulted or in any way disturbed by the frankness of his speech. Rather do I admire him for it.'

Gunn paused, and suddenly he was no longer in the room with the flickering candles throwing shadowy images on the walls behind the silent servants. He was back in *Hesperides* with MacPherson, who had rescued him in the jungle, and they were running in under the guns of a larger, faster Jardine, Matheson clipper to undercut them with their 'mud', to make a deal, and then sail on.

How could he explain to this young shaver how all this felt when you were personally involved? The tang of excitement, and the grip of fear at your heart; money did not matter at all then, did not even enter into the equation. It was a case of your will and determination against that of others. You risked everything; even your life. Many merchants had been cut down by the hired assassins of their rivals in the dark stinking alleyways behind the quay at Macao. Others had suffered gunpowder charges in their vessels, which exploded out at sea. Professional mutineers had been deliberately infiltrated among crews to cut the captain's throat as he slept. It was a rough world; you took your chance of a fortune or a death. There was no middle way; no means of mitigating your risk.

How could he justify such crude and final terms to these gentle cultured people around this table, who could never begin to imagine such a way of life? Or to this young man Greene, who had doubtless absorbed his views from the Parliamentary speeches of others equally ignorant? How could the plump Reverend Royce appreciate the sweat of fear as you came in steadily beneath the guns of a hostile, rival clipper and you saw the tars stripped to their waists, holding ramrods and powder charges strong enough to blow your vessel right out of the sea if their captain gave the word – and eager that he should do so?

You took the risk that the captain would *not* give the word. But this was simply your nerve against his. As with two wrestlers fighting sinew to sinew, the weaker gave in and the stronger excelled; but at the start neither knew who would prevail.

But this was life in a totally different currency, and he had not the gift of tongues to explain it, nor did he feel physically able to argue out the matter. But of one thing he was certain. He had lived; these people only talked about living. Their lives were passed at second-hand, reflection in a mirror of time, without depth of feeling or excitement.

'You are not offended then, sir?'

Greene's voice brought Gunn back to the present.

'Not at all, young man. It is refreshing to meet someone with forthright views. But we all have dark secrets in our minds, about which perhaps, if we were honest to ourselves, we sometimes feel regret and maybe shame. However, we accept these, just as when I was a practising physician I accept failure with certain patients because I learned from failures and, as a result, might not fail a second time.

'Here I feel that the benefits of British penetration and trade with China must outweigh the drawbacks you mention. But we have talked on this subject long enough. Let us turn to other things. In the meantime, sir, I admire your spirit, your turn of phrase, and your conviction. And I would deem it a personal pleasure if you would lunch with me tomorrow at two o'clock aboard my clipper, the *Hesperides*. Mr. Murgatroyd will make the necessary arrangements to transport you.'

'Delighted, sir,' said Murgatroyd in a relieved voice. Like a seatide subsiding after a succession of unexpectedly rough waves, the conversation rolled on smoothly.

CHAPTER FOUR

WHEN the butler had brought Colonel Parker's card to Sir Richard, he had been delighted that his old friend had unexpectedly arrived in London, and come to see him. He had not heard from the Colonel for some weeks, although Gunn had been gone for nearly two months. Now private business had brought the Colonel to London on a brief visit, and he sat with an unease peculiar in such a large, insensitive man, crossing and uncrossing his legs, running a finger between his stiff white collar and his thick reddish neck.

'This is hardly a social call, Dick,' he said at last. 'Indeed, I hesitate to give that reason for it, but as a friend of yours for many years, and owing you a debt I can never repay for the splendid way in which you treated my daughter when she was so ill at the birth of her first child, I felt I must honour my obligation to you, painful and distasteful as this may prove.'

Bankhausen offered him his snuff-box, but the Colonel refused. He had spent a long time rehearsing what he would say, and how he could best say it, and he wished for no interruptions.

Bankhausen took a large sniff himself and sat back. Parker had obviously some problem which he was reluctant to reveal. He would let him speak in his own good time, so long as he was not too drawn out, because he had an appointment with another patient in half an hour.

'It concerns this tenant, Dr. Gunn, you kindly introduced into my chambers.'

'What about him?' asked Bankhausen.

'Do *you* know much about him?' parried the Colonel.

'Well, he is a rich man, a physician turned Eastern merchant. Not possibly entirely a gentleman, as you and I would understand the definition, but of some honour and very rich substances. I trust he does not owe you any rent?'

'Nothing like that at all. I would, however, agree he is certainly not a gentleman, for surely the first rule of a gentleman's behaviour must be that if he engages in any dubious activities, he must never be discovered? "Thou shalt not be found out", eh? The eleventh and most important commandment.'

'What has he done that should not be found out, and which you presumably have discovered?'

'He has used my chambers as a place of assignation, where he regularly met a married lady, the wife of a friend of mine. I first heard of his interest in this particular lady from my brother-in-law, Admiral Critchley. He took his daughter, Sophia, to the de Veres' ball in January, and he noted then that this person Gunn was particularly attentive to this lady, although they were only introduced for the first time that evening.

'I had cause to dismiss my servant yesterday over a matter of petty theft – you know how light-fingered these creatures are – and as a parting shot, he said he had often attended Gunn when he was entertaining this lady. He would serve them luncheon or afternoon tea. They would drink champagne together, and so on.'

'But there is nothing very strange about that, surely?' said Bankhausen. 'After all, Gunn is a young man, and a bachelor. He would assume that any ladies – even married ladies – would find him attractive.'

'I would not doubt that, sir. But would you take such an urbane and civilized view if you knew that this particular lady in this instance was your wife?'

'You mean – Patricia? And Gunn?'

'I mean exactly that, Dick. My servant even gave me the dates and the hours of their meetings. He kept a record for reasons of his own. Perhaps he felt that he might wring some money out of one or other of them in exchange for his silence. I do not know. But certainly Gunn's sudden departure came as a complete surprise to him.'

'And to me,' agreed Bankhausen. 'But at least the fellow paid my bill.'

'Well he might, too, after the disgusting way he had been behaving with his physician's wife. This association has been going on since they first met at the de Veres' ball.'

'Patricia persuaded Elizabeth de Vere to invite this man,' Bankhausen recalled hoarsely, in little above a whisper. 'I might have guessed. And yet I never did.'

'Well,' said the colonel, standing up. 'I feel that I have done my duty as a friend. I have taken the address of my man-servant, should you or your lawyer feel any evidence from him is called for.'

'You have never liked Patricia, have you?' said Bankhausen slowly.

'I would not say that, Dick. I just do not enjoy seeing my friends cuckolded by wives who I consider to be of inferior moral calibre to their own.'

Bankhausen made a move to the rope tassel that would ring the bell in the butler's pantry.

'Don't worry, Dick,' said the colonel quickly. 'I can see myself out.'

He shook hands and left the room. That would teach Patricia a lesson, he thought smugly as he closed the front door quietly behind him. He felt even more triumphant, for he had not felt it necessary to disclose that his dislike of Patricia sprang from the fact that on more than one occasion she had strongly repulsed his own amorous advances. And if he could not possess her illicitly, why on earth should anyone else succeed where he had failed?

For some time after Colonel Parker had left his surgery, Sir Richard Bankhausen remained sitting in the buttoned leather armchair behind his desk. This was not the Sir Richard his patients saw; urbane, attentive, if pedantic, a man in charge, to whom they could easily admit their fears, their guilts, their miseries. This was another man altogether, who lay back, eyes closed, oblivious to the cries of street vendors and the deep crunch of iron carriage-tyres on the sanded street. He looked suddenly very old, with a grey face, flesh sunken on his cheeks like a death mask, sitting wearily as so many patients had sat in the chair opposite him when his diagnosis had drained them of all hope.

There had been other occasions, of course, when Richard, under the humiliation of his own sexual inadequacy, had suspected his wife's interest in other younger or more vigorous men; but never had he received direct evidence of her infidelity, for he had deliberately never sought it. So what did he do now that he knew what he had for so long suspected? Did he stay with Patricia, endeavouring to conceal his hurt, his mounting anger, and continue to endure her supercilious contempt for him – or did he face her with this evidence and then offer her a divorce or a sum of money to leave his life for ever?

They had no children, of course, so this made his decision easier, but there was still the delicate pride of an older man.

He had thought for some time that eventually he might have to face such a decision, but had deliberately given his wife the full benefit of every doubt. Now that the first terrible shock was waning, as time dissipates the pain of a sharp blow, he felt, almost unbelievably, a sense of relief. He could admit now what he had never properly admitted to himself before, that she did not really care for him. She was not simply casual and remote and unpassionate, as he had tried to convince himself for so long; she was warm and passionate – and unfaithful. She had used him, drawing pleasure from his title, from his money, just as he had drawn a thin and increasingly unsatisfactory pleasure from having such a beautiful woman as his wife. Now both their illusory pleasures were at an end. He would be rid of her, cut her off, as he would advise a surgeon to sever a gangrenous limb from a body. The body might not survive the separation in as strong a condition as it had been before the limb became infected, but it would certainly not survive at all unless what had become poisoned was removed with dispatch.

His mind made up, Bankhausen leaned to one side and pulled the tasselled bell rope. The butler appeared in the doorway.

'Convey my compliments to her ladyship,' he told him, 'and ask her if she will be so good as to take coffee with me here.'

The butler bowed. In a few moments a footman carried in a silver tray, with a silver coffee percolator, cups and saucers, and bowls of sugar and cream. He placed the tray on a table by his master's desk, and returned to open the door for Lady Bank-hausen.

'What's the matter, Richard?' she asked brightly. 'I can't remember when you last asked me for coffee in your room. Have you no patients?'

'None for the moment,' he replied. 'Cream and sugar?'

'You know I take both.'

He poured out the coffee, and handed a cup to her.

'Sit down,' he said. 'I want to talk to you.'

'But why all the formality? What's wrong?'

'Should anything be wrong?'

'Well, you look – different.'

'I am – different. I want a straight and honest answer to a question. Have you ever had sexual congress with my patient Robert Gunn?'

His wife's pretty face puckered for a moment, as though she had never heard the name before.

'Gunn,' she repeated. 'Oh, you mean that merchant fellow you introduced me to at the de Veres? That potentate. Of *course* not. How on earth could you imagine such a thing?'

'I did not imagine it.'

'Well, what a *filthy* idea. I am absolutely insulted that you as my husband should ask such a foul and disgusting question – or even conceive I would be unfaithful. I do not even have an address for the man. Where could such an act possibly take place? Why, I have only met him once, as you know.'

'I am asking again for an answer. Is it yes or no?'

'Your answer, Richard, is emphatically, *no*. I repeat that I have never in all my life been so astonished and humiliated by such a suggestion.'

She stood up, smoothing her skirt with both hands, the coffee still undrunk. Her face was pink with rage, but looking in her bright eyes, her husband saw tiny flecks of fear and be-wilderment, and he knew that Colonel Parker's servant had not lied.

'Sit down,' he told her harshly, in a voice of authority she had not heard him use before. She remained standing.

'Sit,' he repeated, as thought speaking to a dog.

She sat slowly, feeling her knees grow weak, and sickness seize her stomach; her body was suddenly chill with fear. So he knew. The old serpent had somehow guessed. But how? Oh God, how *could* they have given themselves away? And to whom?

'You are lying to me,' said Sir Richard in his quiet voice, rather enjoying the turning of tables that had been set against him for so long. What had he ever seen in this woman that he should fawn before her and allow her to dominate him? She was just another silly housewife, the type he interviewed frequently in that same chair and then charged their doting husbands a hundred guineas for listening to their wives' frustrations. His strength was coming back to him, and with it, as feeling returns to a cramped, numbed limb, he found a terrible delight in the prospect of revenge. He would make Patricia cringe, as by her contempt for his performance in their bed, she had often made him sob with humiliation in the privacy of his dressing-room.

'You are lying,' he repeated. 'You have met Gunn regularly in his chambers in Jermyn Street. I could even supply you with the relevant dates – and how long you spent with him on each occasion.'

'You are mad, Richard. I deny it all. You're *insane*.'

But her voice was thin now and cracking. The denial lacked conviction. She seemed to shrink before him and to become not as she was – a young, passionate, desirable – but as she would be when old; discontented, dissatisfied, an unhappy lonely woman concealing pitiful hungers and inadequacies behind a shawl of faded beauty and another man's wealth.

'Do not attempt again to deny anything,' he said sharply. 'You have disgraced your married name. You have humiliated not only me, but yourself. Word of this, believe me, will soon be on everyone's lips. And what will your situation be then?'

She sat silent for a moment, not looking at him, but staring unseeing at the intricate red and blue and brown pattern on the carpet. She felt the roar of blood in her eyes and wondered if she would faint, and she pressed one fist into her palm and forced herself to stay as calm as she could, while her world collapsed about her and the future melted away.

'We did meet there, it is true,' she admitted. 'But only to take tea.'

Her husband said nothing and she blundered on wretchedly.

'But how did you know? Did you have someone follow me?'

'No. That I would never do. But someone saw you and recognized you, and eventually I was informed.'

'Who else knows?' she asked, suddenly giving up all pretence. Her voice was very small, like a little girl asking a petty favour from an adult.

He shrugged.

'No-one, yet. But they will. They are bound to.'

He opened his snuff-box in the gesture Patricia had grown to hate, and pushed a few grains into each nostril. He inhaled noisily and sneezed. The sight sickened her. God, what a man, what a creature! And to think she had ever allowed herself to believe that his wealth, his standing, could ever begin to compensate for love and sexual satisfaction. To think of his soft paunchy body strained uselessly against hers, when she had known a man like Robert Gunn.

'I will give you two alternatives,' Bankhausen told her.

'And if I do not take them?'

'You are in no position to seek concessions, or to alter any arrangements I may make out of the generosity of my spirit. As you know, under English law a wife is regarded as a chattel of her husband. She has no power to enter into any contract or commercial undertaking without her husband's authority and permission. In the eyes of the state, without her husband, she is nothing. And you will be – nothing. Not a maiden, not a widow, but a woman of easy virtue. And how do you intend to live, for you have no money of your own?

'Your mother persuaded me, when I first offered marriage, that you were different from the person events have proved you to be. And maybe I persuaded myself, for I imagined I was in love with you. I was even foolish enough to believe that you

71

might reciprocate my feelings, but your behaviour over the years of our marriage has increasingly brought me to the opinion that you hold no feelings of warmth for me.

'But I do not wish to inflict humiliation on you in addition to that which will be attached to your name in society, so I give you these two alternatives. I can divorce you on the grounds of adultery, naming this man Gunn. But I warn you that the proceedings would be painful and distasteful to you.'

'And the other alternative?'

'Simply that I give you a sum of money – I have in mind 1,000 guineas – and you go out of my life. By this means we are both absolved from disgusting and unnecessary publicity. We have no family, so there are no complications there, and I can change my will, which is simple enough to do.

'You can revert to your maiden name, or marry again bigamously, or disappear, but' – and here his self-control cracked and he beat the desk with his right fist until the lids on the silver inkwells leapt up and down like little mouths opening – 'one thing I insist on – that I never see you or hear from you again.'

'You do not give me much option.'

'I request your reply now. I have a patient who has already been waiting for several minutes.'

'And you have a wife who is waiting to leave you for ever.'

As Patricia Bankhausen stood up, her voice gained strength.

'You like your little power, Richard, because basically you have so little. You are a little man, not only physically, but mentally and morally. I married you, I agree, because my mother persuaded me, and because you seemed kindly and gentle, and I thought that love, or at least some shared warmth of feeling, might grow between us. But what has grown instead is your own high opinion of yourself. You like to feel you have the power of life and death over your patients. And you resent my independence, and the fact that you have neither moral nor physical domination over me.'

Her husband was already writing out a banker's cheque.

'Leave an address and this will be forwarded to you,' he said.

'When you have entered into a proper agreement with my lawyers, of course.'

'I will take rooms at Brown's Hotel, and ask them to forward the bill to you. That will give you an inducement to prevail upon your lawyers to deal speedily with the matter. Goodbye, Richard.'

'Goodbye.'

She walked slowly to the door, still in a daze, unable to accept that the unspeakable had happened. At the door, she paused and looked back at her husband.

Sir Richard Bankhausen glanced up at her.

'One thing I should tell you,' he said casually. 'I never speak about patients, but I feel free to do so now because Robert Gunn has been your lover, and so you have, shall we say, an intimate relationship together. I therefore feel myself free of all constraint to secrecy under the Hippocratic Oath. You should know you were loved by a dying man, Patricia. His seed was mortal, and he has at the most less than a year to live. When you see him again – when you are disposed to love him again – remember that.'

His wife burst from the door, weeping uncontrollably, and rushed up the stairs blindly to her bedroom, and then stood irresolute by her dressing table, heart pounding, one hand on her chin. Her horrified face stared back at her from the mirror.

Was *this* why Gunn had sailed away so suddenly? Had he literally left her to die – or had he somehow learned that their secret mettings were observed and he did not feel able to face her husband?

But no matter why he had departed so precipitately, Gunn had left her a handsome present; a new bank account with 1,000 guineas deposited in her name. Curiously, this was the same sum that her husband now proposed giving her. Was this chance, or could those two men conceivably have arrived at the same figure together? Surely not. She dismissed the idea as preposterous; but then so was the prospect of her future.

With nervous trembling fingers, Patricia unlocked the little drawers in her dressing table, and tipped out of washleather bags the rings and velvet-covered cases containing necklaces and bangles that her husband had given her. She might realize a few hundred pounds on them, and now she would need all the money she could find simply in order to live, for how long could a woman without private means expect to support herself? She desperately needed a key to someone else's wealth, but she could think of no-one, except Robert Gunn. To him, giving her a pension, an annuity, even a small house somewhere with a couple of servants, would be as nothing, if the shadow of death was so darkly upon him. He could not carry his wealth with him beyond the grave, so why should he not leave her some of it?

She had lost everything because of him, so she told herself now; everything. Then he had sailed away, leaving what to him would simply be a token gift. Yet how could she possibly contact him on the other side of the world – and if she succeeded in doing so, would she reach him before his death? She sat down, and her reflection watched her as an idea began to form in her mind. Gunn was ill; no, Gunn was dying – although, she recalled wryly, his performance as a lover would have seemed to contradict this diagnosis. But that was unimportant now; her husband would know the state of his health better than anyone else. It was also extremely unlikely that anyone apart from her husband realized the serious nature of Gunn's illness. He would naturally refrain from telling people himself, in case the news spread. This knowledge was therefore power; surely she could use it as a lever to advance her own situation?

Patricia crossed the room and opened the door a few inches. The butler was holding open the front door for a man she did not recognize – possibly the patient her husband had been expecting. Then Richard appeared, wearing a black top-coat; he would no doubt be going out to dine in his club. She waited until the butler had returned to the servants' hall, and then ran quietly downstairs and into her husband's study. She searched quickly through several drawers, but they contained nothing save bills, two books of bank cheques, and several spare quills. She opened and shut other drawers in his bureau until she found one that contained a folder on his patients. She thumbed through letters and her husband's notes until she came to a letter signed by Robert Gunn. This had been written aboard

74

Hesperides and dispatched when the ship had called at the Cape to revictual on the voyage home. She read it carefully, comparing his signature, the way he crossed the 'T', the way he wrote an 'O', with similar letters in the volume of the text.

She stood for a moment, savouring the thick opulence of the paper, the wealth it represented and how it was going to make her rich and independent. Then she tucked the letter inside her blouse, and went upstairs to her room.

CHAPTER FIVE

GREENE climbed out of bed, crossed to the window of his hotel room in Singapore, and drew back the thin cotton curtain. He was in an upper room of a new hotel above Boat Quay, one of a crescent of buildings overlooking the docks. Beneath him lay a panorama of activity. Half-naked coolies struggled with giant wooden cases of machinery from Birmingham; others rolled casks bound by iron hoops or moved bales of cotton from Lancashire. Singapore was a clearing port where merchandise could be stored safely until a buyer was found or a need discovered – or induced – in Malaya, in the Dutch colony of Java, even in China.

As the busy cranes swung one set of cargoes ashore to be hurried away on trolleys or carts, other bundles of rattan, and containers of gambier, a juice extracted from trees and used in treating leather for shoes and harnesses, with loads of sago and tapioca and spices, were swung back into the holds. No cargo was too strange, so long as it could show a profit. To one side of the main activity stood open metal drums filled with animal entrails, green and yellow with putrescence, pulsating with gas generated by decay, and swarming with flies. These were needed in the manufacture of Chinese love potions and specifics and therefore valuable, for the market was immense.

The tarred hulls of the ships glittered black against the sea, their varnished upper structures and white markings reflected in the oily water. One of these proud vessels must be *Hesperides*. Well, he would soon know which one. Greene crossed to the mirror, and rang a bell for hot water. It was anachronistic that he should appear so idealistic; and he was thankful no-one had remarked on the basic inconsistency last night at Murgatroyd's house, for it was indefensible. Greene had inherited a family shipbuilding and engineering business on the North East coast, and after Rugby and Oxford, enjoying a personal income of several thousand pounds a year, he was undertaking the equivalent of the grand tour of a previous century. It was easy, he admitted, to speak in defence of the poor when you were rich, and even easier, when you did nothing except speak. Possibly you voice radical opinions because you secretly realized that unless you had been fortunate to be born rich, you would be one of the poor yourself, for you possessed neither outstanding ability nor great native talent in any direction.

Just for a moment, Greene contrasted that other grey English sea, so different from the one beyond his window; that dull northern sky, perpetually clouded and clotted by smoke from his factory chimneys. And yet, his managers assured him repeatedly, if Greene increased the wages of workers he so rarely saw, their whole business enterprise, which now supported them as well as him, would almost certainly collapse. Then he put these disquieting thoughts from his mind, as the hot water arrived. God would never have blessed him with such good fortune without a reason. Maybe this reason would reveal itself at his meeting with Gunn?

Robert Gunn sat on the afterdeck of *Hesperides* beneath a scrubbed canvas awning and watched the sampans bob along with their strange fan-shaped sails, and house-boats where water-people lived within their own curious community – charcoal burners, washerwomen, barbers, the keepers of floating food-shops. All their boats, that formed complete floating villages, had broad flat sterns and square blunt bows painted with two eyes. He remembered the Chinese explanation of this: 'No got eyes – no can see.' Soon, he thought, his own eyes would be as useless as these blue and red likenesses. How pleasant it must be to be young and healthy like Greene, to be full of enthusiasm for some project, just as he had been when he first went into business aboard this same vessel! But youth without ambition soon grew dull, like silver that is too rarely polished. Enthusiasm wilted, energy waned; nothing lasted forever. He rang for his steward and asked him to give Captain Fernandes his compliments, and say that he wished to see him.

The ship's captain was a fat man with the dark skin of a Goanese, half Portuguese, half Indian. He had been captain of *Hesperides* when Gunn had been a ship's surgeon, and between them had grown that warmth of feeling which only men know when they have shared the same dangers and the same triumphs.

'What have you discovered about this man Greene?' Gunn asked him bluntly.

'That he is rich, and the owner, through his late father, of Greene & Gowram, shipbuilders and general engineers, in Newcastle. He is interested in helping the natives, but does not know much about them. A harmless, well-meaning, liberal-minded young man in the English mould.'

'I see. And what about Brooke?'

'I can discover very little more than you already know. He is called the White Rajah of Sarawak.'

'But what exactly does he *do* there?' Gunn interrupted.

'Nothing in any way competitive to Mandarin-Gold, sir. Like Greene, he appears to be a wealthy idealist, but of another type. He wishes to keep natives untouched by Western influence, and not preyed upon by any more advanced country. The Dutch do not care for him at all. They regard him as a British spy.'

'Is he?'

Fernandes shrugged.

'I do not know. But the captain of his vessel, *Royalist*, says emphatically he is not. He holds him to be a most fair-minded man, and very brave. He personally led the attack that defeated the rebels threatening the rajah in Borneo.'

'Would you say that Brooke is in fact secretly engaged in carrying out, shall we say, a survey of commercial possibilities, and that these noble thoughts and utterances are simply a cloak to conceal his real interests?'

'I would say exactly the opposite. Brooke is a man of private means, and all I have heard shows that he spends his money – modest as it is by your standards – in furthering his beliefs. Let me give you an example of his independent attitude. The merchants here in Singapore heard what he intended to do, and offered him a large sum of money for a share in his enterprise. He refused to accept this because his plans had nothing to do with commerce or opening up Borneo to the West. They were – in his view – more of a genuinely conservative nature. Keeping the best of the island's customs; teaching the natives how to improve their own standards, and so on.'

'You mean, selling them mud?'

'Never selling them mud.'

'Thank you,' said Gunn, 'I have this young Greene coming to luncheon with me. He admires this fellow Brooke. From what you tell me, I think I could admire him, too.'

'He is not your sort of man, doctor.'

'What do you mean?'

'You are a physician, I know. But you are the only physician I have heard of, apart from Dr. Jardine, who is more concerned with finance than physic. You are a born merchant, a dragoman. You like trade, not simply because you lust after money, but because you savour the excitement it engenders. That, so far as you are concerned, is infinitely more valuable than anything money you make can buy for you.'

'There are some things, Fernandes, that are not for sale because they are priceless,' replied Gunn, thinking of his own condition.

'So I have heard, doctor,' replied Fernandes dryly. 'But I do not think you will be wanting any of those things directly, will you?'

'Anything else?' asked Gunn, ignoring the remark.

'One small thing, sir, which I hesitate to bother you with. But it would mean a lot to the man concerned.'

'Who is the man concerned?'

'Seaman Jenkins, sir. He has been with us for five years, and has a good character. Before we set sail for England, he requested to be paid off in Singapore. I am sorry to lose him. He is honest, willing, but utterly determined to leave.'

'Why?'

'He wishes to see you, sir – to explain the reason. I know that the request is irregular, and there is no need for you as owner of the vessel to involve yourself in personal matters relating to the crew. But I would esteem it a favour if you could spare him a few moments.'

'Of course,' said Gunn. 'Send him up.'

'Thank you.'

Gunn poured himself a whisky, and on impulse left the bottle on the table, beside another glass. Two shadows darkened the doorway. Captain Fernandes saluted.

'Able Seaman Jenkins, sir,' he announced and then withdrew.

'Come in, Jenkins,' said Gunn. The dark-skinned bearded Welshman saluted in the doorway, took off his white cap, held it under his left arm and came into the cabin awkwardly, nervous in the presence of power.

'Sit down,' said Gunn, indicating one of the canvas chairs. 'I am sorry to hear that you are leaving us after so long. Can I persuade you to change your mind?'

'No, sir. It was not an easy decision to make, look you, but then neither was it a swift one.'

'Why Singapore, especially? You come from Swansea, I believe?'

'Yes, sir. And I have seen dozens of clippers from Swansea docks here in Singapore, and I know the amount of trade done is increasing all the time. Singapore is a kind of cross-roads for trade, sir, between West and East.'

'And you're leaving my service to secure for yourself a part of that trade?'

'Not a direct part, sir, but something on the side, if you get my meaning. I have figured that there are any amount of British, American, Dutch and French crews in and out of this port every day, but no clean, proper homely eating-houses for them. Only these Chinese places where they are offered native rubbish like soups made from birds' nests, eggs a hundred years old, and rice, as though they were bloody chickens – pardon the word, sir.

'I had in mind, sir, with my missus, to set up an eating house for food *I* would like to eat, and cheap, too. Like puddings, pork pies – any amount of pigs out here, sir – sausingers, eggs and bacon, tea, good bread, home brewed beer. Not any of your local rice wine.'

'You have an eye for business then, Jenkins?'

'I have not been in this ship in your employ for five years without getting *that*, sir. I have seen what you gentlemen can do, and I think that in a small way I could make this pay.'

'Have you any savings?'

'I have twelve sovereigns, sir, in my sea chest.'

'How is your wife coming out here?'

'She has already taken passage in one of the new P. & O. steamers as a lady's maid. She receives her food and her passage free. The vessel is due at the end of the week.'

'How do you intend to raise money for your venture, Jenkins?'

'I propose, sir, to visit a bank with the good reference Captain Fernandes has kindly given me, deposit my twelve sovereigns, and tell them what I can do, and borrow more money, like other merchants have done.'

'I see.'

Gunn looked at the man, and drummed his fingers on the table. He was touched by his honesty and enthusiasm.

'I have only one thing to find fault with in your proposal, Jenkins,' he said at last.

'Sir?' The Welshman's homely face creased with worry and alarm.

'Yes. It is wrong for you to visit a bank as a stranger and risk insult by clerks who may not know you, and who could therefore quite easily refuse to advance you a penny. Indeed, *I* will advance you what money you need, not as a loan, with interest and usury, but on the understanding that it buys a quarter share in your enterprise. If you fail, I bid farewell to my investment. If you succeed, as I believe you will, I claim a quarter of your profits. Agreed, Jenkins?'

'Why, yes, sir. Most certainly agreed.'

'Good. How much money do you require to begin?'

'My missus and I have worked it out, sir. A hundred

sovereigns would see us clear for rent, crockery, pans, tables, chairs and a little in hand.'

'Once you are in business, Jenkins, you will discover a strange financial truth. When you need money to begin a new enterprise, few are eager to lend. They say that if your proposal is so sound, and you are so sure of its success, why cannot you raise the money elsewhere? But once you succeed, those same people will pester you with their savings, hoping that by some fiscal alchemy you can turn their dross into gold – at no risk or labour whatever, of course, to themselves. So, remember, you can never ask for too much money, only for too little. You have allowed yourself small margin should such plans go wrong, or for setbacks of any kind. I will, therefore, invest not 100 sovereigns, but 200, which should allow you some reserve. How would you propose spending this second hundred pounds?'

'Fifty, sir, I would use at once to buy out my brother from the Royal Navy.'

'In which ship is he serving?'

'The frigate *Aeneas*, sir, berthed at the end of the docks for a refit. He is a cook. Been in the galley for three years. I'd back him as a cook against any ten of these slit-eyed Chinese.'

'When does *Aeneas* leave harbour?'

'On tomorrow afternoon's tide.'

'Then you have no time to lose. What is her course?'

'He tells me she is cruising in Eastern waters, Java way, then up to China, paying calls at Hong Kong, and the treaty ports. Then to Singapore and back to Chatham to pay off.'

'Right,' said Gunn. 'I will instruct Captain Fernandes to order the paymaster to give you 200 golden sovereigns immediately, plus whatever pay has accrued to you. I do not wish for any receipt or papers to be drawn up between us. You have served in my vessel for a long time. We can therefore surely trust each other – which is a second important point in all business transactions. You can have documents and seals and contracts and all manner of legal papers, but without mutual trust, all is worthless.

'Now, there is only one more thing remaining, that we charge glasses and drink to the success of the Brothers Jenkins, Mrs. Jenkins, and your whole enterprise.'

Gunn filled the second glass with whisky and handed it to Jenkins.

'I hope, sir,' said Jenkins diffidently, raising the glass so that their rims touched and clinked, 'I hope we may have the honour of entertaining you, not as a client, sir, but as a guest. You and yours whenever you pass through. It would be a great privilege, sir. I had no idea that you would wish to extend such a very generous gift to me, sir. I do not know how to find words to thank you.'

'The best way,' said Gunn smiling, 'is to make a success of your venture, so that one day Jenkins's pies and puddings become renowned across the seven seas.'

It was exactly two o'clock, four bells as sailors counted time, when Greene climbed up the gangway of the *Hesperides* from the sampan that had ferried him out from the quay. Her hull stretched away impressively, tar shining like a black mirror. All ropes seemed pipe-clayed, and the decks scrubbed with sand and salt until they shone pale as bone. Brasswork glowed like newly minted gold; sails were huge horizontal furled umbrellas against varnished masts that soared up impressively before the cobalt sky.

A sailor saluted Greene and took him down the companionway to a state room in the stern. Wide windows were pegged open and a faint breeze stirred chintz curtains. Gunn, waiting with another glass of malt whisky in his hand, wondered whether he was about to be bored or insulted. He half wished he had never invited the man; and yet this fellow Brooke's attitude and aims interested him. If he and Greene had nothing else to discuss, he would at least find out all he could about Brooke.

Greene appeared leaner in the sun than in black dinner clothes. He wore light trousers, a grey jacket, a white silk cravat, a tall carriage hat.

'Will you take a light wine or whisky?' asked Gunn as they shook hands formally.

'Neither, sir,' said Greene. 'I find that in the heat they disagree with me. By four o'clock I will feel sleepy.'

'You are quite right,' agreed Gunn. 'I never used to drink in the day either.'

And he suddenly wanted to add: And I drink now because it is only when the alcohol is pounding through my blood that I can bear to consider what lies ahead. He poured three fingers of whisky into his glass.

'Allow me to offer you an orange juice, then? As a medical man, I assure you that fruit juice can only be beneficial in this climate.'

A servant squeezed oranges into a crystal goblet.

'I hope, sir,' Greene began nervously, 'that I did not overstep myself in my views last night?'

'Of course not,' replied Gunn easily. 'We are all entitled to our opinions. And yours may well be right. My own concern has generally been limited to hustling a shipload of mud ashore as quickly as possible before the Chinese could open fire on me with guns or arrows, or before the tide changed and the wind dropped. Had I been differently placed, I would have no doubt been in a position to feel greater concern for native customs than I do now.'

'What do you mean, sir, differently placed?'

'Had I been born rich, like you, Greene. The man with wine in his cellar is not generally concerned about a penn'orth of gin. Similarly, it is only when you are poor that money is a magnet. And I must say, it attracted me.'

He thought back to his boyhood in Herne Bay; to his father marking question-papers or preparing the next day's lessons by oil-lamp; to his mother knitting patiently, glasses on her nose. And outside the restlessness of a winter sea, and the wind blowing down the chimney. He had come a long way since those days; but what he would give to have the health and high hopes he had then!

They sat down to lunch; big Malacca prawns arranged like the spokes of a wheel on a bowl of crushed ice; a mild lamb curry, then half-melons filled with port.

'Why I invited you to luncheon, Greene, had nothing to do

with your opinions. I was interested in your remarks about James Brooke. Curiously enough, I recalled that my father had mentioned his name to me before I left England. Apparently, Brooke had overstayed his leave through no fault of his own when he was with John Company, and so was forced to resign his commission?'

'That is quite true. And if he had not, he might still only be a Lieutenant in the Company's army. I mean no disparagement to you, sir, or to any other merchant prince, but I feel that James Brooke's character contains the timeless virtues that have made Britain great, and a leader among less favoured nations. He is not concerned with monetary profit, but with helping those less fortunate. I can think of no better memorial for any Briton in the East — or anywhere else — than to achieve that.'

'Raffles did the same thing in Singapore,' said Gunn, thinking of the strange career of that other East India Company employee who had personally negotiated a treaty with the Sultan of Johore, whereby Singapore island came under British rule, with immeasurable benefits to Britain and to the island. His reward was to die in poverty — and less than twenty years ago — hounded for debts incurred through the bad bookkeeping of incompetent Company clerks.

'His treatment was shameful, I agree,' said Greene. 'But his name will be remembered with admiration long after those who pestered him have been consigned to oblivion.'

'There is truth in what you say,' Gunn agreed. And there was more than truth; there was the unexpected beginning of a wish to do likewise. What was the object in Gunn returning to Macao, simply to increase his fortune further? He had but a few months in which to spend the vaults of money he already possessed. He had neither wish nor need for any more, for when he was gone who would inherit it?

He would make an allowance in his will for his father, of course, but he had no-one else close to him, except perhaps the son he had never seen by the Parsee woman.

This was an opportunity, unasked and unsought, that would never come again. He sipped a brandy, swirling the amber liquid in the balloon glass before he spoke, and when he did speak, his mind was made up.

'The more you tell me about Brooke's intentions, Greene, the more I am impressed. I feel I would also like to use my money to do some good deed, as he is doing, and so leave my mark on the East in a way that future generations will respect.'

'What have you in mind?'

'Nothing specific, but I suggest that we attempt to carry it out in the same island that has attracted James Brooke. It will be for you to make some proposition which you think could usefully unite your idealism and my wealth.'

'Then you wish me to be associated with this?'

'Of course,' said Gunn. 'You are the idealist. I am the realist. But I make one absolute condition. I will pay all bills that I agree, and similarly meet all other outgoings, but you must be swift in this undertaking. We must achieve it within months at the outside – within weeks, if that is possible.'

'I very much doubt that it will be, sir. Brooke was several years before he became the White Rajah of Sarawak.'

'Brooke is a young man.'

'So are you, sir.'

'Yes,' agreed Gunn. 'But I have my own personal reasons for needing speed, which concern no-one but myself. If you believe what you say – and I think you do – then pray act now. And here is my hand on what I say.'

They shook hands. Greene was surprised at the dampness of Gunn's palm; when he had greeted him before lunch it had appeared dry and warm. Maybe the man was ill with one of those latent fevers that burned and throbbed beneath the skin of almost every white person East of Africa? You took physic against it or you drank rum or whisky or some patent concoction in which you believed, but nothing could really rid you of the fire in your blood. Like the lure of the East, it was there with you until you died. And maybe, in the end, it killed you.

'There is a possibility that I can explain,' said Greene slowly, 'but first I must tell you what I know about the island of Borneo. It is largely unexplored and wild. The inhabitants number head-hunters and cannibals, and under their feet lie

86

ores and minerals of a type and value at which we can only guess. I know that antimony is present in large quantities because ships carrying it pass through Singapore. And there are signs that the island has been volcanic.'

'Never mind the possibility of amassing more wealth,' said Gunn dryly. 'Remember your idealism. What about the people there?'

'First, there are Sea Dyaks, who take their name because they are sailors, with a remarkable skill in handling long canoes. They will cut a clearing in a forest, grow rice until the goodness of the ground is exhausted, and then move on elsewhere. They live in curious abodes called longhouses, where as many as fifty families can be accommodated peacefully beneath one roof, and under the rule of an hereditary chieftain.

'The Land Dyaks are smaller in stature, and they divide men's work with women's work to a remarkable degree quite unparalleled in Europe. Women have equal ownership of property and of inheritances, which is more than they possess in our own country. They brew borak, or rice beer, cook the food, draw water from springs and rivers, and cultivate small gardens near the longhouses. The men hunt and sow crops, but both sexes help with the rice harvest, and all important decisions – such as when to harvest, or what to hunt – are made by the villagers as a unit and not by individuals.

'Each individual can accumulate personal wealth, although money is virtually unknown. They count riches in the form of livestock or ornaments, but most of all in huge Chinese pots that date back as far as twelve centuries.

'To own one jar is a mark of respect. To own two is the sign of authority and wealth. They guard these jars as they do their wives' virtue. If they must surrender a Chinese jar to their chieftain for some misdemeanour, it is regarded as a punishment only slightly less onerous than a death sentence.

'There is also a minority community of Chinese. They are peaceful and they abide by the laws. These three peoples could live together without friction and, if they were allowed, might achieve a high level of civilization under British guidance.'

'Who or what stops them?' asked Gunn.

'Malay pirates, for the most part. They molest shipping. They burn villages. They come ashore in marauding bands, rape women, seize what loot they can, and make off again in their fast, vessels, often when the male Dyaks are out harvesting or in the jungle.'

'I do not wish to mount a punitive expedition, although that is in the European tradition,' said Gunn. 'Surely such a measure is what you also seek to avoid?'

'I do, sir, but why should thousands of peaceful people be forced to live in fear through the greed of a handful of predators? There is a sultan on the coast, one Kuan Lung Fai, whose people are at this moment oppressed. The Malay pirates demand that everything the villagers produce or gather, whether it is rice, wax or birds' nests for soup, must be offered to them at *their* price – which is always ludicrously low.

'They then force the villagers to buy their goods, which they neither want nor need, at an absurdly high price. They are ruthless in their dealings. They will commandeer a local boat, and cut a notch in the gunwale, or burn a mark into it and then claim it is rightfully theirs and that the Dyaks have stolen it. Gradually, they are throttling the life of the whole province.'

'What is the sultan doing to stop this?'

'He is an ill man, dying of a wasting sickness in his blood. It is unlikely he will live long – or that he can do much to alter the inevitable.'

'Would you consider that to attack these pirates and drive them out – and keep them out – would be beyond our abilities?'

'Nothing is beyond the ability of a righteous man,' Greene assured him earnestly. 'James Brooke, with only a handful of men from his ship, overthrew an insurrection simply because he was resolute and had right on his side. We could do the same, sir.'

'You almost convince me,' said Gunn. 'But what would be the political consequences? Have the British Government any designs on the island?'

'No, sir, none. Our Empire is large enough and complex enough, without adding to its extent or its responsibilities. The Dutch think differently. They have lost colonies to us in the

East and are anxious to replace them. They have their spies who report on James Brooke, and they or others will doubtless inform Dutch officials in Java of anything we may attempt.'

'I never *attempt* anything,' said Gunn sharply. 'Whatever I undertake, I carry through.'

He paused for a moment, biting his lower lip in concentration. It might conceivably suit the British purpose to let simple heathen peoples fight each other to a standstill, and then negotiate with the victor. On the other hand, it suited his personal purpose best to act now, and he need consult no-one else about his actions. He was his own man. He would risk his own money, and maybe his own life, which was already forfeit.

'What do we need?'

'First, men. How many crew does this ship carry?'

'Thirty able seamen. Six ordinary seamen, four mates and two boatswains, with boys and cooks, stewards and a sailmaker.'

'Are they amenable to strict discipline?'

'Of course. Some of the men are time-expired from the Royal Navy. They can fight and shoot with the best. I can also offer them prize money. I intend to lead this expedition, Greene, as James Brooke led his. Whether I stay in Borneo afterwards will be my decision, and what you do then can be yours. But I intend to supply the men, the money, and myself. And, God willing, with this combination, I think I can promise success to our enterprise.'

Murgatroyd lay in his wide bed, looking up at the ceiling. His wife was still asleep with her back to him, bare because of the heat. He ran a finger gently down her soft moist flesh, but she wriggled away.

'No,' she said drowsily. 'Not now, Thomas. It is too early.'

It was always too early or too late, or she was too tired, too hot. Was this the same with every wife, every marriage? Murgatroyd withdrew his hand, turned on his side, pounded the pillow irritably, and lay looking at the rattan wall. It was five o'clock by the hands of the clock on the bedside table. Already, he heard servants stirring in their compound; the cluck of hens; the Indian *dhobi* hawking noisily. Gunn and that idiot Greene had already been at sea for several hours, for they left on the midnight tide. He felt oddly uneasy about their whole ridiculous enterprise, although it had nothing to do with him. It seemed so unnecessary, so ill-conceived, the sort of journey a man might make for a wager, but never with a serious purpose; and never a man like Gunn.

Why should he suddenly elect to risk his life by sailing to a virtually unexplored island of swamps and crocodiles and poisonous snakes to attempt to right some wrong that was probably either illusory or else not a wrong at all, but merely the consequence of native rivalry? Of course, Murgatroyd had volunteered to go with them, but he had been intensely relieved when Gunn had waved aside his halting offer.

'We need you here,' he had told him. 'Mandarin-Gold demands men who are totally devoted to its interests, pledged, as I know you are, to advance it from one of the biggest trading companies in the East to one of the largest in the world. I could not spare you.'

Murgatroyd believed him because he wanted to believe him, not realizing that Gunn's voice was edged with contempt. Murgatroyd to him was only a clerk, a pusher of pens, a receptacle for other men's instructions. He had no place in a pitched battle when the stakes were high; his place was on a high stool, totting up other men's fortunes, never his own.

Gunn sat in his cabin, under a swaying brass oil-lamp, writing at the pull-out table near his bunk. Beyond open portholes, the ocean streamed past, dark as a sea of ink. Beneath a cold moon a wide and silver path stretched across it to the horizon. The ship creaked, timber talking to timber, as she sped eagerly under full sail like a huge night bird.

'My dear father,' wrote Gunn in a slow careful hand. 'I am writing to you aboard *Hesperides*, outward bound from Singapore, within a day's sailing of Borneo. You mentioned to me at home how a young man, James Brooke, had been forced to leave John Company's service through overstaying his furlough. Quite by chance – or was it providence? – a colleague in Singapore told me more about him.

'Brooke has renounced the pursuit of worldly riches to try and enrich a humble and decent native people on Borneo island. I was so impressed by this act of unselfishness that, on the impulse, I made plans to do the same. We should sight Borneo within the next 24 hours, and then we plan to make our way into the interior to speak with the ruler of this territory, which is half as large as England, and probably without a single hard surface road or continuous track, let alone a railway line, within all it boundaries.

'I do not know how I shall post this letter. Maybe it will have to wait until we put back to Singapore, if I meet no friendly sea captain who will carry it for me. But I felt I should write and appraise you of any plans and my position while I had the time and opportunity to do so.'

Gunn paused, and looked out at the silvery path of moonlight; it seemed like some celestial highway – but leading where? He shivered, but went on writing.

'In my life, I have already had two careers, physician and merchant. Perhaps the most worthy will be my third, as benefactor to people as yet not even known to me. Maybe now our old family name will be remembered in a way that will give lasting pride to those who come after.'

He paused again. This was absurd, for there was no-one to come after him; only a half-caste illegitimate boy somewhere between Bombay and Macao. Gunn was the last of his line. Or perhaps his father would hold that privilege? For, old as he was, Mr. Gunn would surely outlive his son.

Mark Greene stood high in the bows of *Hesperides*, feet braced apart against the rise and fall of the deck. Against the ever-brightening sky, the dark outline of the figurehead rose and dipped again like some strange sea goddess nodding approval at their speed. Above Greene, huge sails were puffed round with wind, like the breasts of gigantic white pigeons, pulling them through the lightening sea. Already, in the mistiness of morning, he could see the knifeblade flash of flying-fish wings as they sped from wave to wave.

Underneath that smooth indigo surface of the sea, all was no doubt in as much turmoil as among men on land. Giant serpents of the deep, huge crustaceans, crabs, squids and rays, some deadly poisonous and others relying for defence upon their frightening appearance, were moving restlessly against the beginning of another day just as he was wondering what the next few hours held for him.

He felt a curious mixture of elation and foreboding. It was one thing to hold forth at a friend's dinner table, primed with wine, about the great things you would do with your life, if you did not need to seek for money. It was altogether another to stand in the bows of a speeding vessel, with a fresh wind moulding your shirt against your body, and realize that within hours you could be facing the blow-pipes of unseen adversaries in some steaming alien jungle. He could be assailed by head-hunters with sharpened bamboos, or speared or cudgelled to death by those same heathen wretches whom it was his intention to help. This had happened to other voyagers; it could also happen to him.

And what had possessed Gunn to decide to lead this mad expedition? It was almost as though the man wished to do some glorious deed and risk death, nay, even court oblivion in its achievement. Money had been spent without thought or calculation. In Singapore, they had bought equipment for every possible contingency; a store of Congreve's rockets, surplus to the Royal Navy's requirements; muskets, grenades, mines; three hundred yards of fuse wire, to detonate explosions, phosphorus paint to allow them to lay a luminous trail to follow through the darkest forest, so that they need not fear losing their way back to their point of landing.

Gunn had even acquired wide-brimmed white hats against the sun, for he believed, admittedly against all recognized medical opinion, that the sun was not harmful so long as the head was protected against its rays. And instead of the serge uniforms prescribed for hot climates, Gunn had ordered a new suit of drill for each man – and insisted that the Chinese tailors had dyed the cloth dark green.

'We'll look like trees in the jungle, sir, when we come ashore – hardly able to see each other,' Greene had protested, thinking that Gunn was attempting some expensive practical joke.

'That is my intention,' Gunn told him shortly. 'Any enemy will have equal difficulty in sighting us. And I am also having paste made up with dark dye so that we can rub it on our faces and hands and then we can travel by night, if danger threatens, and our white skins will not give us away.'

'But, sir, the crew we take ashore to guard us against any native attack should surely dress as soldiers – and the British have *always* fought in red coats.'

'Not always, Greene. Once, we used to fight with clubs and paint our flesh with woad. I know that it is usual for soldiers to advertise their arrival with drums and fifes and buglers and red coats in order to give the other side a chance to prepare their reception – as though a battle were purely a sporting spectacle, like a cricket match between two rival villages. I do not see the sense in that.

'Maybe we will not have to fight. I hope that a show of force will suffice, and a few rounds from the *Hesperides*' guns can convincingly provide that, but if we *do* have to fight, we have to fight to win, and quickly. So I have stolen a page from the book of beasts of the field, that camouflage themselves against their background, and so render themselves almost invisible.'

'As you are paying the bill, sir, I have to agree.'

'You have to agree in any case,' Gunn told him shortly, and that was an end to the matter. Despite Gunn's strange unorthodox ideas, Greene found himself liking the older man. He had guts and enterprise; he acted on his own ideas, and obviously relished his position of power and authority, perhaps because he had achieved it himself, without benefit of inheritance. And yet there was sometimes a sadness in his eyes, a pallor on his skin and a tiredness in his voice that he could not conceal. Was he perhaps unwell, or had he some inner sorrow? Whatever the reason, Gunn kept it to himself, and this Greene admired. He could learn a lot from this man, he told himself, and he would.

The ship's figurehead bowed graceful agreement as the bowsprit dipped after a huge wave; the *Hesperides* sailed on.

Van Vooren, the Dutchman, sat in his hut in a clearing carved out of the forest about 200 yards from the sea on the north coast of the island. The building stood on eight great wooden piles and was reached by a bamboo ladder, and single poles with notches cut for climbers' feet. The roof was of split bamboos, like the floor, which was covered with rush mats. A couple of goats stood tethered to one of the piles, and chickens clucked disconsolately as they pecked in the trodden dusty sand for scraps of food. Two fierce-looking razor-backed pigs snored contentedly in the afternoon sun. Under the floor was a bamboo hutch, where the natives would put the chickens at evening for safety; and no wonder, for only the night before last, a crocodile had come in from the river and somehow raised itself on its back legs to reach them.

The commotion had awakened Van Vooren, who shot the brute in the throat, and he had watched it drag painfully away to the river to die. Van Vooren shuddered at the memory. What if he had not heard the chickens clucking in terror, or the crash of breaking bamboo? The vile reptile might have climbed up into the hut and eaten him. What an accursed island to breed such things! And other evil, unnatural creatures abounded on it as well: the hateful bommi fish that crept out of the water and used their tails and fins to climb and jump along the land; many ant-eaters that would feign death until they were covered with ants eager to reach the soft flesh beneath their scales. Then the foul beasts would close these scales like trap-doors and imprison a colony of ants, to devour at their leisure. No-one in Amsterdam would believe him when he told them of these creatures that were against God and nature. But when *would* he return to tell them anything? That was a question for which he had no answer.

Van Vooren was a fat and usually cheerful man, now incongruously dressed in soft black leather boots to his knees, twill riding breeches and a white silk shirt open at the throat. He wore a stained red bandana around his neck to soak up the sweat that ran down from his long black hair and his soft fleshy jowls. On a table in front of him he had spread a crude map of Borneo, marked by various crosses in red and blue crayon, with a round stone at each corner to hold it flat. The crosses represented villages thought to be friendly or hostile to Europeans. He kept a hammered tin beaker at his right hand near a half-empty bottle of Schnapps. Now and then he belched and rubbed the back of his hand across his mouth, and then he would peer nervously through the open door to the blinding blueness of the sea, and check the hour against a German silver watch. Dark would come soon, and he feared that inevitable moment when day became night with tropical speed, and the jungle, that had been drowsy through daylight, would instantly come alive with hidden whispers and screams, and the rustlings of unseen, unknown animals and serpents.

He had landed here from Java with ten of his countrymen in the previous week, and commandeered this hut. The others had immediately set off along the coast with a native guide who spoke a little Dutch, and who could understand the Malay dialect they only spoke badly. The man had been well bribed with a promise of several thousand square metres of land if their enterprise succeeded, so they trusted him. They could easily afford such a bribe, for if they were successful, they would be able to claim half Borneo for Holland. If they failed, they risked losing their heads to the dreaded head-hunters who inhabited the area. The equation was as stark as that, so what were a few hectares of beach or scrub which the man had demanded as his fee for helping them?

Dutch and British traders and settlers had already divided out vast areas of the East which they claimed as their own, either by treaty or force, for reasons of trade, for national prestige, to protect their existing possessions, or simply to appease local rulers who sought their aid against a neighbour. Their fortunes fluctuated dangerously. In the previous century, for example, the Dutch had controlled Malaya, Ceylon and Java, and had supported North America in the War of Independence, hoping to share the spoils of victory, when Britain was defeated. But to their surprise the loss to the British of their colonies in North America had produced quite unexpected results, which they had completely miscalculated. The British turned their eyes East and drove the Dutch from

Malaya, then seized Ceylon from them and finally blockaded Java with their fleet. They only raised this siege after they had humiliatingly forced the Dutch to sign away most of their markets to them.

Both countries, however, had been careful about claiming Borneo as their own. The island was enormous and largely unmapped, and while the Dutch Government understandably coveted it to help compensate for the lands Holland had lost, the British were not at all anxious to add it to their Empire. Its value was academic. Stories of strange animals and peoples who inhabited it caused unease among travellers, who knew Borneo simply as a valuable source of birds' nests (for Chinese soups), of deerhorns, dried fish and fine animal skins. It was also said to possess one of the world's most fertile soils. Some considered it rich in gold deposits and diamonds and lead and copper and coal. They could well be right, but to extract these buried riches would be a matter of immeasurable cost and complexity. The coast was difficult to land on with safety from a vessel of any draught, and ferocious Malay pirates had already proved they could cut down all but the hardest and toughest adventurers.

What use was a European flag flying proudly from a mast on the highest mountain on such an island if no force or authority could guarantee peace and safety for the Europeans who might work beneath that flag? The British Government was therefore content to let explorers of other nationalities go in first. If they were extremely successful, then they might intervene. If they were not, then they had saved themselves an infinity of money and effort. Shipwrecked British sailors had landed from ships that had broken up at sea, and while some had been kindly treated, others had disappeared for ever. This, of course, was a risk every explorer accepted as part of the debit account of adventure; but still it was better it happened to foreigners.

Van Vooren believed that this present expedition, which he was leading, had minimized all risks as much as possible. They were not attempting to colonize the whole island, but just to reach a possible position of accommodation with the sultan of one province, Kei. The Englishman, James Brooke, posing as a traveller above all thought of personal gain or enrichment but doubtless a cunning British agent or trader, had somehow persuaded a neighbouring ruler to make him a rajah. The cheek of it! Van Vooren did not aim so high; a treaty would satisfy him for a start.

His father was a diamond polisher in Amsterdam, and if he could eventually subordinate this province to the Dutch flag, and then perhaps the whole island, what spoils of diamonds might he not be able to unlock from the earth, not only for Holland, but for himself? An incalculable fortune awaited him, but first he had to persuade the ruler of this remote province that Holland could offer him more than any other European country, if only he would come under the protection of their flag, and trade with the Dutch instead of with other westerners. The sultan had not been at all interested in these proposals when they had first been made some months before. He knew the Dutch from previous experience as brave but hard, and he had no wish to allow his kingdom to fall under Dutch rule, which would mean he was little more than a servant working to make his new masters rich.

The British were known to be less harsh in their dealings and to have some sense of humour, but all they really desired was to expand their trade, to find new sources of minerals to feed the thriving factories in their own country. The sultan believed that the independence of his province was infinitely preferable to either alien rule – but he also realized that inevitably some European country, or even America, whose freebooters sailed eastern seas eager for trade or opportunities neglected by Europeans, might land, bombard them into submission, and then claim his kingdom as their own.

Van Vooren knew this, too, and his task was to make sure that he and his party secured the province for Holland before larger, stronger and more important countries could claim it as theirs. Once they were in possession, they would be almost impossible to dislodge. Two months previously, he had sent out commissioners from Java, and they had returned with the same inconclusive report: foreigners were welcome to trade, but no closer affiliation was contemplated or desired.

The Dutch Governor of Java then produced a second, more devious plan. If the province would not come voluntarily within Dutch control, he would force them to do so before Britain or any other country showed interest in the matter. Already this strange Englishman Brooke had caused the Governor some concern. He must be a British spy or secret emissary, whatever else he might claim to be, for surely no-one sailed all the way from England in their own ship and at their own expense purely for idealistic reasons? Genuine missionaries simply could not afford to do so. Brooke's style of travel was reserved for rich merchants – like this other dangerous Englishman, Gunn, who he had heard from traders in Singapore was also planning a visit to Borneo.

If the Governor was not to be outwitted by these English predators, or others like them, he had to act instantly. For this reason, he had recruited Malay pirates, who lived richly off the coastal provinces, and had come to an arrangement with them. With Dutch guns and a handful of Dutch leaders they would seize the province and de-throne the sultan. The Governor would then immediately declare it a Dutch possession. Having thus obtained a base in Borneo by force, they would swiftly move on from it to secure a second province, then a third, a fourth, until the whole of the island came under the Dutch flag. Then the pirates would receive their reward from the Dutch authorities. They would have the promise of a blind-eye to continued piracy on an agreed scale, and gifts of land for those who wished to leave the sea.

Van Vooren was the Governor's agent, but he was more eager to succeed in his mission because he was uniquely placed to handle the diamonds that the earth was rumoured to contain. This mission could thus win him the respect and gratitude of his country, and personal wealth beyond calculation.

Now he waited impatiently for his companions to return. They had gone to give notice of their intentions to the Sultan Kuan Lung. They knew he possessed few fighting men, because the Dyaks were basically peaceful people. Van Vooren therefore calculated that the sultan would have to accept the proposals made on this visit, for he must realize that it was his final opportunity to surrender his throne without being forced off it. He might then put up a token fight, his loyal forces armed pathetically with bows and arrows and blow-pipes and spears and clubs, but a few controlled musket volleys would soon show these natives where their future lay.

But first, of course, the decencies had to be observed, and the sultan given a chance to accede peacefully and with every appearance of willingness to the Dutch request. Then, if he refused and stubbornly put his life and those of his subjects at risk, they would be fully entitled to use what force might be required to persuade him to change his mind.

This all seemed very simple and even reasonable when the Governor of Java had first discussed the matter; but if it were indeed so easy, and so worthwhile, why had no-one done it before? And why did Van Vooren now feel so unsure of himself, when he should be supremely confident? Instead, he felt lonely and afraid in this hut by the edge of the shore. The wood creaked constantly under his feet with almost human sounds, and the whole building trembled uneasily like a giant nest in some high tree. The sun burned back from the sea like a flame in his face, making his eyes ache, and each time Van Vooren looked through the windows, even though they were shielded from the worst of the glare by long bamboo screens propped open on poles, it seemed to him – doubtless by an optical illusion – that the jungle had somehow crept in closer to him while his mind was elsewhere.

Then he would shut his eyes and open them again quickly, screwing up his face to focus against the glare. Had the trees *really* marched nearer, or were they still standing where they had been on the previous evening? Of course, they must be. He was tired and on edge; it was unnatural to be alone in this wretched place. He would feel better when his companions returned to report how the sultan had reacted. Pray God they would be back before dark. He could scarcely endure another night alone, with the ladders drawn up into the room while he lay half asleep, sweating with heat and fear, ants crawling over his soft flesh, and hearing all around the hut the rustle and call of unknown wild beasts, the flitter of strange and evil birds of night.

Suppose the sultan was a stronger figure than the Governor had led Van Vooren to believe? What if he only pretended to accept their ultimatum – and then sent his head-hunters after them into the forest to murder them on their way? What would happen to Van Vooren then, abandoned and on his own? He could not possibly sail back to Java alone, and yet how could he ever explain his presence here to any natives when he did not speak the language? He should never have allowed all his men to leave him. He should have insisted that at least one remained behind with him as his companion. But it was too late now to think about what he should have done. Van Vooren poured himself more Schnapps and drank it greedily. The alcohol flamed reassuringly through his body, and sweat poured down his back and through his sodden shirt. He reached down to his musket on the floor, already primed and charged, and checked the rounds he had laid out on a plantain leaf to keep them free of sand and dust, and the charges of powder he had measured out for an emergency.

The sun began to melt slowly down the trembling liquid sky, and the tropical dusk rose swiftly from the deep places of the earth to overwhelm it. Almost instantly the day was dark. Fireflies and glow-worms burned and danced like a thousand eyes beyond the open windows. He hated to see them, so he got up from his chair, pulled away the poles and let the screens flap down.

From the beach, now out of sight, he heard the roar and sigh and suck of the sea as the waves pounded in tirelessly. In the darkness, the sound seemed like a giant breathing. Then he heard a footstep outside, and another, and a whisper, and he started up, musket in his hand, aimed at the head of the stairs.

'Who's that?' he called. 'Stand or I fire.'

'It is us, Jan,' replied the familiar voice of Carl Hofmeyer, a corporal in the Dutch army, who had led the party to the sultan.

'Come up then, man,' Van Vooren told him irritably, hoping that his alarm and fear had not sounded too apparent in his voice. 'What news have you brought from the sultan?'

'None. We could not see him.'

'Why ever not?'

Was the man joking? How could the native ruler of an obscure province decline to meet the representative of the mighty Dutch Government, one of the strongest in Europe?

Hofmeyer climbed noisily up into the room. Van Vooren could smell his sweat and the sourness of his dirty body through his filthy clothes; they had made a long march in great heat.

'Why are you sitting in the dark?' Hofmeyer asked in surprise. 'Let's have a light, for God's sake. It's bad enough outside without sitting here like mourners in a tomb.'

He felt about for a flint, struck a spark and lit a small wick that floated in a brass bowl of oil. Their two enormous shadows trembled behind them on the wall.

'Where are the others?' asked Van Vooren.

'On their way. They stopped at a village to get some food. Roast pig, rice, some plantains and mangoes.'

'Why did you not see the sultan? You went there as emissaries, ambassadors. It was his *duty* to see you.'

'It is the duty of the dead to see no-one. Possibly the only blessing death has,' retorted Hofmeyer, pouring himself some of Van Vooren's Schnapps into Van Vooren's beaker without asking his permission.

'What do you mean?'

'The sultan is dead.'

'But he must have some successor, some heir. Could you not see him?'

'There is no heir of age. Only a widow and a young boy.'

'Well, could you not treat with her?'

'She refused to see strangers. We asked. We waited. We offered bribes, but we could do nothing. So rather than lose caste and prestige by staying indefinitely, like petitioners, we returned.'

'So we are back where we started?'

'In a sense.'

'What do you mean, in a sense, man? We either are or we are not. You should have *forced* your way into her presence.'

'With a handful of our own people and two dozen pirates as likely to kill us as the sultan's men? You should have been there to lead us, meinheer. You would doubtless have done better than me.'

'I do not mean that at all,' replied Van Vooren quickly, for he had stayed behind at his own wish. He could not face the fearful horror of cutting a way through the jungle with sharpened knives and Malay parangs and dahs. He hated the prospect of that slow progress, covered with flies, while leeches sucked out his blood, and mosquito bites puffed up his face.

He feared creeping, crawling things. He always had, from childhood. But how could he explain these terrible fears and dreads to a thick oaf like Hofmeyer? Sometimes you had to clothe reasons in a more acceptable garment than truth. You explained you wished to act as a rearguard in case messages were landed for you. You hinted that the Governor might even be sending reinforcements you would have to meet. Van Vooren did not know whether the men in his party believed this, but he sounded so convincing, he almost believed it himself.

'What would you advise if she refuses to see us?' Hofmeyer asked him.

'Nothing. At least until a successor has been appointed. In the meantime, we could seek out some other ruler. There is one a hundred miles inland from here, through the jungle.'

'And what condition would we be in after that journey, pray? We would look like beggars in rags, if we were still alive. There are crocodiles and tigers and wild elephants that have to be contended with, as well as head-hunters with blow-pipes. I suggest we return to the sultan's widow – and attack her palace. It is only a wooden shack about twice the size of this. We could advance from three sides of a square, fire our muskets and then charge and drive the devils out of the fourth side into the sea. There would be little resistance.'

'I would like to speak to the sultan's widow first,' said Van Vooren slowly. 'It would be more seemly to offer her the opportunity of coming under the Dutch flag peacefully, rather than forcing her so precipitately.'

'Who will know what has happened, and no matter who knows, who cares?' asked Hofmeyer realistically, pouring himself more Schnapps, and mentally noting the level in the bottle; Van Vooren must have been drinking heavily to reduce it so much.

'Victory is what counts, not how one achieves it. Our flag run up on the highest tree. Our men with their muskets in control.'

'You may be right,' agreed Van Vooren without enthusiasm.

'I know I am right,' said Hofmeyer contemptuously. 'So do the others with me.'

'You have discussed it together, then?'

'Of course we have. The pirates are in entire agreement. A sharp short engagement and the whole province will be ours. Then we can pay them off, and remain in full control.'

As he spoke, they both heard the chatter of voices, and someone singing in a slurred and drunken voice; the rickety house trembled as they climbed noisily up the ladders. Then they were inside, filling the room with strong animal sweat, striking flints, lighting more lamps. Van Vooren could see metal bowls of rice, steaming hunks of meat, shining with juice, mangoes and plantains and coconuts; they would eat well tonight.

He stood up, and carried his mug of Schnapps to the door, and stood there, looking out, relieved at being no longer alone. Under a rising moon and stars glittering like tinsel in a purple sky, the sea lay calm as a glass floor stretching who knew where. At the sight, his new sense of relief began to drain away. There was something about this island and the immensity of the ocean that combined to frighten him. Hofmeyer and the others did not appreciate that the equation was not simply to attack a virtually defenceless village and seize the throne of a dead man. There were other imponderables, and although Van Vooren could not name them all, he knew they existed just as he knew that the silent and serene sea contained all manner of sea beasts he had never seen and no man would ever see; as he knew that the forest around him was full of eyes and dangers and death.

He sensed difficulties and pitfalls in the plan. What if the Englishman Brooke heard about it and retaliated? What if the sultan's widow had powerful friends and allies? But he dare not speak his thoughts because he could only speak in generalities, and these rough men wanted facts. To them an attack was simple; you won or you lost. How could he explain to such thick dull clods that you *could* win, but then like the ebbing tide, you could almost immediately lose not only what you had won, but everything else you held precious – even your life?

He turned back to Hofmeyer.

'We will march on the palace tomorrow,' he told him quietly, as though this had been his plan all along, as though he had no horror of the jungle, no fear in his heart, no churning in his guts at the thought of what he was saying; and no dread premonition of defeat.

The Chinese widow stood in the receiving room of her long-house, and waited for the spy to approach. She was slightly built, still in her twenties, and her slimness was accentuated by the Malay sarong she wore. Her feet were bare and light brown on the red mosaic tiles; her smooth black hair was drawn tightly behind her head. At the far end of the room stood a sandalwood throne, its gilded arms carved with serpents' heads, their fangs outstretched through open mouths.

The room was built of long hard lengths of nibong palm, and the walls hung with mats held together by thin strips of bamboo. Apart from the tiles on which the Chinese widow stood, the floors were covered with flattened split stems of bamboo with two or three layers of rattan mats thrown over them. As a sign of wealth, strips of red cloth hung around the walls, but the room was otherwise simply furnished, with a few low stools and bamboo chairs. One wide window looked out to sea, and although the hour was late, two bamboos propped open its eyelid-like shade.

The night sky and the sea had fused into one deep blue, but soon the moon would rise, and with the aid of her late husband's glass she would be able to view the strange vessel whose arrival had been reported to her, and for more news of which she had sent out a spy.

A female attendant entered the room silently, bowed and turned to the man who accompanied her. He was a stocky Dyak wearing the special maroon velvet jacket worn only by men commanded to appear before their ruler. It had a stiff collar, heavily embroidered with gold thread and gold-edged trousers to match. He bowed and folded his hands in respectful obeisance, waiting until the attendant withdrew, and his master's widow made known her wishes.

'Speak,' she commanded him. Her voice sounded soft and gentle, but it was also the voice of authority.

'I searched the beach, most exalted one, and interviewed fishermen, but there is no evidence of anyone coming ashore from this vessel. It is too dark to make out the flag, but I would deduce from her general rig and smart trim she is British.'

'The British and the Dutch are like the Cat and the Rat,' said the Chinese widow bitterly. 'One chases the other for the spoils of many countries. But what makes them both so dangerous so far as we are concerned is that we do not always know who is Cat and who is Rat. Why do *you* think this ship is here? Can they know already about my husband, and have come either to offer sympathy – or to attempt coercion because they do not fear his widow?'

'That is highly unlikely, most exalted one. My master was stricken only days ago, when they must have been at sea, even assuming that they have come from Singapore.'

This was true, but then her husband had been in poor health for several months; that could also have been known in Singapore. She did not mention this, but asked another question.

'What if they come from somewhere else?'

'Then they could not have knowledge of the sad event.'

'Might they not have their spies?'

'But how could a spy pass his knowledge on to them, most exalted one?'

'I do not know,' she admitted, 'I do not know.' She wiped her hand across her brow; she was still shocked from the death of her husband and afraid of the dark, and not thinking sensibly. When he had been alive, he had seemed like a towering tree in a forest, bearing all strains, taking all decisions. Men instantly obeyed his commands, for to disobey was death and to linger when the sultan spoke meant a brisk whipping with bamboo staves. He had shrewdly held rival factions at bay, matching one group against another until they weakened themselves with their disputes and arguments and petty wars. Then the victor, exhausted by a campaign he knew he could never win, was forced to admit that the sultan was omnipotent.

But now this man had gone, sinking with terrifying speed into a stupor of fever, his body wasting like a tree without water, covered with the sour sweat that was the harbinger of death. Even the sharpened bamboo needles, by which the ac-upuncturists of her country treated all manner of complaints, could produce no cure.

With him had gone her protector and her protection. Already, the Dutch, sensing the importance of his death with the instinctive nose of political vultures, had landed mer-cenaries who planned to link-up with dissidents and Malay pirates to seize what by right should be held in trust for her seven-year-old son, Kuchin, until he reached manhood. They had even sent a party armed with muskets to seek an interview with her, but of course she had refused to meet them. That way she gained a little more time to absorb her grief and to arrange for a meeting of all the local chiefs to agree that she should rule until her son came of age.

She had no-one among them on whom she could instinctively rely, because all men had their price. This she had already learned from her husband. That price could be power, money, a nubile girl or a willing pretty boy, for even men who outwardly appeared strong were often weak inside like rotten bamboos.

True, she had a bodyguard, but Bula Hassam, who com-manded it, had been her husband's man. Would he serve under a woman's rule? Could she prove herself worthy of loyalty when she controlled only a handful of women servants, a few eunuchs and courtiers whose loyalties would swing like weathercocks in the breeze of any dissent? She feared that they might sell her and her son to pirates; to the Dutch, maybe even to the British, if they offered enough. But these were feeble thoughts, only fit for a woman weakened at her sad time of month; not thoughts for a ruler's widow.

She clapped her hands, and ordered the servant who answered to fetch her husband's glass from his room. An English sea captain had given this to him, and he had been extremely proud of it. When the servant handed the telescope to her on a red cushion, she unscrewed the brass cap, placed the eyepiece to her eye and focused it. The moon was rising slowly, and the ship lay clearly visible on the shining sea.

'No-one will come ashore tonight,' she said. 'But in the morning have a boat made ready. Set out at dawn with plantains and coconuts, as though you wished to trade in fruit. Find out what kind of vessel this is, who is aboard her. And whether they are strongly armed.'

'If they are British,' the spy replied, 'they will come ashore and bring you presents, and seek concessions for trade.'

'You speak truth,' agreed the Chinese widow, 'but I am in no mood to grant concessions at this hour of my sorrow. What if they are Dutch?'

'Then they will open fire first, most exalted one, and blow the tops off some palm trees and longhouses. Then they will come ashore and demand what others seek to gain with gifts.'

'So both could bring harm to our kingdom?'

'Both are in their different ways seeking the same prize.'

'You speak like an honest man.'

'I served your husband loyally, most exalted one, and my father served his father. It is meet and right that I should give my loyalty – and if need be, my life – to my master's widow.'

'I wish the whole province was made up of men like you,' she said, moved by his words and the genuine loyalty that lay behind them.

'Most men are like reeds, most exalted one,' the spy replied. 'They bow to the strongest wind. Yet some men are strong enough to stand apart like trees. They only shake a little. I like to think I am one of those.'

She bowed dismissal to him, and then returned to the window. The sea was turning to silver as the moon slid up the sky. She raised the glass again, but she could not make out the strange vessel, for her eyes were filled with tears.

CHAPTER SIX

WHEN Gunn called Captain Fernandes into his cabin, it was six o'clock in the morning, and he had been awake since dawn watching through his glass the magnificent mountain, Kinabalu, which towered more than 13,000 feet high, apparently a sheer cliff soaring perpendicularly from the sea. The foothills of the range which it dominated were covered with green jungle. Two waterfalls white with foam made the mountain's black rock appear more sombre and impressive.

'That is the Mountain of the Dead,' Fernandes explained. 'At its foot runs the river Koralut. This has giant stones across it, where the ghosts rest on their march to the mountain. When an old man dies, it is said that the tapping of his walking stick is heard clearly against these stones. When a young man's spirit passes over the river, those who live nearby will hear the sound of his *sendatang*, which is a kind of banjo.'

'What happens if a woman or child dies?' asked Gunn sceptically.

'If she is unmarried, they hear the sound of the *toreding*, rather like what we in England call a Jew's harp. If the spirit of a child passes by, they hear only the sound of weeping.'

'Have you ever climbed that mountain?'

'Once,' said Fernandes. 'When I was mate on a schooner, and we called here for water. We had to propitiate the spirits of the dead with an offering of meat, seven eggs and a couple of chickens, and then fire a gun to give warning that living people were approaching their domain.

'I was told that a spirit would then cry out in reply.'

'And did it?'

'I heard a noise from the heart of the mountain,' admitted Fernandes uneasily. 'But I could not say who or what made it.

To me, it seemed to be an animal call. But the local people had no doubt the dead were calling to us. I remember they held the mountain in such sacred regard that none of the streams we crossed or the places where we rested in the jungle on our walk were mentioned by names. The mountain itself is never referred to as Kinabalu, but as Agayon Ngaran, which means Big Name.'

'Has the name a local meaning – like Singapore was originally Singa Pura, the City of the Lion?'

'Yes. Kina means China and Balu is the Dusun word for the home of the dead. In the vernacular the mountain is known as The Chinese Widow. There were once many Chinese on the island, far more than today.'

'A romantic name,' said Gunn, and stood, hands pressed against the rail and the slow roll of the ship, wondering how long it might be before his spirit also began its long march to the eternal mists.

The sun blazed above them, a fire in the sky, and palm trees on the shore shook green branches like huge feather dusters. Fishermen in small boats were trawling nets in the shallow water. One such boat was already coming slowly towards them, propelled by several oarsmen. Gunn fixed his glass carefully on it. The deck was piled with huge melons and coconuts. So the locals were friendly and apparently wished for trade. This seemed an encouraging start.

'See what these fellows want in that boat,' he told Captain Fernandes. 'But do not let any of them come aboard. If they are selling fruit, buy sufficient for us all. Now have the longboat prepared, lowered and made ready. I will go ashore with Mr. Greene.'

'Will you be armed, sir?'

'No, but for safety's sake, the oarsmen will carry pistols already charged. Issue them with powder and ball and also with cutlasses. They can wear their pistols, but place the cutlasses beneath tarpaulins so that they cannot be seen. They are only to be used if we are attacked.'

'Shall I train a gun on the shore?'

'Charge both ten pounders, but keep them out of sight. Train your glass on us, and if we encounter any difficulty on the shore, or should you hear firing of any kind, shoot at the top of that hill. If it is the home of the dead, you will not harm them. But on no account fire into the settlement. Apart from risking our own lives, we have no wish to kill these people. We have come here to help them, not subdue them.'

'They may not readily comprehend the true and unusual purpose of our visit, sir.'

'Which is precisely why I am going ashore to explain it myself to their ruler,' replied Gunn.

The spy stood in the prow of his boat and cupped his hands to shout up at *Hesperides*.

'You want melons? Yams? Fresh water? All I got. All for you.'

The captain called the first mate to the bridge.

'Bargain with these natives,' he told him, 'but do not let them aboard. Buy what they have to sell, even if you have to pay too much for it, but keep them here until Dr. Gunn reaches shore.'

'Aye, aye, sir.'

Both men could see the longboat streaking away from the starboard side of the vessel towards the trembling palms that shaded the white beach. As the boat ran inshore, four of the crew shipped oars and jumped over the side to haul her up through the breaking waves, and hook the small step-ladder on the side so that Gunn's clothes would not be soaked. He strode up the beach, his supple boots sinking up to the ankles in the floury sand. Behind him, Greene looked nervously from left to right, not sure what their reception would be, and lacking Gunn's apparent disregard for hostility. How ironic and unthinkable to be attacked, nay, murdered, by natives they had travelled so far to help!

'Would it not have been safer to wait at anchor until they sent out an emissary to inquire our business?' he asked, his voice hoarse with the intensity of his feelings.

'They can wait on us, not we on them,' Gunn replied shortly, not even looking over his shoulder. If he had waited in Canton or Macao or anywhere along the Chinese coast in the early days, he would still be there, cap in hand, standing on the doorstep of opportunity. A rustle in the trees scattered his thoughts. He stopped, and Greene waited behind him, breathing heavily. A man wearing a white jacket to his knees, with sandals on his feet and a long-toothed tortoiseshell comb in his hair, stood regarding them silently.

Gunn took off his hat and bowed to him. The man bowed in return. He was of middle height and somehow ageless; his face brown and lined, like creased leather. Gunn said in pidgin: 'We wantee quick number one speak. Big chop, big man, sultan.'

'You speak any other number one lingo?' the man asked. 'English pidgin no good. What say number one chop Cantonese?'

'A little,' replied Gunn in that tongue.

'The sultan is dead,' the man explained, also in Cantonese. 'You have landed in a province of tears and grief. We therefore regret we cannot greet you in the manner your rank and dignity demands, but this does not mean our welcome is any the less sincere. It is like a fire within a cave, warm, but concealed from outward view.'

'I am saddened to hear your news. We have brought presents for the sultan. Silks from Surat, stamped velvet, scarlet cloth, gunpowder. And toys and sweetmeats for his children. Must we therefore return with these gifts to Singapore?'

The man bowed again.

'Your excellency is a man of bountiful heart. The sultan had one son, his heir, who is seven years old. It would give comfort to his mother, the sultan's widow, if, from the wells of your generosity, you would think to present his father's gifts to him. As it is written, a gift in friendship is like a lamp in a window. It cheers those inside and outside the house.'

'You speak wisely,' agreed Gunn grandly, easily falling into the flowery talk of the East after his absence in England. 'Let it be done as you say.'

He clapped his hands sharply. Immediately, two lascars swung a sea chest out of the longboat and carried it up the beach, and laid it down before them, on the sand. The sun winked and glittered on polished brass buckles and oiled teak.

Now the stranger clapped his hands, and at the summons, six Malay servants filed silently out of the trees and lifted up the box on their shoulders.

'Can we see the young sultan and give our gifts to him in person?' asked Gunn. 'That is the custom of our country.'

'The royal court is in mourning,' the man replied quickly. 'It would not be seemly.'

'We have come a long way to pay our respects to a great ruler,' Gunn told him. 'Let us therefore at least present our condolences to the sultan's widow. We will not seek to intrude in her grief, but rather to strengthen her in this hour of sadness with the knowledge and reassurance that she has strong friends across deep water. Is it not written, a joy shared is a joy doubled, while sorrow shared is sorrow halved?'

The man hesitated. It was difficult to refuse the Englishman, especially when his ship lay so close to shore, and doubtless had hidden guns already trained on their village. Equally, he did not wish to risk the displeasure of the Chinese widow. However, her annoyance might be tempered by the unexpected and very welcome gifts that this seafarer had brought. He bowed again, his mind made up.

'Please to follow me,' he said.

'I will bring two servants, if I may?' said Gunn. 'They have no weapons, as you see.'

He did not add that despite his words to Captain Fernandes, both he and Greene had strapped pistols to their bare bodies beneath their shirts. The man nodded, and they set off through the trees.

'What is your name?' Gunn asked him.

'I am a pangeran, a prince,' he explained. 'My name is Oya Ali. By marriage, the sultan was my cousin. His blood was my blood; his death is my bereavement.'

'What about his widow?'

'She is a Chinese lady.'

'When will her son be acclaimed sultan?'

'Soon. Perhaps this week. Or next. Whenever the birds of omen say it is fitting. It is impossible to give a firm date for the ceremony. There are many other things to be done.'

Gunn sensed the tone of the man's voice and turned to Greene.

'It would not surprise me if there is some dispute about who actually becomes sultan,' he said in English. 'This fellow is obviously not anxious to discuss the matter. Usually in the East – as elsewhere – victory and succession go to the contender with the strongest sword arm and the most followers. It is not always a matter of descent through the male line, whatever history books like to claim.'

'Do you think there will be trouble?'

'Of course. Man is born to trouble, as the sparks fly upwards, so the Good Book truly tells us. And the odd thing, Greene, is that the older you grow and the more troubles you overcome, the more you expect. But by that time, you do not call them troubles, you dignify them with the name of challenges. I think troubles are like mountains. You must surmount them – if only to see what lies on the other side.'

'That is an individualistic way of looking at things.'

'I know no other way,' replied Gunn with finality. 'Some must always lead so that others may follow. If we did not overcome difficulties, we would still be living in caves, awaiting the invention of the wheel.'

They crashed on through thickening undergrowth. Brightly coloured birds screamed and fluttered above them and the sun turned orange and then green with the increasing density of the leaves, so that finally they appeared to be walking through a deep dark tunnel. Monkeys swung from branch to branch high above their heads, chattering excitedly. The air felt damp and humid; sweat soaked their shirts, and flies and tiny insects stung their faces and settled greedily on the salty edges of their eyes.

Then, unexpectedly, they were in a clearing, facing long wooden houses built up on stilts. Razor-backed hogs grunted in the dirt and chickens clucked beneath their feet. A few fishermen, smoking rolled-up black leaves, squatted in the shade mending nets. They hardly glanced up at their arrival. Children peered at them from behind their mothers' skirts, but did not run away and hide, as Gunn had seen them do elsewhere, when they were unused to seeing Europeans. Because of this general lack of interest, Gunn deduced that they were probably not the first Europeans to visit the sultan or his widow. He wondered when the others had arrived – and what had been their business?

Apathy hung in the air, tinged with something more dangerous; a latent feeling of hostility. Gunn paused for a moment in the shade of the trees, took off his white hat and wiped his forehead with a silk handkerchief. These people were clearly not over-friendly to them. But why not? Was it simply because they had white skins and were European? Or was there some other reason? The clearing seemed depressingly hot. There was no sound except from the chickens and the pigs, and the distant jabber of monkeys, and then a baby began to cry. Blue, bitter smoke spiralled up from cooking fires. The Malay servants waited patiently with the sea-chest on their shoulders.

'When can we receive an audience with the sultan's widow?' Gunn asked the pangeran.

'She may be resting,' he replied evasively.

'We can wait,' Gunn told him. 'Either here, or in our vessel.'

'Please to stay here for a moment.'

Oya Ali padded ahead and climbed a notched log up into a house larger than the others and a little distance from them. The villagers stood silently, watching the visitors. The fishermen worked at their nets. Then all heads turned towards the house; Oya Ali was climbing down the tree trunk.

'Her most exalted highness has graciously agreed to see you,' he announced.

'What about our gifts?'

'Her highness has been moved by your kindness, and accepts them on behalf of her son.'

'Thank you,' said Gunn.

He and Greene followed the man up the creaking tree and into the longhouse. It was surprisingly cool, with a faint smell of tobacco and jasmine scent and the sharp male tang of a raw new-split wood. At the far end of the room stood the Chinese widow. Oya Ali went down on his knees before her. She motioned him to one side and he stood against the wall, hands folded, head down as though unworthy to look at her directly. Gunn and Greene began to walk towards her, holding their hats against their bodies in their left hands. They crossed the rugs. On the bamboo slats of the floor the iron heels of their boots echoed as though they were walking on the taut skin or a vast drum. When they were within six feet of the woman, they stopped and bowed deeply towards her.

The widow said nothing, but inclined her head slightly to acknowledge their greetings. Gunn looked into her dark eyes, trying to guess the thoughts in her mind. Her face was transparent and devoid of all expression, the colour of burnt almonds. Small pointed breasts pushed firmly against her white blouse. She held her hands folded demurely in front of her and Gunn saw that her fingers were heavy with pearl-encrusted rings. He stood about eighteen inches taller, but her eyes watched his, eyes black as sloe-berries, and with as little expression.

Gunn began to speak in Cantonese.

'I am sorry that we have arrived unannounced, at a time of such grief, your highness. This was not our wish.'

'What *was* your wish?' she asked him quietly, as though it mattered.

'We came for a specific purpose, which your highness might find difficult to appreciate, if you form your view of all Europeans from traders or marauders, or if you confuse us as Englishmen with Dutch or Portuguese adventurers. We wished to help your husband's country and your husband's people. No more. But not less.'

'Why? Such sentiments are not usual among Europeans in the East. They prefer, so it is said, to help themselves.'

'That is so, your highness. As I say, you might find our intentions difficult to comprehend, but they are genuine, I assure you. Let me explain my position to help you understand that we come in friendship, and not in search of trade or concessions or in search of any riches your province may contain.'

'First, I am a man of medicine, a physician. I have also been a merchant and have amassed enough wealth to allow me to look at other wider horizons than those that generally limit the view of men of commerce.

'My friend here, Mark Greene, has told me about James Brooke, the White Rajah of Sarawak, whose ideals we both admire. His aims, in helping that kingdom to reach maturity with security in a world of turmoil, and without any thought of personal gain, have inspired in us the wish to do likewise.'

'Why?' the widow asked again.

'It is easy to ask a question in one word, your highness, but you must bear with me if I must answer in many. When I was a younger man, I wished for wealth, not for itself, because gold alone is useless, but for what the gold could buy – pleasure, power, independence. So I made money, and bought these things, and then I realized that money could also purchase other more worthwhile aims. And I owe this discovery to my colleague, Mark Greene. He was born rich and has no need to make more money. And like me, he has no wish to do so. No-one can say when a man enters this world, but some of us may feel we know roughly the time of our departure. I wish, therefore, to leave behind me a memorial not only of commerical enterprise, but a more abiding monument – the knowledge that I have been able to use my money to help others who have not been so favoured by fortune.'

'You speak with a honeyed tongue,' said the Chinese widow. 'What is it you require of me to help you in this aim?'

'Nothing, your highness,' said Gunn, 'save the opportunity to prove that my honeyed tongue speaks truth. It is written out of the strong comes forth sweetness. I seek to show that out of sweet words will come forth strength and prosperity.'

'We have had Englishmen visit us before. One was ship-wrecked, and the only survivor of his barque. He gave my husband a telescope, the only possession he had been able to save from the wreck. My husband sent him back by our own vessel to Singapore. He came here as a man in distress, washed up by the waves, and the gods of the storm. He left as a friend. If you are also such a man, I bid you welcome.

'But we have had other visitors here who have been less acceptable. In their minds they divided my husband's province, seeking how they might take it over to their own advantage. Some also brought presents, others spoke in such a way as you. We have also received missionaries, who diligently tried to instruct us in the ways of their faith.'

'It is not our intention to interfere with your customs or your religion,' said Greene. 'Dr. Gunn and I feel that there is too much change already in the world, and not always is this for the better. We seek to preserve what you already have, to keep safe your heritage from predators of any nationality.'

'But *why*?' asked the widow. 'What is it to you on the other side of the world, how we live here? And how do you intend to fulfil these brave intentions? You must know that my husband, the sultan, has only recently died. His spirit is even now ascending the sacred path that leads to the peaks of Kinabalu. Our court is in mourning. We have many problems to face at a time of tears. Dyaks inland wish their nominee to succeed to my husband's throne, and not my husband's son. There could even be war, one part of my husband's people against another part, a struggle that neither faction could win, but through which all of us would lose. And then the Dutch have sent a party to see me, seeking trade concessions, but I have not revealed my face to them. These are the realities of our situation. Not kind dreams and generous proposals of help, but facts. How could you put your words to the test if I accepted your protestations of good will? If you can answer that, maybe I would then be more disposed to believe you are here for the generous reasons you claim.'

'Your highness,' said Gunn gently. 'We have just arrived in your house. This is consequently the first we have heard of your predicament. What is it you would have us do to show we do not put our faith in empty words alone? We have nearly forty men aboard my vessel *Hesperides* in the bay. She carries some protection against pirates – guns, muskets, fuses and mines. Do you wish us to defend your province as best we can with this armament, to prove that I speak truth?'

'I wish,' began the widow slowly, looking strangely at Gunn as though she was seeing him for the first time. But he did not learn what she wished, for at that moment a servant entered between two draped red curtains at the far end of the room, bowed and waited, trembling, head down, like Oya Ali.

'Speak,' she commanded him sharply. Only a messenger bearing important news would dare to enter her presence unannounced.

The man spoke urgently in a low voice. Gunn could not understand his language, but saw the widow's face muscles tighten at what he said.

'What is the news that he brings, your highness?' he asked her.

'Calamities come like clouds and never alone,' she replied. 'My husband has died. Now it is reported that a force of Malay pirates and white men are approaching this place from the south and the east. Is this part of your doing, Englishman? Is it part of a plan to engage me in talk while my province is attacked?'

'I know nothing of that,' retorted Gunn. 'Nor do I know that any other Englishmen have landed here.'

There were questions and answers, the shrugging of shoulders; then the servant turned his palms towards the roof in a fatalistic gesture of resignation and acceptance.

'One of these white men has been identified,' the widow continued. 'He is not English, but a Dutchman who attempted to visit me some days ago. He was told then that the sultan had died, and he should return after the period of mourning. Seemingly, he has not wished to wait.'

As she spoke, Gunn suddenly heard a faint and distant whistle that reminded him instantly of a steam train on the new railways he had used in England.

'Down!' he shouted, and threw himself flat on the bamboo floor. Greene dropped on his knees beside him. The widow stood perplexed for a moment, and then the whole room trembled and the rugs on the walls billowed in a great hot dry gust of air.

The cannon ball crashed through the trees outside and trundled across the flat, trodden earth, scoring a long straight groove as it rolled. Dust and dead insects showered down on them from the creaking bamboo roofs. Bats flapped in blind terror among the rafters.

'They have arrived,' said Gunn grimly. 'And seemingly voice their demands through the mouths of cannon rather than their own. Do you possess any army to defend yourselves?'

'An army of toy soldiers,' the widow replied bitterly. 'In any dispute here it is the custom for both opposing sides to dig themselves into trenches and then to plant stakes and spikes in the ground pointing at the enemy. Then they fire muskets and shoot arrows in the air to frighten each other. That is how our men play at war.'

'These fellows are playing a different game,' said Gunn. He turned to Greene.

'Wait for the dust to settle, then return to the longboat. Take the two sailors with you. Order them to make ready for my return.'

'You are leaving then?' asked the widow mockingly. 'After your talk of how you wish to help us, you have suddenly re-called another engagement?'

'Yes,' agreed Gunn. 'An engagement with an enemy as yet unknown by name or number. But this means I will add weight to my words. With your permission and approval, your high-ness, my men and I will drive out these invaders in your name, and the name of the sultan's son.'

'How do you propose to do this, Englishman?'

For the first time, the widow's face was animated, her voice more sympathetic.

'Leave that to me, your highness. I will adopt a plan to meet the contingency. But now, pray, give me your authority – and some member of your court who can vouch that I fight with you and for you. I would not wish to be taken for an enemy. And many Eastern races think that all white men look alike.'

'I have heard it said by the old sea captain that Europeans consider all Chinese to look alike,' replied the widow, smiling slightly. 'But I found that difficult to accept.'

'We can discuss such matters at greater length when we have leisure,' said Gunn.

'And safety,' added the Chinese widow. 'Which is not now. I can muster only fifty men armed with flintlocks and arrows. Also, they will consider it an evil omen to fight if they are attacked tonight. They are due to celebrate the Feast of the Dried Heads, which marks that time when a young hunter has severed his first human head from the body of an enemy. By this feat he has crossed the frontier from boyhood and become a warrior. His relations bring sugar, fruit and rice and wild pig, and they all drink tuak beer. Girls have spent weeks making special costumes with brass girdles, and short tunics and special strings of beads. Part of the ritual is for each newly admitted warrior to hold the girl he loves while she pours tuak down his throat. Not even the sadness at the sultan's death can cause this feast to be postponed.'

'How many young men are to be honoured this night?'

'Ten.'

'Then, your highness, please explain to them all that their feast may have to be deferred – but only so that it can be held with even greater glory. For more younger brothers will also be able to lay claim to the mark of the warrior with them. I fear many men will die tonight.'

'Do you think that we shall survive, Englishman?'

'I never *think* about matters,' replied Gunn simply. 'I *know*.'

The Chinese widow clapped her hands and the spy came into the room.

'I have just returned from the English ship, exalted one,' he began unctuously.

'But you could not get aboard,' Gunn interrupted him, 'because I gave orders to that effect, and so you discovered nothing. Now do some more useful task. Take this message.'

He pulled a sheet of paper from his pocket and scribbled on it with a pencil.

'Bear this to my captain Fernandes, the master of the *Hesperides*.'

'What orders have you for him?' asked Greene.

'To pull around the far side of the bay, where our ship will not be seen so easily. It is imperative that these marauders imagine they are simply dealing with native forces, unorganized and ill-armed. If they realize that Europeans are waiting for them, they will be more prepared for what I have in mind. I have no idea how many Dutchmen will accompany them, but presumably the whole band must outnumber us by five or even ten to one.'

'Then have you any hope at all, Englishman?'

'Every hope. This is the sort of situation I will enjoy.'

'You say many men will die this night. You might be among their number. Would you enjoy that?'

'A man's life can be compared to sand running through the neck of an hourglass, your highness. He is dying even before the hour of his birth. I fear death less than I fear other things.'

'What things can be more terrible than death?'

'The answer to that, your highness, can also wait until we have more leisure for discussion. In the meantime, let me see your fighting men.'

The Chinese widow led Gunn down the notched tree trunk. Thirty men clad in loincloths and barefoot, gripping spears or ancient smooth-barrelled muskets, stood around the crater that the cannon-ball made when it landed. Others had surrounded the huge ball where it had come to rest at the base of a palm tree. They all bowed as the widow approached. Dust still hung like a torn shroud in the hot humid air. Little children were crying in their mothers' arms in the shelter of the huts; a few dogs, thin and mangy, skulked uneasily around the perimeter of the village.

'Anyone speak pidgin or Cantonese?' Gunn asked the Chinese widow.

'They only understand Malay.'

'Then please instruct your commander to cut down strong bamboos and sharpen them, and plant the stakes in a fence pointing outwards around the village. Then to build a second similar fence of even larger stakes six feet inside the first.'

'That I will do, but we can improve on that line of defence,' said the widow. 'My men will set spears horizontally at any height you wish, in what we call a blanlek, a spear trap we use to kill deer or wild pigs. Behind each spear they bend back a sapling, and tie this by a rope to a thin cord which the animal sets off as it approaches.'

'Good. Then have them set up these spears at a height to hit men.'

'It is our custom to dig trenches,' pointed out Oya Ali. 'From them we can regard the enemy from positions of safety.'

'So I have been informed,' said Gunn. 'But that can only produce delay at the best and death at the worst; your trenches can too easily become your graves. Put your men instead up in the trees. If you have doubts about their courage, tie them there with jungle creeper lest they feel the urge to flee away. Give them as many arrows as you can spare, and powder and ball for their muskets if they have them. But do not allow anyone to fire under any circumstances until the enemy is only yards away.'

'That is a policy of risk,' said Oya Ali uneasily.

'It is essential, otherwise they will only waste their ammunition – and give away their positions where they can be cut down at the enemy's whim.'

'He speaks truth,' said the Chinese widow. 'Do as he says. That is my command.'

'It will be done, exalted one.'

Oya Ali hurried away. Gunn turned to Greene.

'From a man of peace, you are about to be transformed into a man of war,' he told him.

'So it would seem, sir,' agreed Greene. 'But what of the outcome? I do not put much weight on the performance these fellows show as soldiers. Nor do I believe they will hold their fire as you advise.'

'I agree with you on both counts. But if we do not assume some defensive position speedily, the whole province can be seized by default.'

'If it is, then I would not put a high value on our personal chances of survival.'

'We would have no chance at all,' agreed Gunn cheerfully.

'Does that not worry you?' Greene asked him curiously.

It should, thought Gunn, for I possess the means to buy a lifetime of pleasure, to start new enterprises of infinite and incalculable potential, but I have no time to do any of these things. Already, this anaemia is weakening my blood, which soon will run thin as cheap red wine. Is it not better to die in action on my feet like a man, rather than hold on desperately to a dwindling life, until I sink painfully and slowly, damp with the sweat of illness without cure? Death in battle would have one supreme advantage: it would be quick.

He turned to the widow, forcing these thoughts from his mind.

'Where is your son?' he asked.

'With his *munshi*, his tutor, in a house not far from here.'

'How many other people know that?'

'No-one else but you,' she admitted. 'I feared there might be some disaffection or uprising after the death of his father, and the boy is too precious to me to keep here where he might be seized as a hostage.'

'With your permission, your highness, I suggest your son is removed to my vessel. He will be safer there.'

'Can I trust you?' she asked him simply. Her eyes showed she expected an honest answer.

'That must be your decision. But Mr. Greene can escort him to the *Hesperides*.'

'I trust you, Englishman,' said the widow quietly, and Gunn felt a tightening of his heart; it seemed a long time since anyone had trusted him without contracts and signatures and seals and witnesses. The widow spoke quickly to a servant.

'My son will be here within minutes,' she told Gunn. Another servant brought out a carved wooden tray with oval cups of fresh coconut milk. As they drank the cool fizzy juice, three men appeared at the far end of the longhouse, with a boy dressed in native costume, who carried a small bow with a quiver of arrows.

'My son,' said the widow proudly.

Gunn patted the boy on his bare shoulder.

'Take him back to the *Hesperides*,' he told Greene. 'Give him the spare cabin. And counsel Captain Fernandes to hold his fire whatever may happen here. At dusk, he is to send the longboat in at this beach for me, with twelve men armed with charged pistols and muskets, and cutlasses.'

'Very good,' said Greene. He turned to the boy.

'Come on, young 'un,' he said kindly. 'We have a trip to make.'

Oya Ali led them out to the clearing. The widow watched them go, and then turned to Gunn.

'Now that we are alone, how do you estimate our chance against these attackers?' she asked him.

'You are afraid?'

She seemed so slight standing there beside him, a girl in a world of men and violence and death.

'Concerned,' corrected the widow carefully. 'My husband said I was never to be afraid.'

'He was right, your husband,' said Gunn.

All around them, he heard the cut and thwack of dahs and parangs hacking at bamboo; dry leaves rustled like dead men's teeth.

'I do not think they will attempt anything until nightfall,' Gunn went on. 'And by then they will have lost the initiative – for we will attack them first. If we allow ourselves to be besieged, we could be forced to watch day and night in case of surprise. We are seriously outnumbered, and soon would be weary and easy prey to them. So we will reverse that situation. Surprise will be as good as twenty extra men. Well, almost as good.'

'You are a brave and clever man,' said the widow admiringly. 'Like my husband.'

'You do me too much honour, your highness.'

A servant ran towards them across the clearing and flung himself prostrate on the ground at their feet.

'Stand up and speak,' the widow ordered him sharply. He babbled away in a dialect Gunn could not understand. She translated.

'The strangers are approaching through the jungle, from the east. White men are leading 200 pirates, one of my people has counted them.'

'It is imperative they do not know that any other European has been here,' said Gunn. 'I will therefore retire to your longhouse. They will doubtless wish to speak with you.'

'Then I will listen.'

'So will I.'

Gunn climbed up the tree trunk, and sat on the floor, so that he could watch the clearing through horizontal chinks in the plaited wooden wall. A European carrying a white cloth tied to a bamboo cane came into view with about twenty Malays, who carried drawn swords and bamboo staves. The European wore a pistol in a leather holster at his waist, with a horn of powder and a leather pouch of shot. He was a big man, bearded and running to fat; his face shone with sweat that pasted his torn shirt to his body.

'I come in peace,' he announced to the Chinese widow in Malay. 'I wish to speak with the ruler of this province.'

'What do you wish to discuss that necessitates a guard of so many armed men – if you come in peace?'

'We have marched a long and dangerous way from the coast. We wish to make a treaty with the ruler. To offer him and his people the privilege of joining the Royal Dutch Empire, of serving His Imperial Majesty, the King of Holland.'

'I give you answer as the sultan's widow, and the mother of his heir, who is not yet of age. His people are honoured by your generous proposal, but nevertheless remain content to stay independent. It is our wish to trade by all peaceful means with every person of like mind – including subjects of the King of Holland. Trade is one thing and a treaty of the type you offer quite another.'

'Madam,' replied Van Vooren gravely, hoping that his nervousness did not show in his voice, 'I am the personal emissary of His Excellency the Dutch Governor in Java. I despatched an ambassador to you some days ago, but you would not see him.'

'You sent me a corporal of the Dutch army,' retorted the Chinese widow. 'I do not talk with men of low degree.'

'If you do not accept this generous invitation to join the Dutch Empire, I would be failing in my duty if I did not warn you that your son may be displaced from his throne, and another more generously and realistically disposed towards my sovereign could supplant him.'

'Who is disposed to treat in this way with us? My son will rule as his father wished. There is nothing more to discuss.'

'I do not wish you harm, I simply give solemn warning of

what may happen,' Van Vooren replied, his voice slightly less confident. This accursed heat had dried his mouth. His throat felt hot as the oven of his uncle, the baker at Eindhoven. Why would not this foolish woman be reasonable?

'Therefore, I must make clear that failure to understand and accept the advantages of the Governor's offer could provoke a situation of the utmost gravity to you personally, and to the people of the province. Other rulers have wished most desperately for such a generous invitation, but it has never been extended to them.'

'What other rulers may do is their concern,' the widow replied indifferently. 'I have nothing more to say. I wish you farewell and a safe journey back to your Governor. May the spirits of wind and sea give speed to your vessel.'

She turned away to show that the audience was at an end.

'I am sorry that you thus force our conversation to be continued through the mouths of guns,' replied Van Vooren.

'That appears to be your wish. A cannon has already fired on our village. I cannot prevent you firing again, but for our part, Dutchman, we do not speak with guns. And I find it difficult to accept that a man like you, who says he comes to us in peace, should also stoop to use these iron arguments instead of your own.'

The widow bowed slightly in dismissal and then climbed into the longhouse. Gunn could see she was trembling with reaction, despite her brave replies. She sat down on a cushion on the floor, barely noticing him, her face taut with concern.

Van Vooren shouted up after her: 'That is your last word then, ma'am?'

'It is. I have spoken, and I will speak no more on the matter.'

'On your head then, ma'am, must be the responsibility for what may regrettably be unnecessary death.'

Van Vooren waited for a moment, hoping she would relent, but she said nothing. He led his men back into the jungle; none of them looked behind them. A few yellow-eyed dogs barked and snapped and bared their teeth around their feet.

'What will happen now?' the widow asked Gunn in a nervous whisper.

'First, I would expect a few more shots to frighten us,' said Gunn. 'Then a delay of some hours to increase that fear.'

As he spoke, the cannon boomed again, and a ball trundled down the sky and crashed into a house across the clearing. Children began to cry. Up in the trees, Dyaks started to fire their muskets wildly.

'The damn' fools,' said Gunn bitterly. 'They cannot see any targets, for the Dutch gunners will be at least a mile away.'

Elsewhere in the forest, other muskets crackled in reply. Bullets sang through the air like angry metal wasps, burying themselves uslessly in the tree trunks and piles of houses. The clearing was completely deserted now; most of the villagers were running away to the shelter of the jungle, crashing through the branches in blind panic, like a herd of frightened buffaloes.

'You still believe that you can prevail?' the widow asked Gunn uneasily.

'I do,' he replied. 'But first I must return to the *Hesperides*, for I have a new plan of attack in my mind. Have you two men of courage and resource, who could undertake a special and important mission?'

'Yes,' she replied at once. 'Imi Hassan and Aki Nabula.'

'Please send for them, your highness.'

She clapped her hands and a servant appeared, received her instructions, bowed and left the room. He returned in minutes with two Dyaks, stockily built men, about five feet tall. Their arms and legs were tattooed with stars and the heads of serpents.

'Aki Nabula was my husband's chamberlain, and Imi Hassan is the bearer of the State umbrella – and our state executioner. The families of both these men have been loyal for generations to my husband's house.'

'Here is their chance to prove their loyalty still holds strong,' said Gunn.

He stood up, towering above the two Dyaks.

'I wish you to go out, dressed as peasants, and carrying pots of food so that the pirates will not pay much attention to you should they see you,' he told them. 'Find out the exact position of their encampment, and how it is guarded. Then wait by the headland for us to land, and report to me personally what you have discovered. We will be there at dusk.'

He handed his German hunter to Aki Nabula.

'Watch the larger hand closely,' he told him. 'When it crosses the smaller hand for the fifth time, we shall be on our way. And if you do this deed well, I will give each of you a time-piece like this, so that you will be able to count the hours of sunshine and the hours of dark and chart your lives accordingly.'

'It shall be as you say,' Aki Nabula told him gravely, holding the watch up to his ear before he put it away. They bowed and silently left the room.

'Now is there a back way out of this house?' Gunn asked the widow.

'I will show you.'

She led him through an anteroom hung with red curtains and piled with thick carpets, then through a kitchen lined with scrubbed copper pans and *chattis* of water, and down a second tree-trunk to the edge of the forest. Half a dozen goats tethered to piles butted blindly at him as he headed for the shore.

Near the beach, outside a crude bamboo hut, three old men were gathering in fish that had been split open, gutted and spread on woven bamboo mats to dry. A fourth crouched near a huge clay pot, chewing a cigarette of local tobacco rolled in a wrapper made from a palm leaf. He pounded the rotted fish into a greyish paste with a bone pestle, throwing in a handful of seeds from the kapayang tree from time to time as flavouring. Blue flies swarmed around the stinking mess.

'It is their relish,' the widow explained, seeing Gunn pause. 'Some of my husband's people have tastes that seem strange to Western eyes, although I have heard it said that in France snails and even the legs of frogs are considered fit for food at rich men's tables. These people smoke rats on bamboo spits as a delicacy, and eat snakes and the flesh of tortoises and lizards.'

'Each to his own, your highness,' Gunn replied non-committally. 'But this man has given me an idea.'

As he stepped forward, the old man with the pestle looked up inquiringly, and then prostrated himself on the sand when he recognized the widow. Gunn picked up the pestle and carried it into the dark interior of the hut. As he had expected, the phosophorus in the fish scales made the round knuckle of the bone glow with a weird, ghostly light. He came out into the sunshine and handed the pestle back to the old man.

'I wish to buy that paste and any more pots you may have ready,' he said.

'But it is not to European liking. It will probably make you ill,' protested the widow.

'It would probably kill me – if I ate it. But that I do not intend to do.'

Gunn threw two golden sovereigns in the sand. The old man picked them up, examined them against the sun, bit them with his yellow, sharpened teeth, and slipped them into a cloth pouch he wore at his belt. The Chinese widow spoke quickly to him. He called to his companions; one went into the hut and returned carrying a second pot.

'That is their whole supply,' the widow explained.

'It should be enough. I will now require a canoe from them to ferry the paste – and me – out to my ship.'

The Chinese widow shook her head slowly. Men's ways often seemed difficult to understand, but this man was impossible. Was he seriously capable of defending her village against the Dutch and the pirates – or was he a fool, a buffoon who was brave with his mouth but not his muscles? She sighed; she had better humour him.

'They will take you out to your ship in their canoe,' she told Gunn.

They trusted him, and he felt an almost overwhelming warmth towards these simple people, who did not know who he was. He was a complete stranger, with a different coloured skin, and he could easily be a slave trader. But their ruler's widow had spoken for him and this was enough; they accepted him. Gunn turned away so that they would not see his eyes were moist. He had spent too long with contracts and agreements; too long with soft-bellied companions whose god was money and whose temple the counting-house. It was good to be with men who looked him in the eye, and whose muscles were firm.

'I will return here when the sun is down,' he told her. 'If the pirates should attack before, I will post back at once, but I do not think they will fight in the day. They are creatures of the dark, when few can see their evil deeds.'

She watched as the canoe sped like an arrow across the shimmering sea after the *Hesperides*, now sailing around the foreland. Gunn sat crouched down in the little craft, head down in case the pirates had posted lookouts along this part of the shore. The fishermen turned behind the stern of the *Hesperides*. He climbed up the gangway into the vessel and motioned to one of his crew to carry up the foul-smelling jars. The fishermen paddled back slowly to the island. Greene met Gunn on deck.

'I heard cannon fire, and wondered what was happening,' he said.

'A gang of Malay ruffians under a Dutchman came in to offer the woman the chance of joining the Dutch empire. She refused, I hope wisely, for they will almost certainly attack tonight to take the province by force.'

'And you are abandoning them to that fate?' asked Greene in amazement.

'Far from it,' Gunn assured him. 'I simply give you their intentions. Not mine.'

He turned to Captain Fernandes.

'I will sleep for a few hours, for I find this humid air makes me weary. When I awake, assemble the crew on the afterdeck. All hands, man and boy. Before the light goes.'

'Very good, sir.'

Fernandes gave a disapproving sniff at the two pots, whose mouths glowed faintly with putrescence.

Gunn went below to his cabin, took off his hat, poured himself a glass of water and looked at his face in the metal mirror above the wash basin. His skin still had the same yellow colour, and after the brief spurt of action, his mouth was dry; he felt almost unbearably weary. He uncorked a bottle of whisky and drank greedily from the neck. The raw spirit poured false fire through his body. He wiped sweat from his face with a towel, loosened his shoes, and lay down on his bunk. Almost immediately, he was asleep.

When he awoke, the sun was already sinking towards the sea. He tightened his shoes, dashed cold water on his face and went up the companionway to the afterdeck. Under the pale light of storm lanterns the crew waited, hands clasped behind them, in four silent rows. Gunn peered at the English faces of the officers already dim in the gloom, at the brown skins of the Malays and lascars, the darker skins of Indians, the yellow complexions of Chinese cooks. He counted heads. They were all present and he knew each one by name, just as he knew about their families, and their backgrounds. And not one among them would guess he was living on borrowed time, that his entry in the ledger of eternity was about to close. He would willingly change places with any one of them now, but he lacked the opportunity. Gunn cleared his throat.

'Officers and men,' he began. 'As you know, we have sailed to Borneo with no intention of trading, but to help a simple and peaceful people.

'Mr. Greene and I went ashore this morning to pay our respects to the ruler, but learned he has recently died. While we were engaged in conversation with his widow, Dutch emissaries arrived with armed pirates and other mercenaries to present the lady with a harsh ultimatum. If she did not join the Dutch empire immediately, they would put their own puppet in her son's place as ruler. To protect her son, the sultan's heir, Mr. Greene has brought him here to our vessel.

'Now, you may say that Borneo is a long way from England or China or India, or wherever your homeland may be. And you are right. It *is* a long way – measured in miles. But otherwise these people are like ourselves, in that they do not wish to be bondsmen, but to stay free. And it is my intention, with your help, to assist them in this natural and noble desire.

'I intend, gentlemen, to frustrate this knavish Dutch proposal. And to back my words with deeds, I will pay every man aboard who willingly joins with me in this endeavour, the sum of 100 gold sovereigns, half payable now, half on our return. And I give the solemn promise that should any fall in battle – if there *is* a battle – I will pay this same sum to their dependents. Double for officers.

'You have signed with me as officers and crew. You have not signed to fight unless you are attacked. So I give you this opportunity to all or any of you of such a mind, to withdraw if you so wish. Let us have a show of hands. Who is for me?'

Every hand went up.

'Right,' said Gunn with satisfaction, and turned to Captain Fernandes.

'Take Mr. Burke, the first mate, and draw up a paper paying each member of the ship's company 50 sovereigns now, and 100 sovereigns to each officer now, with the same sum to follow on our return.'

'Aye, aye, sir!'

'You, Captain Fernandes, will remain aboard the vessel with six men in case any pirates should get wind of our scheme and attempt to seize her.'

'What exactly is your scheme?' asked Greene with interest. 'How do you propose to engage and overcome a force said to be 200 strong, and with at least one cannon, while we number barely 40 men and have no heavy armament, whatever?'

'By audacity and surprise, Mr. Greene. Two qualities, which have so far served me well in business, shall now give us the victory in this matter.'

'You seem very confident?'

'Supremely so. I have nothing to lose, save my life, and that I do not hold in much regard.'

'You speak for yourself, sir.'

'Of course. I always do. But everyone else aboard has spoken for themselves by their show of hands. Now – my plan. I have asked the sultan's widow to put out two trusty spies to find exactly where the enemy are encamped. At dusk we will go ashore in the longboats, taking with us the pots of dried fish bought on the beach and the luminous paint I purchased in Singapore. I will send out men with gunpowder and fuses to bind charges to trees and run trip wires from them between the enemy and the village.

'When the pirates attack, they will set off these charges. Some will undoubtedly die as a result, and the others will release the deer traps. You, Mr. Greene, will command the force

I will put within the stockade, so that any who survive the explosives, the spears and the sharpened stakes, will then face your muskets. They should be easy targets.'

'But how will you *make* them move? They may stay still. They may be entrenched – or they may turn and overwhelm you.'

'The operative word in your three alternatives, Mr. Greene, is "may". The operative word in my plan is "will". We *will* coat our clothes with this foul concoction that *will* make us glow in a fearful manner.

'These pirates, like all primitive seafaring peoples, are very superstitious and easily frightened by what they cannot understand. They *will* already be uneasy after spending so much time in the jungle with gibbering apes and serpents and crocodiles. They *will* imagine we are ghosts or evil spirits – and I assure you nothing in our behaviour will weaken this impression.'

'I hope you succeed,' said Greene earnestly. 'We are very heavily outnumbered.'

'But would you not say that one Englishman, or one of our crew of *whatever* nationality, is at least the equal of eight if not ten pirates who only attack when they have such superior numbers?'

'I would not say anything,' replied Greene prudently.

'Good,' said Gunn, slapping him on the back. 'We have both already talked enough. Now – to deeds.'

The tropic dusk dropped its thick short curtain gently over the luminous rim of the sea. In mangrove swamps, bull-frogs and tree frogs began to croak; insects whirred on wide transparent wings, and now and then the listeners heard a heavy slithering splash as a crocodile slid past the rotting stumps into the water.

Van Vooren lit a cigar made from a palm leaf rolled and tied with a single fine thread. Mosquitoes whirred against the back of his hands in the brief flare of the lucifer and he brushed them off irritably. Sweat was cooling on his body now, and his stomach felt heavy with the weight of his own fear. The tobacco should steady his nerves.

Somewhere out beyond the dancing fire-flies, beyond that infinite terrible darkness of the jungle, lay the village he would have to attack before the moon came out. He had argued with Hofmeyer that surely such warlike action was unnecessary. Could they not come to some agreement, some peaceful compromise with these people? But Hofmeyer had been adamant.

'We *have* to strike now,' he had explained with increasing impatience at his companion's lack of perception and courage. 'If we give them time to organize under a new sultan – even the boy – then they will fight fiercely, because they will believe they are fighting for themselves and their whole future. If we can crush them now, when they are still without a leader, it will be infinitely easier.'

'It is not right,' protested Van Vooren unconvincingly.

'Right and wrong do not enter into the matter. We have a mission to undertake, and this is the only way we can achieve it. You know that as well as I do.'

Van Vooren had swallowed then, so that he would not voice the questions that personally tormented him most. What happens to our wounded? What if these supposedly peaceful natives have somehow brought in fierce reinforcements from some other warlike tribe – or even if they were headhunters, as he secretly feared?

He could feel the lead bullet or the sharpened dah slicing his muscles, tearing into his sinews, severing his arteries. He could also imagine being abandoned out there in the dark, to be done to death by stakes driven through him by the women of the tribe; to have his testicles hacked off and sewn into his lips so that even in his giant dying agony he could not cry for help. He would deserve those diamonds if ever he found them. He would have earned them at the risk of his life.

What did the Governor and his officials back in Java with their mistresses and crates of Schnapps know of the dangers that now beset them? Van Vooren was seeing a part of the terrible unspeakable and unspoken underside of every imperial dream; this was the fate of stragglers in all the legions when the tide of action ebbed against them.

Van Vooren looked with distaste at the pirates squatting around their camp fires, faces shining in the glow of the flames. Someone had shot a small barking deer and skinned it, and now the caracase rotated on a horizontal bamboo, dripping fat hissingly into the flames. Van Vooren could not bring himself to touch the flesh. He had no hunger, no thirst, only an almost unbearable yearning to be out of this dark and fearsome jungle and the dread of approaching danger, back among his own kind, in lighted rooms with laughter. Adversity and discomfort and the possibility of an early death might quicken the blood of a different breed of man. So far as Van Vooren was concerned, they only made his blood run thin.

Carl Hofmeyer sat on a tree stump humming to himself as he cleaned his musket, pushing the brass ramrod down the long smooth barrel, twisting and pulling it out again, carefully examining the oil-soaked rag at its end for any trace of corrosion. The climate here was so humid that metal rusted within hours; a pair of new boots left near a sleeper overnight were green with mould by morning.

The thought of being killed or wounded had not entered his mind, which was closed to most other thoughts as well. He was a thick-necked man from the Fens, with no ambitions and fears, just an acceptance of whatever task he was commanded to do. He had been on other such encounters, and he was confident what would happen here. A short fierce burst of fire from their side, arousing a faint, timid, almost token response from the defenders. And then, muskets at the high port across their bodies, those with cudgels waving them, all shouting wildly to add to the confusion, they would leap the pathetic bamboo barricades and overwhelm the natives. Within an hour at most, all action would be over; victory against such primitive savages would not be difficult to achieve, and victory meant native women to pleasure, vats of native liquor to broach, temples to loot of jewels and ornaments, and strange tales to tell when they returned to Java.

The Dutch sea captain stood a little apart from his compatriots, smoking a cheroot, one of a chest he kept in his cabin, brought all the way from Amsterdam. He leaned against a tree, his uniform unbuttoned, watching the Malay pirates carefully. They looked a murderous lot, and he had no doubt that they would easily subdue the village or town or whatever it was they were about to attack. Van Vooren had not acquainted him with its size, and he was not sufficiently interested to ask. But what happened after that conquest? Might not these pirates then turn against the Dutchmen they outnumbered and put them to the sword, and so claim all spoils for themselves?

He had tried to insure against this dreadful possibility by telling everyone – compatriots and Malays alike – that his ship waited in a constant state of readiness, all guns charged, tapers ready to ignite; and he had spoken loudly and often about re-inforcements of regular Dutch troops sailing from Java. But he knew there were no reinforcements. The Europeans were on their own. They would have to protect their lives as best they could, for none of their kind were close enough to help. The pirates had been accustomed for so long to running their schooners and clippers against honest merchantmen, then throwing out grappling irons, leaping aboard to seize what they wanted of the cargo and making off, that once aroused, they could present a fearful problem. Defeat at the hands of the natives was unthinkable; victory might also have its peculiar dangers.

Van Vooren poured himself the last of his Schnapps, and once more went over the plan in his mind, trying to find a flaw in it. They would sleep here by rota, keeping watch in case of any surprise attack. The risk of this was slight, for Dyaks were known to fear the spirits of the dark, but the prudent commander covered every risk, and he was always prudent, never careless.

Two hours before dawn they would awake and advance on the village. They had seen Dyaks sharpening stakes, and Van Vooren guessed that they were desperately trying to build a stockade. If the pirates could not rip these stakes out of the ground, then they would cut down bamboos, trim off their branches, bind the trunks together with creeper and throw these crude rafts on the sticks, and run up and over them. A number of such rafts had already been constructed.

A few native snipers up in the treetops might attempt to shoot them with arrows or their ancient muskets, but the risk of being hit by such marksmen in the dark and on the move was very slight. He had been impressed by the sultan's widow; she seemed a passable kind of woman for a Chinese, and a woman of spirit. Perhaps he would have discovered more about her other attributes before the sun went down next day?

The Chinese widow waited alone and apprehensive in her audience room. A servant had lit a small rush light on a side table, and the tiny flame threw gigantic and somehow frightening shadows on the ceiling and the far wall. She thought of all the uneasy ghosts her husband had believed that darkness set free as soon as the sun went down. She wondered whether her husband's shade was among them, hovering near her like a loving, protective spirit, or whether it had joined the other spirits of the brave on the misty peak of Kinabalu. The thought that it might still be near was comforting, and soothed her, for somewhere out in the darkness, fierce fighting men she had never met, and would probably never even see, were gathered together to attack her settlement, the Dyaks on their own would be powerless to defend it, or her, against such an onslaught.

Elsewhere in that same deep darkness a ship lay anchored behind the headland, and aboard that ship was her son; he at least should be safe, whatever the outcome of this terrible night, And also board that ship was the Englishman, tall and hard and with some strange elusive quality of inner remoteness about him that she had never noticed before in any Red Bristled Barbarian from the West. She could still feel the power of his personality, strong as a physical force. Was he the man she hoped he was – or did he only speak with boldness? It was not fitting for a widow to think about other men, and especially of one other man, so soon after the death of her husband, but still she wondered about Gunn. Whether he was married; what it would be like to feel his body against hers, her legs entwined about him, his body in hers.

She moved on her sandalwood chair. These were unseemly thoughts but surely they were also natural? After all, this man

137

had arrived uninvited, a stranger from the sea, and within moments of their meeting had in some almost inexplicable manner assumed control of her destiny, and the destinies of her son and his people. And the strangest factor was that all this had appeared to be quite natural, almost expected, even pre-ordained. She hoped his deeds would live up to his high promises, but inside her heart she wondered. For how could he possibly overwhelm a force far superior in numbers to those he could bring from his vessel?

Tall as he was, tough as he looked, Gunn was but one man against many. A bullet or an arrow could cut him down as easily as it could kill the lowliest soldier in her pathetic army. But would he fall, or would he prevail? She bowed her head and clasped her hands and drove exciting but unworthy thoughts of his body and hers from her mind, as she prayed to the supreme Deity who controlled the gods, as her husband had controlled his local chiefs.

'Oh, one god of many gods, ruler of the earth, the sky, the seas and all creatures that fly and swim and walk and crawl; creator of all things, timeless in timelessness, without beginning and without end, known before knowledge, the first and the last, the keeper of the keys of eternity, look down in mercy on us.

'Give strength to our arms. Guide our weapons. Drive out fear of this enemy who would so cruelly conquer us. So that under Your guidance, with Your wisdom, through Your strength and power, we can overcome those who are now encamped in force against us.'

She paused, and then added in a whisper: 'And let it be Thy will, god of gods, also to look down and guard this physician Gunn. And for his brave deeds, because of his kind heart – and because I want him – may he survive this night, victorious, unscathed, long to live.'

She opened her eyes. The shadows still flickered on the wall, but now they no longer seemed menacing and strange; they were like the waving of the hands of friends.

The last longboat was swiftly lowered away behind the other

four already heading towards the shore. Captain Fernandes had ordered that old blankets should be cut into strips and bound around the oars to muffle them. The only sound was the heavy breathing of the oarsmen and the faint creak of rowlocks. Soon a distant deepening hum resolved itself into the roar of surf that drowned all other lesser sounds. Instantly, the men were out, oars shipped, dragging the boats up the beach beyond the tide-line. Figures materialized from the darkness, dimly seen against the phosphorescent background on the waves. One was Imi Hassan; Aki Nabula stood near him.

'How many camps do the enemy possess?' Gunn asked them.

'Only one. About two miles from this place, and less than twice that distance in a different direction, from our village. They have six camp fires burning round it and eight sentries posted.'

'You have done your work well,' said Gunn approvingly. 'We will shortly give them a chance to test their alertness.'

He turned to the ship's first officer.

'You go with Imi Hassan, take one sailor and fix charges to the trees, as I have explained.'

They melted away silently into the darkness.

'Now, Greene, you take ten men to the village. Double charge all their muskets with shot, and when the moment comes, only fire five at a time, so there will be no diminution of fire when you reload. Put out the Dyaks in the trees with their bows and arrows, and impress on them through Aki Nabula, under threat of torture or death – and anything else you like – not to fire until *you* give the order.'

'Very good,' said Greene, and put out his hand. 'I hope we meet again later this night.'

'We will not.' Gunn assured him cheerfully.

'Why not?' asked Greene in surprise.

'Because we will be otherwise engaged this night. But we will meet tomorrow morning, never fear.'

Again the party marched off. The forest opened for them and then closed behind them, so that it was as though there had never been any other men on the beach at all. Behind Gunn, waves thundered tirelessly on the sand. The air smelled sharp and damp and salt with spray. His eyes were fully accustomed to the darkness, and the breaking waves gave enough illumination for him to make out the pots of paste and the tins of luminous paint. The second mate was already down on his knees, removing the lids with a bayonet and stirring the thick stinking mess until the round mouths glowed like pale green circles of light.

Dipping his hands in the first pot, Gunn smeared the foul, putrescent slime over his chest, his trousers, his sleeves. Where nothing had been visible in the dark before, there now glowed a ghostly scarecrow, a phantasmagorical greenish figure vaguely the shape of a man. He motioned to the mate to do likewise, and other crew members stepped forward and dipped their hands up to their wrists in the paint or the paste. Soon they were shapeless luminous creatures, grotesque and almost disembodied.

'They will think we are evil spirits,' said the mate cheerfully.

'And they will be right,' Gunn told him. 'Now, charge your pieces.'

A small, trained rattle of muskets; pouches and powder-horn lids were snapped shut.

'All the men are ready, sir,' reported the mate briskly.

'Good,' said Gunn. 'We are going to march round behind Mr. Greene's men so that we can drive the pirates on to their defences.'

'It will be a hard march, sir.'

'I expect nothing less,' Gunn told him dryly. 'If we start up any wild beast, do not shoot. We have some locals with us who will deal with them with their blow-pipes. Keep silence at all times. Now, may good fortune march with us.'

They set off in single file, leaving the angry roar of the sea behind them. Again the jungle opened and closed behind them like an endless mouth swallowing them up. In a darkness too deep to see where they placed their feet, each followed the sweating, green-daubed back of the man in front. Sometimes, clutching, sticky tendrils of jungle creeper would hold a man back so that he lost sight of the glowing phosphorescent back before him, and so had to pause, listening for his breathing and the faint sibilance of boots on fallen leaves. Branches bent like rubber pipes. Fleshy leaves, large as plates, brushed their faces, and occasionally birds, disturbed in early sleep, fluttered frightened wings above their heads. The night felt damp as a warm sponge; their flesh streamed with sweat.

The Dyak guide possessed instinctive knowledge of direction, the result of years of hunting, and he did not stop marching for an hour and a quarter. Then, in a clearing, he held up his right hand and they fell in around him.

'The enemy is encamped in that direction, about five hundred paces from here,' he announced in a whisper.

He pointed, stretching out his left hand like a signpost.

'I can lead you through to them if you so wish?'

'What about their sentries?'

The man smiled, his teeth white in the darkness, pleased at the chance of demonstrating his superiority over a white-faced stranger.

'We have followed you, Englishman, with four of our own trackers. I will send them to one side to make a diversion for you. When the sentries investigate, then – poof! – a dart will deal with them.'

'Good,' said Gunn. 'When your men are ready, all shout together, and we will charge.'

'May all the brave spirits of long departed warriors fight with us and give us victory,' replied the Dyak earnestly. He and his companions melted away into the trees. Around Gunn and his party, the jungle was now slowly stirring in its deep and terrible sleep. He heard faint rustlings of serpents, a flutter as birds stretched their wings in high branches. The croak of frogs and lizards sounded much fainter now. Dawn would be up within the hour. They waited, hands gripping muskets, as sweat dripped unheeded from their faces. Mosquitoes and flying insects stung them, and blind night moths fluttered around their faces. Suddenly, to the right came hoarse shouts; then the crackle of muskets, and wild screams and yells in an unknown tongue.

'Now!' roared Gunn. '*Charge!*'

He led them at a steady pace, muskets held high across their bodies, out of the way of tendrils and branches. Within seconds, he could see the red embers of dying camp fires. Tongues of flames, like orange dagger blades, poked at them from the shelter of big trees: some sentries were still alive and firing. In the growing glimmer of dawn, other men were also starting up, heavy with sleep, groping for muskets, cutlasses, pistols.

'Shout!' yelled Gunn as he ran. Some of his crew roared obscenities and oaths; the rest, wordless animal bellows of rage. The pirates were up on their feet now, and between the trees they saw terrible phantasmagorical shapes running towards them, like ghosts, apparently changing substance and outline as they ran. Some pirates fired their muskets wildly, not taking proper aim, and the blasts blew away branches that crashed down from the tops of trees, and then, without stopping to reload, they fled in front of the attackers to reach higher ground.

'*Fire!*' shouted Gunn. He dodged behind a bamboo trunk thick as a man's thigh, raised his musket, aimed at a running shape and pressed the trigger. The butt jumped in recoil, and the damp air reeked with the sharpness of exploded gunpowder. The pirate spun round, hands in air, and fell. It was impossible to reload again quickly, so Gunn used his rifle as a club, swinging it from the end of the hot, reeking barrel. Some of the crew went down on their knees to reload. Others followed Gunn's example and clubbed the defenders with their muskets or used their cutlasses to run them through.

Crazed with fear at the sight of fanciful luminous patches flickering in the semi-darkness, not knowing who or what they were, but convinced that these attackers must outnumber them, and recalling terrible stories of Borneo headhunters and cannibals and wild men, more animal than human, the pirates headed noisily towards the village. Anywhere seemed preferable to this dark, dripping horror of the jungle, and in the longhouses they could at least regroup, reload and defend themselves. There they would all die at the hand of painted savages or maddened ghosts they could not even see clearly.

'Hold back!' shouted Gunn as some of his men started after

them. His crew immediately stopped running. For a second or so, the only sounds were cries of pain and alarm from the pirates as thorns ripped their hands and faces, and the crashing and splitting of branches as they ran. Then the earth rocked and tall trees trembled with the giant thunder of exploding mines. Three erupted to the right, a fourth to the left. In the violent orange glare that lit up the scene against trees, tall and straight as cathedral pillars, they saw men's bodies disintegrate into separate arms and legs, and shapeless hunks of bloodied flesh. Some were flung into the branches to stay jammed there, food for carrrion birds; others dropped at their feet. Then they heard a monstrous beating of wings, as birds and bats without number, terrified out of sleep, flew like a black fluttering cloud away from danger.

'Now!' shouted Gunn.

The crew started to run behind him through the pall of bitter blue smoke, past trees shorn of branches and leaves, and bushes that burned like huge wicks, towards the stakes. Hofmeyer and some of his men had flattened the nearest bamboos with their wooden rafts; but they had missed others in the darkness and confusion, and now the spears from the door traps were whistling unseen through the air. And crouched on the other side of the second row of sharpened stakes, Greene's firing party picked off the few pirates who hesitated.

Greene sheltered behind a palm tree, musket ready at his shoulder, watching them drop. He had still not fired; he could not bear to take the life of another man. Indeed, he felt oddly remote from the whole struggle, as though he was an observer at some incredible pageant. Then, against fires lit by the mines, he saw a pirate race towards him, swinging a cutlass. The man gave a great shout of anger, and brought the cutlass up above his head. In instinctive reaction, Greene's muscles tightened. His right fore-finger bit into the trigger; the musket butt punched back, bruising his shoulder. And where a pirate had been running, now a headless mannikin spouted blood. The body careered out of control, fell and rolled, and then lay twitching, blood squirting from the trunk into the dust with each muscular contraction of its dying heart. Greene slowly lowered his musket. He was trembling and suddenly felt very sick; he had killed his first man.

The Chinese widow stood in her doorway, looking across the deserted village square. The sun was moving slowly up the sky, and the shadows of the other houses grew steadily shorter as he watched. The village women and their children had fled to the safety of the jungle, and were still too afraid to return. A few chickens pecked hopefully in the dust. She climbed down the notched treetrunk, crossed the clearing, and saw Greene coming slowly towards her.

'Where is Dr. Gunn?' she asked him.

'Out there somewhere,' said Greene wearily, gesturing behind him towards the green wall of trees.

'How has the battle gone?'

'We have driven them off, your highness.'

A few stragglers were still being put to the sword, or bludgeoned to death by musket butts. None of the *Hesperides*' crew saw any need to waste a bullet on a prisoner, and the safest capture was a corpse. Gunn's force now came loping up to the line of stakes, and into the village.

'What are your casualties?' Gunn asked Greene.

'Only two serious ones, so far as I know. A cook had his left hand cut off, and one of the lascars had taken a bullet in his right knee. His friends are bringing him in.'

'I will examine them directly,' said Gunn. 'You look a bit shaky yourself. Are you all right?'

'I have just killed a man,' Greene explained.

'And I have buried more mistakes than I have ever deliberately despatched,' Gunn told him easily. 'And believe me, there are worse ways to die than by a bullet. It has the inestimable virtue of speed. Muslims believe that if you die in battle, you are instantly transported to Paradise. And since these pirates follow that faith, they should have died content.'

'I am not a Muslim,' replied Greene. 'Were you not afraid *you* might be hit?'

'No,' said Gunn. 'As I have said, there are worse ways to die. Many worse.'

He turned away. For a moment, the Chinese widow thought he would say something else, and then, shrugging his shoulders, he threw his musket to the first mate, who caught it deftly. Gunn unbuttoned his pouch and powder horn, and turned towards the member of the ship's crew who had carried the medical supplies.

'Now,' Gunn said to him quietly. 'Let us do a bit of patching up instead of knocking down. Where are the wounded?'

Van Vooren, the Dutchman, stopped running and leaned thankfully against a palm tree, his whole body racked with the effort of breathing. The sun burned like a hot iron; he guessed the time must be nine or ten in the morning, and he had scarcely paused in his flight from that terrible moment when the whole earth had exploded around him. He had been caught in the roaring, blundering vortex of fire and death and yet somehow he had escaped. He remembered the terrible and mangled attitudes of the dead as the pirates had run into totally unexpected mines and musket fire. Everything had gone wrong – but how, and why?

Dyaks had never been known to fight like that before. A few brisk volleys in the air, and by all previous experience they should have fled. Who could have arranged the explosions and those terrifying luminous shapes? They must have been men, of course, carrying some special compound on their clothes, but such deceptions were beyond the capacity and ingenuity of the Dyaks. That sort of artifice was more European than Asian; this meant that the crafty British must somehow be involved.

He must escape and return to Java and warn the Governor that the British should be considered to be moving into Borneo, against Dutch interests and all other expectation. Yet what sort of reception could he expect for this intelligence? A man who brought bad news was often confused with the originator of the ill-tidings he carried?

Van Vooren's heart was beating more steadily now, and he stood up wearily and wiped sweat and insects from his face. He stank like a pig through fear, and his mouth felt dry as the bark of the tree. He narrowed his eyes against the cruel brightness of the sun that flickered like sword blades between overhead branches, and then he started to walk forward, due east by his reckoning.

A few paces ahead of him, in a small clearing, the trees parted. A native, rather taller than average, and wearing a curious coat, the like of which he had never seen before, with maroon sleeves, stood watching him. In his hand he held a small bamboo pipe rather like a flute.

'Who are you?' the Dyak asked him in Malay.

'Your friend,' replied Van Vooren hoarsely, in the same language. 'I am seeking the shore. I am lost.'

'No,' the Dyak answered. 'You are not lost. I have found you.'

'Thank you,' said Van Vooren gratefully. 'Then please lead me to my ship. I will reward you well.'

'Why should I do this thing? You came to my country with pirates, although you do not now appear like a man of war.'

'I am not a man of war,' Van Vooren assured him earnestly, seeking his words clumsily, for he did not speak the language well. 'I assure you I am not. I'm a friend.'

'You are fat and soft from living off the efforts of men like me,' replied the Dyak. 'You are a friend to nobody. Not even to yourself. I spit on you.'

The native hawked and spat on the ground.

'Wait a minute,' said Van Vooren quickly, for he saw the Dyak raise the flute to his lips and in that instant he realized that it was not a musical instrument, but a blow-pipe. The Dyak's cheeks ballooned, and Van Vooren felt a tiny pain as the sharp bamboo splinter pricked his right cheek.

Instinctively, he put up his hand, and when he looked at it, the fingers were red with his own blood. Then his body began to cringe and writhe, as the deadly poison moved in his veins. He sank down on rubber knees, and the trees around him turned blue and yellow, and the sun went black and spun like a wheel in the sky. And all the while he was calling out hoarsely as though down an endless, echoing well: 'I am your friend, your friend! Wait!'

For a splintered second, Van Vooren's mind spanned twenty

years. He saw a procession of vermilion tulips, the familiar yellow sails of windmills long ago and smelled the scents of childhood. Then the taste of poison and of death lay like metal on his tongue and rising dark obscured the turning sails.

Oya Ali watched the Dutchman until his body ceased to twitch and then he stepped forward, unbuttoned Van Vooren's pockets, and took out some papers written in a language he could not read. There were also some guilders and other coins, a watch which he held up to his ear and then carefully put away in his own pouch, some stubs of pencil, a damp, rancid handkerchief.

He rolled the Dutchman over on his side and stood, looking down at him. The busy jungle ants were already exploring the soft wet dead flesh on the back of his fat hands. Oya Ali spat on him again and turned and went back along the way he had come. The forest closed behind him instantly like a green door, and his feet made no sound as he walked.

Already, far above the tops of the highest trees, the carrion birds were circling, answering the silent call of the dead. By nightfall, they would leave little of Van Vooren beyond his bones and his boots.

CHAPTER SEVEN

'So we are victorious, exalted one,' Oya Ali assured the Chinese widow, bowing so low that his nose touched the split bamboos of the floor.

'You are certain?'

'We have broken this attack, your highness,' agreed Gunn, 'but I have no doubt they will mount another, which will be crucial. These pirates have nothing to lose but their lives.'

'A number have already lost theirs,' Greene pointed out.

'But probably not the Dutch leaders,' said Gunn.

'At least one Dutchman will lead no more,' interrupted Oya Ali, and putting his hand inside the front of his loose silk blouse, he pulled out his small leather pouch. He shook out on to the tiled tabletop the items he had taken from Van Vooren. Gunn picked up the papers; they were folded and creased with dirt. Ink had run slightly with the sweat, and in any case he could not read the language.

'Can any of your people read Dutch?' he asked the widow.

'No-one.'

'Then I will keep them until I find someone who can interpret. Now, where are they most likely to land any reinforcements?'

'On the north coast,' replied Oya Ali immediately. 'Their trading vessels have frequently used a bay there in the past for taking on fresh water and fruit.'

'So, if they retreat, they would fall back on that point and await reinforcements or rescue?'

'It is possible.'

'Then we will fall back on their heels and frustrate their plan,' said Gunn.

'When would you propose doing this?'

'Now, of course. As soon as we can make ourselves ready.'

Gunn closed his eyes for a moment. The lids burned red and raw as though he had been staring for too long at the sun. How strange that every comment he made, every action he initiated, had to be in the imperative. Immediately. This instant. Now. There could be no delay, no thought, no rest, for his time was all but exhausted. He would have almost welcomed a quick death out there in the jungle; at least it would have ended this dreadful waiting, this growing weakness which made him drive himself even more ruthlessly, and each day with more difficulty.

'You are tired?' the Chinese widow asked him gently.

'No, your highness,' Gunn replied shortly. 'I am thinking.'

He could not admit to anyone how weary he felt, for once he admitted this, his resolve would be broached like a dam and his courage would collapse. He carefully steered his thoughts away from this dangerous and sensitive area by wondering how he could increase the power of a handful of men with muskets against a forest of enemies. He could not expect any re-inforcements by land; this only left the sea. Yet the *Hesperides* was only lightly armed. What he required was the support from the heavy guns of a navy ship. But how to find such a vessel within hours?

The nearest would probably be the *Aeneas*; but she could be anywhere within a 100-mile radius. And even if he could somehow manage to contact her, he still had to persuade her captain to take part in what the British Admiralty – and, later, Parliament – could reasonably assume to be a private war, on an unimportant island in which the British Government had neither interest nor claim.

Gunn turned to the Chinese widow, his mind made up.

'Have you two fast war canoes that we could borrow?' he asked her.

'Of course.'

'Then pray have them prepared.'

'What are you going to do?' asked Greene.

'The *Aeneas* could be somewhere in the area. If I could

persuade her to change course, and bring her guns to bear on our behalf, our victory would be certain. Even if I could only persuade her to lie off the bay and not even fire a shot, her presence might still prevail upon the Dutch and persuade them not to counter-attack.'

'Surely that might also precipitate a war between Holland and England?'

'The Governments of both countries would have to learn about the vessels' involvement first, and by the time they did so, the issue would already have been decided for months. That risk, I assure you, is very slight.'

'Even so, I am certain that the captain of *Aeneas* would be markedly reluctant to take upon himself such an enormous responsibility.'

'If I can meet the captain, Greene, I will endeavour to make him less reluctant. And I do not care how I do it. A prime value of wealth is that sometimes you can use it to enable others to see one's point of view more clearly and urgently than might otherwise be the case.'

'You mean, you would offer an officer a bribe?'

'I mean nothing more than I say. To offer him even only good advice, we have first to meet the gentleman. And to give ourselves a greater chance of meeting him, you take the second war canoe, Greene, and cover the north-east area. Travel for two hours out from shore, then sweep to the west in a wide circle. I will do the same in the opposite direction.

'I will give you a compass bearing of an approximate position here. If you meet the vessel, which to my recollection is a four-master with twenty-two guns, hail her, then present your compliments – and mine – most cordially to the captain, and tell him that it is a matter of the highest urgency that he changes course to this bearing. If you do not meet the vessel, return here, and we will have to think again.'

'You have not slept this past night, sir, and, with respect, you do not look a well man,' said Greene.

'I look how I look, because I am what I am,' replied Gunn enigmatically. 'Now, to our task. And let us hope that our powers of detection and persuasion are not impaired by lack of sleep . . .'

Hofmeyer stopped running for a moment, and leaned wearily against the warm rough bark of a palm tree. He could hear other men crashing through bushes on either side of him, making as much noise as a herd of frightened elephants. Usually, this would have affronted his instincts as a trained soldier, but did noise matter any more? Were they already surrounded? Or worse, were they being cleverly steered into this clearing simply to be slaughtered in a killing ground of the natives' choosing?

'Hofmeyer here,' he called out hoarsely. 'Who's that?'

'Christiaansen,' replied a voice.

'Who else?'

'God knows. Only pirates, so far as I know.'

'Where is Van Vooren?'

'I haven't seen him. What went wrong?'

'They must have known we were on the march, and they set a trap. We walked right into it. We committed the unpardonable sin in any battle. We underestimated the enemy.'

'So where do we go now? Head back to our ship?'

'Not immediately. They are certain to know the anchorage if they were so well appraised of our plans. We will fall back in that general direction, agreed, but lie up half a mile from shore, where we can watch the ship. And when they come down, believing we are aboard, we will kill them all.'

'The success of that manoeuvre depends on how many there are of them and us,' replied Christiaansen practically. He was a fat man, married to a native woman in Java. Hofmeyer liked him; he considered him a sensible fellow, not one who would frighten easily.

'We have no other option. The tide is at the ebb, so we could not possibly escape, even if we were already aboard our vessel.'

They could hear other men blundering about, calling desperately to each other for reassurance in tongues they did not understand. Humidity hung hot and wet as a steam kettle. Christiaansen's lips had cracked, and his right thigh had been scored by a bullet or an arrow. The wound opened and closed with every step he took, weakening him with pain and loss of blood. What madness this attack had been! Yet it had seemed so easy to mount a quick sharp assault against some virtually defenceless natives. But somehow they had lost their best ally – surprise – and heaven knew how many men besides.

Hofmeyer's plan to retreat towards the beach sounded reasonable – but then so had the original proposal to attack the village. Christiaansen doubted whether they had more than ten or twenty serviceable muskets left between them, and with the first shot the natives on the beach would melt away to draw their darts and arrows and wait for darkness, instantly becoming part of the scenery of the forest, as silent and terrible as death.

'Have you got your compass?' he asked Hofmeyer.

'No. It was on a thong on my belt, but it has been torn off. We will have to march by the sun.'

'We can hardly *see* the bloody sun here, the trees are too thick. We may just go round in a circle.'

'Then we will lie up where we are until dusk,' said Hofmeyer. 'We can see the stars, and they are in any case easier to march by.'

'That does not give us much time.'

'What do you suggest, then? What is your plan? You clearly hold reservations about mine.'

'I have nothing better to offer,' Christiaansen admitted. 'I just want to survive.'

'You speak for me as well. For all of us.'

'The prospect of treasure seemed worth any risk.' Christiaansen went on moodily. 'But now we have abandoned any hope of victory, and are willing to settle for our freedom.'

'In that you speak for yourself, not for me,' retorted Hofmeyer. 'You lack faith in our abilities now, but you will see how the tide of action will turn in our favour. We are trained men, Christiaansen. The rest are only ignorant savages with a few Europeans – probably British army deserters, or the like. You will see, my friend, that I speak the truth.'

Hofmeyer moved away from this sweating and terrified companion. He would never have imagined that Christiaansen's character would weaken and wilt under stress. But then who would believe that heat could melt an iron bar – unless they had seen it happen?

Van Vooren, in Java, had been well regarded as a wise, even cunning servant of the court. But in that house by the beach, and on the march to the village, he had been craven, starting at every strange noise, seeing enemies in every shadow. Hofmeyer could imagine him now, shambling in an extremity of terror and isolation through the trackless jungle, where every clearing resembled the last, and all trees seemed identical. And he might only be yards from him at that very moment. What a terrible country this was. What could be the magnet that so attracted his government to it?

Hofmeyer sat down, back against the tree, and loosened his belt. Almost immediately, he could feel little needle-pricks as tiny red ants swarmed over his sweaty flesh, but he was too tired to care. He would rest here and move on in the late afternoon. War, he assured himself, resembled a bout of fisticuffs, which he had frequently enjoyed back home. Losing one round did not necessarily mean that you lost the fight. And that night, or on the morrow, he would prove this to be true once more.

Lieutenant Richard Blackman, R.N., commanding H.M.S. *Aeneas*, a 22 gun frigate, five days out from Singapore, stood on his open bridge, feeling the night breeze gently fingering his hair. The moon spread a silver avenue over the shining sea; the wind was low and barely filled his sails.

Blackman smelled the familiar tropical sea-scents, salt and tar and rough canvas dried by weeks of hot sun, heard the reassuring creak of taut ropes, and the movement of his ship, one timber groaning against another. He would call at Bangka Island, east of Sumatra, to take on fruit, limes, water, then beat a leisurely progress south between Borneo and Java, then north through the Celebes Sea to skirt the Philippines, and so to Macao and Hong Kong, calling at such ports as he wished to visit.

Blackman was a stocky, sturdily built man of thirty-five who had held command for two years, and had served in the China Seas for all that time. He nodded to the helmsman, received his 'Aye-aye, sir,' with a grunt of acknowledgment, and went down to his night cabin. The swinging brass oil lamp, weighted against the roll of the ship, cast gently flickering shadows on the varnished wooden walls. He sat down on the edge of the bunk, pondering his situation.

Command could be a lonely thing, and he had been alone for too long. Of course, he met his officers regularly in the wardroom, but always he had to initiate any conversation. And as their captain, his opinions were necessarily undisputed and unargued; and now, on his own, with an hour to spare before he turned in, without a book he had not read and lacking the wish to begin yet another letter home, he wondered, as he had recently begun to wonder on many such occasions, just what the future held for him.

He had no private means, no estates in England, no tenants in rows of terraced houses paying him rent, no mills or factories or mines; only a wife with an ailing son. They shared the house of a maiden aunt in Petersfield because Blackman, entirely dependent on his meagre service pay, could not afford to buy and maintain his own establishment. His son was ten years old and still inexplicably unable to read the simplest words or form the smallest sentences; and no-one seemed to know exactly why this should be.

His wife's letters were never much more than descriptions of her visits with young Erasmus to doctors and chiropractors, even to phrenologists who claimed to be able to 'read' bumps or configurations on the boy's head, and from their size and shape deduce the nature of his disability, and how it should be treated.

None of them talked any longer of cures, only of treatment, which to Blackman sounded ominous. Year after year, his modest income had been whittled away by constant medical bills, and year after year his son's condition had grown steadily worse. Or maybe it was just because, as the sons and daughters of his contemporaries grew older, they appeared by contrast to be so much brighter and perceptive; in a word, more normal. His wife's world revolved around Erasmus; the boy's condition overshadowed all other considerations.

Blackman would soon be due for promotion to lieutenant-commander, and while this would bring him more money, it would also bring greater expenses which he could ill afford. There was always the hope of some action at sea that would bring in prize money, according to rank, but action could not be guaranteed; it was only a little more likely to happen than to win a lottery, although in the recent war with China over their reluctance to accept British opium, some captains had done quite well financially.

And yet what was the alternative to accepting promotion? To stay on for two further lonely, aimless years in the East, virtually in exile on the other side of the world from his wife, who already was almost a stranger to him? To meet other captains for a few days every month when they could arrange to be in the same port for revictualling, and then set sail before an acquaintance could become a friend? Was this to be the sum of his life's work, growing steadily older, a passed-over lieutenant, at first accepting being passed-over as an experience that happened even to the brightest and best – and then admitting, if only privately to himself, that he had reached the peak of his profession and only retirement remained?

Now, if he could lay claim to a private income of 500 sovereigns a year (better still, 1,000) he could afford to have his son treated by the best doctors in London. His wife would immediately become altogether more cheerful, and so would he. And because of these fundamental changes in his life, Blackman would then relish the challenge of a new command instead of secretly dreading it. He could afford then to decorate his ship more in tune with his tastes, by adding more brasswork, after the custom of Royal Navy captains with money enough to gratify their private artistic whims. In such a fortunate situation he would have control of his life as a captain commands a ship; not just drifting, sails furled, rudder loose-lashed against indifferent and sometimes hostile tides, but voyaging on with a purpose and a goal.

Through the planking of the decks above, he heard the faint warning cry of the mast-head look-out: 'Ship ahoy!'

Who could this be? Possibly a tea clipper on the Australia run, or an opium vessel on her swift direct journey to the Chinese coast, bringing more wealth to her owners and hours of oblivion to their clients. Even the sight of such a vessel meant an entry in his log, and another image in his mind of a proud ship leaning before the wind, scoring a scar on the sea that would heal even before the vessel herself showed him her high stern and a rear view of a dozen white wind-curved sails.

Then he heard the look-out's second cry.

'Native canoe, ahoy! Stand off!'

Perhaps this was some local fishing boat carried off course by a strong current or adverse winds? Ah, well, he might as well investigate personally as wait down here with his thoughts. Blackman climbed up the wooden stairs to the bridge.

The helmsman saluted him.

'Look-out reports native canoe with 10 oarsmen and one passenger, who is waving furiously, sir, apparently to attract our attention. They wish to draw alongside.'

To discover their intentions, which could hardly be important, was not worth the whole complicated business of sending men aloft in the rigging to slacken sails, and then deliberately drifting until the canoe caught up with them. Instead, he would turn about, and as the wind left his sails, the canoe could row to meet him. He gave the necessary commands briefly with the nonchalant air of the expert. Within minutes, *Aeneas* was facing the other way, and her loose sails thundered disapprovingly against the varnished masts.

'Ahoy, there!' called up someone in English. 'I am Mark Greene, British subject of Her Majesty the Queen, out of Borneo, aboard the clipper *Hesperides*.'

'What do you require, Mr. Greene?' Blackman called down to him.

'Permission to come aboard, sir, on the most urgent mission.'

'You alone then,' said Blackman cautiously. You could never trust strange crews in the east; even these few men might have some nefarious purpose, or be filled with *bhang* and run amok among his crew. If he allowed them all aboard, he might have a battle with knives and axes on his hands. Perhaps this fellow carried a message of some sort, and so he must receive it; and after all, he claimed to be one of Her Majesty's subjects, so some courtesy was due. Blackman gave the orders and a rope ladder was unrolled. Greene climbed up on deck, and made a gesture of salute towards the captain, who shook his hand.

'What is your requirement?' Blackman asked him shortly. 'What precisely is the nature of this urgent mission?'

The young man seemed oddly dressed for a sea passage in a canoe. He wore a shirt and trousers, and near to, he stank almost overwhelmingly of rotten fish. Worse, in the moonlight, his face and lower arms seemed horribly silvered with scales. Had he contracted some foul disease, some dread Eastern pestilence about which he wished to warn them? Blackman took a step back and to leeward.

'I would like permission to talk privately in your cabin, sir,' said Greene.

'Not so, sir,' replied Blackman sharply. 'I do not know your calling, but I must draw attention to the extraordinary aroma of your flesh. Are you diseased?'

'My flesh? Oh, the fish,' said Greene, and grinned. 'We covered ourselves with these filthy scales so we would be luminous at night.'

'Really?' replied Blackman coldly. Was this man a lunatic then, a pale-faced dervish, a maniac from the almost unknown island of Borneo? And who else was involved that he should refer to them as 'we'?

'Yes, sir. This must sound strange to you, but with a handful of British tars from our ship, the *Hesperides*, and her owner, Dr. Robert Gunn, we have just routed a very large force of Malay pirates under their Dutch leaders. They thought we were demons, because we literally shone in the dark.'

'I see.'

Blackman's voice was more conciliatory. The mention of pirates also interested him from a professional point of view. So many trading vessels of the more important maritime countries – North America, Britain, France, Portugal, Spain and Russia

— travelled in constant danger of piracy in eastern seas that any act against these floating murderers was to be welcomed.

'What can I do for you, then?' he asked.

'First, sir, I would ask you, as a matter of grave urgency, to make about and sail on this compass bearing.'

He produced a grubby square of paper on which Gunn had written the bearing of the province.

'Dr. Robert Gunn is also searching the seas for you, sir, in another canoe, but I have been fortunate in finding you. We seek your aid in defeating the insurgents, who seriously outnumber us.'

'Does this province enjoy British protection?'

'No, sir.'

'Then I must tell you I cannot possible intervene. You mentioned Dutch nationals as being leaders of these insurgents, did you not?'

'I did.'

'The Dutch own great possessions in this area, Mr. Greene, which far outnumber ours. And no matter what we may personally and privately feel about their empire and how they administer it, you will understand that, as captain of one of Her Majesty's ships of the line, I could not possibly become involved in a clash with their nationals.'

'I accept that, sir, but I do assure you that this is a matter of life and death for a brave community. Their whole future and their freedom is at stake. I beg of you at least to speak to Dr. Gunn.'

'Who is this Dr. Gunn, exactly?'

'He is a *taipan*, the founder and controlling shareholder of the Far Eastern company, Mandarin-Gold.'

'Opium?'

'Originally he travelled in mud, yes. Now he deals in many other commodities, and controls his private fleet of clippers.'

'I see. So he is man of substance, not one of your shop-keeper type of merchants, eh?'

'He is one of the most powerful men of our country east of India, sir. His personal fortune must be immense, and it is, I assure you, in no way inferior to his personal influence.'

158

Blackman crossed the bridge, opened the locked cabin where he kept the charts in daily use, and unrolled the relevant map. The compass bearing was possibly eight or nine nautical miles north-west of his course; not a great distance in an ocean of maybe a million square miles. And if there were any serious danger involving British lives – Dr. Gunn's, for instance, who seemed an important merchant – and Blackman had not acceded to this young man's civil request for aid, what would their Lordships at the Admiralty say to his excuse that he could not be bothered to sail another eight miles in a voyage of several thousand? Blackman rolled up the chart.

'Proceed on this course,' he told the helmsman, giving him the bearing. 'Under all sail.'

'Aye, aye, sir. All sail it is, sir.'

Gunn looked at his watch, tilting it so that he could see the hands beneath the waning moon. He had been at sea for the agreed two hours, and he had seen no sign whatever of *Aeneas*; he would have to turn back. He sat in the bows of the canoe, the bamboo cross-beam pressing sharply into his spine. Water slopped in and soaked his trousers and his shoes, yet he felt warm and curiously relaxed; not at all tired.

The Sea Dyak nearest to him shipped his paddle and looked over his shoulder. Gunn turned, following his gaze. A ship was bearing down on them, a huge dark shape under a wide twilight of canvas, a phosphorescent smile of foam at her bows.

'Easy all!' he shouted.

Someone understood English and translated; the Sea Dyaks raised their paddles; drops of water trailed like tears from painted, shining blades. The main steersman turned the paddle rudder so that their little craft came up against the side of the approaching vessel, sheer and steep as a tarred wall. A rope-ladder dangled feet away. Gunn stood up in the rocking canoe and grabbed it.

Greene shouted down triumphantly to him from the deck.

'I reached here first!'

So this was the *Aeneas* after all. Greene had found her; now to enlist the aid of her captain. Gunn began to climb up, hand over hand. Sea water had washed away most of the fish scales from his legs, and he was so used by now to the smell, that he had forgotten how foul it was.

'Are you the captain?' he asked the officer who stood by Greene's side.

'I am, sir,' said Blackman. 'And you presumably are Mr. Gunn?'

'*Dr.* Gunn, sir.'

'You are extremely lucky to find us, doctor.'

'I calculated that if Greene and I divided the area to search between us, we might eventually meet you.'

Gunn paused. He needed this man's help desperately and yet suddenly, in some reaction of relief, waves of nausea and weakness were engulfing him. His flesh crawled with fever; his sweat-soaked skin felt chill as a suit of ice in the warm night breeze. Oh, to be well again; to be no longer a prisoner of infirmity!

'I would suggest,' Gunn said slowly, through gritted teeth, 'that we adjourn to your cabin, captain. But in view of the fact that we have had to rub fish scales on our bodies, I would not inflict their smell on you.'

'Mr. Greene has already explained the reason for the odour.'

'Good. Well, sir, let me explain why we are in desperate need of your ship at a bay on the coast of Borneo. I have the precise map reference.'

'Mr. Greene has also already furnished me with it, sir. What exactly would our purpose be when we reach this bay?'

'To subdue an insurrection. To allow a sultan's son, who is still a minor, to succeed to his father's kingdom. To give his mother, the sultan's widow, the opportunity – with my money and my influence – to create in that beautiful province what I would not overdescribe as an Eastern Garden of Eden.'

'*Your* money, sir?' asked Blackman cautiously. What exactly did this fellow mean?

'I am not unknown in the East as the founder of Mandarin-Gold,' Gunn explained. The feeling of sickness was passing; he felt stronger and more in command of himself. 'Prosperity has followed my flag. It is in my mind now to repay to the East something of the wealth I have taken from it.'

'An unusual sentiment in a merchant, sir, if I may say so.'

'Possibly. But then, sir, I consider myself an unusual merchant. Primarily, I am a physician.'

'Qualified in England?'

'No, sir. Scotland. The road south to England may be, as Dr. Johnson claimed, the best sight a Scotsman ever sees, but let us be accurate about our facts. I studied at St. Andrews. Why do you ask?'

'I have a son of ten at home, who is in poor health. I have consulted many doctors there professionally about his disability, but I do not think I have ever met a physician, shall we say, socially? I am therefore pleased to meet you, sir.'

'My social acquaintance with captains of Her Majesty's frigates has likewise unfortunately been limited. Perhaps at some more convenient hour we may discuss the nature of your son's ailment? I would deduce from the way you speak that you are not altogether satisfied with his recovery. I have important friends in the medical profession, sir, and if I could help you and your son I naturally would be gratified to do so.'

'That is extremely gracious of you, doctor, and I appreciate your generous offer to a stranger. I am truly sorry that I cannot reciprocate your kindness. I have explained to Mr. Greene that we are sailing seas, virtually controlled by the Dutch. Our country is not in dispute with Holland and has no wish to change that peaceful and cordial relationship. Holland, of course, controls far more land than we do in these immediate latitudes, and it is clearly in the best interests of both our governments that we maintain friendly relations.'

'So what you are saying, sir, in your diplomatic naval way, is that you must decline our invitation to sail to the shores of Borneo and blast these upstarts from the sea while we tackle them on land?'

'That is unfortunately a correct interpretation of my situation.'

'What you are also inferring, captain, is that while Her Majesty's men-of-war may be dedicated to the release of slaves and to the punishment of insurrection this dedication is only to be honoured in academic terms. Her captain cannot, in fact – or he is unwilling – to discharge a few rounds of grape in order to right a monstrous wrong of which we, as fellow British subjects, have first-hand knowledge?'

'I am sorry, doctor, that you have to put it so bluntly, but I cannot exceed my commission. My strict orders from their Lordships at the Admiralty are that under no possible circumstances am I to show incivility, let alone hostility, to any Dutch national. Within hours of the action you propose – however richly justified it may well be – the news would be on its way to Java and then by fast clipper to Holland. The end of that action, whatever else it might achieve, could conceivably be war between two major European countries. And I could be held primarily responsible. I am not a free agent in these matters, sir. I do not own my ship, as you own yours. I simply hold our Queen's commission to command her, in my country's interests. And, on what you tell me, these interests are not compatible with what you wish me to do.'

Gunn seemed to sag in his disappointment, and he put out a hand on the deck rail to steady himself. He should have expected this all along, of course, but he was so accustomed to overriding indecision and timidity in others by the sheer force of his own personality that he had assumed these tactics would succeed here. He had overlooked the fact that the captain was not a man of commerce, nor was he an employee. He was an officer of the Queen, and so totally beyond Gunn's influence and persuasion.

Gunn understood Blackman's reasons perfectly. There had to be such reasons, of course, for otherwise Her Majesty's ships might become little better than legalized pirateers, ready to offer their guns on any excuse – or possibly even for any large enough bribe – to the service of the highest bidder. Pirateers. *Pirates.* Now here was an area worth further exploration.

'I accept, sir, everything you say,' Gunn replied. 'Let us therefore speak no more about that matter. I apologize for bringing you and your vessel so far out of your course, and I thank you warmly for your courtesy in so promptly acceding to the request of my friend, Mr. Greene. It says a great deal for your thoroughness, sir, that you have done what you have done. After all, we both look mightily unprepossessing.'

'I am told that in South America there are men in charge of countries who do not *look* like presidents,' said Blackman, allowing himself a smile. Certainly, this physician fellow had a pleasing turn of phrase; he was not rough and crude, as were so many Eastern merchants. He also had an aura of power about him that Blackman could respect; and something else, too. A certain look in his eyes, a weariness in his voice that made Blackman suspect he was under some great and barely concealed tension. Well, that was his affair. So far as Blackman was concerned, the routine of the voyage would now return; dullness and loneliness would again claim him. He would bid farewell to this physician who had come providentially out of the sea at dead of night; to this rich man who admitted he had important friends who might help Erasmus, and in so doing he would deny himself the aid that his son so desperately needed. What would his wife say if she ever learned of his decision?

'Before I leave, sir,' said Gunn, cutting into the captain's thoughts, 'May I ask your views on Her Majesty's ships involving themselves with pirates?'

'Again, my orders from the Admiralty are explicit. So far as pirates are concerned, I am to take no prisoners. They show no mercy to unarmed merchantmen. They seize women and children taking passage in ships, and brutally put them to the sword, or worse. They can therefore expect no mercy from anyone else – least of all, sir, from Her Majesty's vessels.'

'And am I right in thinking captain, that despite these sentiments, with which I am in total accord, so few pirates are indeed captured alive in these dangerous Eastern waters that My Lords at the Admiralty have placed prize money of £5 on every pirate's head?'

'That is true, sir. Only five pirates, to my knowledge, have been killed in the last four months in these seas by Royal Navy ships.'

'So on this basis of calculation, if you killed fifty pirates you

– or rather you and your officers and ship's company – would receive the not inconsiderable sum of £2,500 to your credit?'

'That is so, doctor.'

'I ask these questions, captain, because I think that possibly you may be acting too precipitously – although from the highest moral motives – in not seeking to explore my proposition more deeply.

'When I referred to these men as insurgents, I used the word loosely, as meaning men intent on usurping power that legitimately belongs to others. The majority are, of course, simply Malay pirates with a handful of Dutch officers and men, spurred on, no doubt, with glowing promises of grants of land and guilders. I know from the sultan's widow that they are not local malcontents, rising to right some genuine grievance, but pirates come ashore from the seas, for this special and most evil task. And when they have done their foul work on land they will go back to their usual trade or robbing merchants – fortified and enriched by murder.

'You will recall, captain, that I described these invaders as pirates when I first came aboard,' Greene added.

Blackman nodded; now that he was reminded he also remembered Greene using the word. He looked slowly from one man to the other.

'Are you certain of this, gentlemen?'

'I give you my word,' said Gunn. 'And not only mine. The sultan's widow herself will bear out all I say. We do not ask you to fire on disaffected natives in an alien island, but to cut down sea pirates who are temporarily ashore. Indeed, I may say without any fear of contradiction that rarely, if ever, will so many pirates with prices on their heads be assembled together again in one target area – and without their usual heavy armaments to engage your ship, because they are on land. By helping us now, you will also help yourself, sir, and, more important to you as an officer in Her Majesty's Navy, you will also help every vessel that sails these seas, regardless of her nationality.'

Blackman thought for a minute, biting his lower lip. He could see his son's face; the boy's dull uncomprehending eyes. He heard his wife's tears again when she lay awake in bed near him; and laughter from children playing in the next door garden. There always seemed to be so much laughter in that house, compared with so little in his.

He saw the blunt, round muzzles of his guns pointing out like stubby fingers over the shining moon-drenched sea, towards the unseen shore – and to a fortune. Fifty pirates at £5 each; even ten would produce an important sum. And added to this, he would also have the benefit of Dr. Gunn's influence with the medical profession. He made up his mind, grateful for the night in case his visitors might see him blush, thinking he could be bought; and not even thinking, knowing.

'Before I agree, doctor,' he said slowly, 'could I ask one personal favour? That you will help me with my son?'

'You have my word on that,' said Gunn, holding out his fish-scaled hand. Blackman gripped it.

'You think there *may* be as many as fifty pirates?' he asked, trying to keep eagerness out of his voice.

'I am convinced there are two or even three times that number. And to show I believe what I say, I also give you my word that if you do not find so many, I will personally guarantee you and your ship's company the sum of £500. So you will have a fortune either way. You will be able to *buy* yourself promotion.'

'I would rather win that on merit, doctor.'

'Of course. You shall do that, too, sir. But even with merit, money need not necessarily be an obstacle or a hindrance.'

'Tell me, sir,' said Blackman, changing the subject carefully. 'If I had refused your request, what would you have done then?'

'You would have left me but two options, captain. First, as a loyal subject, I could salute the flag, wish you farewell, and be rowed back to the island, to engage and attempt to overthrow the pirates with my crew and what loyal Dyaks could be persuaded to stand their ground and fight.'

'I would not be optimistic about your chances of success, sir, had you selected that course.'

'Quite so. I would therefore have been tempted to follow the second choice. When you were in Singapore, captain, one of your men, Leading Seaman Jenkins, bought himself out of the service.'

'That is true. But how did you know this?'

'Because, for reasons I need not elaborate now, I supplied the money for him to do so. Had you refused my legitimate request for assistance, sir, I would have been forced to inquire how many more of your crew wished to be bought out. I would then have employed them myself to fight these pirates, at my expense and under my command. By the specific order of their Lordships at the Admiralty, if sufficient sovereigns are presented in specie, any serving seaman can leave a ship forthwith.'

'But not to the detriment of any ship in commission. In my opinion, sir, that course would be tantamount to inciting mutiny or treason.'

'I would not argue with what it is tantamount to, captain, because thanks to your own wise decision, it is now purely hypothetical. I submit, however, that it would certainly have been successful. And then, as Sir John Harington, the seventeenth-century courtier, put it very succinctly: "Treason doth never prosper. What's the reason? For, if it prosper, none dare call it treason." '

'You are a cool customer, sir,' said Captain Blackman admiringly. 'Devilish cool.'

'And I will be cooler still,' replied Gunn, smiling, 'when I have drunk that glass of claret I am sure you are about to offer me in your cabin.'

CHAPTER EIGHT

HOFMEYER and Christiaansen had finally reached the heights commanding the bay, and stood, enjoying the welcome breeze on their tired sweating bodies, and watching their ship ride like a toy at anchor on the cobalt sea beneath them. They were so high up that waves breaking on the shore seemed only a wide white smile on an empty beach. The air was so clear, so cloudless that they could hear the crew sing as they sluiced the decks.

Pirates sat, backs resting against tree trunks, or lay asleep in the clearing, muskets by their sides, plaintain leaves carefully wrapped around the hammers to keep out the dust. Hofmeyer glanced at Christiaansen and then at the ship's captain, who had joined their column in the night. He was the only one of the three who had seen Van Vooren's body; he had only recognized it from the shreds of clothing the swarms of red ants had not eaten. The transformation from life to death, to picked bones in bloodied rags, had only taken hours. Hofmeyer had despised Van Vooren alive, but he had not wished him dead; and he would wish no-one a death like his. Truly, this jungle was an accursed place.

Some pirates had already melted away prudently into the trees, and he guessed they would return to their own ships on the western shore. The rest, filthy and unshaven, had stayed, apparently ready to fight a rearguard action. But now it was difficult for him to know who were pirates and who were natives. They all had the same dark skins, the same expressionless eyes, and he shivered at the sight of them. They possessed a total, almost inhuman cruelty – and how could he be certain of anyone's loyalty? Would it not be likely that this scum would simply join the winning side, regardless of previous promises and protestations of friendship to the Dutch?

'How long are you going to give them?' he asked Christiaansen, speaking to drive away such terrible thoughts.

'Until they arrive and fall into our trap.'

'What if they do not oblige? What if they stay at home?'

'Then we will have to attack them again.'

'It would be difficult to persuade the pirates on the wisdom of that course. We assured them once that they could meet no resistance. They would not believe so readily a second time.'

The Dutch ship's captain looked longingly down towards his vessel. He was a man of the sea and felt uneasy on the land, hemmed in by forests and mountain peaks.

'We are playing for stakes in which our own lives have relatively small value,' he pointed out. 'We have the rare opportunity to achieve something for the glory of our king and our country. I would wish I were elsewhere, but my will tells me to stay. Why should we, free-born Dutchmen, flee in terror and confusion from a crowd of savages who live in a mud hut village?'

'They have the help of the English,' Christiaansen pointed out.

'Only a few renegade Englishmen, I am sure of that. Holland and England have a treaty. They have often fought on the same side in Europe, so they do not fight each other out here. Agreed, the French and the English pursue their Western wars here in the East. We more wisely pursue our Western alliance.'

'I hope they feel the same way,' said Christiaansen dryly. 'Personally, it does not matter whether I die at the hand of a pursuer of our alliance, or by a bullet from one of the English Queen Victoria's soldiers. It is the same bullet, it will be the same death.'

'Dying, death, defeat! God, what creatures we are to speak and even think like this?' said Hofmeyer fiercely. 'We command the high ground. We could kill 1,000 men down on that beach and still not be in the slightest danger ourselves up here!'

'If we had sufficient ammunition, yes, we could. But we have barely 300 rounds left between us. The pirates threw away our reserves of ammunition so that they could run faster.'

'Then we will place pirates to cover the beach with their muskets and behind them place Malays with blow-pipes, and when we run out of powder and shot we will draw cutlasses and charge the natives.'

'You make it all sound so simple,' said Christiaansen admiringly.

'Look,' said the captain quietly. 'A four-masted vessel. If only I had a spyglass. She flies the British flag, but I cannot read her name from here.'

The ship sailed in gracefully on the calm blue water. Her huge sails suddenly went limp as though wearied when the wind left them, and then flapped loosely in the off-shore breeze. They heard the shriek of anchor chains running out fore and aft, the cry of orders in English. Then a small boat was lowered and crossed to their own vessel.

'They do not realize we are up here,' said Hofmeyer. 'We could almost pick off the crew on her deck.'

'And risk their guns? Why should we, anyhow – if we are all friends?'

Hofmeyer wiped sweat out of his eyes. His mouth felt like cracked leather, and his body ached with thirst and weariness. Mosquito bites and little red spots painful out of all proportion to their size puffed up his face and bare arms. As he stood, irresolute for the first time, a native runner, naked but for a loin-cloth, padded through the jungle paths up to him and began to jabber something in his unknown tongue.

'Fetch the interpreter,' ordered the sea-captain swiftly.

A Malay arrived and spoke rapidly to the messenger, and then more slowly to the three Europeans.

'He says, sir, that a force of about 200 men are approaching the beach. They are even now within one mile of the shore. Two Englishmen are leading. The rest are Dyaks with blow-pipes and short swords.'

'We have them!' said Hofmeyer triumphantly. 'The Lord has delivered them into our hands.'

Instantly, all tiredness was forgotten. There would be oceans to drink and aeons of time in which to sleep, once they had dealt with these attackers. Quickly, he gave his orders. Half a dozen pirates with muskets climbed out on a promontory overlooking the track from which the men must approach the beach. Ten more waited on one side of this track, with five in reserve; the rest stood in small groups, completely concealed by giant jungle leaves, with strict orders only to fire when he blew a whistle.

The Dyak jabbered something else. The interpreter explained that the man sought permission to run back and then return with a further report.

'Before he goes,' said Hofmeyer cautiously. 'Who is he? He is not the spy we sent into the village.'

'No,' agreed the interpreter. 'That man thought it prudent to stay behind. This man is his blood brother. We can trust him. He is loyal to us.'

'Good,' said Hofmeyer, and handed the native a golden guilder for his purse. The Dyak solemnly raised the coin to his lips, bowed and turned and then ran off as silently as he had arrived.

He was smiling as he ran. How could the foolish fat white man know that his spy lay dead with a blow-pipe dart at his temple, while the runner was loyal to the sultan's widow and the sultan's son? Truly had the Lord Buddha written: 'Company with fools, as with an enemy, is always painful. Company with the wise is happiness.' And he was happy as he ran.

Captain Blackman climbed aboard the Dutch vessel. He spoke no Dutch, but as with many Englishmen in the East, he relied for communication with foreigners on finding someone who knew his language. An officer recognized his uniform and rank, and saluted him smartly.

'You speak English?' Blackman asked him brusquely.

'Some, sir.'

'Is your captain aboard?'

'No, sir.'

'I am Captain Blackman, commanding Her Majesty's frigate

Aeneas bound from Singapore to Macao. I have had intelligence from the shore that a strong force of pirates is approaching this beach.'

'Indeed, sir?'

The officer bowed gravely. He already knew Hofmeyer's plan. How ironic that these stupid pompous English should come blundering in at this moment, intent on killing the very men whom Hofmeyer and the others were waiting to ambush. He must certainly encourage them in this project; the British and the Dutch would make admirable allies for it.

'From my knowledge of the coast, captain,' he said, 'they should approach well east of that promontory. Possibly as much as a mile to the east.'

He pointed to the small hill; he must keep gunfire away from his fellow countrymen and the pirates hiding up the hills or the result could be disastrous.

'Very good, sir,' replied Captain Blackman briskly. 'Then I will tell my gunners to charge their pieces and take aim accordingly. I felt it courteous to inform you of my intentions, knowing the warm sentiments of English to Dutch, world-wide.'

'Which are most generously and cordially returned, captain, I do assure you. In the absence of my captain, could I offer you a glass of Schnapps?'

'You are too kind, sir. But I feel I must refuse. I am on duty. After the engagement – yes, it would be my pleasure. I am grateful that you are able to point out the route these ruffians will take, for my gunners are unfortunately little practised. You Dutch control the seas hereabouts, so they have had small opportunity to perfect their aim. I will order them specifically to lay on the target you have given.'

He saluted, climbed down the rope ladder, and was away in the longboat.

Hofmeyer said: 'That boat's gone back to the English ship. There's activity aboard. They are uncovering the guns.'

Uncertainty and fear tightened his voice.

'It's all right,' said the captain reassuringly. 'The guns are pointing well away. Any fire should land half a mile down.

Probably, they will kill these native swine on their way here. That may even be their intention.'

'My God, what a chance for us!' said Hofmeyer. 'Truly our mission has been blessed with fortune.'

As he spoke, he saw a sudden surprising spurt of flame and then a black beard of smoke, not from any of the guns now being trundled out ostentatiously on deck, but seemingly from another unseen gun beneath the bows of the English ship. Then the charge landed in their midst, and the air was loud with screams and shouts of pain and terror, and the crashing of branches. Then a second charge landed, and a third, a fourth, a fifth.

The birds were stilled and stunned by the unexpected thunder. A faint blue frond of smoke and dust blew lazily away on the morning breeze over the sea.

'That should see to them,' said Gunn from his position down the hill. 'Now we will go forward. And remember this. I will give a golden guinea for each head that is brought in.'

'I feel like a head-hunter already,' said Greene.

'That is how you should feel, for we are in head-hunting country,' replied Gunn gravely. 'And now we can discover just how efficient we are as hunters.'

Tall trees crashed and split and splintered as cannonballs from the concealed guns of H.M.S. *Aeneas* trundled down the hill.

'They've probably selected a target for practice,' said Hofmeyer as convincingly as he could. 'This peak is the most obvious place. But I am certain they are not firing at us deliberately. Even so, we could still be hit. Withdraw after me down towards the beach.'

The pirates gathered up muskets and pouches of powder and ball and began to move down the hill. Dried, splintered bamboos cracked like fire beneath their feet. Some pirates shouted and waved, hoping that the gunners aboard the English vessel would see them and assume they were friendly natives, and stop firing. But the guns boomed on with a dreadful regularity, and Hofmeyer could hear men screaming, but whether through fear or agony he did not know, and he could not stay to discover. Sweat larded his body and insects buzzed around him in a fury. In his stomach, an awful feeling of foreboding hardened like a stone.

Greene watched Hofmeyer through his glass, and saw other men gather round him, all looking fearfully about them, not sure where or even whether to run to escape the bombardment. They presented a perfect target.

'When you're ready,' he told his crew. One by one, they raised their muskets and took careful aim.

'Ready, sir.'

'Fire!'

For a second, the pirates stood transfixed like figures frozen on a frieze. Some dropped instantly, others staggered and ran, and in running, fell. A few fled precipitately into the trees. The rest brought up their muskets and fired first wildly at the undergrowth, not knowing who was attacking them or from which precise direction.

'Charge!' shouted Hofmeyer bravely.

At his command, men rose on either side from behind bamboos, mangoes, plantains, and ran, shouting obscenities, crashing through the splintering green forest. Some waved cutlasses; others, swords. Many had muskets at their hips; more held long boarding swords with spikes coming out of the blades, and used generally to lever themselves up the wooden hull of a ship they wished to capture.

On each side of them, spread out into the inner recesses of the jungle, Dyaks crouched in silence, deadly blow-pipes at their lips, waiting for the pirates to come within range. As they did so, the Dyaks puffed their cheeks. One pirate went down, then another. A severed head rolled like a bloodied cannonball, bulging eyes still wide in disbelief and death. Then the two groups were at each other, too close to load muskets, and so swinging them like clubs.

More cannonballs thundered in from the *Aeneas*, splitting trees and allowing a sharp blaze of blue sky through branches that instantly closed across the gaps. Gunn suddenly saw a tanned face only feet away; a bristling black beard, eyes red from lack of sleep, lips drawn back over yellow tobacco-stained teeth. He fired his pistol, missed and flung the weapon at the man. As the Dutchman dodged to avoid it, Gunn gouged him in the groin with his knee. The Dutchman drew a knife as he fell and struck up at him towards his stomach. Greene yelled a warning and brought down his musket butt across Christiaansen's face.

More pirates came racing down the hill now, alarmed by the explosions, muskets at their hips. They fired as soon as they saw the fighting, but had no time to reload, and so were trapped in the clearing. Other Dyaks followed them in swiftly. Knives flickered through the air; blood spouted from trunks, from the stumps of severed arms. A cannonball landed only feet away and trundled slowly through the clearing smoking as it rolled inexorably between the fighters.

'Fire!' yelled Greene, from the edge of the trees. Six sailors from the *Hesperides*, concealed in the undergrowth, muskets held tightly into their right shoulders, fired and instantly reloaded. Six pirates dropped. The rest began to scatter, running frantically down towards the shore, anywhere must be better than this nightmare of enemies on every side. At the bottom of the track, other Dyaks waited calmly, patiently, blow-pipe dart ready; not a Dyak missed his target.

Suddenly, the clearing was empty except for the dead and the dying. Somewhere, farther down the hill, the cannonball still trundled, crashing its way heavily between the mangroves, and then it stopped, and there was silence except for the frightened scream of birds and the groans of the wounded.

'We have prevailed,' said Gunn. He bent down and picked up the pistol he had thrown into the Dutchman's face.

'Most of us,' agreed Greene. His face was blackened with powder and streaked with sweat. His right sleeve had been cut, almost severed by a sword, and blood was running down his arm.

'You are wounded?' Gunn asked him.

'A scratch,' Greene assured him. 'And you, sir?'

'Nothing at all,' said Gunn. How ironic that he, on whom the mark of death lay so deeply, should have survived unhurt, when all around him fit young men had died in the sudden swift carnage! His training had been to save life, and now he had taken it violently. Yet, he told himself, in taking it, had he not saved the lives of many simple islanders and preserved their freedom? Dyaks moved among the dead, turning them over, cutting off an ear-ring here, often with the ear as well, rifling sweaty pockets for guilders or trinkets.

'Are there many survivors on their side?' asked Greene.

'Undoubtedly. But how long they can survive in the jungle is another question, much more difficult to answer,' Oya Ali assured him. 'It takes a lifetime for a man to learn its secret paths and its dangers. They will not all have a long life.'

'What are the crew's casualties?' asked Gunn.

'So far as I can calculate, sir, two dead and three wounded, one seriously,' replied the first officer.

'Pray advise Captain Blackman that his gunners can cease fire.'

A Dyak bowman stepped forward, his arrows dipped in pitch. Gunn lit three for him with a lucifer and the Dyak fired them up through the trees, out into the bright blue air. Then they heard another noise, a roar of cheering from the *Aeneas*.

'They are coming ashore,' said Gunn. 'Let us go down and meet them.'

The Dutch officer on the bridge of his ship scanned the beach through his glass, then turned to his first mate.

'There is a lot of shouting from the shore,' he said dubiously. 'Maybe they have hit some of our men as well as the pirates? Do you think that it could be deliberate?'

'Probably, yes,' replied the mate at once. 'The English are totally without scruples or honour. A hard people.'

'So are we,' said the officer grimly.

'I agree, sir, but now they out-gun us.'

'What are you suggesting? That we open fire on their Navy ship?'

'Certainly not, sir. But if they *have* harmed our comrades, I fear we will get no more than an apology, although we may personally consider it a deliberate act of war. If they have killed any of our countrymen, they will maintain that the death was an unfortunate accident – perhaps caused by inexperienced gunners. And why were they so inexperienced, pray? Simply because, as their captain has been at pains to explain, the Dutch Navy is paramount in these seas and so they have been unable to practise – for they have a treaty with Holland. I find that hard to accept, sir.'

'We will go ashore immediately, and see the extent of the damage – and if our comrades are injured, whether any redress can be made.'

'There will be no redress, sir.'

'Why not? I will report the whole matter to the Governor of Java.'

'By that time, sir, the English vessel will be miles away, and either in waters the Navy controls, or peacefully at anchor in Hong Kong or Singapore.'

'You advocate a policy of defeat and acquiescence, then?'

'No, sir. Only one of realism. We had the initial advantage. Then the arrival of this gunboat presented it to them.'

'They will not keep it.'

At that moment, the look-out in the crow's nest, up the main mast, shouted: 'Unknown swimmer ahoy!'

The two men looked at each other, puzzled.

'Where from?' shouted the first officer.

'I cannot say, sir, but he is making for the English ship.'

'Shoot him!' ordered the officer instantly. Three marines ran to the edge of the main deck, raised their muskets and fired. The swimmer, naked except for a pair of drawers, heard the shouts as he came up like a pale seal for air, and dived instantly beneath the sea. Bullets sprayed the flecks of foam where he had last been seen.

'Reload and hold your fire. He must surface again if you have not already hit him.'

A slam of powder, ball and ramrods into three smoking barrels, and the three marines waited, sweating with concentration under the burning sun. The swimmer came up for a second time, took a deep breath and dived once more; he had swum about ten metres closer to the *Aeneas*.

'Next time he surfaces, aim slightly ahead. And fire only on my command.'

'Very good, sir.'

The marines waited, holding their breath, muskets at the shoulders, watching the blue water for the swimmer's head to break surface again.

'Fire!' shouted the first officer. He had seen a faint swirl beneath the sea as the man began to rise. The muskets barked. The swimmer's head came up, black hair floated wide for a second like a strange dark weed and the blue water frothed white and red. Then there was nothing but faint, weakening streaks of blood.

'We have killed a British sailor, sir,' said the mate. 'He could have been harmless.'

'Then he should not have been so near our vessel,' the first officer replied, now on the defensive. Shouting to warn or to wound had all the excitement of a hunt; death was always an anti-climax.

'Let us hope . . .' began the mate slowly – and then a roar of explosion drowned his voice. The ship rocked and reeled as though seized by a giant and angry hand.

'A charge!' gasped the first officer as he fell against the wheel. 'He had planted a charge!'

The deck heaved, planks split apart, the whole ship listed sharply, and fell away in the bows as she began to sink. All around, they heard cries and shouts and screams from men wounded or trapped beneath jammed hatches.

'Those bloody English!' cried the mate bitterly. 'Load the guns! Aim at the frigate!' But no-one remained on deck to load them, and because of the list of the ship, the neat pyramids of polished cannonballs had rolled down into the sea, and the guns pointed bronze barrels uselessly at the sky.

The first officer gripped the balustrade of the bridge, unable to comprehend what had happened. The English were allies of the Dutch. *Surely* they could not have sunk the ship deliberately? And if they had, for what possible reason? He had entertained the Royal Navy captain aboard, less than an hour before. A gentleman of his position could not conceivably have held such perfidy, such treachery in his heart? Or was the swimmer from some other vessel he had not seen – or had he even come from the shore? The ship was sinking now, fast. These questions would have to be answered elsewhere – if he survived to repeat them.

'Lower the boats!' he shouted, but again the command came too late. The wooden lifeboats were jammed on their davits. Men were diving into the sea, swimmers and non-swimmers alike, to avoid being drawn down as the ship sank. He leaned over the side and saw with horror that rats were also leaping from the portholes, a whole flurry of them, swimming like a dark furry carpet on the tide. He put his glass to his right eye and focussed again on the *Aeneas*. She rode serenely at anchor, all guns silent now, and he could see the glint of other glasses from her bridge. So they were watching him, the bastards!

Something moved from behind the *Aeneas*, and he saw with surprise the outline of another ship approach, graceful and fast, an opium clipper built for speed. The sun glistened on burnished brass, on polished guns, and sparkling paintwork. The Dutchman moved his glass and read her name beneath the proud figurehead: *Hesperides*.

Gunn and his men stood on shore, watching astonished as the Dutch ship sank. They could see spars, powder bales, hatches and the bobbing black dots of human heads floating on the heaving sea. What had happened? Why had she blown up? Then he saw a longboat coming speedily through the sea from *Hesperides*. He walked down the beach, and waited until it landed. Captain Fernandes jumped out, grinning.

'Have to report one casualty, sir. Seaman who laid a charge beneath the Dutch ship.'

'Why on earth did you countenance such an attack?' Gunn asked him in amazement. 'The Dutch are allies of our country. That was an act of murder.'

'Possibly, sir, but then so is what these people have done to the natives – only on a far larger scale. And if I had not sunk her, what *you* have done could have been interpreted by her commander as an act of war. Then her guns and those of the *Aeneas* could together have set Europe aflame.'

'We are a long way from Europe,' Gunn pointed out.

'Which is why I did it,' replied Captain Fernandes.

'Was the man who died a single man?'

'Yes, sir. A volunteer. Our strongest swimmer.'

'Then see that his dependents are looked after. I would not have allowed his action had I been aboard, but he did what he did in good faith. Instead of sending £100 to his parents, make them a gift of £500. Draw up the necessary draft on my bank.'

'That is a great sum,' said Fernandes, in surprise. Gunn was not usually so generous.

'He has given a great service. All that he had to give,' said Gunn. 'His life.'

And then in a whisper that only he could hear, he added: 'I wish that it had been mine instead.'

Captain Blackman lowered his glass as the first officer reported from the look-out in the crow's nest.

'Dutch vessel seems to have blown herself up.'

'I would not take that as a considered opinion,' replied Blackman slowly. 'I think that our merchant prince physician may have had something to do with it. In the meantime, put out boats and rescue the Dutch officers and crew. Give them all civilities and every comfort within our command.

'If the captain has survived, pray present him with my compliments and tell him he has the hospitality of my ship and my sea cabin. See that the men are entertained respectably. Give them a full tot of grog apiece and some tack.'

'Aye, aye, sir.'

Blackman lit a cheroot, pondering over the matter, and how it might affect him. He had been persuaded to come to the aid of a merchant who, unusually, had once been a physician, and on the perfectly valid excuse that Blackman could thus help to rid the coast of pirates. But unless he were very careful, the monetary profit he had hoped to make of himself, and the more important benefit for his son, could be transformed into the most grievous loss. He must do all in his power to ensure that the Dutch officers realized he was totally innocent of any warlike act against their ship. He drew thoughtfully on his cheroot, wondering whether they would believe him. Why was the truth sometimes so unacceptable? This physician Gunn was certainly a card, because if the Dutch vessel *had* been countenancing any dealings with the pirates – which he as a naval officer found difficult to accept – then they might well have attacked his vessel. As a result, a state of war could most certainly have been created between Britain and Holland. Now, that had been avoided. Gunn wanted watching, however. Well, he had good eyesight. He would watch him.

Monkeys chattered excitedly in the trembling branches of gigantic tapang trees that soared a hundred metres in the air. Hofmeyer felt cold and stiff and old; his joints seemed to have locked in the dampness, like rusty hinges, for the sun was still filtering weakly through the early morning mist. All around him, other pirates were stirring. The wounded, who were unable to drag themselves any further, lay groaning on the mass of rotting leaves that lined the jungle floor. One raised himself on his elbow. He had been wounded in the stomach and blood from his mouth had dried on his chin. Insects crawled insolently over his grey stubbly face; he was too weak to brush them away.

'Water,' he croaked in a hoarse, desperate whisper.

Hofmeyer shook his head sympathetically. All their bottles were empty. The man looked up at the trees and moved one hand feebly towards a branch just out of reach. Hofmeyer could see nests of wild bees, already beginning to hum. He knew that the natives relished the honeycombs and the even greater delicacy of the grubs, so they must at least be edible for Europeans. They were beyond his reach, but with his knife he sliced through a long bamboo and poked at the nest until it fell, buzzing angrily. He ripped it apart, treading on the drowsy bees, and handed half the comb to the wounded man, who sucked at the sticky golden mass. He was dying, of course. Nothing could save him now, but the sweetness gave him some comfort.

Something made Hofmeyer look beyond the blood-stained rags of the dead and dying. The whole ground appeared to move, as though the dead, rotted leaves and soil beneath them had miraculously become fluid. The dying man lay in the path of fire ants. Thousands of ants, maybe millions, had marched down from the trunk of the tree where the bees' nest had fallen. Now they were crossing the ground in perfect formation like a huge moving carpet. They reached the man's body and paused. Then Hofmeyer watched fascinated as they began to crawl over his clothes to attack his raw flesh. He writhed weakly with pain and flung away the honeycomb and began to beat his arms desperately at the moving stream. This made no difference at all, and he began to cry out in agony as they bit him, hundreds of thousands of tiny sharp, deadly, jaws.

'Shut up that man!' ordered a corporal. 'He will give us away!'

The pirate arched his back in mindless agony, thick blood oozing like red treacle through his torn shirt. Ants were everywhere, on his face, his body, eating him alive. His screams grew louder and higher as the pain increased. Hofmeyer swung his rifle butt. The man's skull cracked like an egg, and his screams died in a soft blubbering sob. The ants moved on over his body in a terrible silence, completely covering it.

'You've killed him,' said the other corporal.

'It was the only way,' replied Hofmeyer. 'He was dying any how.'

'We'll all be bloody like him soon if we don't get out of this,' said the first corporal, watching the ants with horror as they devoured the warm flesh from the bones.

The spy climbed up the knotted tree trunk into the ante-room of the Chinese widow's long house.

'I bring you good news, exalted one,' he said, bowing so low he could smell the faint sharpness of resin from the floorboards. 'The pirates have been defeated. An English ship with many guns drove them on to the blow-pipes of our warriors and the muskets of the English traders.'

'And the leader, Dr. Gunn?'

'He is marching back. He should be here within the hour, exalted one.'

'Was anyone wounded?' she asked quickly. 'I mean – *he* is unhurt?'

'I cannot say for certain, exalted one, but although he stayed in the thick of the fight, I believe he is without injury. I did not see him fall, but I did see the slaughter of those who attempted to overthrow your husband's house, and it was a sight my eyes rejoiced to witness.'

'It is well you say this,' replied the Chinese widow. 'Go now, tell others what you saw. Tell everyone you meet, and spare no details of the defeat. Nothing encourages loyalty more speedily than consideration of the fate of disloyal persons.'

'It is well spoken, exalted one. I will do as you command.'

The spy bowed again and withdrew. The Chinese widow crossed the room, her bare feet silent on the carpet. Gunn would be with her very soon, and what price would he then extract for his services? Was he really any better at heart than the pirates he had helped to destroy? Was it not possible that he would demand, in the name of the English Queen, or even himself, a share in her kingdom, or levy a tax on her subjects for his own enrichment? Europeans in the East did not amass huge fortunes within a few years by philanthropy. He was a merchant, and merchants engaged in business, and business meant deals, bargains, arrangements.

Of course, he might really be like that other strange Englishman, James Brooke in Sarawak, who had poured his own fortune into the province which the rajah had given to him as a reward for saving his life. This was a selflessness that had never previously been experienced in any of the Barbarians from over the wider seas.

The Chinese always referred to Western traders and merchants as Red-Bristled Barbarians, and with cause. Had they not ravished China, and then gone to war and humiliated her country, simply because her Emperor had striven desperately to prevent their obnoxious trade in opium that had ruined a generation of peasants? That foul trade had made the Barbarians rich, and with them a whole group of mandarins who had taken their bribes to allow their ships to land illicitly.

Would it be prudent to suggest to this adventurer Gunn that he might care to administer her son's kingdom until her son was of age to rule it himself? Or did he secretly harbour the intention to seize it regardless of her wishes or intentions?

Oh, to have a man by her side, a man such as her husband had been; a person of wisdom and experience, who could advise her on the matter, who would instinctively know the right course to take, and how best to phrase any offer she might make, so that she would preserve the best of the bargain. Oh, to have a man to lie with at night or in the hot afternoons when the bamboo shutters were closed for coolness; when hours could be spent in a pleasant, relaxing dalliance of love! But she had no man now; she was a widow; she must not think of these things. They were thoughts for women to mention discreetly when among themselves, because who would wish to lie with the sultan's widow? And apart from her title, was there not a wise saying among the elders that men should be wary of a widow as of a wild horse, for she had cast her rider?

She heard cries of greeting outside, and then shouts of triumph, and looked out of a window that faced the clearing. The sun was up and the shadows of the palms were short. Across the golden sunlit dust marched a group of Dyaks, naked except for brightly coloured loin-cloths. Many proudly held up the severed heads of pirates in their right hands for all to see and wonder at. Truly, as Gunn had forecast, this encounter had made men from many boys. There would be rejoicing tonight; the beating of drums, the drinking of strong borak. Women would willingly submit to warriors whose prowess and manhood had been proved. Then these heads would hang high in the caves of their longhouses, to be blackened and preserved by the smoke of cooking fires, witness for all time how the man of that house had killed in battle and should never be trifled with lest he should kill again.

Women and children were coming out cautiously from the shelter of the trees to welcome the returning warriors. Dogs were barking and clucking chickens ran madly this way and

that to escape the kicks of the crowd. Then she saw Gunn and
the other Englishman Greene, and two or three sailors with
muskets slung on their shoulders, shirts torn and sweaty. Some,
like Greene, wore bandages around their arms and one around
his head, but Gunn seemed unscathed. She felt an immense joy
at this, and bowed her head and whispered a prayer to the gods
of battle who had shielded him from harm, as her ceremonial
umbrella shielded her from the fierce heat of the sun.

She felt peace fill her heart, as the ocean filled the bay, as the
need of this man filled her body and her mind, and she remembered the words of the Lord Buddha: 'There is no fire like
passion; there is no evil like hatred . . . there is no happiness
higher than peace.'

And seeing Gunn's figure tower above the others, knowing he
was safe and returned, she knew inner happiness and peace for
the first time since her husband's death.

She drew back demurely into the recesses of the building as
Gunn approached, hearing the whole floor creak under his
weight as he climbed the notched tree tunk. His body darkened
the doorway for a second, and then he was inside. He took off
his hat and bowed. She bowed slightly in reply, and looked at
him inquiringly, all expression erased from her eyes. She took
in the strength of his chest, the dark hair on his trunk, his
muscles rippling beneath his brown skin through his torn
sleeves. Only his face was grey as ever, and his eyes had sunk
even more deeply in their sockets. He was ill, mortally ill. She
realized that instinctively, for, having nursed her own husband,
she recognized the symptoms. Gunn's days were numbered,
and she guessed that their number would not be very large. She
had seen the same look in her husband's eyes shortly before he
died; the mysterious footsteps of Death that dog all living
things on their journey through the world had all but caught up
with him.

'Your highness,' Gunn began in greeting. 'I have to report
that your enemies have been totally defeated. Those who have
not fallen to the blow-pipes of your Dyaks or to our bullets and
cutlasses lost their heads – literally – to others of your people.
A few who remain will be hunted down by the crew of the

British frigate, and by some of your warriors who will take pride in their task.'

'Will they succeed in eradicating those who remain?'

'I can assure you they will do their utmost, your highness, and for a very special reason. The British Navy awards prize money to every sailor who can prove he has killed a pirate.'

'I am more thankful than I can utter words to say, that none will return,' said the Chinese widow. 'And you, what are your plans, Englishman?' She paused for a moment, and then continued more gently: 'You look weary.'

'So you told me yesterday.'

Could it only be yesterday, or was it in another life, another world? He felt so exhausted that time had become fluid. Gunn's shoulders relaxed for a moment and she saw the emptiness in his eyes, and crossed the room to him.

'You have saved the throne for my son,' she said. 'You have driven away those who would have killed him and me and made a subject province of our kingdom. I wish to thank you, and through me all my people will demonstrate their thanks as well. It was not by chance that your vessel called at these shores at a time of need; nothing good happens by chance – and nothing bad, either. It was the wish of a watchful god.'

Silence stretched a veil between them. She went on: 'Can I offer you the hospitality of my house? You could bathe here and we have oils and essences from barks that my servants could massage into your body to release your weariness as the birds of night flee at the approach of day.'

'You are very generous, your highness, but we will return to our vessel. We can bathe there, I must tend the wounded.'

'And then – you will take your leave and sail away?'

He shook his head.

'I came here, your highness, to help the indigenous people of your province, as my compatriot James Brooke has done so successfully farther along the coast.'

'You mean – with a treaty?'

So he was just like all the other Barbarians; full of vague insubstantial promises about benefits that would immediately flow once they belonged to their country, or allowed a coloured piece of cloth they called their national flag to fly from a pole on the highest hill. But these promises only cloaked their greed for the wealth of her people, whatever this might amount to.

'No treaty, your highness. Only an offer of help that comes from my heart. In accumulating my fortune, I have inevitably performed actions I regretted at the time, and even more deeply now. I would like to expiate them, or at least mitigate their harm, by helping your highness's people. My money, your highness, could pay for European men of science who could say where new wells should be dug, and teach your people how to build new water channels to irrigate crops unheard of here as yet, but which, with water, would flourish in your climate. Maybe other scientists from my country could examine the earth beneath our feet and find minerals which could bring to your highness's people wealth and prosperity and the benefits of education, without the threat of exploitation.'

'My husband was a Moslem, and told me it is written in their holy book, the Koran, "When a man dies, they who survive him ask what treasures he has left behind. The angel who bends over the dying man asks what good deeds he has sent before him." Do you wish to send your good deeds ahead of you, Englishman?'

'I had not thought of the matter in those terms, but, yes, that is my wish.'

'You wish to stay here and supervise the work yourself?' she asked curiously, still only half believing him. No other Barbarian had ever become involved in such a proposition, except this man Brooke. But she had made her own inquiries about him, and it was said that he had been seriously wounded in Burma, and his masculinity destroyed. Maybe, if that were so, his outlook had also been afflicted. How else could one explain the anachronism of a European wishing to spend money in the East, helping native peoples, and seeking nothing whatever in return?

'Nothing would give me greater pleasure, your highness, but I regret that would be impossible.'

'For a man who produced a plan that resulted in a hugely

186

superior force being routed, I am surprised you consider anything to be impossible.'

Then she thought of a reason, and asked him bluntly: 'You are married, Englishman?'

'No, no. I am not. I am single and unattached.'

'But you have your woman elsewhere, and you grieve for her – or her for you – so that you wish to hurry from this place with the speed of a roe-deer pursued by bowmen?'

Gunn smiled. Why were women always so curious about other women?

'I have no-one,' he answered her.

'Then why cannot you stay, if you are so rich? I would be happy to repay the gift of freedom by declaring you a sultan or a regent, just as the rajah of Sarawak has done for this other Englishman you seem to admire so much, James Brooke. Would you not stay for such a reason?'

Gunn shook his head, unable to speak for the moment. How could he tell her why he had to leave? That, like an animal when its time was come, he wished to be among familar faces and things, so that when the hour of death struck for him, he would not be quite alone.

'Would you stay,' the widow asked, almost in a whisper, 'for *me*?'

Gunn looked down at her. Something glowed in her eyes like coals on a fire when the wind changes. He stretched out his hands and held her gently by her arms. She did not move away, but neither did she move towards him. She seemed immensely proud and lonely, looking up at him.

'I do not even know your name,' he said gently. 'I only know you as your highness. We are still almost strangers to each other, but surely I have given proof to you that I seek to help your people? My men have shed their blood to this end only – not in hope of advancement of their rank or to increase my wealth. As I say, nothing would afford me greater pleasure than to remain here with your people and your son – and you. But I cannot, for a reason I hesitate to say.'

'You have saved this province. You have saved our freedom. You have saved my life and the life of my son. Please tell me therefore why you cannot stay. Is it that I am displeasing to you, or my country is too poor for a man of your standing?'

'Neither of these things are true. It is unworthy of you to suggest that they could possibly be the reason why I must leave. Since you earnestly seek an answer, I will tell you the reason, but it is for your ears only, and not to tell another.

'I am mortally ill, your highness. As a physician, I realize there is no cure for my disease. If I had the slightest hope that any doctor could cure me, I would have sought him out, for I can afford to pay any fee, and have the means to sail anywhere in the world, if a cure existed. But there is none.'

'We have many cures in the East that are not known to you beyond the Celestial Seas.'

'That I do not dispute, your highness, but no cure is known to man anywhere for this sickness. My body is a battlefield now in fever, now in a chill.'

'Truly the Lord Buddha said, "Health is the greatest of gifts, contentedness the best riches, trust the best of relationships." Are you certain that these symptoms are caused by one disease only – and not by another?'

'As certain as I can be. Now, I trust you to keep my secret. You will appreciate, your highness, that since I am living on borrowed time, every day, every hour, every minute, belongs not to me but to eternity. It is strange how the rich use money to buy time, while the poor need time to earn money. I would dearly like to stay here, but I have much to do elsewhere before I can compose myself to everlasting sleep.'

'You speak like my husband. He never did resign himself. Almost to the end he believed that somehow he would recover.'

'Unfortunately, as a physician, I have to accept the truth, which is frequently the most difficult thing in the world to face. So bear with me as I travel on. When I set out from Singapore, I had intended to stay here for a season and at least see my plan established as a farmer who plants seeds looks forward to seeing the shoots burst forth.

'But the exertions of the past two days have wearied me more than I had anticipated. As an earnest of my goodwill, I will leave behind a chest of golden sovereigns. Your son – or you –

may one day require to buy knowledge from the West, and then they will be useful. Or you may wish to deposit the sovereigns in a bank in Singapore as a guarantee for money borrowed against whatever the future resources of your people may be. My friend, Mark Greene, will stay here with you in my name to make sure that any who come from my country whether to trade or to advise you, do not take advantage of a woman on her own.

'When I return to the *Hesperides* I will give orders that this chest is to be brought ashore. I have told everyone aboard that it only contains a special type of tea to which they know I am partial. Never tell anybody how much gold it contains, or your own life could be at risk. The love of money, says the Good Book in our religion, is the root of all evil. Not money itself, for that can purchase much that is worthwhile – except the world's two most priceless commodities, happiness and health.'

'If you would stay, I would endeavour to give you at least the first of those.'

'If I stayed, your highness, I would need the second to deserve the first. I am fatigued. I will drink some whisky, and then no doubt I shall feel better. Not for nothing is whisky the national drink of the country of Scotland, to which my mother belonged. They distil it from malt and pure water, and the natives of that country regard the drink so highly that they call it in their own tongue, *Uisgebeatha*, meaning "Water of Life".'

Gunn paused, remembering a visit with his mother to her relations near Glenlivet in the Highlands. He saw again the spring of pure water cascading 1,200 feet above the Glen, and the Faemussach, a vast field of peat, which contributed so greatly to the whisky's unique flavour, And he recalled his uncle taking him on his knee, and telling him stories about George Smith, the farmer's son who had founded the distillery.

In 1824, after years of illicit distilling and smuggling his whisky south to eager buyers, he took out a licence for the distillery. His old colleagues, the smugglers, resented his new respectability as much as his prosperity, and frequently Smith, a pistol in each hand, had to fight off ambushes as he delivered his whisky.

Gunn felt anew the strange excitement these old stories of adventure, of one man against many, had inspired. Now, he was such a man himself – but how removed from reality was the dream!

'As I draw nearer to the end of the day,' he said, almost in a whisper, 'I find my thoughts continually go back to the past.'

'I have seen the time-piece you presented to Oya Ali, and of which he is so proud. If you liken your day to twelve hours, at what hour of the clock do you now stand, Englishman?'

'In the early evening,' said Gunn quietly, turning away. 'Soon it will be dark.'

The crew lined up naked in the fo'c'sle. Two cabin boys, under the direction of the bo's'n, were still hauling wooden buckets of seawater at the end of a rope and dashing them over the bodies to rinse away the glutinous, stinking mess of scales. The men were whistling, sparring with each other, shadow boxing, making raucous comments about the size of each other's private parts and to what use they could best be put. They were in fine humour, and Gunn listened to them for a moment in the darkness, standing in shadow on the bottom step of the companionway, leading from the main deck. He gripped the handrail thankfully with both hands. The rough male jest by men out of sight above his head accentuated his own sickness. Oh, God, that there were only some cure!

He remembered the childhood story told to him one Sunday afternoon, when his mother would regularly read a chapter from the Bible, about the Roman centurion whose child fell ill, and although the father held power of life and death over everyone in the whole area, only God had power to heal the sick. Now that power was being withheld from him; his time was almost over.

This was not a moment for violence, when the eternal mists loomed so close, but if there was a time to die, there should also be a time to live, a time for freedom and great events. Now at least this widow from China and her son would have the chance to use wealth taken from the East to propel their province into a generation of prosperity. Money. In the end, like a homing pigeon, so many things came back to that; so much and so little. You could starve on a desert island surrounded by chests of gold, while in a great city you could starve because you did not possess a single coin in your pocket. He remembered Macpherson telling him a salutary story about the defeat of the last caliph of Baghdad, Al-Mostansir Billah (He Who asks Help from God). Ghengis Khan's armies had smashed open his treasure-house, the greatest store of gold and jewels in the world, and were amazed that he had not used his wealth to pay an army large enough to defend him securely. And, to reinforce their lesson that gold had no worthy merit except for what it could buy, they had imprisoned the fallen Caliph in his treasury, and as he starved, had jeered, 'Eat the gold you have stored so carefully!'

Gunn would willingly give all he had acquired in return for health, as the Caliph would have bargained all his bullion for a loaf of bread, but who could honour such an exchange?

He swallowed great gulps of the cool night air and salty sweat dripped from his nose, his chin, and trickled down his back. He had so very little time, and so much still to do. He went on up the stairs. The raucous comments stopped instantly as he appeared. Gunn clenched his teeth against pain and sickness and both temporarily receded. Mind could always beat matter, he assured himself, until the last battle, when death beat both.

'Gentlemen,' he addressed his crew. 'You have acquitted yourselves like men. An entry will be made in each of your pay books and there will be 100 sovereigns a man on demand.'

They began to cheer, stamping their bare freet. The strength from their bodies, their muscles rippling under flesh shiny with sea water, seemed a cruel commentary on his own wasting frame.

'What is the next move, sir?' asked Greene.

'My compliments to the captain,' replied Gunn. 'Please ask that he instructs the galley to prepare a hot meal for everyone who took part. Then post sentries, two hours on, four hours off, until half an hour before dawn, when everyone will stand-to in case there is another attack.'

'What will they attack us with, sir?' asked one man cheerfully.

'I could tell you!' shouted another. 'The only weapons we've left 'em with!'

Gunn smiled, despite his sickness. These were good men to sail with; he felt a sudden warmth towards them all. He would write each man into his will and leave them another 100 sovereigns apiece, regardless of rank.

'I think we have a final victory,' he assured them modestly. They began to cheer again, chanting the word.

'Victory! Victory!'

Gunn turned and went down the stairs, along the creaking board of the deck, still warm from the burning sun, and into his cabin. Victory over whom? For what? O, Death, where is thy victory? And he knew he could not bring himself to answer.

CHAPTER NINE

SINGAPORE shimmered in a heat-haze on the port horizon, and seabirds dipped and called to each other across a sea stained yellow by sand. Gunn, through his porthole, could make out the new buildings on the quay, white in the sun. More ships were anchored in the harbour. The business the city handled increased every week; he had been wise to buy some freehold land and build an office there. He called for Captain Fernandes.

'Take on water and provisions,' he told Fernandes. 'Then give the crew twenty-four hours shore leave, half on, half off. We will probably sail within two days.'

'Where to now?' Fernandes asked him.

'Macao,' said Gunn. 'I will pay a visit to my main office.'

'And then, doctor?'

'Who knows, captain? We have seven wide seas to choose from, have we not?'

Gunn poured himself four fingers of neat whisky. He would like to tell Captain Fernandes that he believed it certain he would never leave Macao, and so far as he was personally concerned, *Hesperides* could drop anchor and stay in that port for ever. But he did not wish to explain this, for he would then show his own vulnerability, and rumour would spread like a forest fire. The predators of the East would move in like vultures on all he had built, hoping to salvage rich pickings for themselves.

The longboat carried him ashore. He was surprised that Murgatroyd was not waiting on the quay for him. Surely the man must have seen his vessel approach, flying the red and gold flag of his company and the other flags that made the signal 'Owner Coming Ashore'? Gunn ordered his first officer to call a doolie and in this he was carried to his office. He had not visited it when he had landed in Singapore, before going on to Borneo; he had not even met the staff. Now he could rectify this situation.

An Englishman with a pale, sweating face and a red boil on the side of his nose came slowly out from the inner office, and looked at him inquiringly and in none too engaging a manner. Gunn disliked him on sight.

'Well?' the Englishman asked him truculently. 'And what is your business?'

'My own,' replied Gunn shortly. 'Who are you?'

The man bristled and fingered his nose gently as though to reassure himself that the boil had not moved.

'I am Mr. Wilberforce,' he replied. 'And who are you?'

'What do you do here, sir?'

'I am in deputy charge of the counting house. On what matter can I help you?'

'I wish to see Mr. Murgatroyd.'

'Mr. Murgatroyd is not here, sir.'

'Where is he?' asked Gunn.

'He has gone to Macao.'

'Why?'

'Please, sir, these are matters of domestic concern to this company. I cannot divulge to strangers the reasons why senior members of the staff move to different offices of the firm.'

'You can to me,' retorted Gunn. 'I am no stranger. I founded the firm.'

'I do not understand,' said Wilberforce nervously, his pale albino eyelashes fluttering like moths near a candle flame.

'I pay you to understand,' said Gunn coldly. 'I am Dr. Robert Gunn. Now fetch me Murgatroyd's deputy. And speedily.'

Something was afoot here that he did not like; something smelled like an open drain. The antennae in his mind, that had so often warned him of danger or treachery when he was building up Mandarin-Gold, were instantly on the alert.

'Can I have proof of your identity, sir?' asked Wilberforce.

Gunn laid his stick on the counter, and then whacked it down.

'You shall have proof, sir, directly,' he told him, and pushed his way past into the office. As he did so a wave of nausea overcame him. He hated acting like this; shouting and bullying menials. After all, Wilberforce had every right to speak as he had done, and was no doubt working for Mandarin-Gold's best interests; but equally Wilberforce could not understand the turmoil in Gunn's mind or his desperate wish to keep an outwardly calm face while eternity yawned and gaped just beyond his feet.

A man wearing a dark suit and a stiff uncomfortable collar hurried importantly across the floor on long, bunioned feet.

'What is all this?' he began angrily, and then he recognized Gunn.

'Why, sir . . . Dr. *Gunn*.'

He reeled against a desk and put out a hand to steady himself. His face was grey with shock.

'What is the matter?' Gunn asked him. 'Are you ill?'

'Why, no, sir. It was a shock seeing you, sir. I did not know you were ...'

'I was – what?'

'I regret to report, sir, that we have recently received intimation that – that – you had *died*.'

'Died? Life, I agree, is a transitory thing, Mr. Symonds. But I am pleased to say I have not yet reached the end of its journey. Who gave you this false news?'

'I understand it came from Macao, sir.'

'Macao? By what means? A letter?'

'No, sir. Word of mouth.'

'Whose mouth? Whose word?'

'There was a clerk, sir, Baxter, who came through here on his way to England on furlough. He told me personally that he had been notified you had died in Borneo at the hand of pirates.'

'Is that why Mr. Murgatroyd is in Macao?'

'Yes, sir.'

'When did he leave?'

'A week ago exactly, on last Wednesday's high tide. Virtually as soon as he was given this news.'

'Well, I am happy to say the news that Mr. Baxter brought was wrong. I trust that his book-keeping in Macao was more accurate.'

'Will you be staying long in Singapore, sir?'

'So long as I wish. Have you anything to discuss that demands my attention?'

'Why, no, Dr. Gunn. I was just very pleased to see you are still fit and well, sir. Very relieved too, sir.'

'Thank you.'

As Gunn turned slowly and walked to the door, the whole office fell silent behind him. A dozen heads craned for a glimpse of the founder of their firm, the man who had done what they all yearned to do: make a huge fortune in half a dozen years, while he was young enough to enjoy it. He heard a voice call over his shoulder.

'Oh, one more thing, doctor.'

He turned.

'Shortly before Mr. Murgatroyd departed, he received a message for you of a personal nature. When he heard of your decease, he passed it to me, sir, in case it should be handed to your executors. I have it here.'

'Give it to me, please.'

Symonds opened a drawer in a wooden cabinet and brought out a sealed envelope, marked 'Personal and Private'. Gunn took it, walked to the doolie, climbed inside and then ripped open the envelope. The note inside was on paper fragrant with lavender water, a scent recalling English gardens, under a pale English summer sun.

'Dear Doctor Gunn,' he read.

'You may remember that we met briefly at a party in Sturry in Kent some months ago? You gave me reason to believe that our short encounter touched some warmth in your heart, as you knew it did in mine.

'My husband, being old and of a jealous nature, suspects that, subsequent to that meeting, our relationship was untoward and your conduct unbecoming from a gentleman lately introduced to a married woman.

196

'I find myself in Singapore, and realizing you will have no means of knowing of my arrival, I have ventured to write this letter, which I am leaving at your company's office.

'I hope that you will visit me at the Rosary Hotel in Orchard Road, where I have taken a room myself under my maiden name, as Mrs. Oxford. I would like to meet you again, and to thank you personally for your most kind and quite unexpected gift.

'I do not know the etiquette in the East of a gentleman calling upon an unaccompanied lady, but should you call or leave a message, to avoid any breath of scandal, might I suggest you choose the name of a county, a stay in which I recall with warmth, and which I hope strikes a similar cord in your own memory – Kent?

Patricia.'

Gunn folded up the letter slowly, replaced it in the envelope, and then buttoned it into an inside pocket. Two weeks had passed since the date Patricia had written it. Would she still be in the Rosary Hotel – and if she were, why should he visit her now?

Of course, he remembered their lovemaking, but impersonally, as though two other people altogether had been involved, for theirs had been a physical reaction, the attraction of iron to a magnet, nothing deeper, at least on his side. Was this feeling due to his illness – or to the fact that, once a man arrived in the East a door closed behind him on everything that had happened in England? Whatever the reason, he owed Patricia a meeting. He wondered whether her husband was in Singapore, too; and how much Sir Richard really knew about his wife's infidelity, or what he only guessed.

Gunn glanced at his hunter. Twenty-five minutes after ten o'clock. He would visit Patricia, and then call on Mrs. Murgatroyd in the hope that she could enlighten him about her husband's sudden departure.

The Rosary Hotel was a two storey building built in Continental style on the north side of the main thoroughfare of

Orchard Road. The front, of white painted wood, backed on to less attractive mud outbuildings and a verandah shaded by split bamboos. He told the coolies to wait and pushed his way through the front door. A punkah creaked above his head and lazy flies buzzed slowly against dirty windowpanes. There was a faintly sour smell about the place. He ran a finger along a window ledge and examined the dust with distaste. A Chinese clerk came out from the back room behind the low wooden counter, and bowed deeply.

'Can I help you, tuan?' he asked.

'Yes,' said Gunn. 'I am Dr. Kent. I understand an English lady is staying here, a Mrs. Oxford?'

'You are a physician, doctor?'

The man was small, thin and prematurely wizened, his skin the colour of a walnut.

'Why do you ask?'

'Because the lady has been unwell for some days, I advised her to consult a European doctor. But she did not wish to do so.'

'I am also a friend,' said Gunn. 'Pray show me to her room.'

'It is number three on the verandah,' said the clerk, suddenly surly, opening a ledger and prodding a quill pen into an inkwell.

'Do me the courtesy of showing me to the lady's room,' said Gunn, the edge in his voice sharp as a sword blade. From the man's attitude, Patricia Bankhausen was not a very important guest.

'Certainly,' replied the clerk with alacrity, instantly recognizing the voice of power. 'Please to come this way.'

Unpainted wooden stairs, stained with slops, creaked under their shoes. Behind one bedroom door a man was coughing softly and wearily, as though his spirit was trying to escape with each expectoration. A naked Indian child with long earrings and gold bracelets played on the rush floor of the verandah; she did not look up as they passed. This was a strange place, surely, for Lady Bankhausen to stay, when she and her husband could have been the guests of a dozen rich merchants delighted to entertain such distinguished visitors? Or had she just booked the room for herself for her own reasons? The clerk tapped on a painted door.

'Yes?' asked a woman's voice.

'A gentleman to see you. A physician. Dr. Kent.'

'Show him in,' Patricia commanded.

The clerk turned the handle; Gunn went inside. The room looked out over a yard where three kit-hawks perched on the kitchen roof and waited for scraps, cleaning their curved beaks on their wings. The room was sparsely furnished; a single bed, a tallboy and a wardrobe with a stained yellowish mirror screwed to the door. A marble-topped washstand with a bowl of grey scummy water beneath it stood near the window. Patricia Bankhausen waited in the centre of the room, wearing a shabby silk dressing-gown. Her hair had not been combed, and hung down greasily over her shoulders. She looked tired and ill-groomed. She held out her hand. Gunn took it. The skin felt dry and hot; maybe she had a fever?

'You are not well,' he said gently.

'No,' she agreed. 'I have been in this place for two weeks and I have been unwell nearly all the time.'

'I would have visited you before, but I have been away from Singapore. I only found your letter on my return this morning.'

'I heard you were away,' she said.

'What about your husband? Is he staying here?'

'No. I am on my own. I had nowhere else to go.'

'But it is a long way from Sturry to Singapore. Surely you could find somewhere more congenial – and nearer home? Perhaps you have private business here that brings you on a three months' voyage?'

'I have left Richard,' she said dully.

'I am sorry to hear that.'

'He discovered about – us. He gave me the option of leaving him at once, otherwise he would divorce me. I had your generous gift, which was an enormous comfort to me. I realized some more money by selling my jewels, and on a mad impulse, I took passage here. I wanted to see you, and as I say, I have been ill almost from the day I set foot ashore. I had not wished you to discover me looking as I do.'

'Let me arrange for you to stay in a hospital,' said Gunn. 'You will never be cured in an hotel like this. With proper care and treatment you will soon he restored to health. You probably are only suffering from a minor fever. They are very common in this climate.'

Gunn looked at her with compassion, and no other feeling. He was far closer to death than she was. A week in a clinic with plain food and good nursing, and Patricia would be well. He put his hand into a washleather pouch he wore around his belt, took out five gold sovereigns, and scribbled a note on one of several sheets of Mandarin-Gold notepaper he always carried in his wallet.

'This will guarantee any bill you may have. Just show it to the clerk downstairs when you leave and sign for whatever you may owe, and my company will deal with all your debts.'

'I could spend a fortune,' she said, smiling. 'And you would never know.'

'That is true,' agreed Gunn. 'But then what is the use of a man having a fortune unless he allows a lovely woman to spend it as she wishes?'

He bowed in farewell.

Patricia watched him go, keeping out of sight behind her window curtain until his doolie had disappeared. Then she sat down at her dressing-table, opened a japanned metal box, put the five sovereigns inside and carefully turned the key. She had been totally surprised by Gunn's visit, and had not known how best to handle the situation. She uncorked a flask with a silver label, 'Eau de Cologne', poured three fingers of brandy into a tooth glass, and drank greedily. Her illness was not entirely feigned; she had indeed felt unwell ever since she had landed in this accursed, humid place, but this was largely due to conern about her financial situation and her future, since Gunn was apparently away indefinitely. She had travelled a great distance and did not possess sufficient money to finance a prolonged stay in the hope he might return. And knowing how ill he was, the risk increased with every day's absence that he would never come back.

This wretched Chinaman only suffered her in his filthy hotel, suspecting she was a whore. He demanded payment every morning for the previous night's lodging. He guessed this was all she could afford and to think how recently she had been mistress of a magnificent house in Harley Street! Why, had he shown his slit-eyed fawning face at her back door there, hawking silks or scents, she would have had him trounced by one of her footmen and flung into the street. But now these days of exile were surely all numbered. Not knowing whether Gunn would ever return, she had put into action the plan that she had worked out in London. Hearing how that insignificant clerk – what was his name? Baxter? – was passing through Singapore on his way from Macao to London, had been an unexpected piece of good fortune. When she learned he was not returning East, but was leaving Mandarin-Gold to take employment in an uncle's grocery firm, she had made him an offer. And for one night spent with her, plus twenty-five golden sovereigns, he had magnificently carried out her bidding.

Let Gunn foolishly imagine that she would simply spend a few more sovereigns on buying some feminine fripperies or a bottle or two of port or patent blood restorative! His gift would never buy her off. And why should it, when it meant as little to him as a halfpenny meant to her when she would throw one to a blind beggar in a London street?

It was probably his clumsy way of attempting to compensate for what she had lost through their folly. What did that matter now? Life was like a long game of chess. You moved a pawn, and you lost a bishop; you stole a knight, and you compromised a queen. And if you were clever enough, in the end you won the game, as she would win wealth now. The heady prospect made blood roar in her ears; she emptied all the brandy into her glass and drank it thirstily, partly as a toast to her future and partly to steady her nerves.

Gunn sat well back in his doolie as the coolies jog-trotted with him towards Murgatroyd's house. He had left instructions with the Chinese clerk to order a closed carriage to take Lady Bankhausen – or Mrs. Oxford as he must grow used to calling her – to the best clinic in the city. The clerk, sensing Gunn's power and influence from his manner of speech, assured him that he would give the matter his personal attention; he would even visit Mrs. Oxford there twice each day, to take her instructions, in case she wished for sweetmeats or fresh fruit.

The sun now hung vertically in the sky, and all the shadows were short; the road ahead burned like a long white flame. The coolies trotted along it in their tireless gait, bells jingling on their leather harnesses. Gradually, the big new houses of the merchants fell away on either side, and then they passed empty plots of land still for sale, and then the jungle came in greenly and they were outside the Murgatroyds' bungalow.

Gunn climbed down stiffly under the porch. He felt grateful for its shade, and wiped his damp forehead with his silk handkerchief. For a moment, nausea again almost overwhelmed him, and he swallowed back the taste of bitter vomit, and leaned, head down, eyes shut, against one of the whitewashed pillars. Thank God he was out of the sun. It seemed to burn him up nowadays, to heat his blood, to dry out his whole body as though he were perpetually too close to a furnace. He had never disliked heat before; rather had he welcomed its warmth, and revelled in the fiercest glare of the sun. Now, with illness upon him, he feared it as an enemy of finite and tireless strength, while he daily grew weaker.

A tame green parrot chattered in its bamboo cage.

'Hallo! Goodbye!' it repeated endlessly in English, head on one side, then rubbing its beak in its feathers.

Beyond the porch, two Indian gardeners squirted water from glistening black hogskins across the dry grey soil. Gunn looked up and saw a Malay servant standing silently in the doorway.

'I wish to see Mrs. Murgatroyd,' he told him.

Mrs. Murgatroyd had heard his arrival, and came out of the drawing-room. She had been sewing and still held a needle and red thread and a small square of tapestry in her hands. Her face showed amazement as she recognized her visitor.

'Why, Dr. *Gunn*!' she said with just the same surprise that Symonds had shown in his office.

'Indeed, madam,' he replied, bowing. 'At your service, as always.'

'I thought . . . I thought . . .' Her voice tailed away.

'You thought, perhaps, that I was dead?' said Gunn. 'Well, I am not quite in that condition, although my office had also heard of my demise. Apparently this rumour emanated from Macao, by way of a member of the staff passing through on his way to England. Can you give me any enlightenment on the matter?'

'I am sorry, but I cannot. My husband heard it from Mr. Baxter, and he told me. We were both very distressed at the news. I knew you were unwell, for you had previously told me as much.'

'Quite so. But there is a drastic distinction between illness and death, Mrs. Murgatroyd. I hear that your husband is in Macao? What precisely is he doing there? His office is here in Singapore.'

'He had intelligence that all was not well at your head-quarters in Macao and that his presence there was necessary, as some changes required to be made.'

'What sort of changes?'

'He did not confide in me, doctor. He simply said he had to take the speediest ship to Macao.'

'Was this before or after he heard that I was apparently dead?'

'It was just after Mr. Baxter passed through Singapore that he left.'

It was possible, of course, that Baxter had brought out some confidential letter from MacPherson on an urgent matter that needed his personal intervention; or maybe the letter had been addressed to Gunn, and Murgatroyd had opened it, believing him dead? In these circumstances, he would not necessarily confide in any of the staff in the Singapore office, or even his wife, for rumour ran wild in the East, and bad news could cripple a company even as large as Mandarin-Gold if it were not swiftly checked. Gunn had no reason to doubt Murga-troyd's loyalty, and yet the rumour of his death must have been deliberately spread by someone. He felt again the feeling of unease he had experienced when he had gone into his office in Singapore. But – why?

'Can I offer you a *nimbu pani*?' Mrs. Murgatroyd asked him nervously.

'No, thank you.'

Gunn could not bear the thought of the bitter lemon juice in his mouth. His feelings were bitter enough already. He would go back to the *Hesperides* and lie down for the rest of the day. By evening, the attack might have passed.

'Please,' she said, sensing his indecision, his loneliness, seeing his face grey and the drops of perspiration, which he had so recently wiped away, burst out again on his forehead. He looked so ill, a man whose determination and spirit kept him alive when others would have long since succumbed.

'You are too kind,' Gunn said. 'But I will return to my ship.'

This confounded fever fumed in his blood like poisoned wine and clouded his mind and reasoning powers.

'One last thing, Mrs. Murgatroyd. I would greatly appreciate any help you could give me on a private matter. I have just seen a woman friend of mine newly arrived in Singapore, a Mrs. Oxford, who is in poor health. I have given her a letter to say I will be responsible for her hospital bills and any other expenses she may incur.

'I would esteem it a personal favour if you could interest yourself in Mrs. Oxford and visit her. I will, of course, reimburse you for any expenses you may incur, and should she wish to buy clothes or rent suitable accommodation when she leaves the clinic, or if she has any other expenditure whatever, please see that her wishes are carried out. My letter will be your guarantee to honour any of her debts.'

'I have already met the lady, doctor. She visited David in the office, and he brought her home to dinner because she said she knew you in England.'

'I am glad she is not a stranger to you.'

'Is she to have *anything* she wants?' asked Mrs. Murgatroyd enviously. No man had ever issued such instructions on her behalf, and no-one was ever likely to. She repulsed short savage stabs of jealousy.

204

'Anything she asks for,' Gunn assured her. 'And now, madam, by your leave.'

He bowed and turned on his heel, and Mrs. Murgatroyd followed him to the doorway and watched him climb into the doolie. He did not look back. He was thinking that he really had little interest in discovering who had put about the rumour of his death. The way he felt, by the time he discovered its author, the rumour could be true.

'Hallo,' called the parrot inanely after him. 'Hallo! Good-bye!'

CHAPTER TEN

MRS. MURGATROYD watched Gunn's doolie out of sight and then turned back into her own room. She sat down and put her tapestry and the needle back in her workbox, for her hands were trembling and she felt faint. When she was a little girl, her mother had frequently told her that she worried too much, and took other people's problems as her own, and she never denied that this was so. But now surely her concern was justified? Something here frightened her; she sensed danger and an unwanted involvement in events that neither she nor her husband could even begin to control.

She had nagged at her husband to seize what opportunities he had of promotion and advancement before Gunn died, because the knowledge of Gunn's illness was her secret and his, and they must use it as a lever to further their own advancement, but now this woman Patricia Oxford had appeared. Mrs. Murgatroyd had not trusted her, for Patricia was everything she admired in a woman; bold – some would say almost brazen – voluptuous, and capable of making decisions which many men would shun. Mrs. Murgatroyd feared Gunn's reputation for ruthlessness. One word from him and her husband could be out of his employ, and where else would he find a place that paid the salary offered by Mandarin-Gold? If only I knew Gunn better, she thought. If only I had dared to tell him. She caught sight of herself in the cheval glass; a pale, nervous woman, not pretty, not plain, simply nondescript. The thoughts were without meaning. Had not her mother also told her that the two saddest words in the language were 'if only'? And if she possessed the courage for such an action, she realized, she would never be a clerk's wife, living in a rented bungalow near the mangrove swamps on the unfashionable side of Singapore Island.

She remembered Gunn's first visit, when he had clearly been ill. 'What is the matter with him, do you think?' she had asked her husband before the dinner party, as they took tea on the verandah together.

'Some sort of fever,' said Murgatroyd. 'I heard he wasn't too good when he called here on the way back to England, just before I joined the firm.'

'He is a lot worse now. Who takes over if anything happens to him?'

'Anything happen to Dr. Gunn? Why, he's in his prime. And tough as old boots. Everyone says so.'

'Mrs. Robinson down the road lost two children under eight last spring,' his wife reminded him. 'They seemed tough, too, until the fever killed them. He is ill, very ill. I sense it in the way he walks – slowly, every step an effort. The way he likes sitting down whenever he can. What I want to know is, who takes over when he goes?'

'He has left a will, I expect, in which all that should be dealt with. He is not married, of course.'

'Why is it called Mandarin-Gold? Is there someone called Gold involved?'

'No. Gunn was once marooned by a Parsee who hoped the Chinese would kill him. I don't know all the ins and outs of it. But Gunn was lucky – he met an old Scottish sailor, MacPherson, who had jumped ship and was living with some woman and acting as interpreter for the Chinese. Mac-Pherson apparently saved Gunn's life and Gunn in return persuaded him to join him and they formed their company.

'They chose the name because a mandarin represented power to the Chinese, and gold seemed the most powerful force in the world. Or so they believed. I don't like MacPherson. He's a crude fellow, a bottle-a-day man.'

'But it could be that he takes over?'

'It is possible,' agreed Murgatroyd slowly. 'I would not personally be happy with that prospect. I do not think he has a great regard for me, either. Now I'll see whether the doctor is well enough to join us for dinner.'

'No, I'll go,' said his wife quickly. She went into the bedroom. Gunn was still sleeping, and for a moment she stood looking at the outline of his long body in the bed, noting the blueness around his eyes, the sallowness of his skin, how thin his hands appeared on the coverlet. Her gaze pierced his sleep, and he opened his eyes.

'I hope I haven't disturbed you, doctor,' she said nervously. 'I wondered if you wished for anything before dinner?'

Gunn shook his head.

'Nothing,' he replied. 'But I thank you for your kindness in asking.' He lay, eyes closed, for a moment and then he looked at her again.

'Have you any experience in nursing?' he asked.

'A little,' she replied. 'My father was ill for many months before he died.'

'Then you will appreciate the meaning of the Hippocratic Oath we doctors take. Let me tell you something then under the bond of that oath. I am dying, Mrs. Murgatroyd. I have a disease for which there is no known cure, with at most a few months left to live, at worst possibly only a few weeks. I called at Singapore not meaning to become involved with social entertaining, for I fear I am poor company. You have been kind to me, Mrs. Murgatroyd, in inviting me to your home.'

'I have done very little, sir,' she said.

'Many people have done far less,' replied Gunn simply. 'Now, if you will excuse me, I will sleep a little longer.'

Already his voice was heavy with slumber. She stood up, but he did not open his eyes again. She tiptoed from the room.

That night, after their party, Murgatroyd lay with his wife in their high-ceilinged bedroom listening to the whirr of cicadas, the croak of frogs. The relief of having overcome the awkward moments between Gunn and Greene, the warmth of the night and the proximity of his wife's soft voluptuous thigh, stirred his desire, and he rolled gently against her, reaching out his hands for her breasts. She drew away slightly.

'No,' she said briefly. 'It's too hot.'

'It was too hot last night,' Murgatroyd said grumpily, wanting her all the more, yet hating himself for showing his weakness, and his need of this flaccid, stupid creature who could so amazingly transport him into a brief paradise of ecstasy.

'Let me tell you something,' she said. 'About Gunn.'

'Oh, him,' he replied, moving farther away from her. If she did not want him, then by heavens he would not so much as touch her flesh. His mind flitted over possible prospects in the Chinese quarter; girls with almond eyes and passive faces who would be willing to accede to any whim, however outrageous. The thoughts inflamed his longing and despite his decision he again moved restlessly against her smooth, soft shape.

'He told me a secret,' she said. 'He is dying.'

'Dying? What of?'

'Some wasting disease, I fancy. He did not give me the name. But I watched my own father die of a similar complaint. If you are to make your mark in this company, you should sail to Macao once Gunn goes and see this man, MacPherson. Ingratiate yourself with him. Show him how useful you are.'

'He would see through me in a minute.'

'Nonsense. All men are lonely. They welcome the offer of friendship from a younger man, because in the younger man they can see themselves as they once were.'

'I wouldn't dare,' said Murgatroyd.

'Wouldn't *dare*?' she repeated contemptuously. 'Then don't touch me. Prove yourself a man first, not a male creature with the organs of a man, lying there, willing to spend your life in second-class subservience, while others seize the fruits above your head. If *I* were a man I would be on my way already.'

'You don't understand,' he said. 'There are so many difficulties.'

She snorted, her contempt too great to translate into words.

'MacPherson is a hard man,' Murgatroyd went on. 'He might want the company for himself, to promote his own people.'

'Then fight him. Why, you are only half his age. Think what it would mean to us to be rich, to be a *taipan* of Mandarin-Gold, not just a clerk!'

'But how could I possibly be a *taipan*?'

'Good God!' she retorted angrily. 'Why do you find so many reasons for *not* doing something? You could have done what Gunn did and made your own fortune years ago, but you always were too cautious. You wanted another man to pay the bills, to take all the risks, while you sat on your ridiculous high stool clerking away, adding up *his* fortune. Now Gunn is dying. MacPherson, you admit, drinks heavily. Some clever young man will take over the whole thing – someone like Gunn, only in good health. Cannot you see yourself as that man – in that position – with that power? Must I explain *everything* to you?'

Murgatroyd lay for a minute, fear knotting his bowels. He had heard how tough Gunn was, and how could he be certain he really was mortally ill? He feared Gunn, even if he were dying, more than he feared other men in the prime of health.

MacPherson and Gunn had succeeded because they were ruthless; they played for the highest stakes and they did not complain when they lost. They would give the winner his loot and then start again – and beat him. Murgatroyd was not like that. He was a clerk and craven; he envied them, sometimes hated them, but he feared to take their risks. Yet what had he to lose but his own servitude? Surely he could always find another job clerking? He would try. *My God*, he would try. And with the thought, blood rushed through his body and he rolled against his wife, not diffidently now, not even as a man, but as a beast, and did not pause until he was above her, forcing open her legs, and then his body was in hers, thrusting like a piston. She turned away her face, eyes shut, enduring the humiliation without response; and yet in a curious feminine way, she felt fleetingly proud of her husband, because at least he was behaving like a male. And that, if it was nothing else, was an improvement on past performances.

Just as clearly as she remembered that night, she recalled Mrs. Oxford coming to visit her. It had taken Mrs. Murgatroyd nearly half an hour to convince her that Gunn really was not in Singapore, for Patricia had been certain he was hiding from her, refusing to meet her, and no-one could readily persuade her otherwise. For a moment she had been surprised at the consternation on Mrs. Oxford's face, and then, equally unexpectedly, this had changed to relief, as though she had reached some decision, some acceptance about his absence. She had excused herself and had returned later in the day, when she appeared infinitely more friendly, even seeking Mrs. Murgatroyd's advice on small things in a most flattering way. And then, when the servants had gone to their compound, and the two women were alone, sitting in cane chairs on either side of the little table with its delicate china tea cups and plates of Bath Olivers, Mrs. Oxford had opened her handbag and taken out a letter, and, in the strictest confidence, had allowed Mrs. Murgatroyd to read it. The contents astonished her.

'Is this letter legal?' Mrs. Murgatroyd asked her nervously.

'Of course,' Mrs. Oxford assured her, sipping her China tea with the little finger of her right hand delicately curled. 'Perfectly legal. I have had the advice of the foremost lawyers in London. So you can see how important it is for me to reach Dr. Gunn.'

'I do not know what his plans are,' said Mrs. Murgatroyd frankly, 'or when or even if he will return here.'

'That is precisely what your husband told me. But I was anxious to be quite sure, which is why I came to see you.'

'Dr. Gunn rarely confides in anyone, or takes anyone's advice. He seems self-sufficient,' explained Mrs. Murgatroyd. 'One day, the look-out on Flagstaff Hill will see that his vessel *Hesperides* has arrived in harbour. That is all the notice Dr. Gunn usually gives his staff.'

'But do you personally believe he will return from Borneo?'

'I simply do not know. If he leaves the island, maybe he will go to Macao instead, to the main office of his company.'

'And your husband is in charge of his company's operations here?'

'He is in charge of the office here,' corrected Mrs. Murgatroyd. 'Dr. Gunn is always in charge of the company's operations.'

'If what this letter foreshadows came to pass, would your husband be willing to take a greater say in the control of Mandarin-Gold?'

'I cannot speak definitely for my husband without discussing the matter with him, but I am certain he would be eager to better himself. We have one child, and I have reason to believe another is on the way.'

'I congratulate you,' said Mrs. Oxford. 'I never bore my husband any children, much to his regret. He used to say that a child is man's best hope of immortality. Not that I doubt the essence of the Christian faith, dear Mrs. Murgatroyd, but I have since sometimes thought that there was wisdom in his remark. This news, therefore, of a second expected happy event, makes it even more important that you listen to me carefully.'

She leaned across the table, looking into the pale bewildered face of her hostess, despising all she saw.

'You are the only person in all the world who has seen this letter, apart from lawyers, of course, and obviously I must ask you not to pass on the contents to anyone else. But you could mention the broad outlines – only the intentions – to your husband. Then let him take ship to Macao.'

'But on what pretext, Mrs. Oxford? What if Dr. Gunn comes back and finds him gone?'

'Dr. Gunn is dying. Every day that passes diminishes his will and his ability to create controversy or trouble. When he has gone, it will not be for him to say who controls the destiny of the company he has left behind him. You have read this letter yourself. You know what it means, and you also know what I mean. You have been kind to me, Mrs. Murgatroyd, you have offered friendship to a stranger in a strange land. I, in return, would like to repay your generosity. Send your husband to Macao. I will give him a letter of authority – my authority – and when that which is about to happen comes to pass, I will return your kindness – with interest. You and he, and your child and the child you tell me is already within you – all will reap the benefit of your act of kindness to an old friend of Dr. Gunn.'

Mrs. Murgatroyd well recalled the conversation, and the memory, which had been sweet and warming, like ginger syrup, now lay like a stone in her. What was behind Gunn's return? Did he suspect anything? Worse, could he *know*?

The Chinese widow stood watching the afternoon sun fall slowly into the sea, a sight that never failed to move and sadden her. One moment, the sky would burn red as new-shed blood, then it was streaked with orange and the first faint white feathers of cloud; next, all was dusk and the sea was but a deeper darkness against the darkening sky. She felt like that sky, that sea; dark, empty, alone. Gunn had been gone for weeks, and she had received no word from him. But then, of course, she kept telling herself, writing would be difficult, and no ship had called with any provisions or mail.

She wondered – as she found herself wondering every evening, when she could be alone with her thoughts – what Gunn was doing; what business he was transacting; how he was feeling – and whether he ever thought of her. Or was he pleasuring himself, ill as he might be, with another woman, other women? Truly had Lord Buddha written: 'From affection comes grief, from affection comes fear; whoever is free from affection knows neither grief nor fear.' But how could she stop this ache she felt for this strange man? And who, having known affection, would wish to be free of that delicious bondage?

After his ship had sailed out of sight, even beyond the long eye of her husband's telescope, she had resolutely attempted to put Gunn from her mind, hoping to busy herself entirely with the affairs of her little kingdom, but it had proved impossible. Her son was now accepted, even by dissidents in the province, as his father's successor, and she would help him rule until he came of age. Increasingly, as day followed day, she found herself wondering what Gunn's advice would be in some situation, or how he would react to some unexpected happening.

Greene was a pleasant and agreeable young man, and so clearly anxious to help in every way he could, without thought of profit for himself, that she inclined to the opinion that perhaps Gunn had also been sincere in his expressed wish to help her people in ways where they could not help themselves. Gunn. All thoughts eventually returned to him, like trained birds winging to one nest. Where he was, how he was, when – or whether – he would return.

Her head-hunters had sought out the pirates who had

unwisely fled into the forest, and had brought back their heads in triumph as a warning to others. Several Dutch sailors who had swum ashore from their ship had been kept prisoner for a week, while she hoped to interrogate them, but the language barrier made this impossible. Two had been beheaded before she could prevent their death, and village drums had beat so strongly that night, and there had been such gaiety at the far end of the village, that she guessed their bodies were being roasted and eaten.

The others she removed from the bamboo jail and handed them over to Oya Ali, who had prepared a long canoe with a matting sail, and packed it with hogskins of fresh water, coconuts and plantains. They had set out to sail to Java by the stars and sun and by now, if the gods of the sea and the winds were friendly to their voyage, they should have reached land, and reported on their strange adventure.

She heard a foot on the bottom notch of the tree trunk that led up to the longhouse. The spy came in through the door and bowed. A servant was lighting rush lamps and he waited until the woman had withdrawn before he spoke.

'If I may have your ear, exalted one?' he began diffidently.

'Speak,' she commanded, over her shoulder, still looking at the indigo sea, wondering where Gunn was, imagining the lights of his vessel growing stronger on the horizon, sailing towards her, wishing that her dream was real.

'I have done as your excellency commanded,' said the spy. 'I have two men waiting below, well skilled in their special arts, ready to go wherever your wish may send them.'

'Let them present themselves.'

The spy bowed and half turned to the door, and called down into the darkness. The house trembled again as two men climbed up and stood by his side. They bowed deeply as the Chinese widow came towards them.

'Look at me, eye to eye,' she commanded. 'Bear yourselves like men.'

A servant came in and held up one of the rush lamps, and by the light of flames that burned like topaz eyes, she peered into their expressionless faces. They were both in late middle age, with wispy beards and the long moustaches of Chinese aristoc-racy. Their nails, she noticed, were not long enough to be en-cased in the jewelled sheaths which the very rich Chinese wore to protect them, to show they had no need to stoop to manual labour, but the softness of their hands showed that they were of an intellectual class.

They were tall for Chinese, and both wore grey robes of rough cloth. Their wary intelligent eyes met her own; she guessed they were the best who could be found for this as-signment.

'You know your orders?' she asked them.

'They are engraven on our hearts, exalted one,' replied the elder of the two.

'If you treat well with this matter which is committed to your charge, and your acts succeed, as you assure me they may, my debt to you will indeed be great.'

Both men bowed, but said nothing.

'The tide is running high, exalted one,' interrupted the spy nervously. If their vessel missed it, they would have to wait until morning for the next one.

'May the gods of all the winds fill your sails, may kind sea spirits guard you on your mission.'

'It is as the gods wish,' said the elder man simply. 'Success or failure, life and death, are not ours to command. We can only speak with the voices of others who have gone before us. We only act with the knowledge of those who now are at one with the gods themselves. We of all people are the instruments of ancient learning, and the repositories of past wisdom.'

They bowed briefly and she watched them walk down to the shore. There was some shouting as the ship put out, and then there was only the suck and boom of the great waves on a beach she could no longer see. She became aware that the spy was still with her.

'Is there anything else?' she asked him.

'One more thing, exalted one, which I hesitate to mention. But I would fail in my loyalty if I kept silence on the matter, although my tongue is reluctant to form words that may add to your distress.'

'Speak on, and speak the truth.'

'The god who lives beneath the island has also been heard to speak. Old men say he is at last awakening from his long slumber. They have heard him groaning. And today, there was fire and white smoke seen at the top of the hill.'

'There has often been fire and smoke from that hill,' replied the Chinese widow. 'Ever since I came to the island I have been told that this God of the Inward Mountain is about to awaken. But every time, like an old man, he only groans in his sleep and turns over, and goes to sleep again. That is the voice the old men heard – what you and I have often heard. This god will not awake in our lifetime.'

'With the utmost and most reverent respect, exalted one, some of the elders believe that the God of the Inward Mountain is now much nearer waking than ever before in their long lifetime. I have told them that, as you say, he is like an old man groaning in his sleep, but they shake their heads. They say he is groaning because his sleep is done, because his work is about to begin.'

'Old men talk foolishness,' replied the Chinese widow. 'Their blood runs thin, their love grows cool, their muscles are soft, and while they wait for death they talk of things that do not concern them, matters of which they have neither knowledge nor understanding. It has always been so. Their themes do not alter. Present times are not like past times, which were on an altogether more noble level. Young people lack the respect that they in their youth willingly accorded to their elders. And soon some great calamity will be upon us all as a reminder of ancient values and honour that the present has abandoned. Is that not so?'

'It is often as your excellency says,' agreed the spy, and bowed and turned to leave. He had no stomach for an argument, but although he outwardly agreed with the widow, in his heart he knew the past because so far as they were concerned what had been was more important than what was to come; and for them time past always exceeded time to come.

The widow called after him.

'Do not speak to the elders of what I have told you. Remember, age also has its pride. Old men have little left but their thoughts, and it is natural that they should speak like this. Do not mock them, but consult the priests discreetly. Find out their views on this matter.'

'It will be done, exalted one,' said the spy, and then he melted into the warm night, and the widow was alone.

As she listened to the sounds of darkness – the rachet-like whirring of insects' wings, dogs barking, a gong beating in the warm distance, the endless chorus of bullfrogs and tree-frogs against the lullaby of the waves – she thought, almost wryly, how much of her life had been spent alone. Her husband had frequently been away on visits to the interior, or meeting the rulers of other provinces, and she had grown accustomed to no company but her own. She hoped that her son would have a less solitary existence. Or maybe all rulers, like people who dwelt of their own will in the high peaks of every mountain, were by their nature doomed to stand apart from the crowd?

She recalled her own childhood, first in Canton, and then in Macao, with brothers and sisters and cousins and aunts and uncles and four grandparents all crowded together in a tiny house. She did not remember much quarrelling, although there must have been some; there was in every family. She remembered instead the happy times: combing her sisters' hair, sailing toy boats with her brothers, hearing two grandmothers tell tales of long ago when all Chinese women of any rank bound their feet so that they were no larger than children's fists, before the Red Bristled Barbarians had forced their country into a war that no-one wanted.

Her father had once likened the members of a family to the different parts of a human body. If the father represented the head, the mother should be the neck to turn the head. The children were like arms, and grandparents were like legs, bearing the strength of years of experience. All members of a human body had their special tasks, and worked together, so surely they gave a good example to each human family?

Her father had been full of such homely instances. He was a trader, filling his junk under its fan-shaped sail with sago from Borneo and bringing back bales of gaudy cloth which Indian shopkeepers resold to make skirts for young girls. She had been fifteen when she had first visited the island, and the drums had been beating, because an oracle had declared that a woman from over the sea would marry their ruler. Even then, she suspected the truth of this prophecy. More likely, some Hindu trader had crossed the astrologer's palm with gold, and then the man had spoken words people wanted to hear, for such news was an excuse for a feast, with a day and a night of drinking.

On the evening they made port, while their cargo of cloth was still being unloaded on the quay, her father had called her to him in his cabin and closed the door. She remembered so clearly the scent of sandalwood and joss sticks in the small square room; the friendly creak of wooden planks, and shouts from the coolies on the shore. She remembered her father just as clearly, for she had loved him; and a girl's love for her father is only equalled by a mother's love for a son.

'My daughter,' he had said gently, setting her upon a stool. 'You have heard the drums, and you know why they beat so strongly. The sultan of this country seeks a wife, not of his own people but from the mainland. We have been approached by emissaries, for he has seen you when he visited my godown in Macao last month. That is why I brought you with me on this voyage.'

'You mean he wants to marry *me*?'

The idea was so incredible that she could not believe her father could be serious. Her father nodded gravely, and she sensed the strange masculine pride in the fact that *his* daughter had been chosen from far off by a rich and important prince.

'But I have never even met him, father.'

'It is the custom here not to meet your future husband. That way, you both start on an equal plane.'

'But he may not like me. I may not like him.'

'It is not wise to question the decisions of elders.'

'But who has decided? You?'

'It has been agreed,' he replied non-committally. 'He will make you a kind husband. In addition, he will personally guarantee that we continue to have trading rights for our produce above all competitors from Canton and Macao. And you know, little one, you have many brothers and sisters whose mouths are ever open for food.'

Something of the dancing excitement of the sun on water had gone out of the day. She feared the unknown, married to a stranger of another race, another religion, another background. Would she ever see her parents again, or her family, and, most of all, what would the sultan be *like*? She said nothing, for no-one could answer these questions to her satisfaction, and since an agreement had already been made, there could be no going back.

So she sat, head lowered, knowing she had said goodbye for ever to girlhood.

'Does everyone here know about this in advance?' she asked.

Her father nodded, and put his hand fondly on her shoulder.

'Our people on the island are very pleased. They have arranged a special Wang Kang tonight to celebrate the honour that has been done to us all by the ruler wishing to marry my daughter.'

The Chinese widow remembered that strange, colourful procession, A Chasing out of Devils, led by musicians beating drums, blowing trumpets and fifes, followed by carts trundling on big wooden wheels, all the spokes decorated with gaily coloured paper and flowers. The carts contained huge papier mâché likenesses of fantastic beasts – goats with bulls' heads, elephants with men's faces – and young Chinese men ran alongside waving polished swords to show how brave and dashing they were. The evening was warm and the men who pulled these carts, harnessed between the shafts like two-legged horses, sweated so heavily that sympathetic spectators passed cups fixed on long poles to them over the heads of the crowd.

At the heart of the procession came a crimson and green paper dragon, before a gaudily painted junk. The dragon was at least fifty feet long, with a man inside the head to snap its jaws continually at a gold ball that hung just out of its reach, symbolizing mankind's yearning for a happiness he can never quite achieve. Behind this Dragon of Elusive Happiness marched two lines of young men in purple tunics, carrying purple banners on either side of the huge wooden junks on wheels.

In this ceremonial vessel stood a paper captain with his paper crew. They stood tall as men, but they had long painted tusks in their mouths instead of teeth, and swollen tongues bright with gold lacquer. Around them were stacked all manner of provisions that spirits might need on a long journey from this world to the other unseen, unknown worlds that revolved endlessly in the vast eternity of space. A live pig, two clucking chickens, firewood, rice, three sets of sacred swords to ward off evil ghosts, eight monkeys bearing flags by which spirits would realize their friendly intentions, fans, even bedsteads with netting pulled down against mosquitoes. Hundreds of Chinese marched behind this huge junk, swaying as they walked to the rhythm of the drums in a trance of opium and rice wine. And behind them again came pony carts and rickshaws filled with wood and paper to set the junk alight and keep it burning. She had watched, enthralled, amazed and humbled that this procession should be staged in her honour.

People knelt or flung themselves to the ground as the cavalcade passed by, holding up joss sticks that flared with pungent purple flames, acridifying the night air with their peculiar incense.

On the edge of the sea, the whole parade halted, while the wood and paper were emptied from the carts into the junk. For a second, as an elder in long robes held a lighted taper to them, all was silent save for dogs barking on the outskirts of the crowd. And then the flames caught, and the paper and the wood blazed and burned and the paint on the junk blistered and bubbled, and the pigs and monkeys squealed in terror and pain. The flames swiftly grew taller than the grotesque paper figures, and licked the sails, devouring the masts, and finally the heat grew so great that the people fell back from the roaring inferno. Then, as swiftly as they had arisen, the flames dwindled and shrank and died. Now and then the wind fanned the charred paper and wood into a sudden fierce incandescence, but the heat was all gone out of the fire, and only ash was left.

A great sigh of relief arose from the crowd at that moment, and the girl watching it thought the sound was like the beating of many wings. And, of course, it was; for all kinds of spirits had now been set free. All evil things were gone into the endless upper darkness, and the night could be made over to the delights of wine and love. No woman refused a man at this special celebration.

'This is a good omen,' her father told her with satisfaction. 'The junk has been completely burned. Nothing remains but its memory. So will it be with your troubles in the years ahead. However fierce they may appear, little one, when you face them bravely, they will speedily wither and burn and disappear away, even as the spirits have gone from this sacred place.'

'When you told me this morning, father, that the sultan wished me in marriage, I was afraid, because I thought I might not see you or our mother again, or my brothers or sisters. Now I am certain it will be even as you say. I will be a good wife to this man who saw me, when I did not even know his eyes were upon me.'

'Blessed will you be among women,' her father answered her. 'Your husband is kind and strong and rich and powerful. How many wives can say this with honesty of husbands who lie with them? For some have fat husbands, or boasters, or lazy men or weaklings who can no more satisfy their love than an empty calabash can quench the thirst of thousands.'

'But will I *like* him?' she still asked herself with a small inner voice. She did not seek any answer from her father, for how could he possibly know? She was the only person with the answer to that question.

Next morning, the sultan sent his highest official to greet her, the Umbrella Bearer, who also held the more gruesome post of Executioner to the State. He was an old, thin, uncommunicative man who chewed on an unlit cheroot with his yellowed, worn-down teeth. He wore a blue jacket edged with gold, and black velvet trousers striped with gold on the outside of each leg. He carried as his mark of office a yellow satin umbrella with a fringe of beads around the edge, and he held this above her head solemnly as he walked down the narrow gangway, along the beach and up into the longhouse where her future husband awaited her. It would not be fitting for the harsh rays of the morning sun to bring colour to the pale skin of the face of the girl from over the seas, whom his ruler had chosen as his bride.

After the wedding, when they were alone in a room so thickly decorated with flowers that the air smelled sweet as honey from their scent, the sultan had moved against her body, his sensitive fingers sliding down her back, across her small breasts, along her stomach, and then to the inside of her thighs. She had a vague idea what would happen, from listening to the veiled accounts of other brides, and expectation was sharpened by slight fear and dread. But he had been gentle, and afterwards he had said something which she knew she would always remember; and maybe, one day, she would repeat the words to another shy, innocent girl about to be a bride for her son.

'It is with a man and a woman as with an archer and his bow. A man is the drawn bow, back arched, all muscles tense and firm. His arrow is the seed he plants.'

'And the woman – who or what is she?' she had asked softly.

'Why the woman is the target,' her husband had replied, and taken her in his arms again. And they had both laughed, and the elders, squatting outside on the edge of the jungle, had nodded sagely to each other, puffing at damp chewed cheroots, sipping strong borak, while the drums beat against the night as strongly as the hearts of the sultan and his bride had beaten against each other's bodies.

Months melted swiftly into a year; their son was born. They were both certain that he would be but the first of many sons and daughters. But there had not been any others. Now, there never would be.

She moved closer to the window. Outside, a grove of casuarina trees trembled in the evening breeze from the oceean. Their frail branches, thin and delicate as a tracing against the sky, rustled with a peculiar sound, unlike the noise of any other tree in all the world.

Her husband had explained why it was so different.

'When you are troubled, listen to these trees. Through the wind in their branches speak the voices of unknown people who have lived and died long before us, telling us secrets they have learned in the past that can help us.'

'But will I know the language they speak?' she had asked.

'Listen,' he replied gravely. 'Be still, and you will discover that they speak to each of us in a tongue that we can understand.'

Often, since then, she had waited in the evening on the edge of the forest, listening to these delicate trees, but the wind had no message for her, no single voice filtered through with words of warning or comfort. It was as though voices were there, striving to be heard, but she lacked the ability to comprehend their message.

Then, on the evening following her husband's death, when his sarong had been ceremoniously torn into strips that fluttered from poles so that it could not be used by unfriendly spirits, but would protect his own spirit on its journey to Kinabalu, Dutch emissaries arrived unexpectedly, and she feared their return; she had listened to the trees and at last had understood the voices of the dead.

'Be of brave countenance,' was their message. 'You have no need for fear.'

'I have every need for fear,' she had replied, speaking in a whisper lest other human ears should hear and know she was afraid. 'I am a widow with a young son. My husband's people were loyal to him because he was a man, and strong. I do not know whether they will be loyal to me. I am not of their people, and my son shares his blood with me. What counsel have you for me now?'

'We have the counsel of the ages. We have seen kingdoms larger than yours rise to power and wither like trees without roots, because their rulers – and sometimes their widows – lost faith in the past and hope in the future. Courage is like a hot coal. It can burn the hand that meddles with it lightly, but brings forth fire under the hand of steadfastness.

'As heaven is for height and the bottom of the sea for depth, as are the ways of the brave unsearchable, so is the heart of a king. And you are the widow of such a ruler, and the mother of his son. The spirits of the past will watch over you and see your enemies confounded. Out of the sea shall come strength and succour. The hands of strangers shall prove stronger than

223

the hands of friends. It is written in the tables of eternity, on the face of the wind of time. The wind cannot see, the wind cannot read. But you can understand the message it brings, and this knowledge will be your most precious shield.'

Then the voices grew faint and faded away completely, and there was nothing but the sigh of the wind and its faint rustle in the casuarina leaves. She remembered one of her husband's stories about a Haji, a holy man, whose soul was so pure that whenever he cut himself with his perang, hewing trees to make canoes, his blood ran white as milk. One day, this man met the Daughter of the Moon, a spirit who lived on the peak of Mount Santubong in Central Borneo, who could turn herself into a cloud or a woman at will, and they married and lived on a hilltop in great happiness.

From this height, the Haji could see the lights of the village he had left, and he recalled when he was a bachelor, and re-membered friends of that time, and yearned to be back with them. So he said goodbye to his wife, and set off for his former land, assuring her he would return. But once he reached his village, he quickly put her out of his mind, until one day, glanc-ing towards the Santubong, he saw a dark cloud forming over the peak. Then he swiftly remembered his wife, and summoned his servants, and set off back to beg her forgiveness.

But when he reached his house, he found it empty, for the Daughter of the Moon had lost patience with her husband and returned from whence she came. So the Haji dwelt in lone-liness, until a stranger told him one day that she had been seen on another mountain peak. He rushed there to seek forgiveness, but arrived too late to see her.

From peak to peak he travelled, seeking but never fated to find the woman who had vanished from his life for ever.

'*You* would never leave me, would you?' the Chinese widow had asked her husband when he had finished this story.

'Only death will carry me away,' he had assured her. And now this had come to pass. The numbness she had felt at the ceremonial funeral had worn away, for was it not written that only the dead should live with the dead?

Her husband had been buried after local custom, for he was a

Dusun, and his relations believed it imperative to be rid of his ghost speedily in case it should come back from the grave and haunt them for their lack of despatch.

After the Dusun fashion, his body had been placed in a huge jar and buried with its top just beneath the surface of the soil. This would allow his spirit freedom to leave for the sacred Mount Kinabalu, the home of the dead. The bamboo bier on which the sultan's body had been carried from the house was then slashed to pieces, everyone bathed in the river, and the room where he had died lay empty for a week to discourage his spirit from making a home there.

His spirit should by now have crossed the River Karaput, across the stepping stones on which only spirits trod. Thinking of this now, imagining the rushing roar of the river, and her husband's ghost crossing it in silence, she realized that already her thoughts about him had faded, like the voices she had heard in the casuarina trees. Like those whispers on the evening wind, he belonged to the past. She belonged to the present. And was the English physician Gunn to be part of her future? Or when he decided to return, would she also have departed, like the Daughter of the Moon?

CHAPTER ELEVEN

THE Chinese clerk, his face yellow as an unripe lemon from chronic malaria, came into MacPherson's office overlooking the Praya Grande, the main thoroughfare that bordered the bay in Macao, and stood obsequiously, head down, his thin-boned hands folded as though in prayer.

The shouts of Chinese carrying doolies, like sedan chairs with pagoda-shaped roofs; the cries of sweetmeat sellers; the sharp crack of whips as coachmen drove their rich European masters through the crowded afternoon thoroughfare in splendid carriages, filtered gently through the green shutters drawn across the windows.

The background of the city sounded far louder down in the clerk's office, on street level, while MacPherson's office on the top storey was high above the bustling shouts. And the clerk thought philosophically, it was only just that this should be, for MacPherson was Dr. Gunn's partner. Together they controlled Mandarin-Gold, now one of the three most important commercial companies in the East.

'What do you want?' he asked gruffly.

'My apologies for just now intruding,' said the clerk in his high-pitched voice. 'But Mr. Murgatroyd is here, tuan. He seeks to see you urgently.'

'Murgatroyd? From Singapore? Why? What does he want?'

Murgatroyd had no more authority than any other clerk required to forward on a cargo, or make out a bill of lading, or exchange. What had caused him to come to Macao from Singapore without instructions?

'He has a special message to give you which he refused to impart to me,' the clerk continued. He did not like Murgatroyd.

The man was no better qualified than he was himself, but he gave himself airs.

'Show him in, then,' replied MacPherson. 'And quick about it.'

He looked up irritably as Murgatroyd entered, closing the door carefully behind him.

'What is it you want, man?' MacPherson asked him brusquely. He had no time for trivialities and the accepted inanities of what so many people dignified by the title of conversation; asking how people were, and about their families. If they weren't fit, why the devil had they come to see him, anyhow? And if they were fools enough to marry and raise families when they could not afford them, what was that to him?

'Why have you seen fit to leave your office to come here?'

'I have an important letter to show you,' said Murgatroyd.

MacPherson made a mental note that he had not called him Sir. There must be a reason. Well, he would no doubt soon discover it.

'Then pray show me.'

Murgatroyd took a sealed envelope from his jacket pocket and passed it to MacPherson, who ripped it open. As he read the letter, his leathery face creased in astonishment. He punched a brass bell on the desk. The Chinese clerk, who had been listening outside the door, appeared instantly.

'Bring me the last Bill of Lading for Hong Kong that Dr. Gunn signed,' MacPherson told him.

'That will go back many months, sir.'

'I don't care if it goes back a hundred years. Get the bloody thing.'

The man scuttled away like a thin dry crab, and returned, carrying a sheaf of documents bound with pink tape. MacPherson tore off the tape and skimmed through the pages of copperplate writing until he came across Gunn's signature. Then he growled to himself and put on a pair of glasses he sometimes used for reading, but more often simply as a means of impressing subordinates, because by putting them on, then taking them off to polish the lenses and solemnly replacing them, he could make inferiors wait for at least a full minute in silence. He had found that in these sixty seconds their self-confidence wilted, while his ascendency increased.

Robert Gunn's signature leapt out of the page at him. He compared it carefully with the signature at the bottom of the letter. They seemed the same, but written with a different pen, of course. There were some other minor differences, perhaps because the notepaper was smoother, but nothing significant.

'Are you satisfied?' Murgatroyd asked him, smiling.

'No. I am not. And I am bloody well amazed that Gunn should have chosen a woman to run his side of this business.'

'Since he holds the controlling interest, he is entitled to do as he wishes, whether this causes surprise to you or not,' replied Murgatroyd silkily. 'And here is another letter from the *lady* in question which doubtless will provoke the same reaction from you, or maybe even a stronger one.'

'A lady, is she?' retorted MacPherson. 'If I know Gunn, Mrs. Oxford is more like a doxy, with big tits and the habit of spreading her legs.'

'Please,' said Murgatroyd in a pained voice. 'There is no need to judge others by your own standards.'

'His standards have often been mine. He is a tough man. Not a pusher of pens, like you, Murgatroyd.'

MacPherson would have said more, for something about Murgatroyd's superior smile and the man's smugness riled him like a broken tooth. Gunn must be insane if he had done what this letter claimed. No doubt he had pleasured this woman, whoever she was, but what a price to pay! Or maybe he genuinely *was* ill unto death? That could put a different colour on his actions, of course.

'Any more lip from you, young fellow,' said MacPherson, 'and you will be run back to that wife of yours in Singapore, and very glad to be there.'

'I would suggest that you peruse this letter before you make offensive and insulting suggestions of that kind,' Murgatroyd told him tartly.

MacPherson scanned through this second letter with astonishment he now found quite impossible to disguise. He had been amazed at the first letter from Gunn to some woman he had never heard of, Mrs. Patricia Oxford, in which he made over his controlling interest in Mandarin-Gold to her because, as he explained coyly and uncharacteristically, of what lay between them, and in view of the fact that he knew he had not long to live.

Well, none of them had, come to that; not when you drank a bottle of whisky a day in this accursed climate. Now this second letter, signed by this unknown woman in the presence of an attorney, appointed Murgatroyd as her nominee in all matters relating to the running of Mandarin-Gold. According to her letter of authority, this unctuous, ingratiating, weak clerk would now be able to give orders to MacPherson, despite the fact that he and Gunn had founded the firm. Why, he had only given Murgatroyd a job because he thought he would be steady and hard-working, a drudge without any ambition to rise above the safe rut of clerking. Now the man could apparently wield control over the entire company.

Gunn must indeed have been so ill that his judgment was gravely affected, if he gave any woman control in such a rich company. Did he possess no relatives to whom he could have willed these shares and the power and wealth they represented? MacPherson and Gunn had quarrelled shortly before Gunn had sailed from Macao for England. Now he could not even recall the cause of their argument – there were so many in the heat, with valuable cargoes at so much risk from pirates, humidity, even mutiny. But this brief coolness had prevented him from noticing whether his partner was ill or not. And in any case, quarrel or no quarrel, few Europeans looked really well in that climate. They drank too much, like him, or they suffered from one of a dozen incipient fevers. Whether Gunn had seemed healthy or ill when he had sailed for home, he must certainly be at the point of death now, which was all that mattered.

'Has anyone else in the company seen these letters?' Mac-Pherson asked Murgatroyd.

'No-one. Yet.'

'What are you proposing to do now you are here?'

'There will be some changes,' allowed Murgatroyd carefully.

'Indeed? And of what nature?'

'For many months, MacPherson, in fact, almost since I joined the firm, I have been irritated by your crudity and your attitude. I have had to endure both since you were my superior. Now I need tolerate them no longer. I will recommend that you resign.'

'That recommendation would be ironic, considering I engaged you in the first place. However, as you may yet discover, Murgatroyd, life is compounded of ironies. What other changes will you, as you say, recommend?'

'Some of the older type of merchants you employ as agents I consider to be ill-suited to present trading conditions. We need more tact and finesse, not their rough and direct approach to business.'

'Your bloody tact and finesse would have got you nothing further than a Chinese arrow up your arse or your throat cut in Lying-Pig-Alley, if you had been with us in the early days.'

'That is as may be, but we are no longer in those early days. Our enterprise is no longer confined to selling opium, but embraces a dozen more worthy cargoes.'

'If you sack these men, you will soon have none remaining but lick-spittles and pen-pushers to buy and sell these worthy cargoes. Any hollow husk who is able to read and write can compose a letter in copperplate saying they beg to introduce some new cargo or some commodity. But it takes a different breed to *find* and *sail* it across the world so that it arrives at the right time in the right place, and most important of all, at the right price. You are so tied up in paperwork you think *that* is business. It is not. That is only one unimportant result of business.'

'Your comments are your own, Mr. MacPherson, and therefore crude. But as I now control the workings of the company, I must impress on you that it would be easier for all of us if you resign in a civil fashion, rather than awaiting a formal notice of dismissal from the controlling shareholder.'

'I am not resigning in any fashion, civil or otherwise. Gunn once told me six useful words he had found good, which I pass on to you to live by. Never explain. Never excuse. Never resign. You can dismiss me, if you like, but remember I still own 40 per cent of the shares. And if I leave, your fancy lady's 60 per cent would not be valuable, because I would take my know-how with me. I might even start up again in opposition next door.'

'You could do what you please. Your future actions will not influence my decision in any way. I leave the thought with you.'

'That's all you will leave with me,' said MacPherson sharply.

'In the meantime,' continued Murgatroyd, ignoring his remark, 'I require an office, so I will take over Dr. Gunn's, since he will not be requiring it again. I will then interview senior members of the staff and make my recommendations known to them.'

MacPherson bit back a retort. His mind was so fuddled with drink and stupefied by surprise that he still could not clearly assimilate what this young upstart meant, or the true and dreadful importance of the letters. Yet the fact remained that this ridiculous clerk was in control of the company, and could do apparently as he pleased.

MacPherson possessed enough enemies in other firms who would readily jeer at his discomfiture, and do all in their power to prevent him setting up a new concern successfully. And, to be realistic, how could he ever hope now to compete with Mandarin-Gold?

Gunn had produced most of the original ideas. He had decided what risks they should take, what new cargoes they should carry, and which contracts they should sign. MacPherson would have to think for a day or two. If he could only get at that bottle in his drawer, he might feel more able to cope with this extraordinary news. He was a man of deeds not debate. Gunn had the sharp mind for such discussions; but Gunn was dying – might already even be dead – while he was left on his own. He felt his heart fluttering in his chest, like an imprisoned bird, and sweat on his back, not just from the heat of the day, but from the shock of dismay and defeat.

'I see you are already considering what I have said,' Murgatroyd told him superciliously.

Really, this was all too easy. Was there genuinely no more to being a *taipan* than this? Once you assumed control of the company, you could do anything with it and the men who worked for it; and MacPherson, whose rough tongue had so often lashed him, was nothing but a drunk, foul-mouthed old Scot. What a fortunate chance it had been, meeting Mrs. Oxford! Of course, he would have speedily risen in the company on his own merits, but this meeting had certainly accelerated his advancement.

Murgatroyd gave a curt dismissing nod in MacPherson's direction, left the room and crossed the corridor, under the creaking punkahs, to Gunn's office. This was the first time he had entered it. He sat down in the controlling shareholder's red leather chair behind his wide, gold-edged desk. On the wall behind him hung a large map with the last-known position of every vessel in the company's trading fleet marked by red-topped pins. Two watercolours, on the opposite wall, showed different views of the fishing village of Herne Bay, in Kent. One had smacks drawn up neatly on the beach; the other was of the church and school. Clearly neither had much monetary value or artistic merit, so perhaps they had some sentimental association for the doctor? Whatever it might be, that belonged to the past. Gunn would be the late doctor soon, Murgatroyd thought, as he took them down from the rail. He would replace them with paintings chosen to his taste as soon as he had finished with the more urgent task of dismissing the men he disliked.

MacPherson thankfully wiped his mouth with the back of his hand and replaced the bottle in his drawer. Whisky was wonderful stuff. He felt better already; not much, but a bit. How could anyone possibly be teetotal?

He thought back to his early days with Gunn; about their first attempts to run ships heavy with opium against the organized might and power of their rivals – and how, against all advice and probability, they had succeeded. And to think that this doctor with his enormous energy and ambition, now stood at the edge of extinction; dying on his feet, if, indeed, not already dead.

MacPherson desperately needed someone to discuss the situation with, but he had nobody. What use was a Chinese mistress, or these pathetic Chinese and Eurasian clerks he employed? She could not begin to understand the special agonies of a man's world, while they just did their job and then scuttled back to the refuges they called homes, while others took the risks. They were made in the image of man, but they were not men, as MacPherson understood the definition. They were content to live in the shade of life and not the sun; to make do on other men's leavings. MacPherson and Gunn were not. That was the difference – possibly the most important one. MacPherson admitted he had travelled far under Gunn's protection, as pilot fish advance by the side of a shark. Now, the protector had relinquished his power, and MacPherson felt alone and vulnerable in unknown and dangerous waters. He reached down to the drawer again and gripped the bottle.

The fire was dying, but the scented logs still glowed with a fierce orange incandescence. All round this rim of light lay darkness, and in that darkness Greene sensed rather than saw the waiting Dyak servants, the warrior courtiers of the sultan's widow.

Mosquitoes whined disconsolately on the edge of the dark, fearing the acrid wood-smoke, yet envious of the warmth. The forests croaked with bullfrogs, and the whir and creak of lizards. The night was never still in the tropics; only a man's mind could be still, never his surroundings.

'How long have you known the doctor?' the widow asked Greene, breaking into his contemplation. They were sitting on cane chairs behind her longhouse, and had just eaten a meal of barking deer roasted on a spit above the flames, with rice and red peppers. Now, bamboo cups of tapai – a drink made from fermented rice flour and sugar – in their hands, they relaxed in front of the fire.

'Not for very long, your highness, if you count time in days and weeks. But long enough to admire him greatly, although when we first met I admit I did not care for the man.'

'What has given you reason to change your opinion?'

'His example, nothing less. In my country, your highness, I

233

am a man of wealth. I have no need to work, and indeed I live on the efforts of others. Yet I have always thought of myself as a person of liberal views, and as such I have wished well for my less fortunate fellow men. I have assumed that I was in sympathy with their needs and aspirations, although I must admit I had rarely met these people – usually when I visited a factory I had inherited, or inspected property others had acquired for me.

'I realize now that my feelings for these seldom progressed beyond the vague thought that someone should do something to ameliorate their wretched lot. I knew that they had been exploited – but I had never considered myself as one of their predators. Managers, bailiffs, overseers – they dealt with them for me. Then I met Dr. Gunn in Singapore and I took a strong and instant dislike to him.'

'Why?'

'Because I felt he represented a type of man and a way of life I had been brought up to hold in contempt. He was brash, and the rough corners of my character had been smoothed away by generations of wealth and education. He took risks, and all the risks in my family had been taken by my ancestors, long ago. He was hard, when I could afford to be lenient. He wanted wealth, while I already was accustomed to what it could buy. Then I sailed here with him, and saw him in a different light, when, with only a handful of men, he accepted the challenge of the pirates.

'By every law of war and probability Dr. Gunn should have been annihilated, but he has a special quality in his character, your highness, which I had not met in any other man. One might call it courage, or simply an inability to accept what others would assume to be a virtual certainty. He is a fighter who cannot recognize defeat.

'He quite incredibly appeared to enjoy the conflict – just as he enjoyed making money – not just for the sake of victory or wealth, but because he savoured the challenge of pitting his daring, his brain against others who considered themselves superior.'

'You clothe my own thoughts with words,' replied the

widow. 'In part, he reminded me of my husband, but my husband was a far simpler man. He had been born to rule, and when, like you, one comes from a long line born into privilege, it is very different from being the first of that line. Dr. Gunn is in the position of being his own ancestor.'

'That is true,' agreed Greene. 'Because I have inherited my wealth, and my father before me, we never thought of ourselves as fortunate, for money and all it could buy had always been ours to command. But my grandfather, who founded our fortune, must have been a man like Dr. Gunn. He was a smith, shoeing horses and then he worked with other smiths and finally formed a co-operative and built a factory. And from that small beginning our family's wealth grew as a tree grows from a tiny seed.

'I can more easily imagine what my grandfather thought, and how he felt, since I have sailed with Robert Gunn.

'I have also learned something else from my time with him. He is brave and generous – and he is ill. He conceals this infirmity as best he can, but I have seen him grip the ship's rail in a calm sea, as though he feared for his balance. He maintains that he is in fine health, but his eye is dull and his skin sallow. Maybe he flung himself so vigorously into the front of the battle partly because he did not care whether he lived or died.'

The widow sat in silence for a moment, watching the dying flames.

'It is truly written by the Lord Buddha: "Sons are no help, nor a father, nor relations; there is no help from kinsmen for one whom death has seized." None of us can say where or when we enter this world, and only a few know the date of their departure. Maybe Dr. Gunn is also one of these?'

They sat without speaking for a few moments, then she asked a question that had been in her mind for some time.

'What are your plans, Mr. Greene, if Dr. Gunn dies in Singapore?'

'I understand, your highness, he has left a chest of gold with you, and it is my wish – if it is yours – to remain here. I do not speak your language, but that can be remedied. I will learn it.

'I could be helpful to your people – your son's people, I

should say – in that I can meet my own countrymen on equal terms. I know their thoughts. I can sense from a man's eyes, from the firmness of his handclasp and the tone of his voice, whether he is to be trusted, whether his word and bond can be honoured. This is not always easy for an alien to discover. If it is your wish, your highness, it would be my pleasure to stay here, to build – as James Brooke is attempting to build in Sarawak, as Dr. Robert Gunn also proposed – a genuinely independent kingdom, where all can share in whatever wealth the earth and the sea around us may possess.'

'What do you seek for yourself, Mr. Greene?' asked the widow quietly.

'Not wealth, which I already possess. Shall I say the inner peace and satisfaction which come from helping others less fortunate?'

'I would be pleased for you to stay here, Mr. Greene,' the Chinese widow told him, 'and perhaps you could teach my son English and the ways of your nation, which are so difficult for one born in the East to comprehend?'

'Then that is agreed, your highness,' said Greene with satisfaction.

They sat silently watching the arched logs crumble and fall with a shower of sparks. The heat began to die quickly now and darkness, the chill from the sea was deepened by their wintry thoughts. Dr. Gunn was dying, and the knowledge lay like ice within them.

'Make the signal,' Captain Fernandes ordered the mate. 'Owner coming ashore.'

'Very good, sir.'

As Fernandes watched the coloured flags break and flutter at the mast-head, the *Hesperides* bowed to the wind and sailed gracefully into Macao harbour.

The Chinese clerk came into MacPherson's office, his face shining with excitement.

'With your permission, tuan,' he began, 'the *Hesperides* is out in the bay, flying the company flag and "Owner coming ashore".'

MacPherson started up in amazement.

'But Mr. Murgatroyd is now the owner. He is already ashore, is he not?'

'Read the signal for yourself, sir,' said the clerk, and handed him a glass.

MacPherson focused on the mast. The message from the flags fluttered clearly into the room. MacPherson lowered the glass in bewilderment. Surely Gunn would not have flown these flags if he did not still control Mandarin-Gold? Or maybe he had not yet told his crew he was relinquishing control? Or maybe he was already dead, and this woman Mrs. Oxford was aboard?

'Shall I tell Mr. Murgatroyd, tuan?'

'No,' MacPherson replied firmly. 'Tell no-one. Go back to your stool and continue with your work. I see their longboat is already coming in. We will know for certain, you and I, within minutes who *is* the owner. Truth must always banish rumour.'

He picked his stove-pipe hat from its peg behind the door, brushed the side with his sleeve, rammed it on his head, and went out of the office. He paused for a moment, and then turned and locked his door, a thing he had never done before in all the years he and Gunn had been together. They trusted each other, and admired each other, even if sometimes in a grudging way, admitting that part of their value to each other was that their characters and outlooks were complementary. But Murgatroyd was a horse of a different colour; and not even a bloody horse, thought MacPherson sourly, more like a serpent on two legs.

He went out into the heat, across the Praya, where matched greys in fancy harnesses pulled the lacquered carriages of rich Portuguese ladies, and on down to the quay.

The white-painted longboat with its full crew was already drawing alongside. Gunn stood up in the stern. So he was still alive, thought MacPherson with relief, but he looked ill and as pale as one of his own counting house clerks. A steward helped Gunn carefully on to the stone steps, green with sea-slime, and the boat backed off smartly. Gunn came slowly up the steps using a strong walking stick. He's devilish ill, thought

237

MacPherson. I've never known him need a stick before. He waited until Gunn was level with him before he spoke.

'Morning, Robert,' he said. 'I saw your signal, and thought I would come down and welcome you myself. It is many months since you were here.'

'Why, MacPherson,' replied Gunn, his face creasing into a surprised smile of pleasure. 'You are looking well.'

MacPherson said nothing.

'I noticed you do not say the same for me,' said Gunn dryly. 'Well, I can tell you as an old friend, I am glad you do not pretend. For I do not feel well at all. Have you a carriage here, or a doolie?'

'No. It is only a few paces to the office.'

'I am out of condition,' explained Gunn quietly. 'I have been aboard ship too long.'

'I would like to talk to you privately before you go to the office,' said MacPherson. 'Before anybody else even knows you are here.'

'You're talking to me now,' said Gunn peevishly. 'What is this matter that must be discussed so secretly?'

The heat seemed to beat up from the paving stones, burning him, drying out his flesh like the split, gutted fish that lay in rows on the quay. He must get out of this sun, into somewhere sheltered, somewhere cool.

'I cannot discuss it here,' said MacPherson. He turned and hailed a gharry and ordered the driver to take them to his house. They sat in silence under the scrubbed canvas hood, smelling the familiar scents of hot varnish and harness oil, and two sweating jades.

MacPherson opened his front door and showed Gunn into a cool, tiled room overlooking the bay. Green silk blinds filtered the heat from the sunlight, and Gunn sank down thankfully in a cane armchair. MacPherson noticed that his hands were trembling slightly. He rang for a servant, who brought two glasses of nimbu pani, the juice of fresh lemons in iced water and poured in huge measures of whisky.

'Now, what do you wish to see me about?' asked Gunn, sipping his drink gratefully.

'Something of paramount importance to me, and to Mandarin-Gold,' began MacPherson. 'It concerns a letter you wrote. Murgatroyd brought it to me himself from Singapore. It was addressed to a Mrs. Patricia Oxford.'

'A letter from *me*?' said Gunn, sitting up, instantly alert, his eyes burning in his pale face. 'I have never written a letter to that lady, or received one from her.'

'But you do know her? You admit that?'

'I saw her in London on several occasions. And again in Singapore before I sailed here. What does this letter say?'

'Knowing you are suffering from a mortal illness, you have made over to her your controlling share of Mandarin-Gold.'

'But this is *impossible*,' protested Gunn. 'Have you got this letter?'

'No. But I have seen it and it certainly appears to be your writing — and to have your signature. I have compared it myself with your signature on another document.'

'But what is Murgatroyd doing here? I heard in Singapore that he had travelled to Macao on some urgent business, but no-one could apparently tell me what it was. Pray enlighten me.'

'He is here on his own initiative to bring me that letter, with a further communication from this lady, giving him authority to run Mandarin-Gold on her behalf, since she claims she is principal shareholder. He has already dismissed a number of our older employees, and even asked for my resignation, to spare me the embarrassment of similar treatment.'

'Is this some kind of jest on your part, MacPherson?' asked Gunn irritably. 'I am not well enough for foolery of this kind. I have a disease which so far has eluded the skill of medicine, but I am not dead yet. And before I die I, as the principal shareholder, will decide who runs Mandarin-Gold. My intention is to make over to you sufficient shares to give you the majority holding. The rest I would like to donate partly to charitable purposes in Borneo and partly to securing an income for my father in England. As for Patricia Bankhausen — or Oxford, as she now calls herself — I simply cannot comprehend what you are saying about her. As I told you, I saw her in Singapore and she mentioned not one word to me about any of these matters.'

'You will hear plenty about them from Murgatroyd when you come to the office. If he can spare time from reorganizing the firm.'

'But Murgatroyd is little better than a clerk,' said Gunn. 'You know that. You engaged him.'

'He was admirably suited, so I thought, to his post in Singapore,' said MacPherson, 'where he had no decisions to take without reference to us, and no personal responsibility to shoulder. I think he is an honest man, but this good fortune has excited him and made him obstreperous, whereas before he used to be a man of mild manner. But although I dislike his arrogance and what he is doing to our company, I cannot think he would dare to act in this way unless he genuinely believed that this woman Oxford had full authority to declare him a principal.'

'He must be speedily disabused of this grave misapprehension,' said Gunn grimly. He stood up suddenly, too suddenly, and the room spun like a multi-coloured top. Nausea gripped his throat; he sank down again shakily into his chair. A little yellow vomit ran out of his mouth. He dusted it away quickly with his silk handkerchief.

'I apologize,' he said weakly. 'As I said, I am not well, MacPherson. It must be this accursed heat.'

'Please rest here for an hour or so,' said MacPherson, watching his partner with pity and depression. 'You will feel better if you can sleep. I also have some laudanum if you wish it.'

'Laudanum,' repeated Gunn with a wry smile. 'To think of the tons of mud we have shifted on to those wretched Chinese peasants, and the hundreds of thousands of pounds it has made for us. But not all our poppy fields in Bengal, nor all the clippers stacked high with it at sea, nor the mountains of the drug we have in our warehouses here and in Hong Kong can bring me recovery now. Thank you for your offer, but I will sit here for a little longer, and then I will return to my ship.'

'What about those letters?' MacPherson asked him. 'Do you feel well enough to come in and tell Murgatroyd they are both forgeries?'

'I will come in when I am able,' promised Gunn. He felt so

weak he could barely open his mouth to speak, but he forced the words out through clenched teeth and bloodless lips. To start an argument now over letters he had not seen was beyond his power. Tomorrow he would interview Murgatroyd – if he felt well enough. If not, then the matter would have to rest until he had gathered his strength.

'I will send a carriage to the quay for you,' MacPherson told him.

Gunn nodded.

'I apologize for my weak condition. I have been resting for most of the voyage, but walking up the steps from the quay has proved too much for me.'

'Why not seek a fresh medical opinion? We have three new doctors here since you left – an Austrian, another Englishman, and an American. They would all be honoured to wait upon you. Surely one might be able to help you?'

'You are very kind,' said Gunn. 'But I am a doctor, too. I know that only God can help me now.'

'Perhaps He will,' said MacPherson. But he was not a religious man, and he spoke sadly, and without conviction. Murgatroyd was right; Gunn was dying.

The southern cross moved three feet to the left in the indigo sky, and then the same distance in the opposite direction, as *Hesperides* rolled lazily at anchor.

Gunn had ordered Captain Fernandes to sail half a mile off shore and then drop anchors fore and aft to hold her steady against the tide, for he wished to be away from the smells of the quay, the noise of Chinese firecrackers and the constant complaining whine of mosquitoes. He lay in his silk pyjamas on a truckle bed beneath a canvas awning that stewards had set up for him on the after-deck. At his right hand stood a small table with a glass, a bottle of The Glenlivet, another of boiled water, and a book he had been reading by the light of an oil lantern. He had wearied of the close print and turned down the wick. Now he lay, between sleep and wakefulness, alone with his thoughts.

The night was cool, with a spice-scented breeze blowing off

the shore. The creak of ship's timbers and the chuck of water under the stern were soothing, but still not sufficiently soporific to make him fall asleep. MacPherson had brought him back to *Hesperides* by carriage, then helped him into the longboat, and now, physically relaxed although still mentally in a turmoil at the thought of his worsening physical condition, Gunn lay watching the stars, wondering at the possibility of life beyond the grave. Could anything or anyone exist on those far planets? Now and then a meteor flickered briefly between them, to be swiftly extinguished in the dark immensity of the sky, as his own spirit would soon be snuffed out like the flame in his lantern, when finally he wished to sleep.

He felt a faint remote jarring against the stern of *Hesperides* and a muffled warning shout from the look-out. Then there came an annoyingly high-pitched jabber in Chinese; the creak of a rope, more voices speaking, but now in urgent closer whispers, and then a padding of feet towards him. He turned wearily on his side, fully aware of the interruption. Captain Fernandes stood at the head of the companionway, regarding him.

'I apologize for disturbing you, sir, but two Chinese dignitaries have come aboard.'

'What do they wish with me at this hour?' asked Gunn, glancing at his hunter. It was midnight, which the Chinese called pan-yeh, or yeh-pan, depending on whether they referred to the end of the night or the beginning of the day.

'They say they desire to see you on the most urgent personal business.'

'To whom is this business said to be most urgent – to them or to me?'

'To you, sir. But it is not business as we understand it, concerned with trade,' explained the captain. 'They say it is a personal matter.'

Could this be something concerning Patricia and this man Murgatroyd? Whatever it was, it would keep until morning, nothing could be decided now.

'I do not wish to see them,' replied Gunn shortly. 'The hour is late. Ask them to address me with a petition through a letter-writer, or to visit me again at some more reasonable and convenient time.'

Captain Fernandes turned and spoke in Mandarin to two men Gunn could not see standing on the deck below. They replied in soft but insistent voices. From what he could hear of their accents, and the fact that they spoke in Mandarin, Gunn judged them to be men of class and education. He saw the captain nod and turned back to him.

'They are most reluctant to leave, sir. They claim they come on a matter of life or death.'

'For them?'

'No, sir. For you.'

'That is a matter which I fear providence has already under urgent consideration,' replied Gunn. But the determination of these visitors impressed him. With this persistence, they could not just be ordinary bum-boat men, trying to sell him fruit or trinkets. Had they perhaps come to warn him of some approaching catastrophe? He would not sleep now until he knew.

'Show them up,' he said at last. 'Then perhaps we may be rid of them.'

The flip flop of toe-thonged leather sandals slapped wooden steps. Two Chinese, tall for their race, dressed in grey silk pantaloons and long tunics with crimson cummerbunds scattered with gold thread, bowed to Gunn.

'What is so important that you must present yourselves to me at this hour of night?' he asked them. 'Please state your business as speedily as you may. I am weary and in poor health.'

'Your excellency,' began the elder of the two, speaking in a deep, curiously soothing voice, that reminded Gunn of the booming of a deep and distant bell, 'I apologize most humbly for disturbing your rest, but I visit you at this unexpected and uncivilized moment of darkness, The Hour of the Rat, as we count time, to give you thanks for a kindness you have generously shown to one of my family.'

'Gratitude, I have read, is a burden to our natures. But you certainly choose an odd time to relieve yourself of it. Pray, what was the kindness?'

243

'Something that a man of your noble and bountiful spirit would doubtless dismiss as commonplace, and immediately erase from the tablets of your memory. You administered your barbarian physic to a younger son of an elder sister who was grievously ill. As a result he is now recovered and a man of substance, able to help support his widowed mother in a manner befitting the mother of a successful son. Truly, his ancestors have been pleased with this progression, and with your kind act that made it possible.'

'Thank you,' said Gunn. He would not ask the man's name; he could not, in any case, recall the fellow. He employed too many people to know them all, and indeed most of them had been engaged by hirelings. And what did it matter? If this relation had been cured from whatever disease had afflicted him, that was the important point. Would that someone could cure him in return!

'Your gratitude warms me,' he continued, in the flowery way the Chinese appreciated. 'Was this the only reason for your visit?'

'I wish – we both wish – to express our thanks in a more tangible form. Like you, my colleague and I are physicians. The tongues of rumour declare that your excellency has recently been denied the priceless benefit of robust and lasting health.'

'For once, the tongues of rumour speak truth,' admitted Gunn. 'I am indeed denied the benefit of which you speak. I also know the nature of my disease, as a physician, and I despair of the patient's chances.'

The two Chinese placed the palms of their hands together and bowed deeply from the waist towards Gunn.

'We are not acquainted with the nature of the ailment that so cruelly afflicts your excellency, but with the deepest and most earnest deference, we would wish to hear its symptoms from your lips. It could be that we might be able to help alleviate its mortal effects.'

'That is indeed generous of you, and would that I could accept your kind offer. But I have already consulted the greatest specialist on the matter in the West. And his opinion –

and my experience with others who suffered similarly and placed themselves in my care – is that there is no cure.'

'The East and the West,' replied the elder Chinese, 'are like two halves of a melon which, although fitting together perfectly where they are divided, may otherwise be of different aspect. The West has its learned teaching and so does the East.'

'Our conversation is like a cat that chases its own tail and so makes no progress in any direction,' Gunn told him. 'Were I in better health, I would be delighted to engage in a prolonged discussion on these matters. But, as I am, even speech and concentrated thought becomes an effort. Please do not think me ill-mannered or rude in the manner of some Red Bristled Barbarians, when I ask you to take your leave.'

'Before we bid you farewell, your excellency – and we leave with agonized reluctance – may I ask you one question to which the answer is "yes" or "nay"?'

'What is the question?'

'Do you read your holy book, the Bible?'

'I was brought up so to do. But I must admit that in manhood I have somewhat neglected its teaching.'

'It is thus with many men and all religions. In youth and the shadow of eternity they find comfort in the wisdom of the word. But when they are engaged in the business and pleasures of manhood, they put these matters to the back of their minds, as a householder stores away umbrellas – until the rains appear.

'Your excellency will nevertheless be acquainted with the story in your Old Testament about Naaman, the leper?'

'Pray enlighten me,' said Gunn. The name rang a faint bell in his memory, recalling Sunday School meetings at the church hall in Herne Bay. A cold stone-walled room, with a small burning fire in a black-leaded grate, and a winter sea grumbling at the end of the road.

'Naaman was a distinguished Egyptian warrior who contracted leprosy, for which there was no known cure. His wife employed a Jewish maid who informed her that her husband could be cured if he visited a prophet in her country. He did so, and this holy man advised hime to bathe three times in the waters of the River Jordan.

'Naaman scorned this proposal. The Jordan was a tiny stream compared with the great Egyptian rivers, the Abana and the Pharpar. But the Jewish girl persisted, and so did Naaman's wife. He had tried all known medical opinion and found it wanting.

' "Surely," the wife told her husband, "If you had been asked to do some daring feat and so be cured, you would gladly do so. So why should you hold back from such a simple suggestion?"

'Finally, Naaman accepted that since his life was already forfeit, he had nothing left to lose. So he did as they suggested, and either through the strength of her God, or the strength of unknown salts and minerals and elixirs in the Jordan River, Naaman was miraculously cured.

'I submit, your excellency, that just as in every country there are regrettably men of education who have never left its shores, and so greet the tales of travellers with disbelief, so some who practise medicine, whether in the East or West, also regard with unnecessary reserve reports of cures that may be alien to their teaching and unknown to their experience.

'For example, I have heard it said, your excellency, but find this difficult to believe, that some surgeons in your country have actually discovered a gas which a patient can breathe like air. And when he breathes, he sleeps, and in his sleep he can feel no pain – even if a leg or an arm are removed. Can that be so?'

'There have been several instances of this working,' agreed Gunn.

'Yet if I told many colleagues about this, they would say I lied, that death was the only sleep powerful enough to stifle such terrible pain.

'I submit, therefore, your excellency, that just as the West makes great advances in its cures and treatments, unknown through distance to the East, the reverse way also is true. I believe that our eastern treatment might help you.'

'What is your specific treatment?' asked Gunn, interested now despite himself. The man spoke sense. He had seen fakirs in India who could drive long nails into their bodies, and even walk barefoot through fire without the slightest ill effect. Who would easily believe that if he had never left home? Science could not explain such happenings, but he had witnessed them himself, and believed the evidence of his eyes.

'Thousands of years before your Jesus Christ was born,' replied the Chinese physician, 'our ancestors, almost by chance, discovered a means of curing many ailments. They believed – and we in China have based all subsequent medical learning on this belief – that the human body contains twelve meridians which rule its various functions. They can be likened to the lines of latitude and longitude on an atlas. Where they cross and recross are points where we can press golden needles and so influence their actions. This ancient healing art we call in translation, acupuncture, from the Latin word *acus*, meaning needle, and *punctura* meaning a hole.'

'But how can digging holes with golden needles in a patient's body help anyone – least of all the patient? I have neither time nor inclination to discuss the theories of unqualified practitioners. We have many pedlars of potions and pills in my country.'

The Chinese doctor smiled.

'Here we also have specifics made from rhino horn and insects and the flux of cats and many other ingredients without medicinal value, but in which the ignorant and simple put their faith. Acupuncture is not to be confused with such bazaar remedies.

'There are several hundred points of acupuncture, and its study, as with the study of Western healing methods, can take a lifetime. We have spent our lives seeking its knowledge and new ways in which to apply our learning. I have never attempted to explain this to a brother physician – indeed, I never needed to, since the art of acupuncture is taught to students of medicine throughout China. I must therefore crave your indulgence, if, with the deepest respect, I may now appear in the role of teacher and you in the role of seeker after knowledge.

'Five thousand years ago, Englishman, we in China already possessed an advanced culture and civilization. Basically, we were lovers of the arts of peace, but nonetheless we repelled invaders vigorously with weapons made – like those of your ancestors – from sharp flints and stone. After examining the

247

wounded of many battles and border encounters, our high priests, who were also the physicians of the day, noted certain things that puzzled them.

'A Chinese soldier might receive a slight wound in a certain part of his body, and on recovering from it would discover with astonishment and delight that some other specific ailment in quite another part of his body was also cured.

'To give two examples, a wound in the side of the knee would relieve severe headaches in men who had suffered from this affliction for years. A cut in a man's foot could relieve the pressure of blood. At first, the priests considered these incidents to be accidents, but as they increased in number, and were confirmed in different parts of our country, and elsewhere throughout the East – always after a wounding – our priests arrived at this conclusion. The nature or severity of the wound received was irrelevant. What was important was the site of the wound – whereabouts in his body the man was struck.

'They then deliberately started to treat patients who suffered from disabilities that had responded to wounds in others, by inflicting their own small incisions with sharpened bamboo needles or fishbones. And in many cases, lasting cures were effected. Over the centuries, something like 1,000 specific points of the body, each one carefully named after the practitioner who discovered it, were listed as having a close relation with other parts of the trunk. This system of treatment has now been brought to a high art.'

'Was it widely practised by anyone else, besides you Chinese?'

'Of course. Men of science, enjoying the same background and the same training all around the world, frequently reach the same conclusions at the same time. Thus, a discovery in one part of the globe is often closely followed by a similar realization elsewhere. Knowledge is like blossom that blows on the winds of heaven, to every country. But whether we all make use of our discoveries may depend on other factors and conditions often beyond our power.

'The Egyptians, 1,600 years before your Christ was born, had already made their own medical deductions about acupuncture. In South America and in Africa, medical men of other civilizations also worked on the same theories. In Brazil, cannibals would shoot tiny sharpened arrows through a blow pipe at specific parts of the body of a person in pain. Bantu natives in South Africa inflicted scratches on their bodies in precisely the same regions we have marked as our points of acupuncture. Arabs treated various aches by pressing hot metal probes to part of the ear. These things we learned from travellers. We were not alone in our discovery, but we were alone in the wide recognition that our wise rulers of the past determined this art should receive.

'The Yellow Emperor decreed that all other medical treatment and teaching should cease. He also decreed that every case cured by acupuncture should be fully described, so that those who came after could benefit from these accounts.

'As a student I was taught his words. "We desire that all remedies apart from acupuncture be suppressed. We command that this method and knowledge should be recorded and transmitted to future generations and that its laws also be recorded, so that it will be easy to practise and difficult to forget."

'During our Sung dynasty, the Emperor Wei Te commanded that special bronze likenesses of the human body should be cast and set up in all centres of medical learning, each one clearly marked with the points of acupuncture.'

'I have heard a little about this medical treatment,' admitted Gunn. Shortly before he had finished his medical training at St. Andrews University, the first issue of the new medical magazine *The Lancet* was published with an article by a Dr. John Tweedale, of Lyme Regis in Dorset, who made the remarkable claim that he had successfully treated a case of anarsarca, or dropsy, by acupuncture.

As a medical student in Scotland, Gunn had also heard how doctors in the Royal Infirmary in Edinburgh had experimented successfully with acupuncture at around the same time. An English doctor, John Elliotson of St. Thomas's Hospital in London, claimed success with upwards of 100 patients whom he had relieved of chronic rheumatism by pressing sharp needle-points into their bodies.

Of course, eminent physicians had ridiculed these claims. One remarked scornfully that the needles were simply hat pins, and another declared dramatically: 'I refuse to have my "seat of honour" used as a pin cushion.' In his usual good health, Gunn would probably have agreed with these sturdy critics, but now he felt weak and ill, and this mellowed his scepticism. The treatment might be absurd and against orthodox medical belief – but was that important? Surely the only consideration should be if the treatment worked? After all, if a man were dying of thirst in a desert, and a stranger offered him water, would he query whether he drank from a crystal goblet or a cracked glass?

'I accept that many cures are claimed for such treatment, gentlemen,' he said, 'but how can this possibly help me now? You will also recognize the symptoms of my malady. I believe that my blood has weakened and grown thin like sour wine. It can no longer maintain its richness and strength, and my body has become a battleground between life and death. My training tells me that this battle must soon be over, and death will be the victor.'

The two men had listened intently; now they bowed in agreement.

'It is as you say, Englishman. All our bodies are battle-grounds, and we all fight the same battle, life against death, and every hour the tide of eternity encroaches a little farther on the time we have remaining. We are dying as soon as we are born and death must always win the last battle. But the date of that final and irreversible defeat can frequently be postponed, just as a meeting between a debtor and his creditors can be deferred until he has funds again, and so can purchase freedom from their usurious demands.

'We believe that the basic principle of the entire universe is contained in what we call *Tch'i*. This is the beginning and the end of everything; the opposing poles of life and death. We might call this invisible substance energy, for consider what the word embraces. Many substances possess the same ingredients, but still present a different outward experience. Water and ice, for example, have the same constituents, yet when ice melts, energy is liberated; when water freezes, energy is trapped.

'Man is made of many essences, and into these inert substances the eternal gods have breathed the magic of life. He thus possesses two sources of *Tch'i*, or energy. One stems from the continual changes between his essential cells when he eats or drinks or passes waste matter out at the draught. His other source is the basic energy of life which has been his since birth – otherwise he would not be alive at all.'

'I agree with that,' said Gunn. 'But you are still not answering my question. How can sticking me with needles cure my condition?'

'Now you wish me, as your teacher, to run, before you, the seeker-after-knowledge, have learned how to walk upright! I explain with all convenient speed. In China, time is measured against the infinite movements of the stars and the seas and not the swift movement of springs and cogged wheels, or a weighted pendulum, as you in the West choose to do, for as living beings we must all obey the rhythm of the world.

'Consider my words, physician. We speak now at night. But within hours, day will drive away the dark. Spring turns to summer, and then to autumn and winter. There is a continual cycle of positive and negative forces, light and dark, warmth and cold. We are more active in the daylight hours or in a warm climate. Night is a period of inactivity when we sleep. Some simple animals even hibernate throughout the whole winter, and only stir when the warmth of the sun bids them move. There are thus two phases of our universe, the positive active one, which we call Yang, and the negative phase we call Yin.

'The first represents masculinity, heat, the sun. The second stands for night, for cold, for the moon and winter. As I say, a man is active in the day and sleeps in the dark because his body follows this cosmic pulse. His bladder contracts or relaxes. His digestive organs, his respiratory rhythm, all are subject to these two forces, Yang and Yin. If one of these forces gains temporary supremacy over the other, then one part of the body also gains similar supremacy over the other parts. To give an example. In England, I am told the climate contains many dull

251

days, and houses are damp, and rain falls even in the summer. Old people feel water in their joints, like rust in an iron hinge. By the nature and severity of their pains, they act like human barometers and can even forecast a change in the weather, either to rain or sunshine.'

'I would agree with that,' admitted Gunn.

'Then you are in agreement with our teachings of the two forces, the positive and the negative. Your blood may well be thin, and you may be beyond all treatment any man born of woman can give, for our lives are poured into unequal vessels. Some are finished long before others have drained the cup.

'But if you accept how all living things obey the rhythm of the stars – the positive and negative energy of day and night, warmth and chill – would you not also accept that your own ailment might be caused by an ascendency of one or other of these forces? If you feel your blood is thin, might not this be caused by a slothful, sluggish liver – that Western specifics have not treated or Western physicians did not even suspect could be at fault?'

'That is of course possible,' agreed Gunn. 'But I have consulted the hightest authority in London on this matter. Since he is also arguably the best qualified specialist on this illness in the world, it is not likely that he would confuse an inadequate liver with a terminal disease.'

'You mean the *Western* world,' replied the old man quickly. 'If your liver could be stimulated from its unnatural torpor by means beyond a Western practitioner, might not your blood be enriched, and charged with a new vigour, and then course through your body like brave, young reinforcements eager to fight the battle of your life against your death? Our treatment is simply to note your symptoms, and to place our needles accordingly.'

Gunn poured himself another Glenlivet. The theories the Chinese practitioner was expounding were alien to what he had learned as a student, but this did not necessarily mean they were the views of a charlatan. Only a few years earlier, people would have ridiculed the idea of iron floating in water, but now great iron ships were sailing on every sea. And what about the extraordinary experiments into electricity that Michael Faraday was conducting? Would they not have been held to be beyond belief only a few years previously?

'Gentlemen,' he said. 'Your treatment is not one with which I am at all familiar, but then neither are the ways of the East necessarily the customs of the West. What is strange to one has become habit to another. I only know that I am ill, and if you can cure me I will not argue about the nature of the cure. How will you proceed?'

'We wish you to bare your body from trunk to the feet, and then we will insert our needles at the points laid down by our teachers. There will be no pain, nor do we draw blood, so have no fear. We may not cure you – but at least we can cause you no harm.'

'Not all physicians can promise so much,' said Gunn dryly.

'You may feel a certain drowsiness, like the soporific approach of sleep. We do not claim to give you back your health immediately, but we will return tomorrow morning at the Hour of the Snake, nine o'clock as you count time, and with your permission, later in the day, at the Hour of the Horse. If by our third visit you can truly say there is no improvement whatsoever in your condition, then we will admit the disease has defeated us, as it has repulsed the treatment of your own practitioners, and we will depart from hence.'

'You speak fairly,' said Gunn. 'Do as you will.'

He could lose nothing now. So little was left of his life that these men could scarcely accelerate his demise. And it was just possible, although improbable, that they might be able to halt the dreadful lassitude he felt as he slid slowly down towards the shores of the last eternal river. He turned to Captain Fernandes, who still hovered in the darkness, just outside the circle of light from the oil lamp.

'Have a cabin made up for these gentlemen,' he told him. 'They will be staying aboard.'

'Very good, sir.'

Gunn waited until the noise of his footsteps diminished down the companionway, then he turned to the practitioners.

'I am ready,' he told them. 'And may the old gods of medicine, whoever they are in China, view your treatment with more approval and success than have the doyens of Western physicians, Galen and Aesculapius and Hippocrates.'

They bowed ceremoniously and then rolled down the sheet on the bed. The younger man produced a small leather pouch, which he placed on the table and opened. Gunn saw a dozen gold needles, fine as long quivering hairs, set into a square of dried sponge. The elder man selected one and nicked Gunn's thigh with its point. The needle trembled with every beat of his heart. Gradually, they moved down his legs, jabbing their tiny needles into his skin. The points were so sharp and the incisions so gentle they did not draw one drop of blood. He thought inconsequentially that his legs must look like strange flesh-coloured gooseberries, with these long gold prickles glowing in the lamplight.

As they reached his ankles, Gunn felt a tremor pass through the nerves of his legs and his spine, and he shivered, as though he had been douched in cold water. And then, from the innermost parts of his being, he felt a welcome drowsiness spread out through all his body. He was a boy again in Herne Bay, running along the wet, shining shingle between fishing-boats and the sea. He was eating supper on Sunday evening after church in the kitchen by the fire; his mother, glasses at the end of her nose, was mending a hole in one of his socks, and looking up now and then to smile at the extent of his appetite. He was sailing in the second-class Indiaman on his first and last commission as ship's surgeon. Then the tide of sleep rose swiftly and washed away his dreams.

The two Chinese stood looking down at Gunn, watching his face, now curiously relaxed, all pain and tension gone. The older man held an hour-glass, and as the last of the sand ran through, he nodded to his companion. The younger man began to remove the gold needles and replaced them, points up, in the sponge. Captain Fernandes stepped out of the shadows.

'Is he all right?' he asked anxiously.

'He sleeps,' replied the old man briefly.

'Well, I tell you, he had better awake, otherwise you two gentlemen will not leave this ship.'

The old man looked at Captain Fernandes scornfully.

'From the colour of your skin,' he said, 'you appear to have been born in the East, and have no doubt lived here all your life. Have you then so little faith in our skills that you seriously imagine we would kill our patient?'

'It seems odd to me,' persisted Captain Fernandes doggedly, 'to attempt to cure a man by digging needles in him.'

'Odd? Would it not have seemed curious, captain, if only two or three years ago someone had told you that one man could sit in a room in Macao, and by tapping a metal key connected by metal wires through coils of the same to a glass of acid eating into lead and copper plates, he could instantly deliver a message to another man 100 miles away?'

'Yes, it would,' agreed Fernandes.

'But that is now possible, as you know. And is not that capability far stranger than this treatment, which has already been practised with success for more than 5,000 years? Do not concern yourself with matters beyond your knowledge and experience, captain. You are a sailor and a man of deep waters. We could not attempt to guide your vessel by sun and stars to any destination across the trackless seas. But such a task to you is easy, because you are trained for it, and you have studied the arts of navigation.

'Why should you therefore presume to know the secret workings of our bodies and our minds? Let us each contemplate our own concern, and in this way arrive at a true sense of our value to our fellow men. I heard Dr. Gunn ask you to prepare a cabin for us. Pray lead us there. We have made a long journey, and we are fatigued.

Greene lit a cheroot and threw the lucifer out of the porthole of Captain Blackman's day cabin aboard *Aeneas*. Hofmeyer sat in a cane chair opposite him, holding a glass of Martell. The Dutch sea-captain sat by his side, looking worried. Captain Blackman poured them all out another measure. They had already discussed for hours the matter of the swimmer and the explosion that had sunk their ship, the *Orlando*, without reaching any conclusion that was satisfactory to them all. They were being studiously polite, speaking slowly in English, deferring to each other, and secretly concerned at the possible outcome of what the English carefully called an act of piracy by an unknown person, and the Dutch dignified by describing as an act of war.

'I appreciate your concern and your feelings, gentlemen,' said Blackman earnestly, 'but I can only repeat what I have already put in my report to their Lordships at the Admiralty in London, which I will dispatch as soon as I make port. I had no prior knowledge whatever of this dastardly outrage, and I can assure you, as an English officer and gentleman, that I would never have countenanced any action of this kind. Nor, I am sure, would Dr. Gunn, the owner of *Hesperides*.'

'I agree with that entirely,' said Greene pontifically. 'The swimmer must have done this on his own, and since he perishes we shall never hear what possessed him.'

Which, Greene thought to himself, was just as well, for Captain Fernandes had told him he had asked for a volunteer to place the charge against *Orlando*'s hull. He would never have cast Fernandes in a role of violence or intrigue. He had done what he did with the best of intentions – but did not good intentions supply paving for the road to hell?

'I tell you, Mr. Greene,' Fernandes had assured him. 'If we had not sunk her, those damn' Dutchmen would have defeated us. They could either fire on our Dyaks under any pretext they wish or they could have put about and returned to Java, to take on 100 or so mercenaries and come back to destroy us.'

'Could not Captain Blackman's frigate deal with the vessel in a more open manner?'

'Of course, but it would be the height of unprecedented imprudence to involve one of Her Majesty's ships. We could start a war by such an action. My way, the Dutch cannot prove anything. They may suspect. But suspicion is one thing, proof another, and by the time they reach Java, the whole situation here will be changed forever – in our favour.'

In a court of law, in the quiet safety of England, before judge and jury, the counsel wearing wigs, and solicitors pressing spatulate fingers together and nodding as each delicate legal point was made, Greene would have spoken out roundly against such a dastardly outrage. But 10,000 miles away from the luxuries of English safety and English law, when he knew in his bowels that Fernandes spoke truth, such considerations, such shadings of legal opinion, became totally irrelevant. What might or might not happen in England, was play-acting, life in a mirror. This was life as you lived it, winner take all.

Now that the *Orlando* lay at the bottom of the sea, her Dutch crew would have to accept Captain Blackman's offer of safe passage to Java, or make their own way home in native canoes. Honour had been upheld, if you could dignify the deal by such a shining name. But nothing in any human negotiations, Greene had been forced to admit, was ever entirely all black or all white. It was a medium shade of grey, and the most one could do was to strive to keep the colour as light as possible. How easy it had been in England, far away, to take a detached view of other men's problems and follies! But equally, how dull his life had been then, reading about events instead of influencing them, watching the action instead of being part of it.

'I will make my own full report to our Governor in Java,' Hofmeyer was saying for the fifth or sixth time. 'I have already told you I must do so, and while I am personally grateful for your courtesy and hospitality, captain, as a Dutch citizen I must reserve my rights.'

'Of course. I would do the same in your position,' Captain Blackman assured him. 'But in the meantime, gentlemen, we are forced into each other's company, and I am pleased to welcome you as guests aboard Her Majesty's ship *Aeneas* for as long as you care to stay with us.'

'When do you intend sailing?' asked the Dutch sea-captain.

'During the next few days,' Blackman replied evasively. He was not sure how long Gunn wanted him to stay at anchor off the island, yet he could not delay his passage indefinitely. Already, 82 pirates had been killed and their bodies counted, and he had noted this figure in the ship's log. He and his officers and crew were thus richer by £8,200, to be divided strictly according to rank and seniority of service. Everyone aboard was understandably reluctant to leave, while any more pirate corpses might still be counted. Indeed, Blackman had argued that it was his duty to stay until he was assured by Dr. Gunn, as a British subject, or the sultan's widow, as the ruler's mother, that no more pirates remained alive, lest they should regroup and offer further violence either on land, or – as he stressed in his report to the Admiralty – they could present a further danger to peaceful merchant ships. But even so, he could not delay his departure for much longer; he had other ports to visit, other seas to sail, and the monsoon, with the possibility of hurricane and typhoons, was only weeks away.

Yet it would be sad if his itinerary forced him to leave without seeing Gunn again, without thanking him for the letter he had handed to Greene for him, addressed to the senior physician at the Royal Hospital, asking him to accept Captain Blackman's son as his patient – and to send the bill, whatever it might amount to, on to Gunn's bank in St. James's for immediate payment.

How strange that a totally unexpected meeting at sea, the rare chance that he had been awake when a native canoe crossed his ship's path in the night, could change the pattern of his future life, and not only his but also his son's entire future!

'When do you think Dr. Gunn will return?' Greene asked him, making conversation.

'I have no idea,' replied Blackman. 'I would not be surprised if he goes on from Singapore to Macao. He is a busy man.'

'*Must* you wait until he is back, then?' asked Hofmeyer. 'He might be away for many weeks.'

'I will wait for one more day, Meinheer.'

'If your departure were to be delayed further, captain, then I think that my colleagues and I should withdraw from your ship and negotiate privately for a Dyak canoe with a dozen strong oarsmen, and seek Java on our own. We have lost a very valuable vessel, captain, and important as the Dutch navy is in these waters, we can ill afford a loss of this serverity.'

'That would be a brave voyage to make, Meinheer, and well in accord with the great sea-faring traditions of your nation. But the tides are treacherous and the monsoon is due soon, which causes havoc with trade winds.

'Our next port of call could be Macao, if this would be of convenience to you. Would it, therefore, not be easier and safer if you and your brother officers took passage with me as my guests, and then in Macao you could doubtless find a Dutch merchantman bound for Java?'

'You are very generous,' said Hofmeyer. 'I must agree that, impatient as we understandably are to report to our Governor, your proposal is more agreeable than ours.'

'Good,' said Blackman, and poured him another Martell. 'Then it is agreed. Whether Dr. Gunn returns or not, we will sail to Macao on tomorrow's afternoon tide.'

CHAPTER TWELVE

Captain Fernandes poured the last of the rum into his first officer's glass and tossed the empty bottle through the open porthole.

'I tell you, Mr. Deakin, I saw it all myself,' he said. 'Those two Chinese fellows dug little gold needles all over Dr. Gunn's legs and even into his body. They did not seem to cause him any pain, and presently he just dozed off. Then they took out their needles and went down the companionway and into their cabin. I set a watch on the door, in case they meant any harm to the doctor, but they stayed in the cabin all night.

'I let the doctor sleep, and when he woke this morning he told me he had enjoyed his best sleep for months. And damn me if those two Chinese fellows weren't back again after sun-up digging their needles into him for the second time. They are going to do the same thing again this afternoon and again this evening, and every day thereafter until he is cured. He will still feel a bit weak and shaky, they say, but soon that will pass. A bloody miracle, I call it. A bit of good joss.'

Fernandes used the local word for a benign happening, a corruption of the Portuguese word, *deos*, for God.

The first officer nodded gravely. He was slightly drunk and to move quickly made him feel dizzy.

'It would cause concern to certain parties if the doctor were to be cured, I can tell you, captain. I was ashore buying victuals this morning, and I heard that that clerking fellow, Murgatroyd, from Singapore had taken over the company. He claimed he had some letter of authority from the doctor, so it was said. I thought that Dr. Gunn must have been very ill if he ever signed that. I'll give you ten to one that if he is cured, he tears it up. I know I would, in his shoes.'

'I did not even know Dr. Gunn was ill. He kept that as quiet as he could,' said Captain Fernandes. 'I only discovered by accident when MacPherson brought him back. I had to help him aboard.'

'Thought he was drunk myself,' said the first officer, banging his empty mug on the table. Captain Fernandes uncorked a second bottle and poured out another five fingers.

'We don't all drink like you, Deakin, and it's a damn' good thing we don't. And I'll tell you something else, too. There will be good days ahead if Dr. Gunn is cured. We'll see some changes then, you mark my words.'

Gunn opened his cigar box, selected a Cuban torpedo, pierced its end, and lit up, savouring the rich heavy flavour and the fine blue smoke.

'This is the first occasion for six months that I have smoked a cigar with any enjoyment,' he told the two Chinese physicians. 'It is also the first time that I am completely without sickness or weariness.'

They bowed gravely to show their appreciation of the compliment. They had been aboard *Hesperides* for two weeks, and had treated Gunn each morning and evening. Now his cheeks had a healthy tan, and he had gained weight; he felt that, almost unbelievably, he was out of the shadows and in the sun once more, with a lease renewed on his life.

'You said you have previously consulted some of your most esteemed physicians in your own country, without benefit of cure?' the younger man asked him.

'That is indeed so.'

'Therefore maybe Western physicians could follow a rule we obey in the East. Only Chinese physicians of the second class ever accept a fee when they treat a patient for actual illness. First-class physicians are paid by their patients – only when they are well. If patients fall ill, then they feel that their doctor failed them. He is therefore unworthy of even the most meagre reward. As one of our great doctors of time past, Sun Wen, said: "To administer medicines to diseases which have already developed is comparable to the behaviour of those persons who begin to dig a well after they have become thirsty, and those who begin to make weapons after they have already engaged in battle." '

Gunn smiled cheerfully.

'I have colleagues in London, where a thoroughfare, known as Harley Street, is becoming the home of many medical and surgical specialists, who might disagree with that.'

'But it is truth,' said the older acupuncturist simply. 'How can anyone disagree with truth?'

'It is also true that you have cured me, yet I still cannot understand how you have done this so quickly, when by my own diagnosis, and that of a far greater specialist, my disease was beyond all human cure. When I go back to England, they will not believe that I ever was ill at all.'

'Years ago, your excellency, very worthy, eminent persons also most sincerely believed that the world was flat. If you sailed too far, your ship would fall off over an endless precipice into a bottomless hole. Other equally eminent persons – as I have had cause to remind this ship's captain – knew that iron would sink. But look now at iron ships that float perfectly, and are even propelled by steam instead of the winds of heaven.'

'There are many things that are mysteries now which one day will be explained,' agreed Gunn. 'And I would be obliged if you can tell me the answer to one simple mystery. Did the widow of the Sultan of Kei in Borneo send you to see me?'

At the mention of her name, both the Chinese doctors gravely bowed their heads. They placed their hands in the wide loose sleeves of their robes and said nothing.

'Your silence I take to be an affirmative answer?'

The old man lifted up his head and looked Gunn in the eyes.

'A man hears no words from a silent thought, and may read what he will from an empty face. But that is up to the man concerned,' he said enigmatically.

'Well, then,' Gunn went on, 'answer me another question, if you will. When you arrived here, you said I had done some kind service to a relation. Was that so?'

'It was not exactly true, your excellency. No doubt your kind heart would willingly have helped such a relation of mine had

262

the chance arisen. I invented this reason because every man is warmed by the thought that a good deed he has done is remembered – even though he may have lost all recollection of it. Gratitude is like honey. All relish its sweetness.'

'You know the workings of our minds,' said Gunn, amused at the answer. 'Now, I am sailing back to Borneo. Can I offer you both passage with me?'

The old man shook his head.

'You are very generous,' he said. 'But we travel to the north. One day maybe our stars will cross with felicitous results, as the meridians Yin and Yang crossed in your body. Without doubt, Englishman, we will again meet. May the kind gods of the earth and the sea and all the spirits of fair winds attend your voyage.'

MacPherson slammed shut the bottom drawer of his desk, turned the key and then wiped whisky off his lips with the back of his hand. The Chinese clerk knocked on the door of his office and entered.

'We have had a messenger from the quay,' he announced. 'Dr. Gunn is already ashore.'

'He made no signal of his intention to land?'

'No, tuan.'

'Is he alone?'

'Entirely. And walking briskly.'

'Is he now?' said MacPherson. 'Go back to your stool and say nothing. Express no surpise as Dr. Gunn enters, and do not inquire after his health. Such inquiries are rarely welcomed by the seriously ill, only by those who suffer from imagined ailments. Where is Mr. Murgatroyd?'

'Out, tuan. He is seeing a merchant about a cargo of sago. He should be back within the hour.'

MacPherson nodded. As soon as the man had left the room he unlocked his drawer and took half a dozen more swallows of the neat whisky. As its fire exploded in his blood, and he closed the drawer, Gunn came into the room.

'How are you today?' MacPherson asked him, as though it was the most natural thing in the world for him to be there, although they had not seen each other for the weeks in which *Hesperides* had lain, anchored fore and aft like a barge, in the mouth of the bay.

'I am extremely fit,' said Gunn cheerfully. 'Almost in rude health, as our novelists would say.'

'Do you mean that, doctor? You were far from well when we met last. You even thought then that your condition could be mortal.'

'That is true. But I have literally been brought back from the edge of the grave by an ancient Chinese medical treatment known as acupuncture. Two of their physicians dug golden needles into my body, and I was cured. That treatment may sound absurd, standing here in this office, but it is exactly what happened. And I venture that my present state of health is the best possible proof of its efficacy.'

'So it would seem, although for a doctor with a Scottish qualification to speak highly of treatment by Chinese wielding golden needles would no doubt surprise some of your former medical professors at St. Andrews. However, I see what I see. And I see a healthy man, although I personally maintain that the best medicine for any disease from which *I* have ever suffered is contained in a bottle of pure malt. Not by the spoon twice a day before meals, but by the mouthful through each of the twenty-four.'

'You have a short memory,' Gunn retorted. 'When we first met, you were concerned that you might have the pox and I treated you. But not with whisky.'

'Aye, so you did. But it was not pox either, doctor, and if you think it was, your memory is also short as a Chinaman's arse. It was just flux from which I suffered. And, while your physic cured me, for which I am grateful, whisky played a noble part in rehabilitating me, I'll have you know.'

'Well, come into my office, MacPherson. I want you to be by me when I see this clerk Murgatroyd.'

'Murgatroyd is not here. He is out interviewing a merchant about a cargo.'

'Then pray have him sent in to me directly he returns.'

MacPherson followed Gunn across the corridor, under the

creaking tapestry punkah, and watched him turn the polished brass handle of his office door. His office was locked.

'Fetch the key,' Gunn called to an Indian peon, sitting on the bench outside the room, ready to run errands.

'*Ata*, sahib,' replied the man, and ran off to the main office. He returned with the Chinese clerk who had warned MacPherson of Gunn's approach.

'We have no second key, tuan,' he explained.

'Then fetch a locksmith forthwith to unlock the door, and instruct him to make a new set of keys.'

The clerk looked beseechingly at MacPherson, who deliberately studied the plaster carvings of fruit and flowers on the ceiling, and so did not need to meet his eyes.

'What's the matter?' Gunn asked, glancing from one to the other. 'I can give you an address of a locksmith myself, if you do not know of one.'

'Oh, I know the address, tuan,' the clerk admitted quickly. 'It is just ...'

'Just what, my man? Speak up.'

'Well, tuan, Mr. Murgatroyd keeps the only key to that office,' said the clerk. 'He is using it.'

'That is my office, and whatever Mr. Murgatroyd was doing in it, he will have to do elsewhere in some place of his own choosing. But why bother with a locksmith when we have our shoulders and our feet? Break the door down, and then fetch the smith.'

'Mr. Murgatroyd would dismiss me, tuan, if I did that. He has already given notice to four of my superiors in the counting house. And they were English-born.'

'Then I will have to see about that, too, if you will give me their names. English-Scots-Chinese-born, we are all employed according to our abilities, not our nationalities or the colour of our faces, in my firm. Now, your shoulder, if you please.'

'Very good, tuan.'

The clerk pressed his thin bony shoulder half-heartedly against a panel.

'Here, out of the way,' said Gunn in exasperation, and barged the door with all the force of his six foot three inches. For a moment the door held firm, but on the second blow it burst open with a crash of splintering wood. Gunn looked over his shoulder before he went into the room. Every doorway along the corridor framed frightened faces brown, yellow, white – all watching his action with horrified fascination.

'Back to your work!' he called to them cheerfully.

'Now, you,' he said to the clerk.

'Tuan?'

'After that locksmith, and have this door repaired.'

He paused, looking round the room, once so familiar and now unfamiliar. His desk was not where he liked it, back to the wide bay window overlooking the sea, so that he would not be tempted to watch the ships instead of concentrating on his work.

The two prints of Herne Bay had also been taken down and stood, backs outwards, against the wall. He crossed to a bureau, opened a drawer, fingered through some of the contracts written on oiled parchment, and sniffed at the mustiness in the room. It smelt of cloves and camphor, of caution and carefulness, attitudes as anathematic to him as the lack of fresh air. He opened the window wide, and all the cheerful noise and chatter of the crowds in the Praya below rushed into the great room. Gunn motioned to MacPherson, and together they manhandled the desk back to its original position. Gunn sat down behind it and indicated MacPherson to take another chair.

'What are you going to do when Murgatroyd returns?' MacPherson asked him.

'Demand to see that letter, and then inform him that it is a forgery.'

'You may have to prove that in law.'

'Then I will do so. But I hardly think that such a course will be necessary. The law out here is generally a last refuge for scoundrels.'

'If you and I had ever been given such a letter – and such a chance – we would have fought for it through every court in this country and our own.'

'Possibly. But if Murgatroyd were like you or me he would

266

not still be a clerk at his age. Maybe he acted in good faith, and let us assume that he did. Then, in good faith, he can be persuaded that the letter is a forgery. Where I take strong issue with him is over the harsh way in which he has misused authority by dismissing older employees, by seeking your resignation, by changing contracts, and attempting to alter Mandarin-Gold's whole pattern of business.'

Gunn leaned back in his leather chair, drumming his fingers on the red top of the desk so that its two brass oil lamps rattled in their green glass shades. MacPherson stared uneasily out of the window.

'I do not know what the law is about this,' he said, the whisky in his blood suddenly counselling caution.

'I do not give a damn what the law is,' retorted Gunn. 'This is my firm, in that I hold the controlling shares. I started it with you, and until you and I declare otherwise, it will continue in the same fashion.'

'But you have apparently declared otherwise when you were ill. You *must* have written that letter. It was witnessed by attorneys.'

'I have never written a letter to any woman in my life, except to my mother. That has always been a cardinal rule in my philosophy, and it still remains one. I have been a victim of some kind of treachery. As for attorneys witnessing it, you and I know lawyers here and in Hong Kong who will put their names to anything so long as the man unfortunate enough to employ them will put *his* name to a large enough bank cheque in their favour.

'I hope for Murgatroyd's sake that he is innocent. After all, I have stayed in his house as a guest; I have dined at his table. I would not like to learn that he is a man of duplicity, and that he forced me to return past hospitality with harshness.'

The clerk knocked at the already open door and came in hesitantly.

'Mr. Murgatroyd is arriving, tuan.'

'So I should hope. But what about the locksmith?'

'But the door is already open, tuan?'

'Do not let me see you here again unless you bring that lock-smith.'

'Very good, tuan.'

The man melted away, the flap of his footsteps decreasing down the polished blue and white tiles of the corridor. Gunn heard the sound of excited breathing from many clerks as they peered in anticipation from office doors. He winked at Mac-Pherson. He enjoyed this sort of situation, just as he had enjoyed the climb from obscurity to power. He thought it was a strange commentary on other men's ambitions that so many, like the fascinated clerks along the corridor, could find sufficient satisfaction in watching other men like him take risks, perhaps even secretly wishing they would fail, but content to live their own lives at second hand, watching the world through a window.

Murgatroyd came along the corridor and saw their heads and wondered why they were not working. Really, he must speak sharply to them, most sharply indeed. He paused at the open door of Gunn's office.

'What is the matter with this door?' he called to the nearest clerk. 'Why has it been broken?' The man did not answer, but simply stared at him, swallowing slowly, as though mesmerized by the question and the man who had asked it – and the man inside the room who could best give the answer.

'I will tell you,' said Gunn quietly. 'I kicked it open.'

'Dr. Gunn!' Murgatroyd's voice was shrill with surprise. Gunn selected a cheroot from the box he kept in the right hand drawer, lit it, put his feet up on the desk, and flicked the lucifer over his shoulder.

'That is correct, Murgatroyd. And in fine health and good spirits. I understand you have a letter you wish to show me?'

'It is not my wish to show it to you,' replied Murgatroyd sharply, 'but I am prepared to do so. Mr. MacPherson has no doubt informed you that I am now in charge of this company, by reason of Mrs. Oxford's letter of authority, following your assignment to her of your controlling interest.'

'I have heard some nonsense of that kind,' agreed Gunn. 'But

I never put much weight on rumour. Pray let me see the letters, so that I may read these most interesting and valuable documents and form my own judgment on the matter.'

Murgatroyd crossed to the maroon safe which stood on a low-legged black lacquered table. He selected a key from his chain, and opened the door. Then he took out the letters and placed them on Gunn's desk. Gunn read them both in silence, and looked up at him.

'Are you not afraid I will tear them up?' he asked.

'It does not matter if you do. I have, of course, had them witnessed by attorneys as Mr. MacPherson has possibly told you, and I keep the copies in the safe.'

He took back the letter, replaced it in the safe, locked the door, and turned to face Gunn across the desk.

'Attorneys,' said Gunn easily, 'are tongues to be bought. Like dogs, they will bay for any man who feeds them with a fee.'

'I have in the past heard it voiced that you disliked legal brethren of the robe, and no doubt at some future time we discuss such matters agreeably either in your house or mine,' replied Murgatroyd. 'In the meantime, doctor, as representative of the controlling shareholder in this company, I have important work that demands my attention. I would therefore ask you to vacate my chair and my office.'

'I represent no-one, but then I do not need to, since I *am* the controlling shareholder. And you do not represent me, either,' said Gunn quietly, drawing on his cheroot.

'What puzzles me is how you, as a man of affairs, could ever seriously imagine that I would write a letter to Mrs. Oxford, making over to her everything I had built up in my working life.

'If you had come to me, Murgatroyd, when I first returned here two weeks ago, and told me that you had received this strange communication from her, and had acted on it with honesty and integrity, astonishing as its contents must have appeared to you, I would have accepted this explanation. But you made no attempt to visit me aboard my clipper, although you knew I was there. I am, therefore, driven to the reluctant but inescapable conclusion that either through personal vanity or duplicity or even some personal involvement with this woman Oxford, you have conspired to overthrow me because you believed I was dying, and too ill to fight back.

'The dead command no attorney, Murgatroyd. You calculated that even if I were not quite dead, I was as nearly in the grave as made no difference. You were right. I was too ill to care greatly about business matters. But even grave maladies bow to cures, and against all expectation, I was cured.'

'I am pleased to see you restored to health, doctor, but that does not alter the situation in any way,' said Murgatroyd. 'I have this letter to Mrs. Oxford, which you signed. I have shown it to various people in this city who recognized your signature – attorneys, clerks in counting houses, bankers and merchants who have frequently seen your autograph on other documents. And I have Mrs. Oxford's authority to act on her behalf since she now controls this company.'

'I tell you categorically, Murgatroyd, that the letter to her is a forgery. But since you choose to dispute this by claiming that others know my signature better than I know it myself, I will simply destroy the letter.'

'The copies will stay in the safe, until I decide to remove them.'

'All the copies?'

'Yes. There are three.'

'Then we will open the safe,' said Gunn, and punched a brass bell at the side of his desk. The Chinese clerk instantly appeared at the doorway, a task that presented no difficulties for him, since he had been eavesdropping behind the door, wondering who would win the argument, for his own future could depend on the outcome.

'How much do I pay you a week?' Gunn asked him.

'Ten rupees, tuan.'

Gunn nodded. It was roughly what he had expected; the equivalent of fifteen shillings.

'I think you are due for promotion,' he said. 'You have the air of a keen and alert and ambitious man of figures. I will give you one hundred rupees now.' He opened his wallet and threw the note on the desk in front of the clerk. 'Order in sufficient coolies to remove that safe.'

'No-one who touches that safe will ever work for me again,' said Murgatroyd furiously.

'Since you have never worked for Mr. Murgatroyd, that threat or promise should present no particular hardship,' remarked Gunn. 'Now fetch those coolies and look lively.'

The man nodded.

'Very good, tuan.'

He returned within minutes leading six Madrassi coolies wearing loin-cloths, turbans in the Mandarin-Gold colours of red and black and huge brass numbered discs around their necks. They were chewing betel-nut; its juice reddened their lips like life-blood.

The clerk spoke to them quickly in their own tongue, and four immediately bent bare black shoulders to the safe. The other two pushed bamboos beneath the metal base and as it was slowly raised, they all moved to the door, calling words of admonition and advice to each other, to make plain to the sahibs how adept they were at moving such a heavy load. The strange procession left the room, and padded barefoot down the corridor, lurching from side to side, but never quite losing control of their burden.

'Where do you want it taken?' MacPherson asked Gunn.

'Out to *Hesperides*. What do you think I was going to do with it? Dump it in the sea?'

The clerk went out to direct the coolies to the quay, and Gunn drew thoughtfully on his cheroot.

'If you want to play attorneys, Murgatroyd,' he said, 'you could do so in Singapore, where all this seems to have started. There you could also look to your patron lady, Mrs. Oxford, for the matter of putting you in funds. Lawyers are like leeches when it comes to fees. You will discover that they are never satisfied.'

'I acted in good faith,' said Murgatroyd sullenly. 'Mrs. Oxford introduced herself as an intimate friend of yours. Knowing that you were seriously ill, I had no reason to disbelieve her. I stand by your letter to her and hers to me. And I warn you, doctor, I will fight you all the way through the courts.'

'That may be a long and expensive journey. If I were in your position I would think again.'

'You are not me.'

Even as Murgatroyd uttered the words, he could have bit them back, because he knew that had Gunn been in his position, he would have somehow managed to manoeuvre the situation, however unfavourable it might initially appear, to his own ultimate advantage. That was one reason why Gunn sat behind the desk and Murgatroyd stood in front of it.

Murgatroyd sagged visibly, his bright hopes already crumbling around him like one of the hot-air balloons the Portuguese sent up from the Praya on saints' days. Mrs. Oxford's story had sounded so plausible that he had eagerly welcomed her suggestion and accepted the letter as valid. Also he had wanted to, because for the first time in his working life he felt he was being properly appreciated and valued at his true worth. This had been his opportunity to grow rich, like Gunn and MacPherson. It had seemed so easy, so straightforward. But nothing that brought great rewards was ever really simple or undemanding, whatever outward appearances might suggest. Now he thought uneasily of his wife in their lonely bungalow on the edge of the mangrove swamp outside Singapore; their child fractious in the heat, and the possibility, at which his wife had only cautiously hinted before he sailed for Macao, that a second baby might also be expected.

Murgatroyd's whole future would depend now on whether a court of law believed his story or Gunn's; and on his small salary, how could he conceivably hope to engage advocates eloquent enough to plead his case successfully? Slowly, he looked from Gunn to MacPherson. Their eyes met his, and he saw hostility and contempt in their gaze. He turned silently and walked out of the room, down the corridor, past the clerks who did not now bother to conceal their amusement at his discomfiture.

He had been one of their number, and he had tried to better himself; he had dismissed older men and insulted former colleagues, and after all that, he had still failed to gain power. The dead, as Gunn had reminded him, had no attorney; now Murgatroyd realized bitterly how few are the friends that failure can command.

MacPherson poured out two glasses of The Glenlivet, and handed one to Gunn.

'To your continued health, doctor,' he said cheerfully. 'And to the increased prosperity of our company. Bad cess to our enemies.'

'To you, old friend,' said Gunn. 'I have no doubts that the two first wishes will be realized. But let us not admit to any enemies. Rather let us attempt to convert them to our view and so claim them as friends.'

'Do you include Murgatroyd in that category of missionary endeavour?'

'I include everyone. He is not an enemy, simply a small person who aspired to greater things. Like the frog in the fable who took deep breaths to try and make himself grow as big as a bull.'

'Aye. And he blew himself up by so doing.'

'I hope that nothing so dramatic and final happens to Murgatroyd.'

'I do not agree, doctor. I started the morning as his employee, beholden to a man half my age, whom I despised – because he despised me. I had given up all hope of you returning in good health, for the last time we met, you were seemingly at the point of death, a ghost of the Gunn I knew.

'You were indeed so damned ill, I wager you did not even feel able to face this pipsqueak Murgatroyd, but merely crawled back to your vessel, as I thought, to die. Then, damn my hide, a couple of Chinese joss-men stick you all over with bamboo needles like a bloody porcupine, and you come bouncing back and show young Murgatroyd who's boss. Now, what are you going to do with him – not try to claim him as a friend surely? Not after what he has done?'

'In fact, MacPherson, he has done nothing. He failed

abjectly in what he tried to do. A year ago,' agreed Gunn, 'I would have ruined him. I could not afford to have a rival or even a weak enemy, because a weak enemy can grow strong, or ally himself to another man of strength. I would have made certain that he never worked again for any other firm in the East. But that was a year ago. When I first returned here, I did not greatly care about the letters, or what he had done or wished to do. I was simply too ill. Believe me, life's greatest problems seem as a spoonful of sand when weighed in the fearful balance against eternity.'

'I am not talking of last year or last week. I am talking about *now*. What are you going to do with him now?'

'Nothing,' replied Gunn. 'Nothing at all. I will dismiss him, as much for his own good as for ours. Having discharged so many older clerks and behaved so abominably when he thought he controlled our firm, his life would be made exceedingly miserable at the hands of his colleagues if he remained in our employ.

'As for myself attempting to punish him, no! I will not do that. The sultan's widow mentioned to me her view of punishing those who had fought against her. She would leave that to others. As she said, the sword of heaven is in no haste to smite. But equally it never leaves a debt unpaid.'

'But you will re-engage all these clerks?'

'Of course.'

'Do you think Murgatroyd will sue you about that letter? I'll wager he has kept another copy in his quarters, or some sly attorney has made one for him.'

'He may attempt some legal manoeuvres, and he is welcome to do as he wishes. The person behind this causes me more concern.'

'Mrs. Oxford, whoever she is?'

'Yes. The former wife of Sir Richard Bankhausen. The specialist I consulted in London. And I am the reason she is his former wife. We had an association, which her husband discovered. No doubt this was not the first she had enjoyed, but so far as he was concerned, it was the last. I will make amends to her, so far as I can.'

'But she tried to seize the company! Are you going to let her get away with that kind of roguery – and still pretend she is a friend?'

'You and I have got away with much worse in our time, have we not?' Gunn reminded him gently. 'And she did not succeed in her ploy, which is most salutary. I will visit her on my return to Singapore, and see that she has sufficient to live on. She has been punished enough.'

'I think your recovery has weakened your resolve. This is surely not the hard Robert Gunn who persuaded me, against all my Scottish judgment, to seize the Parsee's ship and then his trade?'

'You may be right, MacPherson. But have no doubt that as my strength increases, my resolve will also return in full. Mercy rarely lies in the gift of the weak, only the strong.'

'Mercy is a very fine quality, but does this woman deserve it? She tried to swindle you out of a fortune, doctor. Out of vessels on every sea, and buildings, docks, warehouses, godowns – here and in Hong Kong and Singapore – and you are to let her go and give her funds. You're bloody mad. You need golden needles in your brain, not in your body.'

'We have pushed mud and given bribes and broken those who stood against us in our time,' Gunn replied. 'She was desperate and I was dying. And if I had died, it would not have mattered a damn to me, would it?'

'It would have mattered to me.'

'Possibly. But you view things differently when you stand on the edge of your own grave. Matters that seemed highly important before, suddenly become extremely unimportant. Agreed, I might extract some crude satisfaction by destroying both Murgatroyd and this woman. But in Borneo, the sultan's widow told me one of Buddha's sayings that seems apt in this situation. Buddha declared that if by abandoning a small pleasure one sees the possibility of a great pleasure, "let a wise man leave the small pleasure and look to the great . . . He who wishes to obtain pleasure for himself by causing pain to others will become entangled in the bonds of hatred and will never be free." '

'Fine words, doctor,' said MacPherson caustically, pouring out a third glass for himself. 'Though I personally have never attached much weight to native gods and idols or their sayings. The Shorter Catechism was always good enough for me when I was young. Well, it is your affair – I nearly said, your *funeral*!'

He started to roar with laughter, slapping his thigh at the incongruity of the remark.

'Now, where will Murgatroyd find employment?'

'He has a wife in Singapore, and a house, which I understand belongs to the company. I shall not put them out on the street. There are always clerking jobs for Europeans to find – if they search hard enough.'

'How long are you staying with us in Macao?'

'I must return to Borneo shortly. I have some unfinished business to transact.'

' 'Tis a terrible place, man,' said MacPherson, his face wrinkling with distaste. 'Those headhunters will cut off your head as soon as look at you.'

'You could say that about us, too, the way we have sometimes conducted our business dealings,' replied Gunn. 'I certainly found them friendly enough. But I will come back here. I have plans to discuss with you for advancing our enterprise, for establishing offices farther west. For example, we only maintain agencies in Calcutta and Bombay. Why not establish full branches there – giving the managers autonomy to occupy themselves with any local trading they feel may be lucrative? And what about engaging in trade along the coast of Africa? That is a huge, new, almost entirely undeveloped continent.'

'If there is any local business worth looking at there, I would instantly agree.'

'There is business everywhere,' said Gunn, 'if you only search hard enough.'

'I am getting too old to search,' replied MacPherson. 'I am content with what I already have. My Chinese woman, my house here, another up the coast, money in half a dozen banks.'

'Now that is another area into which we could move with positive advantage. Why not start our own bank? Then when a client repays a loan, interest has doubled your principle. If he does not repay on time, you seize his assets for a fraction of their worth. The risks are minimal and the profits maximal. Why should we leave these riches for others to collect?'

MacPherson said nothing, but poured himself another whisky. Dr. Gunn had made a remarkable recovery. Why, he seemed even more full of ideas than he had been before his illness.

CHAPTER THIRTEEN

HOFMEYER walked slowly along the Praya Grande, reading the names and ports of registration painted on the sterns of the vessels that lay at anchor. He saw clippers from California, opium runners from Calcutta, merchantmen from Tilbury, and Chinese junks painted with eyes and their names written in indecipherable characters; but not a single Dutch vessel in all the line.

He turned away, disappointed. He would have to wait until one arrived, but that might not be for hours or for weeks, and already he had waited longer than he had wished to make his report to the Dutch Governor in Java. Resentment at the way he and the others had been outwitted in Borneo still smouldered like a slow, dangerous fuse inside him. He would get even with those accursed British who had sunk their ship and ruined their plans; if he waited all his life, he would have his revenge on them.

Captain Blackman had landed him and the *Orlando*'s officers and crew earlier that morning, and then had sailed on to a Royal Navy anchorage out in the bay. Hofmeyer's companions were in a chop house in one of the steep cobbled alleys near the shore, drinking rice wine and eating a native meal of prawns and turtle steaks.

Macao at first glance seemed a fine and prosperous city, and no place for Europeans with so little money they could not afford the price of a Portuguese whore. They could survive for a few days, sleeping rough in doorways, perhaps begging from any rich merchant generous enough to give them alms. But unless a Dutch vessel arrived swiftly, they would soon have to resort to stealing to keep alive.

Hofmeyer stood to one side to let six coolies run past him,

their dark bodies glistening like seals with sweat. On their shoulders, braced by two thick bamboo poles, they carried an office safe, painted maroon with a gold line and fancy lettering on the door. The sight seemed so incongruous that he stopped and stared. He read the words, Mandarin-Gold, and repeated them to himself. He had heard them before somewhere, surely? Then he remembered. This was Gunn's company; this was the firm of the man who had led the Dyaks to victory against them in Kei. As he stood, he heard English voices, and quickly walked up two steps into a porched doorway, and pretended to be examining the list of occupants of the building painted on a panel of the door. He glanced carefully over his shoulder and saw a man, middle-aged and with a red florid face, gesticulating and speaking English in a strange accent. Behind him came two other Englishmen in stove-pipe hats and long black coats so grotesque in the heat, and in the middle he saw Gunn. Hofmeyer had last seen him in the jungle, from a distance and through a glass, and now his stomach tightened and his arm muscles stiffened with animal hatred for an enemy. Close to, Gunn seemed infinitely more relaxed, younger, almost jaunty, than he had appeared in Borneo. But then he had been at war, and wary. Now, he was at peace, never suspecting that a mortal enemy stood less than a yard from him.

The florid man was saying: 'That poor devil Murgatroyd. Somehow, I can't help feeling sorry for him now. Maybe you are right in being merciful.'

'I should imagine he is also feeling sorry for himself.'

'Now, if I were in his shoes, I would feel more inclined to get my own back in some way . . .'

They walked on out of earshot. Hofmeyer came down the steps and walked slowly in the opposite direction, anxious to put as much distance between them as possible. Three hundred yards up the road, beyond a row of stalls piled high with sugary sweetmeats, swarming with flies, with melons split open and paw-paws incongruously red inside against green outer skins, he paused near a grander building. This was obviously the house of a merchant of the richest kind, a *taipan*, and he stood looking up at it admiringly, comparing the wealth it represented with his own wretched predicament. Ornate metal railings on the balconies gleamed with new black paint; the door was freshly lacquered in deep blue. A brass knocker in the shape of a dolphin glowed like molten gold, and beneath its glittering snout was a small brass plate, also highly polished, bearing two words engraved in the metal: Mandarin-Gold.

So this must be Gunn's headquarters. This was the heart of the huge business he had built up, which, so Captain Blackman had told him, had provided him with the two essentials that Van Vooren craved for himself, power and money, and which had almost been his before Gunn had torn them from his grasp.

Hofmeyer stood, fascinated by the sight of the house, and consumed and corroded with envy. This was his enemy's lair, this the castle he had built, the nub of his power; and he hated him with an intensity that made his body tremble as though gripped by a high fever. Gunn had prevailed, had lived to grow even richer, no doubt, while half of Hofmeyer's contingent were dead and the rest shared his defeat, waiting about the docks like paupers, happy to beg a lift to Java in any craft, while Gunn commanded clippers on every sea.

Hofmeyer climbed the steps without realizing why, only that he felt he had somehow been guided here, that he had seen Gunn in the street only because a merciful Providence must be offering him a chance of revenge.

The entrance hall was high-ceilinged, with pink marble pillars and a tiled floor of great black and white squares like a gigantic chequerboard. A turbaned Sikh wearing a red jacket edged with gilt, huge polished brass buttons and a belt with a buckle in the shape of the letters M-G, saluted him. As Hofmeyer returned his salute, he realized why, all unknowing, his feet had brought him to this house in preference to all others. And in that same moment he knew what he had to do. An idea had developed in his mind; he would go forward and translate the thought to action.

A Chinese clerk, sitting behind a wide desk to the left of the door, looked up inquiringly, not very impressed by Hofmeyer's appearance, his shabby clothes, his face raw and red from sun and sea winds aboard the *Aeneas*.

'I wish to speak to Mr. Murgatroyd,' Hofmeyer informed him.

'You have an appointment, tuan?'

'No. I am the representative of a Dutch consortium. I have been at sea for some time, and only made port this morning.'

'I am sorry to have to tell you, tuan, that Mr. Murgatroyd has just now left the building.'

Hofmeyer frowned; he had not expected this. 'It is very important – to your company – that I see him. I have letters and special credentials for which he has been waiting. Is he likely to return shortly?'

'I could not say, tuan.'

Hofmeyer paused, biting his lower lip. He had never heard of Murgatroyd until a few minutes previously, but now he must see him to discover whether he could use him for his plan. He experienced the same feeling of depression when he doubted Van Vooren's ability to negotiate with the sultan's widow. He had not been wrong then, and he was not wrong now. When you had nothing else to follow, you followed your own star, the lodestone of natural intuition, the animal sense that told you which move could be profitable and which could be dangerous.

'I could give you his home address, tuan – his lodgings – if that would be of any assistance?'

'I would be much in your debt if you would do that,' Hofmeyer assured him. The clerk dipped his quill in a silver inkwell decorated with the Mandarin-Gold monogram and wrote swiftly on a sheet of blank paper. Hofmeyer took it, read the address and bowed his thanks. Then he walked through the cool hall, down the wide white steps, back into the baking heat of noon.

He found the lodging house by asking his way through a variety of quaintly named streets – The Road of the Twelve Stations of the Cross, Avenue Vasco de Gama and Stinking Dog Alley – all so narrow they were more like spaces between houses than proper thoroughfares. The walls of the lodging houses were scabby with peeling stucco. Blue shutters had been fastened tightly over narrow windows, and he beat imperiously on the door, noting the peculiar Portuguese knocker in the shape of a clenched fist. That seemed symbolic; his clenched fist would soon smash the dreams of this Dr. Gunn.

A half-caste Portuguese woman with a baby at her right breast rattled a chain in a bolt and opened the door a few inches.

'Mr. Murgatroyd,' said Hofmeyer.

The woman opened the door fully and beckoned him inside. The hall floor was covered with uneven, greasy tiles; a green cockatoo fluttered madly in a cage of bamboo slivers. She pointed upstairs, and made an animal noise in her throat, a strange, horrible choking sound. Hofmeyer realized she was dumb. He walked up the stone steps, black with trodden food droppings, taking care not to touch the damp and stinking walls. It was twilight behind the shutters, and he beat hastily on the door. This was no place to linger. A man's voice called out in English; a disappointed voice on the defensive.

'Who is that?'

'A friend,' replied Hofmeyer, watching beetles scurry like polished chips of coal across the floor. 'I wish to speak with Mr. Murgatroyd.'

The squeak of a rusty lock, and the door was opened. A pale-eyed, sandy-haired man looked at him warily.

'Who are you?'

'My name is Hofmeyer. I am a Dutchman, briefly here. I seek an interview with Mr. Murgatroyd.'

'I am Mr. Murgatroyd. What is it you wish to discuss?'

'I cannot speak my business in doorways,' said Hofmeyer urgently.

'Well, come in.'

Murgatroyd opened the door and locked it behind him, and then leaned against it. The room was small; an unmade bed in one corner, a dressing table with two horn-backed brushes and some folded copies of *The Macao Times*. A wash bowl, still full of soapy water, stood on a bamboo stand.

'Not much of a place,' admitted Murgatroyd, guessing Hofmeyer's thoughts from the expression on his face. 'I have been lodging here for a week or two, until I selected more salubrious quarters.'

'But you are not taking them now?' asked Hofmeyer.

'No,' said Murgatroyd, and his face tightened briefly at the thought of all he had lost. 'Not now. There has been a change. A change of plans.'

'I have a proposition that might interest you,' said Hofmeyer softly. 'It might even mean another – perhaps more felicitous – change of plans. I have close connections with certain powerful members of local mercantile communities representing Holland, Portugal and even your own country.'

'What brings you now to see me?'

Hofmeyer paused. It was all so simple; the wheel of fortune was turning, and he was moving up again.

'I have received intelligence that some members of these communities consider you may have been dealt an unjust blow at the hand of fate,' he said gravely. 'Or, shall I be more specific and say you have suffered this outrage at the hand of one Dr. Gunn? Pray, before I continue, would I be correct, sir, in this basic assumption?'

'If you have heard that, Mr. Hofmeyer, your intelligence system is extremely quick, and as accurate as it is speedy. Please speak on.'

'It is as I thought,' said Hofmeyer with satisfaction. 'But before I elaborate my proposition, which I make bold to hope will meet with your approval, please inform me of the circumstances concerning this cruel blow you have received at Dr. Gunn's hand. I will recount a similar misfortune which I have recently suffered through the activities of that gentleman. And then I will explain how we could both not only ameliorate the effects of his behaviour, but turn his crude hostility to our mutual and lasting advantage.'

The spy came into the Chinese widow's longhouse, bowed, and waited until she turned to face him.

'Well?' she asked.

'The acupuncturists have returned, exalted one,' he told her.

'What success do they report?'

'It would seem considerable, exalted one, but they await your pleasure to explain to you personally what happened.'

'We will see them at once.'

The spy turned and clapped his hands twice. The two Chinese physicians entered the long room, and bowed to the widow.

'Speak,' she commanded them. 'And tell me all that transpired, leaving out nothing.'

The elder one cleared his throat nervously.

'We found the English vessel lying off Macao, exalted one, as it had been described. We hired a local boat from a Chinese waterman who took us out. We climbed aboard and presented ourselves to the Barbarian physician, Gunn.'

'What was he doing at that moment? What was the hour?'

'It was roughly pan yeh, midnight as the Barbarians measure the passage of time. He was lying on a bed on deck, alone. His ship's captain brought us into his presence, and he listened to us in a civil fashion. When we proposed that we should treat him, he offered no resistance. He did not view our approach to healing with the contempt some of his rough and red-bristled countrymen have elsewhere shown to our methods.'

'And then?'

'And then he removed his shirt and we administered our needles.'

'Your treatment was successful?'

'It was, exalted one. We remained with him for two weeks, to give him comfort, and to assure him that we had administered a lasting cure. To leave too soon might have sown the seeds of suspicion or alarm that we had done him some harm. We thought it best to wait.'

'He was still friendly towards you?'

'Most definitely so. He even offered us passage back here in his clipper. But we excused ourselves by explaining we wished to travel north.'

'So he will return here – and not as an invalid, a man resting on the way to Kinabalu – but as a man in strength?'

'He will, exalted one.'

'That is good, better than I could have wished for. It is written, "As a cowherd with his staff drives his cows into the stable, so do age and death drive the life of men." You have shown this good man a different road to march, a way to health, maybe to happiness. Rich indeed will be your reward.'

'We have done our duty, as the Barbarian physician did his,' the older man replied. 'That is our reward.'

The sea shimmered like a golden floor beneath the afternoon sun. Gunn lit a cheroot, and savoured the saltiness in the wind as the bows of *Hesperides* dipped slowly, and then rose and dipped again. The newly gilded breasts of the figurehead pointed west to Borneo. Three days hard sailing, all canvas high, and they would make landfall. Captain Fernandes stood on the bridge opposite him.

'It is good to have you so fit again, doctor. A tonic for every man in the crew. The best physic you have ever prescribed to any of us.'

'Thank you,' said Gunn. 'All the wealth in the treasure houses of the world are as nothing when weighed against health. I cannot express my gratitude at being brought back from the edge of the grave. And the experience has taught me something important, Captain Fernandes, which I offer also to you.'

'And what is that, sir?'

'To live every day as though we were going to die at dusk. Never to look forward to future enjoyments or deeds we may do tomorrow, because that dawn may never rise. Today is the most important day. Now is the most important word.'

'You speak as a philosopher, sir.'

'You do me too much honour. I speak like a physician who became a merchant, who nearly became a corpse.'

A cry echoed from the crow's nest high up the main mast above their heads.

'Ship ahoy! Starboard bow!'

Fernandes adjusted his glass.

'Who is she?' asked Gunn, wondering whether this might be one of his own vessels, northward bound.

'I cannot read her name, but she is a clipper, flying the British flag. And she seems to be becalmed.'

'There's enough wind to carry her,' said Gunn. 'What do you make of it?'

'I don't know, sir. Could be mutiny, but that is unlikely. Maybe they have sickness aboard, or maybe she is just changing course.'

'They would not do that in mid-ocean, surely?'

Fernandes shrugged. Sometimes, with a combination of heat and loneliness and too much alcohol, captains in tropic seas made the most unaccountable decisions. Or cargoes could shift and smoulder in the heat beneath battened hatches; ships turned in mid-ocean and momentarily lost the wind for an infinity of reasons.

The clipper grew larger. Shabby sails beat against the masts like slack drums. Her rudder stood firm, so someone was presumably still at the wheel, but the ship had an air of dereliction and decay. Her tarred sides were scummy with green weed; rope ends flapped uselessly from unvarnished spars. The British flag at the stern post was faded and almost threadbare, the sails patched and dirty.

'Pull alongside,' ordered Gunn. 'Maybe the crew have been overcome by some sudden fever, and we can give aid.'

'Ahoy!' shouted the boatswain. Gunn could read the ship's name: *Ethiope: Hong Kong*, painted in chipped white letters on her stern. A European appeared at the rail of the bridge. His face was dark with several days' beard, and his clothes from a distance seemed nondescript and shabby. He wore a naval hat crammed down over his eyes. He waved and shouted to them excitedly, but the wind blew away his words.

'What do you make of that, sir?' asked Fernandes.

'A problem of some kind. Put six men aboard with our compliments to their captain to discover whether we can help them in any way. This fellow is European, and presumably English, if he is sailing under the Jack.'

Gunn borrowed Fernandes' glass and focused it. There was something familiar about the man on the bridge, but who could he possibly know aboard a strange ship a hundred miles out at sea, becalmed on a burning day? He had met so many strangers whose lives had briefly crossed his in building up Mandarin-Gold, that it was impossible to remember all their names.

'Stand by to come alongside,' ordered the first officer

286

sharply. Half a dozen of *Hesperides'* crew waited along the port rail of the main deck, tarred ropes in their hands, ready to throw them across the swiftly narrowing gap of sea and then leap after them and make them fast on *Ethiope*'s deck. Thirty feet, twenty, fifteen. They could see now that on the unscrubbed decks, ropes lay like long, knotted serpents, not neatly coiled. Copper trim was green with verdigris, the brasswork cloudy and dull. Something was wrong here, and a warning drum beat in Gunn's mind. There was danger and death aboard this ship, but in what guise? Pestilence or mutiny – or something else altogether?

Ten feet. Eight. The crew bent their bodies like discus throwers, ready for the order.

'Let them go!' bellowed the mate.

Instantly the tarred ends of the ropes flickered through the air, like obedient serpents. Then, as the men prepared to jump on to the main deck of the *Ethiope*, it suddenly and amazingly swarmed with crew.

They leaped up from bales of canvas and the rough coils of rope that had concealed them, from behind masts and the wheelhouse. And as they jumped they seized bamboo poles, twenty, thirty, even forty feet long, which had been hidden down out of sight in the scuppers.

'Hard to starboard!' roared Captain Fernandes.

'Starboard it is, sir.'

The helmsman spun the polished spokes of the wheel. The *Hesperides* heeled over, sails booming like cannon above their heads, but the order came too late.

In perfect, unhurried precision, born of long practice, *Ethiope*'s crew swung their poles like lances, and Gunn saw with dismay that each pole had a hook at its far end, like a shepherd's crook. Now these hooks moved and twisted, and gripped the necks of his men, or delved under their armpits. A sharp tug, a push to knock them off balance, and then a fierce heave, and they were hauled over the rail before they had a chance to realize what was happening.

He heard a shout of agony as one man was crushed between the grinding hulls as the vessels collided. Others were already down in the water, screaming with the pain of dislocated necks and shoulders. Behind the men wielding these bamboo hooks stood a second line of dark-skinned men, swinging ropes around their heads like lariats. At a shout of command, they released their ropes and the sharpened, weighted hooks to which they were bound whistled through the air and dug deeply into *Hesperides'* wooden decks, or wound themselves around stanchions.

The two ships were locked together now. Sailors aboard *Hesperides* hacked desperately at the binding ropes with sea-axes, but as fast as they severed one rope, another whistled over their heads and a new hook buried itself into the woodwork. There was no escape, and even if they would release their vessel, this shabby clipper carried a vast expanse of sail, and might well have the edge on them in a chase. They would have to fight it out to the end with these pirates.

Gunn kicked open the locked door of the deck cupboard where he kept emergency weapons; three pistols already charged, a musket, and two swords. He flung one pistol and a sword to Fernandes, the second sword to the mate, and grabbed the other two pistols himself. Then he jumped from the edge of the bridge down on to the deck of the *Ethiope.*

A lascar came at him, brandishing a fighting knife, honed to a needle point. Gunn fired at a yard's range. The man's face disintegrated into a raw red mass of blood and pulp and he reeled away. Gunn jumped to one side, and using his empty pistol as a club, cracked the skull of a second pirate who jumped from the lower rigging with a cutlass between his teeth. The man rode the blow, and attacked Gunn, using the edges of his hands like hammers. Gunn kicked him in the crotch with the toe of his boot, and as the man folded, his mouth opening to choke out his cutlass, Gunn punched him with all his force in his Adam's apple. The pirate fell back, a froth of blood bubbling at his mouth. Another man jumped on Gunn's back, and swung him off balance. As Gunn fell, he fired his second pistol. The ball scored the deck uselessly, carving a smoking, reeking groove in the wooden planks. He threw away the gun and fought with his elbows, his hands, his knees. One hand clamped round the pirate's throat, he forced two fingers of his other hand into the man's nostrils, and flung his weight against him until the pirate's neck snapped and he collapsed.

Gunn leaped to his feet, seized the pirate's cutlass, and jumped towards the mast, anxious to have its protection at his back. Fernandes was fighting a pig-tailed Chinese sailor in the fo'c'sle and, as Gunn watched, *Hesperides'* first mate, on the foredeck, raised a musket and fired. The charge at such close range carried away one of the Chinaman's legs. The man spun like a top spraying blood, and then fell. He rolled over the side beneath the rail, and down into the sea.

The air crackled with shots like a firework display, as the two ships rocked uneasily on the swell, creaking and groaning like huge sea-beasts in pain as their hulls ground together and then spread apart at the short extent of the ropes.

A pirate crept round the side of the second mast, dagger in one hand, cudgel in the other. He was a half-cast wearing his long hair tied in a knot and brass ear-rings. Gunn saw him a second before the pirate realized he was there, and flicked the club from his hand with the tip of his cutlass. Then he pressed the blade at the man's throat until the skin tightened.

'You speak pidgin? Cantonese?'

'English,' gasped the man, almost choking beneath the blade. 'A little.'

'Drop your knife.'

His dagger clattered to the deck.

'Who are you? Malays? Chinese?'

The man did not answer. Gunn pressed the blade until it nicked the flesh; a thin spatter of blood dribbled down the man's chest.

'Speak,' Gunn ordered him. The man spoke.

'Mostly Malays. A few deserters from a British Navy frigate. And some Chinese.'

'How many altogether?'

'Thirty-five.'

As he spoke, he suddenly jerked his head backwards and swung his left leg in a vicious kick at Gunn's stomach. Gunn jumped sideways to avoid the full force of the blow. As he jumped, he brought down the cutlass across the man's knee. He screamed in giant, unbearable agony as the stropped blade bit through cotton trouser, through flesh, deep into pink bone. Gunn twisted the blade free. The man writhed soundlessly on the deck, unable to walk, or even to crawl, leaving a trail of blood as he moved.

Fernandes, behind Gunn, wrenched open one of the main hatches, flung down half a dozen fire-crackers and then slammed the lid shut. After the explosion, they heard faint screams through the thick teak deck planks, then long blubbering moans, and then there was silence as blue, acrid clouds of smoke billowed out from portholes. Resistance was failing now, and the crew of the *Hesperides* were laying about them with clubs and spiked boarding swords, and the butts of their muskets. Gunn seized one pirate by his pigtail and held his cutlass into the small of his back. The man flung up his hands and shouted something in a tongue Gunn did not understand. Other pirates held up their hands in surrender, letting pistols and knives clatter on to the deck.

'Who is captain?' Gunn asked in Cantonese.

A man taller than the rest heard the question and pushed the others aside.

'I am,' he said in the same language. He was half Malay, half Chinese, a burly swaggering fellow in sea boots, wearing loose silk trousers, a dirty silk shirt open at the throat, and brass-bound leather thongs on both wrists. A black skull cap was clapped on his thick dark hair.

'What was your object in attempting to seize my ship?' Gunn asked him. As he spoke he held out his left hand. Fernandes instantly placed a charged pistol in it. Gunn pointed the barrel at the captain's head an inch from his mouth.

'Speak or die.'

'I was given a promise,' the captain said sullenly.

'Of what?'

'A share in what your vessel carries.'

'We have no cargo,' Gunn told him. 'We carry nothing but victuals for our own sustenance.'

'You carry something else of greater value,' insisted the captain.

'I'll tell you what it is,' interrupted Fernandes. 'Your office safe. That is the only thing we took aboard at Macao, apart from food.'

'Yes, for something it contains. I had a firm promise . . .'

'Who gave you that promise?'

'Two men. One English, one Dutch.'

'Are they dead or alive?'

'They were with me on the bridge.'

Gunn turned to Captain Fernandes.

'Send up four men to bring down whoever they find. If they are armed, disarm them. But be careful not to kill them – yet.'

'Very good, sir.'

'As captain of a vessel engaged in piracy,' said Gunn, turning to the man, 'you will accept responsibility for this attack. There is only one punishment for piracy. Death.'

The captain clenched and unclenched his fists.

'I do not shirk responsibility. But I would ask one small request – that first you give me leave to say my prayers.'

'Your request is granted.'

The captain removed his round cap, and knelt down on the deck, and then slowly swivelled his body to face the sun. He raised his arms straight above his head and bowed, and then, muttering a prayer, brought forward both arms slowly and lowered his head between them. Gunn watched him, wondering at his thoughts, what it must be like to know that certain death lay only minutes away. He could imagine the fierce intensity of the pirate's feelings; he had come as close as he cared to the end of his own life.

'*Look out!*' yelled Captain Fernandes suddenly. Gunn jumped as the pirate's right leg shot backwards, kicking him off balance. The captain rolled over, seized Fernandes by the ankles, brought him down, and then was on his feet, racing for the bridge. The mate raised his musket, took careful aim, and fired. For a second, the pirate kept on running, as though he had not been hit. Then his arms shot out in a last beseeching gesture, and he collapsed on the deck. Gunn picked himself up, and helped Captain Fernandes to his feet.

'We should be more careful next time, captain,' he said gently.

'I agree. It is fatal to parley with such men.'

Captain Fernandes turned to the mate, who had already re-loaded his musket.

'Thank you for saving my life,' he said. 'Now put that body over the side.'

Four sailors heaved the corpse up to the rail, balanced it for a second, and then threw it down into the sea. The rest of the crew from the pirate ship stood, some with hands bound behind their backs, some barefoot, clothes torn, others lacking even shirts or hats against the beating, blinding sun. The crew of the *Hesperides* were already feeling in the pockets of the dead for coins and trinkets, ripping gold rings from ears, leather belts from their trousers.

'Shall I put them all over the side, sir?' asked Captain Fernandes. 'Sink or swim?'

'Wait,' said Gunn. 'They only obeyed orders.'

'That is no excuse for piracy.'

'I agree. But let us first discover who gave the promise that their captain accepted.'

Along the deck came two Europeans, clothes blackened with powder, shirts dark with sweat across their chests, faces unshaven and sunken with defeat.

Gunn recognized Murgatroyd. The other man was a stranger, standing head and shoulders taller than Murgatroyd, with blond hair and blue eyes and a proud bearing. Gunn addressed him first.

'You speak English?'

'I do.'

'Then who are you, sir, that you should persuade a captain to commit an act of piracy on a peaceful British vessel?'

'I am a Dutch subject.'

'What has that got to do with it?'

'Everything, Dr. Gunn.'

'How do you know my name?'

'Because I was in Borneo with several of my countrymen when you were leading the Dyaks. I learned your name then –

and also that you had designs on a province which the Governor of Java sought to persuade to join the Eastern Empire of the Netherlands.'

'So you were one of the leaders of those mercenaries? You tried to bully the widow of the ruler into accepting a suzerainty which would mean that she and her people became your country's slaves?'

'Not so, sir. She would enjoy all the other benefits that came from belonging to the empire of a European kingdom.'

Gunn turned to Murgatroyd.

'And you? What is your explanation for your presence here?'

Murgatroyd spread his hands wearily, as though words and explanations were all beyond him. And what did they matter now? He had gambled, and he had lost. He had stepped out of the safe anonymous ranks of security, and he had been cut down for his imprudence.

'Speak,' ordered Gunn sharply. 'What is your involvement with this Dutchman?'

'I was in my lodgings in Macao,' began Murgatroyd reluctantly, as though he was speaking about something that no longer concerned him, had never concerned him, 'This Dutchman Hofmeyer came to seek me out. He had somehow heard that I was in dispute with you over the control of Mandarin-Gold. I explained what had happened – I had no-one else to tell. I was grateful for a sympathetic ear.'

'And then?'

'And then he introduced me to the captain of the *Ethiope*, who your first mate has just murdered. I told him that certain papers which could change all our fortunes were in the safe aboard your ship.'

'I could have punished you in Macao for attempting to seize my company, but I gave you the benefit of every doubt. You rewarded that generous action by joining forces with common pirates to attack my vessel. As a result, several of my crew have been killed, and it is only by the grace of God and the strength of those around me, that we are all not dead with them.

'The penalty of piracy is death. Even so, I do not care to condemn a fellow countryman, however evil I may consider his actions, however craven his conduct, to death by drowning or by sharks. Yet a crime like yours cannot go unpunished.'

'What do you propose, then?' asked Murgatroyd. Could there be a glimmer of hope that he might not die here, that somehow he might be granted a pardon?

'I propose to put you in the charge of Captain Fernandes. He commands this vessel, and under English law the captain gives every order while at sea.

'As for you, sir,' he turned to Hofmeyer. 'I feel no constraint to mercy. You landed with soldiers of your own country and pirates owing allegiance to none, with the intention of seizing what you believed was virtually a defenceless province. Had you not believed this, then doubtless you would not have been so eager in attack. Unknown numbers died as a result of that warlike expedition. You then introduced my employee, Murgatroyd, to pirates so that he could attempt to seize this vessel *and* my trading company. There is but one punishment for you, sir. Death.'

'I have only acted as you and English robbers like you have acted for many years throughout the eastern hemisphere.'

'That may be so, or it may not,' replied Gunn. 'But when the attempts of English robbers have not been blessed with success, they have also faced the same supreme penalty. You played for the highest stakes. The loser in that game forfeits his life.'

'What about the rest of them?' Captain Fernandes asked him. 'It is the custom to put pirates over the side of the ship. If you treat them with mercy, they will only attack another innocent merchantman.'

'Then deal with them as you will,' said Gunn. It seemed a pity that Captain Blackman and his ship's company were not present to claim their reward.

Captain Fernandes walked slowly along the line of pirates. Some stared at him beseechingly; others with hostile, contemptuous eyes; a few natives, blissfully doped with *bhang*, looked dreamily over his shoulder at visions no undrugged man could imagine.

'You are to be punished according to the law of the high seas,' he told them, speaking in Malay. 'We will put you over the side, where you have a chance of survival. It will be sink or swim. If you can swim or simply keep afloat, you may be picked up by another ship, or carried by the currents to land. If you do survive, then no doubt the memory of this punishment will make you change your evil ways. If you do not, then may your heathen gods have mercy on you.'

He nodded to the first mate.

'Cut their ropes,' he ordered. Two sailors stepped forward and nicked the cords with their knives. The pirates thankfully massaged bruised, cut, numbed wrists. Ten of the crew had meanwhile fallen in behind them, cutlasses drawn, while others had dismantled a section of railing at the edge of the deck. The ocean lay thirty feet beneath. Gunn, glancing down at it, saw a floating shirt and some rags around what had been the pirate captain's body, and then two black triangular fins scored the surface of the sea, and were gone, and the sea was empty.

Captain Fernandes gave a quick nod to the sailors, who dug the tips of their blades sharply into the buttocks of the pirates, some to a depth of an inch or more. Some pirates stayed where they were, as though rooted to the deck, until blood streamed through their clothes, and the cutlasses finally forced them forward reluctantly. Others, who had not seen the sharks, jumped over the side readily, welcoming any escape from humiliating captivity, and the chance of freedom. They splashed into the sea and then surfaced, flailing the blue frothing water with their hands.

The watchers saw a flurry of huge, dark, glistening sharks gather around the swimmers, encircling them; then the white undersides of the sharks, mouths open to display serried rows of white teeth, sharp as saw blades.

They heard screams and shouts of terror and pain, and then the water bubbled and boiled and turned pink as men and man-eaters threshed in a frenzy. Gradually the turmoil ceased, and the water was blue once more, and calm as though its peace had never been disturbed.

Fernandes turned to the two Europeans. Their faces were grey with horror, shining with the sweat of terror at what they had seen and heard.

'As the instigators of this attempt at piracy, you should expect no more clemency than your crew. But I will give you both a greater chance of survival. You are not heathen. You may yet live and learn from your misdeeds.'

He turned to the first mate.

'Fetch me a coil of half-inch manilla rope twenty fathoms long,' he told him. 'We will keel-haul these two.'

'No!' cried Murgatroyd hoarsely. 'No! I beg of you. *Anything* but that.'

'You have no choice of punishment, Murgatroyd. But you will have some chance of survival.'

Two sailors carried up a coil of new rope, cut the cords that bound it and lowered the rope in a huge loop over the bows. Each man took one end and slowly they walked back amidships, pulling it and letting it go, until the rope ran smoothly beneath the clipper's keel, from starboard to port.

'You will go first,' Fernandes told Hofmeyer. 'As the leader, that is your prerogative.'

Two other sailors tied one end of the rope tightly round Hofmeyer's waist, while a third ripped off his shirt. His pale body glistened with sweat as though it had been varnished. He turned to Murgatroyd and then looked at Gunn, as though half expecting a change of orders, a reprieve. Surely no white man could do this to a fellow Christian? Gunn looked back at him stonily. Hofmeyer spat on the deck.

'You English bastard,' he said bitterly. 'May you rot and burn in hell for ever.'

The mate and the boatswain each took an arm and propelled him to the edge of the deck. Then they flung him forward. He landed heavily in the water, sending up a great gout of foam. Before he had time to surface, half a dozen sailors on the far side of the deck gripped the rope, and pulled steadily, passing it damp and dripping through their hands, coiling it neatly behind them. Suddenly, they slackened their efforts. Hofmeyer's body came up. They drew it up and stretched it out on deck.

He lay in a spreading pool of water, streaked with blood. Barnacles had scored his bare chest like barbs. Some sharp projection from the hull had torn through the muscles of his right arm from shoulder to elbow, and the sinews were exposed as Gunn had seen corpses prepared for dissection when he was a medical student. His left eye had been gouged by a bolt-head on the keel; the socket was filled with a blackish bloodstained jelly, that trembled like frog-spawn. Captain Fernandes knelt by his side, felt his pulse, and stood up.

'He is dead?' asked Gunn.

'Yes.'

'Untie him,' ordered Captain Fernandes, making the sign of the cross.

The same two sailors loosened the rope, now red and slippery with blood, slipped it over the bows again, walked back amidships and bound one end around Murgatroyd's waist.

'Shoot me rather than this,' he screamed. 'I beg you, have mercy.'

'A bullet is final,' replied Captain Fernandes. 'Under the custom of the seven seas, if you survive, you may go free when we reach land.'

'That is the chance you offer me, is it?' Murgatroyd asked bitterly. 'A chance in a million.'

'It is a better one than you hoped to offer us.'

'Have you anything to say?' Gunn asked him.

'I have. Please do not tell my wife how I died.'

'I give you my word.'

'And tell me one thing,' Murgatroyd continued as the men wound the rope three times around his waist, pulling the knot so tight he could scarcely breathe.

'If this had not happened, what would have been my future with Mandarin-Gold?'

'What would have been your future with yourself? Had you been content to push your pen on your high stool, you could have continued to do so. You would have been promoted, no doubt, and might eventually have been put in charge of a bigger office. But you were not content. Your envy was greater than your abilities.'

'Are you ready, sir?' asked the first mate.

'When you are,' Captain Fernandes replied.

Half a dozen sailors frogmarched Murgatroyd to the rail. He glanced down at the warm sea swirling against the tarred hull. Just beneath the surface, he could see green beards of moss and white encrustations of barnacles on the underside of the vessel. He wondered how far down the keel would be, what death would be like. His guts writhed at the thought; then his bladder loosened and his bowels ran like water from fear.

'Get him over and have that mess cleared up,' ordered the mate shortly.

'Heave-ho! A one, a two, a three – and over he goes.'

Swarthy men stripped to the waist – Lascars, Chinese, Malays – seized Murgatroyd by his arms and his legs and flung him as far as they could into the sea. He hit the water sideways, like a log, in a great white spout of foam.

'*Heave!*' roared Fernandes. The rope tightened like a living thing in the strong brown hands of the crew waiting on the starboard side. It came swiftly over the rail as they pulled, making the varnished rail smoke with friction.

Murgatroyd gasped desperately for air as he went under, swallowed water, choked and then felt the first ferocious jerk of the rope around his trunk. His eyes were still open, his hands waving frantically to hold himself away from the cruel, razor-sharp edges of the barnacles. The sea was green, then blue, then black with depth.

He struck his head against one of the hull's underwater ribs and cried out in pain. Air bubbled in huge balloons from his throat. Then his face was ripped against the shells and an un-bearable weight was at his chest and his eardrums. He forced his body away from the hull with his hands, then stuck, heart thundering, lungs bursting, jammed against the main keel.

I must get free, he thought. *I must get free.* He opened his eyes and the weight of water impelled his aching eyeballs into their sockets and exploded his eardrums as a child bursts a toy balloon.

His head, his body, even his brain seemed only a mass of channels forced full of water by the immeasurable pressure of the salt sea. Another jerk almost cut his body in two. The rough raw rope bit into his flesh like a knife. And then he was round the keel, bouncing with his knees folded, using his hands, his elbows, even his head to keep the rest of his body away from the sea shells that would tear him to strips. Such wounds would weep streams of blood which the sharks could follow before he was hauled up.

Dimly, choking, unable now to stop swallowing water, he realized that the deep of the sea was growing lighter; and then the green brightening glare of the sun was agony to his tortured eyes, and he was vomiting bile, sea-water, gobbets of food. When he opened his eyes fully they refused to focus properly. He could see a wild painful blaze of light, an iridescence of water, a black hull, and above it, vague phantasmagoric figures. Men were mouthing words at him, and waving their arms, but whether in anger or advice he did not know and could not comprehend.

He could not even see them clearly and he could hear nothing because now he was deaf. But at least his head was out of the water, and he began to breathe and look down at his torn knuckles, at the shreds of flesh stripped from his bare forearms, and the streaky wisps of blood his heart pumped like huge red feathers into the sea.

'Haul him up!' shouted Fernandes, but Murgatroyd did not hear the order. He only saw the captain's lips form words like a face moving behind glass, he was imprisoned in a world of total silence, as serene as the depths of the sea.

They pulled him over the rail and let him drop, dripping, on the warm wood of the deck. Then they untied the rope. He lay, totally unaware of his surroundings, only knowing dimly that somehow he had survived, but why or how and for what purpose or what future he had no idea whatever.

'What about the pirate ship, the *Ethiope*?' asked Captain Fernandes, looking down at Murgatroyd, wondering how long he would take to recover.

'I want nothing to do with that,' Gunn replied.

'Then have I your permission, doctor, to put a prize crew aboard?'

'Put who you like aboard, and keep what profit you may reap, but I do not wish to be involved,' Gunn told him.

'Aye, aye, sir.'

Already sailors were hacking the ropes and grapples that bound the two ships together. Others swarmed up the masts to set *Ethiope*'s sails. There would be a fortune to share if they could bring her safely to Borneo and then to Singapore before the monsoon broke.

Captain Fernandes read a hasty prayer over their own dead before they were rolled up in a blanket and then dropped unceremoniously over the rail. Then, sails proud with wind, like the breasts of gigantic white pouter pigeons, the two ships leaned over as they headed for Borneo.

Gunn stood in his familiar position on the bridge, feet apart, body braced against the roll and dip of the deck. He felt no remorse at what he had done, any more than he would have felt regret at severing a gangrenous limb from a patient. Any pirate who endangered the arteries of trade, and the safety of the seas which mariners of all nations should be free to sail in peace and safety, deserved neither pity nor consideration. They lived by the sword, so it was only just they should die by the same. And as the Chinese widow had said, while the sword of heaven might sometimes seem slow to smite, it never left a debt unpaid. He drew thoughtfully on his cheroot. What a far cry his life was now from serving as surgeon aboard a second-class Indiaman! In a few years, he had travelled the immeasurable distance from obscurity to riches, from saving life to taking it.

Gunn looked back across the wake of the two ships. The sun was falling now, and the sea glowed like melted gold. Its smooth heaving surface gave no sign of the men who had been thrown overboard, alive and dead; and no sign of the sharks that had devoured them, or the other creatures of the deep that teemed beneath that deceptive calm.

Gunn turned his back on the sun, and felt it warm through his shirt. The whole world is like that sea, he thought. Battles raged, passions and lusts burned incandescent behind bright friendly smiles. Hatred seethed beneath many a placid brow. He smiled to himself at the incongruity of mankind. The sun slid steadily down into the sea, turning the gold to blood, then to ink. The two ships sailed on like friends, close together for company, into the gathering dark.

At 10.35 on the following morning by Gunn's silver hunter, *Hesperides*' main-sail cracked like a gun against the varnished mast. Then the other smaller sails above him began to bang in response like angry cannon-fire. Gunn looked up in surprise; seconds before, they had been rounded by the breeze and now, inexplicably without a wind, they were flapping like stricken truce flags.

'We have lost the wind, sir,' explained Captain Fernandes.

'Well, put about,' said Gunn shortly. 'Can you not tack?' He could not bear to endure any further delay; he must needs be in Borneo as speedily as his ship could take him.

'No, sir. The wind has dropped all round.'

Gunn glanced up at the Mandarin-Gold company flag; it wilted without movement or life. Now the heat of the sun was reflected from the surface of the sea as though in a giant magnifying mirror. Sweat trickled from the roots of his hair down his neck to his back. The air felt hot and curiously dry to his nostrils, like a blast from the mouth of a brick kiln.

Behind them, the pirate ship rolled heavily on the swell. No waves were breaking, and no flying fish spurted like silver darts from the blue, oily sea. The water seemed heavy as though it was not water at all, but some other glistening viscous liquid.

'What do you make of it?' Gunn asked. 'A tropical storm?'

'I don't know,' replied Captain Fernandes frankly. 'There is usually wind with a tropical storm, and the monsoon is not due just yet. I have only once had a similar experience, when I was south of Java, about ten years ago.'

'What caused that?'

'A tidal wave. An earthquake. We rocked a bit, and then the wind returned and we were on our way.'

'Damn this delay,' said Gunn irritably. Every minute spent unnecessarily on the journey was a minute away from the woman who he believed had saved his life. He wanted to be with her; to grow in knowledge with her, to explore her mind and her body. He had never felt like this about any other woman; this was not a physical attraction or a mental affinity, but both. Together, they would build up her son's province until it was the richest and most flourishing in the East, with her son's people prosperous and without envious eyes on any other nation, and completely unsubjugated by any European imperial power. And in striving for this together, might not they both find the basis for something even more important – a lasting relationship of their own? This was something that Gunn had never imagined or even envisaged with any woman. What surprised him was the fact that he thought of the widow constantly; that he even found himself wondering how she would react to this or that situation; that he heard her quiet voice in his mind, and knew he would never grow tired of hearing that voice; of hearing her laugh. And yet he had only met her on a few occasions, and had not spent more than a dozen hours in her company. What was there about her that made him eager to spend the rest of his life discovering the secret of this unbelievable attraction, when every moment parted seemed a moment lost, wasted, thrown away?

The shout of the lookout scattered his thoughts.

'Mist approaching! South, south-east!'

'What do you mean, man – *mist*?' shouted back Captain Fernandes.

'It's all I can see, sir. Whole horizon looks yellow. Regular London peasouper.'

Fernandes turned to the first officer.

'Batten down all hatches. Furl sails. Loosen those you cannot furl in time. Warn *Ethiope* and shut all ports. Tropical storm's coming up.'

'Aye, aye, sir.'

Gunn heard other men repeat the orders. He raised his glass and focused it in the direction of the lookout's pointing arm. The whole horizon trembled and merged, sea with sky, into a curious roller of fog which the sun had incongruously coloured light yellow.

Gunn glanced to the left and right, but the haze extended on either side for as far as he could see. Even as he watched, he heard a faint rumbling, like the breaking of giant waves on a distant shore. And then this hum increased steadily to a drone, and then to a deafening roar. The crew were up the masts now, furling the great sails, working with speed and silence. Other sailors lashed ropes across the hatches and bound to the deck all coils of tarred rope and the latticed crates of live chickens and other provisions; anything that might shift position dangerously or could slide overboard if the ship rolled steeply.

Captain Fernandes took over the wheel from the helmsman.

'Main sails furled, main hatches battened down, sir,' reported the first officer.

Fernandes nodded.

'Good. Everybody not on duty, go below decks. Everybody on duty, to attach a rope around his belt secured to the main mast, in case seas break over the decks. I have seen waves as high as a house, that can sweep a man away like a spent match.'

'Aye, aye, sir.'

Gunn braced his legs against the slow sluggish roll of the vessel on the oily sea, watching the yellow mist approach them. There was something inexorable and fearful about the sight: the *Hesperides* could not escape it. They might turn turtle or be pounded to splinters, but they possessed no way of avoiding whatever destiny might be theirs. Captain Fernandes considered that his best hope was to hold the bows right into this yellow, roaring fog, and trust they could ride whatever tidal wave it concealed. Now Gunn felt a breeze on his sweating forehead, and this wind steadily grew stronger so that it moulded his damp shirt to his body. It blew like no other breeze he had experienced before; neither cool nor moist, but hot and dry and foetid like the fevered breath of a dying giant.

He found himself breathing and choking and sucking in gasps and gulps of the air, for the wind that rode ahead of the fog was sulphurous and dead.

He glanced sideways at Captain Fernandes.

'We shall know our chances in a couple of minutes,' he said.

Captain Fernandes made the sign of the cross.

'I have lived all my life at sea, doctor, so I suppose it is only fitting that I should also die in deep waters.'

'To hell with that,' said Gunn. 'I intend to live. None of us is going to die. Do not be so confounded fatalistic.'

303

'To accept one's fate without argument is a custom of the East. And remember I was born in the East. Here is my hand, doctor. We have enjoyed some good days together. And I had hoped that as many more lay ahead of us both. It is indeed ironic if you have been cured of your disease on land, only to die days later at sea.'

'I have been cured to live,' retorted Gunn, but before he could say more the yellow fog, which had appeared to be a comfortable hundred yards from them, suddenly surrounded them, blotting out all sight of sun and sea. It clouded the masts and the rigging, and brought a throat-clutching sulphuric heat that prickled Gunn's eyes and burned his nose and made him choke.

The *Hesperides* reared up like a terrified stallion. Ropes as thick as a man's wrist lashing the crates on deck snapped like string around a Christmas parcel. The heat of the wind was now almost too much to bear. Gunn dropped down on his knees to escape its full ferocity, and Fernandes threw a metal hook through the wheel spokes to lock the rudder firm. He crouched beside Gunn, both men gripping a brass footrail as the deck heaved and trembled and shuddered beneath them.

Somewhere high above them, out of sight in the swirling choking mist, a mast head snapped like a bent dry stick, and rigging and halliards crashed down around them, like a huge tent falling.

For a second Gunn could see the gilded hair of the figure-head at the bows rise up and keep on rising in a terrible way so that it seemed the ship must stand vertical on her stern and crash backwards. Then a boiling frothing wall of water blocked his view. It was churned to a yellow foam, and in this swirling spume, high as the roof of a great house, he saw with horror the bodies of men and beasts; great spars of wood, bamboo trunks, whole trees with branches and roots peeled pale as bone by the anger of the sea.

One palm tree smashed against the main mast, and its roots gripped the rigging like immense writhing fingers. A huge beam, the main rafter of a longhouse, crashed into the mast and split in two. Against the bellowing thunder of the furious foaming sea, the noise of the beam breaking sounded as light as the cracking of a twig.

The water hit the wheelhouse with the force of a solid brick wall. White wooden sides split like paper; the yellow sea poured on over the superstructure. Now Gunn breathed half a lungful of hot salty air, and then the water overwhelmed him. The stream of the sea stretched his body taut and flung him down against the boards. Driftwood hammered his hands on the rail, and he held. on desperately, knowing that if he relaxed his grip for an instant he would be swept away for ever.

The decks dipped alarmingly. He glanced back and saw the sails billowing backwards with the force of the flood, and then the sea was beneath him as though he was up on a cliff top looking down at a whirlpool. Bowsprit, figurehead, bows themselves dipped beneath the water. The deck fell away like a trapdoor opening. For a second, the ship trembled, and then she rolled, slid sideways and righted herself. Water boiled like a cauldron. Gunn had lost all sense of time or distance. All he knew, all that mattered, was that he was still alive; bruised, stunned, soaked, but breathing.

And then the wave passed them, and they were rocking like a toy boat in a child's bath, turning, heaving, dipping. Now bows dipped beneath the sea, now stern, while water spouted from the scuppers and the smashed portholes in great yellow gouts. As the ship steadied herself slowly, he guessed at the enormous quantity of water she had taken aboard, for he was at least six feet nearer the sea than he had been before the arrival of the wave.

He stood up, gripping the ruined and splintered rails, and glanced behind him. The pirate ship was half a mile away, as though bound in the opposite direction, her sails blown clean off the spars, so that her three masts looked like three trees, bare of leaves on a nightmare seascape.

Beyond the *Ethiope*, receding into the distance, north towards the mainland, raced the golden fog and the diminishing roar of the tidal wave. All around them bobbed pieces of wood, split tree trunks and the bloated revolting corpses of natives, pigs and cows, even chickens with bedraggled feathers. The sea was no longer blue, but yellow. The tidal wave had ruffled the bed of the ocean that had lain undisturbed for centuries.

Captain Fernandes was pulling himself slowly and shakily to his feet. His right arm hung loosely by his side, and his face was cut and pitted where nails on a piece of driftwood had scored and lacerated his flesh. Blood mingled with sea-water on the chest of his sodden uniform.

'We survived,' said Gunn. 'I said we would.'

'Praise be to the Lord,' said Fernandes, and again gave the sign of the cross.

'Also a word of thanks to the men who built the ship.'

'Also to them,' agreed Fernandes. Then he saw the extent of the damage, and the vast amount of water they had taken.

'To the pumps!' he shouted urgently. 'All hands to the pumps.'

Voices answered.

'Aye, aye, sir. To the pumps it is.'

Unsteadily, his broken arm swinging like a puppet's limb from his sleeve, and still so numbed by shock that he felt no pain, Fernandes went down the companionway to inspect his vessel. Gunn followed him. He bent down, drew his knife and cut the ropes from the nearest hatch. The crew began to appear, soaking, cursing, but cheerful and thankful to be alive.

'Anyone seen the first officer?' asked Gunn.

'I saw him. He was hanging on to a stanchion, sir,' said a seaman. 'Then a spar hit him and he had to let go.'

'What about the first mate?'

'Here, sir.'

'Get all the wounded up on the aft deck,' Gunn told him. 'I'll treat them there.'

Captain Fernandes was also giving orders.

'When you have the pumps going, clear the galley, and brew up tea. Then issue a double tot of grog to all hands.'

'And you had better come to my cabin,' Gunn told him. 'I'll set your arm.'

306

'My arm?' repeated Fernandes in dazed amazement. He looked down at his sleeve. 'Oh, my God, I can't use it.'

'You will,' Gunn assured him. 'You will.'

'When the ship has been baled, send three men across to the *Ethiope* to report their casualties,' Fernandes told the mate. 'Then tell them to drop anchor and we'll put about and take her in tow.'

In Gunn's cabin, with the wind cool through the smashed glass porthole, and everything sodden with sea-water, they sat in damp canvas chairs, sharing a bottle of whisky. Fernandes' face was grey with pain from his arm, now bound in two driftwood splints and a sling from a torn sheet.

'That was the largest tidal wave I have ever seen,' he said, shaking his head at the memory. 'It will make a strange entry in the log.'

The *Hesperides* trembled and leaned to starboard and then righted herself and began to turn slowly.

'Main sail up, ahoy!' they heard the mate shout.

The wind seemed intermittent and undetermined, now blowing forwards and now back, so that three hours passed before the *Ethiope* was in tow, and they could set on their way, all hatches wedged open to let the sun dry out their drenched vessel.

Gunn spent that night in a damp bunk, sleeping lightly, now and then starting up uneasily as he dreamed of a yellow mist and a yellow roaring wall of water. At twenty-five minutes to ten on the following morning, he heard the call from the lookout for which he had been impatiently waiting ever since they had raised anchor at Macao.

'Land ahoy! Land ahoy on the port bow!'

He left his day cabin, which he had converted as a temporary hospital for the wounded among the crew, and went up to join Captain Fernandes on the bridge. In the distance, on the utmost edge of sea, lay a long smudgy streak: the island of Borneo. He focused his glass on it. The trees seemed fewer and less green than when he had seen the island for the first time – could it be only a matter of weeks previously? But perhaps this was because summer was almost at an end? He lowered his glass and the look-out called: 'Small boat to starboard! South-south-west.'

Gunn leaned over the side of the bridge; a large Dyak canoe with a big triangular sail hoisted in her stern was approaching. In the bows a European crouched, waving frantically to them. Captain Fernandes gave orders to lower sails. The *Hesperides* lay becalmed, awaiting their arrival. The crew threw down a rope ladder. Gunn watched Greene climb slowly, almost wearily up the side of the ship, like a man moving in his sleep. He went down the companionway to meet him. But was this Greene – this gaunt man with sunken eyes? As he drew near him, Gunn saw that his hair had turned as grey as his skin.

'Welcome aboard,' Gunn said brightly, to conceal his dismay at the appearance of his younger companion. 'What news do you bring?'

'The very worst,' replied Greene. His voice was toneless, little above a whisper.

'How do you mean, the very worst?' asked Gunn. 'We have had a not uneventful voyage ourselves. First, we were attacked by pirates and then we were hit by a tidal wave.'

'That wave was the result of what has happened here. The province as we knew it is no more.'

'But I can see it on the horizon.'

'You can see a stretch of land, a few trees, a promontory here and there. That is all.'

'But what has happened?'

'An earthquake or some ferocious volcanic eruption. I am not clear about the cause, only the result. The islanders, so I am informed, believed that some great god slept beneath their feet, and now and then moved in his sleep, and the island trembled lest he should wake. Two days ago, he awoke.

'I was in the longhouse when I felt the whole building move on its supports. I thought that a storm had arisen and the wind was shaking it. I heard people outside shouting, and so I glanced at my watch. It was four thirty in the morning. I immediately dressed and went out. One or two of the smaller houses had already fallen down, and old women were wailing and crying, and mothers clasping little children to them, while the whole ground shook like the deck of a ship caught in cross currents.

'The motion increased so severely that one of the piles supporting my own house cracked and the corner collapsed. Someone had let loose their chickens and these were running everywhere in terror, and dogs and pigs were howling and squealing. There was an odd sulphurous smell in the air – hot and dry, like a blast from an oven door. I could not conceive the cause of this extraordinary phenomenon.

'I went to the Chinese widow's house, and she had called for the local priests and the astrologers and asked their opinions. They replied that the god beneath the earth must have been angered or slighted or somehow insulted, and he was moving in his sleep and about to awake.

'It seemed to me a poetic explanation of what was happening. Coconuts were dropping all around us like huge stones, and then the branches of the palms split and finally the trees themselves came crashing down. A foul, hot, ash-like dust filled the air. Now it seemed grey, now sandy coloured, and it made us choke as we breathed – a most alarming and disagreeable manifestation, doctor.

'The women and children were weeping on all sides and the priests were down on their knees, beating their chests and wailing in an attempt to placate this angry god. I felt we must be experiencing some kind of volcanic eruption, and I told the widow to marshal her staff and give the strictest orders to everyone to lie down flat on the ground as far away as possible from trees and houses, and to place their hands over the backs of their heads, and shield their ears with their arms, to save them from falling trees and coconuts. Hundreds did this, but then they grew terrified as the earth tremors increased, and many of them fled into the interior. I do not know what happened to them. Maybe they escaped with their lives. I pray they did.'

'And what about those who stayed?'

'Some survived, but as we lay with our eyes shut against the stinging dust, I heard people near the edge of the jungle begin to shout and scream. I opened my eyes and saw a sight I hope I may never see again.

'A thick tide of grey molten substance – lava, I assume – came rolling towards us. It was burning white-hot at the core, and orange at the edges, with tongues of flame leaping up under a heavy pall of black smoke. The earth itself had caught fire and melted, and was moving like some terrible Biblical prophecy of the last days before my eyes.

'The tide was at least ten feet thick and fifty feet wide, and those nearest to it had no chance whatsoever of escape. They were simply petrified with terror, and the heat roasted them yards before the lava reached them. Some others managed to run into the forest, but by then the trees were burning like giant torches, and the air was so hot it scorched our throats as we breathed.

'I could not see the Chinese widow anywhere, but I found a handful of people, including her son, and I ran with them until we reached the beach, and we plunged into the sea. Even the water was too hot for comfort, but it was still safer than the land. We kept ducking our heads to avoid clouds of red-hot ash that drifted away from the tide of lava, which still came rolling on like some river out of hell.

'Trees burned down, and ash and dust covered the beach and floated on the sea like scales, but, thanks be to God, we survived. Hair and eyebrows were singed, our faces scorched, but we were alive, when countless others had perished.'

'What about the Chinese widow?' asked Gunn.

'I do not know what happened to her,' said Greene. 'I searched everywhere, but the bodies were unrecognizable, for the most part just burned, blackened bones. Some, of course, were buried by the lava which gradually cooled into a kind of pumice-stone lake. I pray she escaped to another part of the island.'

'I pray the same thing,' said Gunn. 'And her son? Did he live through all this?'

'I am thankful to say that he did. He is an extremely brave lad,' said Greene warmly. 'And the chamberlain, Oya Ali, the man who helped us against the pirates, is with him. When I saw your ship approach, I immediately put out to tell you the news.'

'I appreciate that,' said Gunn. He turned to Captain Fernandes.

'Have Mr. Greene's canoe brought aboard, and all his crew. See that they are given food, and put any who may be injured in my day cabin, where I will examine them. In the meantime, clap on all sail you can, regardless of damaged masts and rigging. It is imperative we reach the island as speedily as possible.'

Captain Fernandes nodded, and turned to give the orders. The two ships leaned forward as all possible sails were rigged, and with a fair wind behind them, the island ahead grew steadily out of the sea. Gunn scanned the shore through his glass. All leaves had been burned from the trees, and now they spread bare branches grey with lava dust. Some trees had burned right down to charred stumps, with wisps of smoke still curling from them. The surface of the sea was dark with charcoal. Calcined branches floated on scummy water, black as melted tar.

When Captain Fernandes dropped anchor in the bay, the crew immediately lowered the longboat and waited, oars shipped, for Gunn and Greene to join them. They climbed down the ladder and sat in silence in the stern. Gunn trailed one hand in the water; it felt much warmer than any tropic sea. As they drew nearer to the beach, he could see a thick line of burned thatch and branches twenty feet up on the beach. Here and there lay bloated, burned bodies of pigs and cows. The sweet, sickly smell of burning flesh, of roasted fat and scented woodsmoke, drifted towards them as they landed. Both men jumped out without waiting for the boat to be pulled up the beach, and waded ashore.

'I will take you to the widow's longhouse – or what remains of it,' said Greene.

All landmarks that Gunn remembered – trees, longhouses, huts – had disappeared. The island seemed desolate, a desert of grey dust. There were no birds, no cries from children or chickens, no homely gruntings of hogs. Most of the longhouses had crashed to the ground when their piles had broken with the early trembles of the volcano. Others had burned through as they stood, and then fallen in on themselves.

A handful of islanders, with damp rags tied around bare feet against still-burning wood, faces and bodies coated in ash, eyes red with weeping and wood smoke, prodded listlessly amid the wreckage. Others attempted to recognize the identity of a relation from a pair of melted gold ear-rings near a blackened skull, or to rescue cracked clay cooking pots and metal pans and other humble possessions.

Gunn stood in the midst of devastation, unable to assimilate the full extent of the tragedy. A man limped towards him, using a branch as a crutch. Gunn could see that his right leg was fearfully burned; the flesh black and shiny with great crackling bubbles like a side of overcooked pork. Oya Ali raised his hand in salute.

'It is a time of great sadness, Englishman,' he said simply. 'The gods were angry with us, and when that is so, no-one can escape unscathed.'

'That is surely a time for other gods to show friendship and kindness,' replied Gunn. 'Not even gods can be angry for ever. Where is the sultan's widow?'

Oya Ali bowed his head.

'She is no more, Englishman. She has gone to join her husband in the world beyond this world. She has climbed the slopes of Kinabalu, the mountain that bears her name.'

'You are certain?'

'I am certain, for I saw her die. She had led many of her people through the trees and away from the burning earth into the sea. But some of the women were great with child, and their hair was alight and they held back in fear of the merciless anger of the god beneath the ground whose terrible rage had turned the soil to liquid, and caused the whole earth to bake like a giant oven-lid.

'She returned to reassure them, to tell them that they would all be safe and their children within them, and the children they carried in their arms, if they would only follow her swiftly into the sea. Some agreed, but others could not overcome their terror at the sights all around them – fierce flames fanned by wind, trees ablaze, a river of fire consuming all in its path.

'And while she argued, the whole island trembled as the god within the earth stood up, and spewed from his mouth a tide of fire. It overcame them all, a river of flame streaming to the edge of the sea. I was quicker than the tide, or very nearly so. I escaped with my life, but I nearly lost my leg.'

'Do you know exactly where the sultan's widow died?'

'I can take you almost to the place.'

'Please do so.'

Gunn turned to Greene.

'Be so good as to convey my orders to the officer in charge of the longboat crew. They are to return to the ship and collect all medical stores – bandages, medicines and ointments – and bring them ashore.'

As a physician, Gunn's place was with the living, not the dead, but first he had to see where this woman who had so impressed him had met her death. He followed Oya Ali between charred and smoking tree stumps, like a forest for dwarfs, past widows who wailed and beat their heads and hands among the reeking ash, in their extremity of grief. The sea seemed much closer now the trees had disappeared, and soon Oya Ali halted.

'It was about here, Englishman. I find it is difficult to say precisely, because the whole outline of the beach has changed, such was the anger of the god.'

Gunn walked slowly along the shore. The tide was out, and the waves seemed very small; the sun danced on the water, and the smell of burning hung strong on the still air. He walked for twenty paces before he saw the huddle of skeletons protruding from the solid grey tide of lava, about fifty feet wide and high as the height of a man.

Some bones still had blackened rags clinging to them. Sinews had fused to joints so that hands were raised, even after death, in abortive attempts to hold back the tide of melted lava that had passed over them for ever.

Death, he thought, was a great democrat; all skeletons looked much alike. Yet one set of these pathetic and almost identical blistered blackened bones had been clothed with the flesh of a woman he would have given all his wealth to meet again. He had hoped to ask her to share his life, as he had wished so earnestly to share hers.

He stood, head cast down, shoulders hunched, not seeing the bones, but trying to picture men and women and children; people with dreams and desires and secrets and hopes, now all frozen forever in a solidified river of death.

Ironically, he had been cured by the kindness and wisdom of a woman who had herself died in this inferno. Perhaps the gods had indeed been angry because he had amassed power and wealth through forcing a degrading and dangerous drug on pathetic and simple peasants? Maybe these same gods had felt cheated that his death had been postponed.

We all owed the gods a death; that was the only fact of which anyone in this life could ever be certain. And gods, like bankers, would never be denied the collection of their just debt when it fell due. He had received extra time for payment of his debt, through a woman's kindness; but then her own life had been summarily demanded long before any would have imagined.

He remembered her smile and her kindness and her courage; and he knelt down in the hot bitter dust, with the smell of burnt flesh in his nostrils, and prayed as he had not prayed since he was a boy, conscious meanwhile of a further irony, that a man who had frequently declared he did not believe in God, should, in his ultimate loneliness, call upon that God for the greatest favour of all.

'Oh, God,' he prayed haltingly, dredging for words in the depths of his misery and loneliness. 'Oh, God, look down on all of us who have survived the witness of your power on this island and at sea. May the spirit of this dear lady be treated kindly in whatever after-life you command. Although I pray to you as one God, she prayed to you under another name. But you are the same God, under whatever name, just as we are all your people, your children, regardless which nation we call our own – or the colour of our skin, or the names we give to your abodes on earth – temple, mosque, synagogue, church.

'You created all of us in your image, so let us who are left keep your vision and your guidance, and build our lives in memory of those who have gone before and beyond us.'

Oya Ali said gently: 'You are grieving for the sultan's widow?'

'Yes,' admitted Gunn. 'I am grieving.'

'Remember, Englishman, in your holy book it is written, man is born to sorrow as sparks fly upwards from the fire.'

'But rarely is a man born to bear a loss so needless and unexpected.'

'All loss is needless to those who lose. All loss, at the last, is also a surprise. But no-one is ever alone in the sorrow of death they have to bear. Long ago, Englishman, there lived a widow whose only son died young. In the extremity of her grief, she went to the Lord Buddha and sought his aid in bringing her son back to life. And Buddha, knowing her great sorrow, told her first to go to every house in that city, and in his name ask for grains of mustard seed, with which he would make an elixir for the boy. But the Lord Buddha added one strict condition: the widow was not to take a single seed from any house that had known bereavement.

'In the first house she visited, she learned that the father had recently died; in the second, she heard of the death of an aunt; in the third, a sister. And soon she realized that she could not gather *any* mustard seed, for sorrow and death were universal. That realization helped her to bear her own sadness. I pray, Englishman, that in your hour of sorrow it may also help you.'

Gunn stood up awkwardly, and glanced beyond Oya Ali towards the sea. The water seemed much calmer here, and from its colour was obviously very deep. This was not a part of the coastline he had visited before, and he thought inconsequentially: this would make an ideal site for a port, for godowns and warehouses. Here is where I would build the quay. And he asked himself in bewilderment, why am I thinking about commerce and trade at a moment like this?

The reason must be that these are the matters about which I am most concerned. And these would be the ways in which I could give greatest help to those of the province who have survived. A port would also be a constant abiding memorial to a

315

widow who had wished so well for her husband's people that in the end she gave her own life for them.

Even the rock-like river of lava could be of use; it had hardened into a wide thoroughfare leading to the edge of the waves. Not only was this ideally placed for the line of a new road; it would be its firm foundation.

To develop this place would be Gunn's next endeavour. He had been given back his life in order to use the time for some worthwhile purpose. Even before his cure he had wished to help the people of this province; now he knew best how he could do so.

He turned and walked slowly up the beach, busy with his thoughts. As he entered the charred ring of tree stumps, he saw a servant leading a small figure towards him, and he recognized the widow's son.

He felt the boy's hand go into his, and looked down. The Chinese widow's son stood looking up at him appealing. Gunn squatted in the dust, at the little boy's level.

'You are the sultan now,' he told him.

The boy nodded gravely.

'You are going away, Englishman?' he asked Gunn.

'Only for a season. I will come back,' Gunn promised. 'I will help you to improve the prosperity of your kingdom as I told your mother was my intention when I first landed here.'

He pulled out a piece of paper and scribbled an address on it with a stub of pencil.

'If you need me before I return, send a messenger to Singapore with this note. All aid in my power will be yours for the asking. And, in any case my friend – our friend, Mr. Greene – will be staying here with you.'

'And my mother?' asked the boy and his voice began to quaver.

Gunn put his hand around the young shoulders and drew him gently towards him.

'She is dead, as we humans count death,' he agreed, speaking slowly, trying to formulate his thoughts as he went along. 'But in the religion of my people, we believe that only the body dies. The spirit lives on, sometimes, I think, in other people. I believe that her spirit lives on, too – and your father's – in you.

'You are a man now, sultan, if not yet in years, in responsibility. Soon you will have to make your own decisions. You will have also to make your own friends, and they will be very few, for no leader can ever afford to listen long to voices that tell him only what he may secretly wish to hear.

'And sometimes, as you grow older, you will wonder which course you should take. Whether you should follow this direction or that, whether a man is a friend or an enemy pretending friendship. And you will think of your mother and your father, and wonder what they would have said or done. And then their spirits will advise you. That way, some part of us, the best and kindest part, lives on forever.'

'Do you believe that, Englishman?' asked the boy gravely.

Gunn nodded.

'If I believe anything,' he said sincerely, 'I believe that.'

Gunn stood up.

'In your country I hear you shake hands,' the boy said. 'In mine, we bow.'

'The meaning is the same,' said Gunn. 'Let us now do both to show we are in agreement. And may God – yours and mine – be with us both until we meet again.'

The boy watched Gunn walk across the clearing. He did not look back. Then the boy turned and scuffed his feet in the dust, seeing glittering particles of silica flash like brief sparks. What the Englishman had said was true. He was a man now, and men did not weep. Only women wept, and he had watched his mother cry silently on two occasions; after the death of his father, and when Gunn had not returned.

Perhaps if the Englishman had come back quickly, his mother might still be alive; or perhaps they might both have perished. He had lost his mother, and his father, but he still had friends; the Englishman Gunn was his friend; so was the Englishman Greene. And he had a special piece of paper which he had only to show to other English people in Singapore, and all means of aid would be given to him. The thought cheered him, and he turned to Oya Ali and put a hand in his hand. The spirits of his father and his mother were indeed by his side. They would stay firmly by him, as Kinabalu stayed firmly on the edge of the sea. There was comfort in the thought and also in the local name for Kinabalu; the Chinese Widow. His mother had been Chinese and a widow. Truly it was written, as his *munshi* had often told him: All things are altered, but no-one really dies.

Gunn walked slowly down the beach, his soft leather boots sinking over their ankles in the white sand. The longboat was waiting for him; men held it steady as he climbed in. Greene asked him curiously, waiting on the beach: 'Are you coming back soon?'

'Not immediately,' Gunn replied. He thought without enthusiasm that in Singapore he would have to meet Patricia Bankhausen and Mrs. Murgatroyd. The future stretched bleakly ahead – and only days ago it had seemed so bright.

'I have things to attend to in Singapore,' he went on. 'When they are satisfactorily resolved, I will return.'

'Will that be long?'

'I hope not. I promise you, Greene, I will be back. Later.'

The eight oarsmen bent to their varnished oars, and the boat scored a white arrow of foam through the cobalt sea. Later. How much later, Gunn could not yet say; his heart and mind were still in turmoil. He had found one woman above all others whom he believed he might love, and yet he had never touched her. He did not even know her name. But he had admired her, had been drawn to her by an affinity that bridged chasms of race and upbringing and belief. He did not look back, although he wanted to. But to look back would mean weakness and irresolution; and in the empty months ahead he would need to be strong. And then, when he had grown accustomed to his grief, when work had sweated sorrow from his soul, when he felt he could speak to her son without tears in his heart and longing in his voice, then he would come back to build his port. When that might be, he could not say, but he would return. He had given his word, and he would keep his promise.

Later.

THE END

MANDARIN-GOLD
by
JAMES LEASOR

'Highly absorbing account of the corruption of an individual
during a particularly sordid era of British imperial history.'
The Sunday Times

'James Leasor switches to the China Sea more than a century
ago, and with pace and ingenuity tells, in novel form, how the
China coast was forced to open up its riches to Englishmen, in
face of the Emperor's justified hostility.'
Evening Standard

'... the nasty story of opium – European and American traders
made fortunes taking the forbidden dope into nineteenth century China, and this novel tells the story of their deadly arrangements and of the Emperor's vain attempts to stop them.
Mr. Leasor has researched the background carefully and the
detail of the Emperor's lavish court but weak administration is
fascinating. The white traders are equally interesting characters, especially those two real-life merchants, Jardine and
Matheson.'
Manchester Evening News

A SELECTED LIST OF FINE BOOKS PUBLISHED BY CORGI BOOKS

All these books are available at your bookshop or newsagent, or can be ordered direct from the publisher. Just tick the titles you want and fill in the form below.

CORGI BOOKS, Cash Sales Department, P.O. Box 11, Falmouth, Cornwall.

Please send cheque or postal order, no currency.

U.K. send 19p for first book plus 9p per copy for each additional book ordered to a maximum charge of 73p to cover the cost of postage and packing.

B.F.P.O. and Eire allow 19p for first book plus 9p per copy for the next 6 books thereafter 3p per book.

Overseas Customers: Please allow 20p for the first book and 10p per copy for each additional book.

NAME (Block letters) ....

ADDRESS ....

(JULY 77)..

While every effort is made to keep prices low, it is sometimes necessary to increase prices at short notice. Corgi Books reserve the right to show new retail prices on covers which may differ from those previously advertised in the text or elsewhere.